T0083590

LADISLAV FUKS
OF MICE AND MOOSHABER

LIMO
Kiosk

Ladislav Fuks

Of Mice and Mooshaber

Charles University Prague
Karolinum Press 2014

ISBN 978-80-246-2216-3

I

The Land of the Elves, which was the name of the local hostelry, had been hired out for the afternoon. The window into the courtyard was wide open and in the courtyard itself a tethered horse was at work on a sack of oats. A wedding party was sitting in the saloon.

They were seated at a table covered in a white cloth and decorated with flowers, candles, glasses and a dish full of fancy cakes or kolaches. At the head of the table, under a portrait of the sovereign, the Dowager Princess Augusta, and the Prime Minister, Albinus Rappelschlund, sat a man with big hands that had seen a lot of toil. He was dressed in black with a white shirt made of tow-cloth and was turning this way and that in a clumsy fashion, throwing out nods and smiles in all directions and even through the window towards the horse. This was the bridegroom. Next to him sat someone smaller and fatter, a blonde with a face that was puffy from laughing at nothing. A laurel wreath lay on the table in front of her, while she squirmed and swaggered and put on airs and rolled her eyes this way and that. This was the bride. Next to the happy couple sat a friend of the blonde called Rona, a girl of twenty who had collapsed in giggles, and the two witnesses, swarthy and strange.

The daily papers hung on the wall alongside the wedding table, full of assorted vignettes and titbits about Prime

Minister Albinus Rappelschlund, because today was his name-day. A few side tables had been placed beneath the newspapers.

At the bottom end of the table sat a young man with a dark chequered jacket and a white silk shirt. Delicate, ill at ease and taciturn, this was Lothar Baar. A second young man sat next to him, also well dressed and even more taciturn and ill at ease. This was his classmate from school, Rolsberg. And then right at the end of the table sat an elderly lady in a black and gold scarf, black waistless jacket with sleeves and a long black shiny skirt. She had shoes without heels on her feet and a smallish bag in her lap. This was Natalia Mooshaber.

'My daughter talks about you all the time', said Mrs Mooshaber to Lothar Baar at the bottom end of the table. The remnant of wine she'd been given – her glass had been almost empty from the start – was about enough to moisten her lips. 'She is always talking about the tape she sold you in the shop.'

'The tape recorder,' nodded the young man with an embarrassed look towards the head of the table.

'Just so,' nodded Mrs Mooshaber, 'surely you live in a palace somewhere, Mr Baar.'

'I have private lodgings', said the young man as he threw another look of embarrassment at the head of the table, 'my friend Rolsberg and I are staying with a rich merchant who has a villa here.'

'Do you also take meals with this merchant?' asked Mrs Mooshaber, while she leaned forward in order to get a view of Rolsberg's face.

'Just breakfast,' said Lothar Baar. 'The rest of the time we eat in the student canteen.'

'And you eat well there,' agreed Mrs Mooshaber, 'to be sure there'll be ham and Italian salad, not to mention wine and lemonade. I would like to invite you to our own home, gentlemen, but we are just simple poor folk. We don't live in a villa but in a run-down house. Why, even now there are masons around repairing the shared balcony...and as for food, we eat oatmeal...' Mrs Mooshaber glanced through the window into the courtyard where the horse had its sack of oats, '...cornmeal too. Now and again I do a bit of baking. I bake, Mr Baar, it's something I like. That dish of kolaches,' Mrs Mooshaber pointed discreetly at the table, 'that was all my own work. For my daughter's wedding, you see. No one has taken any yet, but wait and see what happens after they've eaten the meal. In a little while....' Mrs Mooshaber suddenly leaned forward and whispered to Lothar Baar, '...in a little while the banquet will arrive. The banquet, Mr Baar. They ordered ham and Italian salad,' she repeated in a whisper, 'wine and lemonade too. And ice cream, but that comes at the end. Oh yes,' said Mrs Mooshaber laughing, 'I like to bake. But other than that, Mr Baar, it's bread for the likes of us.'

The bride at the head of the table, the plump and simple-minded blonde, was meanwhile laughing and fooling around with Rona and the witnesses. Her new husband beside her, the big hands that had seen much toil resting on the tablecloth, was spinning round, nodding and saying 'yes' to everything. When there was nowhere else to spin, he span to face the horse through the window.

'So you'll be keeping your own name', said one of the witnesses to the wedding party, a swarthy fellow with black hair and a low forehead. The plump and simple-minded blonde laughed and gave a bridal nod.

'He'll still be a Laibach.' She gave him a shove and he gave a nod. 'I'll be whatever I'm called already. Food's on its way now.'

'You see, Mrs Baar,' Mrs Mooshaber addressed both Lothar Baar and Rolsberg, 'there'll be food in a moment. Ham, salad, lemonade, they've got it all at the front behind the bar counter. Now there's something I must tell you, gentlemen,' and once again she leaned forward for a view of Rolsberg's face, 'when I went to school, which will be sixty years back from where we are now, I had a friend called Maria. She was so tiny and frail, the poor crooked thing, but she was bright and kind and the children loved her. She came from a rich family, her father was a farm steward and he had this watch, made from gold it was. Anyway she got married and took her husband's name but then he died shortly afterwards and she became a housekeeper for a rich family. And she was the housekeeper in this family for two generations. I haven't set eyes on her in fifty years. Fifty years,' she nodded as she glanced over the wedding party at the portrait of the sovereign, the Dowager Princess Augusta, hanging on the wall with that of Prime Minister Albinus Rappelschlund, whose name-day it was, 'fifty years. Did you know, Mr Baar, that I always wanted to be a housekeeper myself, just like my friend Maria? I can set a table and make it fancy. See here...' she pointed at the white table laid out with candles, posies, wine and kolaches, 'I could have managed this table too, only they went and ordered everything from the publican.'

'And you will also be living apart.' The voice that could now be heard at the head of the table belonged to the second witness, another swarthy fellow with black hair and a low forehead. The blonde bride gave another foolish laugh and said:

'He will carry on renting from that Klaudinger woman and I'll be where I am now. What's funny about that, eh?' She gave the bridegroom another nudge and he just responded with a nod and a smile.

'He's a nice hard-working fellow,' Mrs Mooshaber said to Lothar Baar in a quiet voice, 'well brought up. He's a mason. He was never in any school for troublemakers or house of correction and he'd do anything for our Nabule. He said that she can have everything he earns. He'll just keep a bit back for his smokes. She'll live with me and he'll have lodgings with Miss Klaudinger, but only at the start, they're saving up for a flat in the Elizabethan district. I would so like to invite you to our place, gentlemen,' Mrs Mooshaber repeated, 'but we are just poor people living in a run-down house with masons repairing the common balcony. All their tools are lying in the passage right in front of my flat. But let me finish telling you about this housekeeper. That's what I'd have liked to be, just like my friend Maria. I always wanted to have one of those kiosks. You know, those covered stalls where I could sell ham, salad, even lemonade perhaps, but there again....' Mrs Mooshaber gestured with her hand and glanced up at the newspapers hanging from the wall, 'I'd rather not tell you about that now. I'd rather tell you what I'm actually doing. I'm working at a cemetery. I water the plants and tend the graves. And I'm attached to the Mother and Child Support Service.' Mrs Mooshaber suddenly reached into the bag on her lap and took out a card with her name on it.

'Miss said something about your dealings with the Welfare,' confirmed Lothar Baar, taking a hesitant peek at the card which Mrs Mooshaber tucked away again. He cast a somehow bitter glance at the blonde at the head of the table and continued: 'Actually she's a miss no longer but more like a missus.'

Then he spent a while looking at the portraits towering over the wedding party, at the old princess and Prime Minister Albinus Rappelschlund, whose name-day it was, before saying:

'So, Mrs Mooshaber, you have practical experience of children.'

'Indeed I do have practical experience of children,' agreed Mrs Mooshaber, while she took a peek at the head of the table and was going to elaborate further when Rona, the friend of the blonde bride, piped up: 'Where is Wezr, Nabule? Why isn't he here? Where could he have got to, that he was unable to attend his own sister's wedding?' And the blonde bride laughed until the horse behind the window to the courtyard turned round. Then she nodded in the direction of Mrs Mooshaber and said:

'Let her tell you where he is. Let her tell you' (this came with a shake of the head) 'where Wezr is, why he's not here. Why he's not at his sister's wedding.' Mrs Mooshaber gave a start and her eyes opened wide as she blurted out:

'No, my son Wezr is not here, he's elsewhere. He's got work to do...'

The guests at the head of the table squealed with laughter.

'Her son Wezr is not here,' they shouted, 'he's elsewhere. He's got work to do....'

'They want to have a good time,' said Mrs Mooshaber in an apologetic voice to Lothar Baar and Rolsberg, 'you know what it's like with weddings, gentlemen.' Then she went on:

'Well then, besides what I do for Mother and Child Support, which is unpaid, I work in the cemetery. The one in the centre in Anna Maria the Blessed Square. I water the plants and tend the graves. But you know, gentlemen,' she went on, once again leaning forward a little in order to catch sight of Rolsberg's face, 'I look after something else too. I mean the fact that our building's caretaker keeps a banner in my flat. A real banner, even two... well, one's a spare as they say. Two banners, but you know, gentlemen ...' Mrs Mooshaber was looking at the white tablecloth, 'they're black. Black, something you hang from the house when someone dies. I hang the banner from a long pole which I keep in a corridor behind the wardrobe. I have a little pension from my husband, who worked as a coachman for a brewery. I had my children late. There's Nabule, the bride here, and Wezr, who's not here because he's got his work to do. I had them late, after I was forty...'

At this moment a waiter entered the saloon and went up to have a word with Nabule. She gave the bridegroom a nudge and stood up.

'The feast is here,' said Mrs Mooshaber in a quiet voice to Lothar Baar and Rolsberg, 'the feast of ham and salad, which has all been ordered, lemonade too. And once they've eaten their fill, they will take my kolaches. Did you know that I spent a whole day baking them for my daughter's wedding? I added vanilla, almonds and raisins, they'll taste a treat. When the children were small, Mr Baar, I mean our Wezr, who's not here, and Nabule the bride, I did what I could for them. I even sang them a lullaby. Just look, Mr Baar,' Mrs Mooshaber suddenly glanced up, 'the waiter's bringing it already. Look, real ham, salad, and such a lot of it, wine and lemonade, oh my...' Mrs Mooshaber looked at the plates which the waiter was setting down on the unused side tables beneath the newpapers, 'I've only eaten ham and salad once in my life – and that goes for lemonade as well. You know...' She leaned over towards Lothar Baar and whispered. 'It was at my own wedding. And fifty years have gone by since then...'

'It's like being in the Metropol!' yelled Rona with a glance at the ham and salad, 'we could be in the Ritz! And oh crikey! Look at those fancy pastries...'

'Pastries,' spluttered Nabule, her face at this moment looking even more bloated and banal, 'pastries. Ask her who did the baking, she'll spout it all out. Just start her off...' she nodded towards the lower part of the table.

'Yes, I baked them' said Mrs Mooshaber from the other end of the table, 'My daughter's quite right. I spent the whole day baking them for my daughter's wedding. I added vanilla, almonds and raisins, they'll taste a treat. But of course they're better saved for after you've eaten,' she gave a sudden smile, 'after all this salad and ham or we'll be too full up for the main course.' I like baking,' she said with a smile, 'but only now and again. But when dear Rona gets married,' she smiled again, 'I'll bake for her too.'

'Oh isn't she a one for baking,' shrieked Nabule, 'did you hear all that? When little Rona ties the knot she'll be baking pastries for her too. And she cares for the children and she tidies the tombs,' she yelled. 'And what's more, she could offer us a song,' shrieked Nabule.

The place went quiet for a moment and then gales of laughter broke out again.

'A song?' laughed one of the witnesses.

'She can sing?' laughed the other.

'Yes, she's a hoot' screamed Nabule.

'So make her sing,' shrieked Rona, 'make her sing...' And in the twinkling of an eye they had gone quiet and turned to face the end of the table.

Mrs Mooshaber clasped hold of the bag in her lap and spoke in an apologetic and hesitant manner:

'No, I don't know how to. I only used to sing when the children were little. A lullaby. Of course I could sing that if you like, just for fun. After all this is a wedding and we're supposed to be having fun, aren't we?' She smiled and everyone gave way to spluttering laughter and Nabule did one of her twirls and then stood up and bounced over to the tables below the newspapers where the plates of ham and salad were laid out.

While she started doing the rounds with the plates of ham and salad, setting them down in front of the guests, Mrs Mooshaber sat up a little straighter at her end of the table and started singing:

Now it's good evening and now it's good night
Now by the power of angelic might

Everyone was in stitches, laughing, shouting and shrieking. Only the bridegroom sat nodding and smiling, and only Lothar Baar was bewildered and subdued, alongside his even more subdued and bewildered friend Rolsberg, while Nabule went on doing the rounds with the plates of ham and salad and setting them down in front of the guests. And Mrs Mooshaber looked at the guests while she sang:

Tomorrow in the morning-time
You will once more rise and shine

She was so determined that the song was as good as she was able to make it, that she didn't even notice that Nabule had put plates of salad and ham in front of everyone else while there wasn't so much as a morsel on the table in front of her. Lothar Baar and Roslberg, on the other hand, did notice and they looked at the blonde in astonishment. But she just exploded in cackles and then all of a sudden burst in unexpectedly on her mother's song.

'Cut it out,' she broke in, 'that's enough howling from you. Shut your gob. Tuck in then, 'she said to the guests before going back over to her mother and saying:

'That's enough of the wailing woman. Now get out.'

Lothar Baar and Rolsberg were struck dumb. So was Mrs Mooshaber. But before Lothar Baar and Rolsberg knew what was happening, and before Mrs Mooshaber could recover her composure, with a huge cackle Nabule had reached over to the plate of kolaches, got one into her claws and had hurled it at the ceiling. The kolache rebounded from the ceiling like a ball, fell amongst the flowers and candles on the table and leaked cream cheese and even its raisin topping onto the tablecloth. And then, to the accompaniment of another huge cackle, Nabule took the whole plate in her claws, flounced over to the window and hurled the plate of kolaches at the horse. Then she seized hold of some wine and yelled at the lower end of the table:

'Aren't you gone yet, for Christ's sake? Aren't you off to water your corpses or cosset those mothers and children? Scram!'

Mrs Mooshaber, who up to this point had been sitting stock-still staring at the tablecloth, now showed the first signs of coming to life. The bag shaking in her hand, she stood up and slowly made her way to the door. She left the room looking like an old and withered tree. The pub dissolved into shrieks and yells.

'She's off,' they shouted, 'she's going to water the graves.'

'She's leaving,' they screeched, 'to care for her children.'

'And make sure to stop at Wezr's,' laughed Nabule, 'the one who's got work to do.'

'Tell him to get himself here, Mrs Mooshaber,' laughed Rona, 'his work has taken him long enough.'

Lothar Baar and Rolsberg came to life only when Mrs Mooshaber had gone through the door into the bar. They glanced up at all the people chuckling and shouting at the top of the table and looked out of the window at the horse wolfing down the kolaches in the courtyard, and then the two of them jumped up from their chairs.

'Where do you think you're off to?' shrieked Nabule, 'it's not curtains yet. The party's just beginning!' But Lothar Baar and Rolsberg were already running through the door from the saloon into the bar and from there into the street, only to find the street outside the pub deserted. Of Mrs Mooshaber there wasn't a trace. They rushed round the nearest corner, but there was still no trace of Mrs Mooshaber. They went back to the bar, but the bartender told them that the lady had definitely left. Back they ran into the street, but there wasn't a soul to be seen there. There was nothing but a single withered old tree on the pavement opposite.

Mrs Mooshaber had been hiding behind the door of the next house. Only long after Lothar Baar and his friend Rolsberg had finally departed in a shocked and disturbed state, did she herself venture out and hurry home along the street.

II

It was a beautiful September afternoon as she hurried through street after street, past banners hanging from the public buildings in honour of Prime Minister Albinus Rappelschlund's name-day, until at last she reached the square named in his honour. The statue here had been hung with flowers and ribbons of various kinds, but the people going by didn't so much as glance at it, each one preferring to look at the pigeons swarming over the ground. Along the main avenue she had to make her way past a crowd of people in front of the editorial offices of *Our Blooming Homeland*. There was always a crowd of people here discussing sport or breakthroughs in transplant surgery or the different types of seaweed and sky, or even swapping stamps. They were chatting on this occasion about the fact that despite the banners on the state buildings and the fully beribboned statue in the square, the windows of apartments were empty and deserted...indeed they were really empty and deserted, lacking not only people but a single flower, candle, glass of wine or piece of cake, such as were to be found on the name-day of the Sovereign Dowager Princess. And for once no one was so much as burning a stick of incense in their apartment. Mrs Mooshaber made her way past the crowd in front of *Our Blooming Homeland*. Then she passed the glass and laminate fronts of the street stalls, where people were eating ice cream, ham and salad or drinking lemonade.

Keeping her head down, she quickly passed them all and was glad when she found herself running over the white stripes of the asphalt crossing by the *Sunflower* department store. Then she hurried down three drab alleyways and was near to the place where she lived.

It was really an old and dilapidated two-storey house with a large cavernous passageway. This was where a pile of masons' tools was to be found and some bricks, a wheelbarrow and a tub of lime. A woman in her fifties wearing a short summer skirt stood in the passage. Another woman was beside her with a lad of perhaps twelve in ragged clothes. His eye was swollen and he was looking unhappily up and down the street.

'My God, Mrs Mooshaber,' called out the woman in the short summer skirt as Mrs Mooshaber went by, 'have you come back from the wedding already? Is it all done and dusted at *The Land of the Elks*?'

'It was *The Land of the Elves*' said Mrs Mooshaber as she shook her small black bag. *The Land of the Elves*. I had to leave, I wasn't feeling very well. I probably had too much to eat. You know what it's like with weddings. But what's up, Mrs Faber?' Mrs Mooshaber threw a quick glance at the other woman and pointed to the lad. 'What happened to him?'

'He's daft as a brush', said Mrs Faber coldly, without a muscle twitching in her face, 'fat-headed, dim-witted, always answering back, never able to stay still and not the slightest idea of what he's doing. Climbed the scaffolding used by the masons and could have put his own eye out. Brainless halfwit but bold as brass, so he's off to the eye specialist as punishment.'

'Perhaps he doesn't need to,' said Mrs Mooshaber looking at the young lad standing there looking gormless, 'I tell you what, Mrs Faber, I'll make him an eyebath and then when it's cooled you can use a piece of cloth to dab his eyes.'

'I'm not dabbing his anything', Mrs Faber replied in her cold voice, still without so much as a muscle twitching in her face, 'he's going to an eye doctor. Let the doctor cauterise it.'

'Now then, Mrs Faber,' laughed the woman with the short summer skirt, 'Mrs Mooshaber knows a thing or two about these things. She works in the cemetery and for the Welfare, she's got a card to prove it. Mrs Mooshaber, don't you have a card? Anyway, Mrs Faber, you know that much yourself. And besides,' the woman suddenly added, 'it's a national holiday. There won't be any optho treating eyes today.'

'There will be somewhere,' said Mrs Faber while she examined the card which Mrs Mooshaber had taken out of her bag, 'after all, my husband's working as usual.'

'Just stay where you are,' said Mrs Mooshaber as she slipped the card back into her bag, 'I'll sort out his eye. Let him come and see me in the evening. And you can come too,' she said to the woman in the short summer skirt who was the building's caretaker. Then she gave a quick nod and hurried through the front passage.

Mrs Mooshaber's flat gave directly onto this passage. The pile of mason's tools, the bricks, the 'barrow and the barrel of lime, stood right at her front door. By the door was a corridor containing a pantry and wardrobe, with a very long pole towering up from behind the latter. The corridor led to the kitchen, which had a frosted glass window facing back into the corridor where some stairs began and another door leading to a further room. This further room had a window facing the courtyard, just next to the main staircase. Dark and meagrely furnished though it was, it was kept tidy. Mrs Mooshaber made for the kitchen, put her bag on a chair and looked at a large cake lying on the table. Then she opened a cupboard and pulled out a threadbare old bag containing a few coppers in savings. She opened it, took a look at its contents and returned it to the cupboard. Then she moved on to the other room. A few bits of clutter were lying around under the bed and the mirror, left there by her daughter Nabule in the morning when she rushed off to the wedding. Mrs Mooshaber went back into the kitchen and, with a glance at the table, the chair and the clock above the stove, seated herself on the ottoman.

'So that's how it was, she threw me out', she said to herself, 'without so much as a crust to eat, and the kolaches I baked she chucked at that horse. And she did it in front of all those people, including those students. And Wezr,' she was shaking as she spoke, 'Wezr will get here any minute now.'

Mrs Mooshaber got to her feet again, looked at the cake lying there on the table, picked her bag up from the chair and tidied it away in the cupboard. Then she took off her black-and-gold scarf, her waistless jacket and her long, black, shiny skirt, before putting on her house clothes and an apron. She proceeded to get the stove going with wood from a box, put a mug of water with a smattering of herbs down on the stove top and poured some more water into a bucket. She then took the bucket next door in order to clean the floor. When she had finished wiping the floor as far as the mirror, she got up to take a breather and that was when she looked through the window at the stairs leading down into the courtyard. And there was scruffy little Master Faber. She wiped her hands and went to let him in.

The lad glanced nervously around the kitchen. Perhaps he had never been there before. He looked at the ottoman, the table and the cake on top of it, and walked up to the stove. Mrs Mooshaber bent down to the stove and fed the fire a little.

'So your mother says you've neither manners nor sense,' she said as she dunked a piece of cloth into the mug on the stove, 'if she says that, I suppose it must be so. Otherwise she wouldn't say such a thing. After all, she wouldn't torture herself like that if you were a good boy, would she.'

Having wrung out the piece of cloth Mrs Mooshaber went up to the boy, who was standing by the stove looking at the cake on the table and didn't move an inch.

'Your father will be in for a surprise when he gets back from work,' said Mrs Mooshaber as she applied the cloth to the lad's eye. 'You normally go and get some beer for his dinner. Hold the cloth for a moment while I tie it on.' Mrs Mooshaber went over to the sideboard for a bigger cloth, a chequered one, and fashioned a bandage from it for the boy.

'How can you learn anything at school when you fool around so much?' she asked and for the first time the lad ventured a reply.

'I do my lessons', he said in a whisper as he continued to shake a little.

'Lessons about what?' asked Mrs Mooshaber. 'About trees?'

'About the life of our Prime Minister,' he whispered, and went on shaking.

'So you know all about him?' asked Mrs Mooshaber as she sat down at the table.

'Oh yes,' the lad whispered, standing gormlessly by the stove with the compress on one eye and the other on the cake, 'we had to know his biography for his name-day.'

'Tell me then, if you know it all', said Mrs Mooshaber.

'Albinus Rappelschlund was born, that is to say he was born....' With one hand on his chequered bandage, the lad began to recite in a timid voice, 'he was born...when he was fourteen he was apprenticed as a tanner, and then he left to go to a military school in order to become an officer, but then he left again and went to learn waitering and he was learning to carry plates, plates... but then he moved on again and went to a Protestant college. But then he left it and went, and went...' the lad went on shaking and speaking in a whisper and staring at the cake, 'when he was twenty he entered the service of Princess Augusta who had just acceded to the throne. He was promoted to be her valet and then colonel and then minister, minister....and he brought law and order. Five times he took part in a voyage to the Moon...'

'Go on,' said Mrs Mooshaber when the lad stopped and couldn't go any further, 'what happened next?' and the lad shifted the dressing over his eye a little before continuing in a whisper, 'he went on bringing law and order, he gave the people more work...he founded a museum....he built the biggest airport, the Albinus Rappelschlund airport, in the Stadium district of the city....the one the spaceships fly from. Then, then....' The lad's eyes wandered nervously here and there and especially towards the cake on the table, and then he ground to another halt.

'Go on,' said Mrs Mooshaber, 'what happened next...'

'Then,' the boy finally spoke up, 'he discovered the traitors who plotted to assassinate Princess Augusta. He brought them to justice and he himself became the Prime Minister. Ever since he's governed as the only high and mighty one after our sovereign Princess Augusta, who has been widowed in the meantime. But people say...' suddenly the lad stopped and now he was shaking like a leaf, 'people say...'

'Just what do people say,' asked Mrs Mooshaber, 'what do they say...'

'They say,' now the lad was shivering with fear, 'they say that the only one in charge is him. They say that the princess has gone into hiding or has already been dead for a long time.'

'I see,' said Mrs Mooshaber as she rose from her chair, 'I'll get the mug for you.' She took the mug with the potion off the stove and handed it to the boy. 'Before you go to bed, wet the cloth with this and apply it three times. You'll be as fit as a fiddle. And don't be naughty,' she went on, 'your mother must have reason to say you're naughty, she's not going to worry herself silly about nothing. You climb up the masons' scaffolding and you misbehave and what can she do with you then? You'll go to the school for troublemakers and then the house of correction and you'll end up a labourer, an unskilled pair of hands like as not hired for the day, and you know how it will all end. You know where you'll end up,' said Mrs Mooshaber with a shake of the head, 'behind bars.'

'Madam,' began the lad all of a sudden in a pleading tone of voice, as if he had managed to build up some courage, one hand holding the chequered compress and the other holding the mug with the potion, 'it's been said that you....' And then he dried up again.

'Said that I what', asked Mrs Mooshaber, 'what exactly....'

'It's been said that you.... the lad geared himself up for another attempt and glanced up pleadingly, 'that you keep live mice.'

'Live mice?' Mrs Mooshaber shot him a glance, 'live mice? I have mousetraps,' she went on, 'mousetraps to catch them with.'

‘Where are they?’ came the boy’s beseeching question, while he kept his eyes on the cake on the table.

‘Right here.’ With a flourish of the hand Mrs Mooshaber indicated certain key strategic areas of the kitchen. ‘Behind the stove, behind the sideboard, behind the sofa. Then there’s the other room and the pantry. In fact everywhere.’

‘Could I see one of these mousetraps?’ asked the boy in a quiet voice. ‘I’ve never seen one. I’ve only seen cages.’

Mrs Mooshaber went over to the sofa, bent down and picked up three mousetraps.

‘But there aren’t any mice in them,’ said the lad in a disappointed tone when Mrs Mooshaber put the traps down on the ottoman. ‘There’s nothing inside them. At least inside cages you can see lions.’

‘They’re empty because no mice were caught in them yesterday,’ explained Mrs Mooshaber, ‘but perhaps some will be caught this evening....’

The lad put the mug containing his potion down on the table for a moment. With one hand on the dressing and the other on the sofa he examined the mousetraps. It seemed as though he had begun to lose his shyness somewhat.

‘How do the mice walk inside?’ he asked, looking at Mrs Mooshaber.

‘They don’t walk inside, they crawl inside, through this little gate-like thing.’ Mrs Mooshaber showed him. ‘The gate snaps shut behind one and there you are. The mouse is trapped inside.’

‘And what do you do with them in the trap, do you kill them?’ asked the boy with another shudder.

‘I don’t kill them, they die of their own accord’ said Mrs Mooshaber, ‘they succumb to the poison.’ She pointed at the pieces of bacon on the board. 'The mouse gobbles this up, runs around for a bit inside the cage and then falls over. That's when the poison begins to do do its work.'

'And where is it, this poison?' asked the youngster, while with one hand on the dressing he examined a mousetrap.

'The poison's on the bacon,' said Mrs Mooshabr, 'you can see it right there – that white powder.'

'And you buy this bacon?' asked the boy, who was now taking another look at the cake on the table. 'You get it from a butcher?'

'Indeed I do get it from the butcher,' replied Mrs Mooshaber, nodding in agreement. 'But without the poison. I sprinkle that on top here. There's a few pieces of treated bacon on a plate in the larder.'

The lad opened his mouth in surprise and looked very warily at Mrs Mooshaber. It was as if he couldn't believe his own ears. And then he suddenly and unexpectedly asked:

'But why exactly do you poison the mice?'

'Because of all the harm they do,' said Mrs. Mooshaber.

The lad went quiet again, held on to his dressing, looked at the cake on the table and then spoke up again in a diffident voice:

'But there are other things that do harm. Many things are harmful but they don't get killed. Why is it the mice that get killed? Is it because,' (he added quietly) 'they don't speak?'

Mrs Mooshaber fixed her eyes on the trap and nodded.

'If they weren't poisoned,' she said, 'then before you knew it there'd be a whole regiment coming after us. They're desperate and they're bold as brass. They'll eat anything, potatoes, corn, bread – why, they'd even eat that cake on the table... they'd gnaw away at the furniture and bite holes in the bedclothes. This divan too. They must be poisoned. Otherwise they'll worry us to death.'

'I have to go now', whispered the boy. Putting the mousetrap down on the ottoman, he took the mug from the table and once again fixed his eyes upon the cake. Mrs Mooshaber guided him to the front door and sent a final remark into the passage:

'Wet the cloth and apply it to your eye three more times and by tomorrow you'll be back at school and fit as a butcher's dog. Don't get up to mischief, don't upset your mum. You know what will happen to you if you do.'

The clock was striking above the stove when Mrs Mooshaber returned to the kitchen. It was one of those clocks that struck not only the hour but the quarter, half and three-quarter hours. Mrs Mooshaber hurried into her other room in order to finish her washing before darkness had fallen. 'That boy doesn't seem to be so bad,' she said to herself while she was cleaning the floor around the table, 'perhaps he isn't, but then again maybe he's pulling the wool over my eyes. It's only because he was climbing scaffolding that he hurt his eye, and when his mother says he's naughty perhaps he is just that. And don't I know enough and more about naughty children!'

Evening had arrived by the time Mrs Mooshaber finished her washing. Having wrung out the cloths, she draped them over the bucket and left the bucket behind in the room. She went back to the kitchen, rinsed her hands and sat down at the table. She eyed the cake on the table and then the mousetraps on the divan and was on the point of stirring herself to put the mousetraps under the ottoman again when she suddenly froze. Someone was knocking at the front door. Then she heard a woman's voice from outside saying: 'May I come in?' Mrs Mooshaber sighed with relief. It was just the caretaker.

The caretaker was wearing a longer blouse as it was now evening but as ever she was still in the short summer skirt that she had sported during the afternoon.

'It's just little me,' she said in the corridor and headed into the kitchen. Once there she parked herself cheerfully on the ottoman next to the mousetraps.

'You've been baking,' she said, pointing at the table.

'Help yourself', said Mrs Mooshaber while she fed the stove, 'I'll make you some coffee to go with it. It's six o'clock. I've just finished cleaning the room.'

'You've been sprucing your room up,' said the caretaker with a shake of the head. 'That I can see, given that you've got your apron on. Your Nabule is getting married and you stick on an apron and scrub the room. You'd have done better to take a breather, at least on her wedding day. Tell me all about it, Mrs Mooshaber. What was it like? A lot to eat and drink, you said. So much you even overate a little. What treats did you have? Spaghetti?'

'Wine,' said Mrs Mooshaber as she closed the little door of the stove, 'ham, Italian salad, lemonade, and some kolaches at the end. As for the table...'

'Laid out for a banquet, was it?' The caretaker shook her head and adjusted her blouse, 'tidy and trim...'

'Tidy and trim all right,' agreed Mrs Mooshaber, 'white tablecloth, flowers and candles, glasses of wine, kolaches...'

'All you were missing was the incense, then,' laughed the caretaker, 'like we have in the windows for the royal name-day. One other thing, Mrs Mooshaber, your Wezr wasn't there at all, was he? Do you think they didn't let him out?'

'You know they wouldn't do that,' said Mrs Mooshaber as she moved to the sideboard to prepare coffee, 'they don't let people out of gaol for someone's wedding. But he'll be here soon. It's been three months now. You gave me a fright when you knocked – I thought it was him. I was afraid that he was on his way here already.'

'You should call the ratcatcher,' said the caretaker as she looked at the mousetraps right next to her on the sofa, 'cats won't do the job and with you being next to the courtyard and the passage you're right in the front line.'

'A ratcatcher...we'd be waiting till the end of time', said Mrs Mooshaber with a dismissive wave of her hand as she took the coffee over to the stove, 'I don't suppose there'll be anyone from that profession in this city. Ratcatchers were a feature of my youth but they're not around any more. Nowadays everyone has to look out for themselves. Suppose the mice go climbing up the scaffolding which we've got here. Suppose they go crawling right up into the Fabers' place. '

'Did he come for his concoction?' laughed the caretaker as she adjusted her blouse.

'He did,' nodded Mrs Mooshaber while she stood at the stove making coffee, 'I had to show him these here mousetraps lying on the sofa. He'd never seen a mousetrap before, only lions in cages. He wanted to see a mouse, but as luck would have it none was caught yesterday and so I showed him how the mice crawl inside and eat the bacon. He didn't seem such a bad lad to me,' Mrs Mooshaber went on with a sudden shake of the head, 'but what would I know? It's always Mum knows best and when she talks the way she does it must be because she worries about him. I expect he only does what she tells him when she sends him to fetch beer.'

'When he goes for beer he sneaks some himself', said the caretaker with a smile, 'when you see him on the way home, Mrs Mooshaber, it's always with just half a jugful. Mind you it seems to me sometimes....' the caretaker stopped abruptly for blouse adjustment, 'it seems to me that perhaps he only drinks the beer on his way home because they don't feed him properly. It's out of hunger that he takes the beer.'

The caretaker fell silent and fixed her attention on the cake on the table. Then she started up again:

'He drinks beer on the way home simply because he's not getting enough to eat. And did you notice his clothes? I wouldn't bet my life that he'll even have a coat to wear this coming winter, because the way that Faber woman lets him go round he almost looks like a beggar. And you know all about this eye business today,' said the caretaker with more shaking of the head, 'I'd say there was more to this than meets the eye. I mean she drags him off to the eye doctor and she tells him that the swelling may have to be burned away. The poor lad was in such a fright at the thought, shaking all over he was. I had to find some way of keeping him away from this doctor. And as for the drinking,' the caretaker went on nodding as she spoke, 'as for the drinking there may be another reason for it. Perhaps it's not just that the lad doesn't get enough to eat. His father doesn't know when he's had enough to drink either, decent fellow though he is.'

'He drinks', said Mrs Mooshaber with a deep sigh as she brought the caretaker's coffee to the table, 'the lad may well take after him. And then it will be doubly bad that he's been like this from childhood. He be at the schoold for troublemakers and the house of correction and he'll work as an unskilled pair of hands like as not hired for the day until he ends up...' Mrs Mooshaber gave a heavy shake of the head and removed the mousetraps from the ottoman, kneeling down with them on the floor beside the caretaker.

'I'll put these back where they belong,' she said as she put them under the ottoman, 'perhaps they'll catch something during the night.' And then Mrs Mooshaber sat down on a chair opposite the caretaker and said:

'I've still got to empty the bucket of water in the next room, but it can wait for now. Mrs Kralec, I want you to know why I got back so soon from the wedding. I want you to understand that I wasn't at any banquet. They threw me out.'

'Good God,' said the caretaker, and gave such a start that she nearly fell off the sofa, 'threw you out?'

'Threw me out,' Mrs Mooshaber confirmed, 'I was singing a lullaby while Nabule was handing out the ham and salad. She gave the food to everyone except me and then she grabbed hold of the kolaches which I'd baked for the wedding and flung them into the courtyard before throwing me out. She said that I could water my corpses and cosset children. And I was wearing my one and only best clothes for the occasion.'

The caretaker sat stunned for a while until she finally came out with:

'What about the bridegroom Laibach? Didn't he do something about it? Slam the table or shout something?'

'No slamming or shouting,' said Mrs Mooshaber with a shake of the head, 'he's a nice enough chap but he's not one for speaking out. But that's the way it is. There were also two students there, the ones who got served by Nabule, and that was the worst thing of all. I felt so ashamed about it happening right in front of them. She threw me out right in front of their eyes, without a bite to eat and no more than a drop of wine.'

'Mind you, Mrs Mooshaber,' began the caretaker, still shocked at the news, but at last finding words, 'mind you, don't you think they might have been a bit sloshed?'

'It was too early for that,' said Mrs Mooshaber with another shake of the head, before going silent for a while.

'What a terrible thing to happen,' said the caretaker, breaking the silence, 'really terrible. So she chucked the kolaches you made for the wedding into the courtyard....'

'At the horse,' insisted Mrs Mooshaber, 'flung them out for the horse to eat....' And then Mrs Mooshaber rose all of a sudden, went over to the sideboard and opened a small door lower down. 'Drink your coffee,' she said as she extracted three new mousetraps from the sideboard. 'Drink your coffee,' she repeated and bearing the mousetraps made her way slowly towards the door.

'Where are you going with them, Mrs Mooshaber?' asked the caretaker.

'To the courtyard,' replied Mrs Mooshaber, 'to the courtyard. To set traps in the courtyard under the scaffolding. So that those mice don't climb up the scaffolding. Suppose they got to the Fabers. It will be half six,' said Mrs Mooshaber as she took a peek at the clock above the stove, 'I will put the traps in the courtyard while I can still see a little out there, and then I'll take the bucket out of the room. Have some cake with your coffee, I'll just be a moment.' Mrs Mooshaber left the kitchen with the traps and went through the corridor into the passage.

Night had already fallen in the courtyard – it was half past six on a September evening – but it wasn't completely dark. It was a darkness broken by the lights from windows on various floors, so although night had fallen it was possible to see. In what was essentially half-light the courtyard also retained a September evening warmth, while silence reigned everywhere, even on the shared balconies higher up.

Mrs Mooshaber went round the steps at the end of the passage where the dustbin was standing, before continuing through the silent twilight of the courtyard beneath the scaffolding. She was on the point of bending down to set the snares when she heard a brief and feeble whistling sound from up above. She lifted her head just in time to see a pair of green and black lights high up in the sky, lights which then suddenly disappeared as if they'd slipped away into the stratosphere. Mrs Mooshaber gave a nod and was already bending down when she heard a sort of subdued snapping sound up above her. A plank came down into the courtyard. Then another subdued snap could be heard, followed by a thin board falling into the courtyard. At this very moment the clock above the stove in the kitchen struck the half hour, it being half past six and it being possible to hear the sound through the open window of the room. Silence reigned in the courtyard and on the shared balconies. Carrying her mousetraps, Mrs Mooshaber wrenched herself away from the scaffolding beneath which she'd been standing and edged forwards into the courtyard. She turned her head to look up at the scaffolding on the first and second floors and at the shared balconies. Everything remained enveloped in silence, although she suddenly had the impression that up there on the scaffolding something was moving. Moving around somewhere up there among the planks and boards and posts, breathing in quick and terrible gasps, panting while it persistently, so persistently, kept eyeing her, eyeing Mrs Mooshaber, down in the courtyard below. All of a sudden she shivered strangely.

'If it's a cat', she said to herself as she shook, 'that will be all right. Let it be some cat on the prowl up there, it must be a cat on the prowl.' Surprisingly enough Mrs Mooshaber suddenly made her way back, mousetraps in hand, in the

direction of the scaffolding. When she reached the steps, however, she turned round and ran home.

The caretaker was sitting at the table drinking coffee just like before, though by now she was also eating cake. She glanced up when Mrs Mooshaber appeared at the door.

'What's up, Mrs Mooshaber,' she inquired, 'has something happened...haven't you set the traps in the courtyard?'

'No, I didn't set them.' Though Mrs Mooshaber was getting over her shock, she seemed suffused with a strange unease. 'It's dark out there, you can't see any more. I'll set the traps tomorrow. The thing is, Mrs Kralec...' Mrs Mooshaber continued as she carved an anxious path towards the table, 'the thing is...'

‘I heard something fall,’ said the caretaker as she gulped down a mouthful of coffee, ‘something wooden, I think. Did something fall off the scaffolding?’

‘A plank,’ said Mrs Mooshaber as she put the mousetraps down on the table and parked herself on a chair, ‘a plank of some kind and a thin piece of board. I expect there’s a cat up on the scaffolding. It was panting in a timorous way while it looked down at me. But it’s good that it’s there and on the prowl. There was another thing up there,’ Mrs Mooshaber added, ‘a spiceship’.

‘Spaceship’, agreed the caretaker, ‘it’ll be on its way to the Moon. They’re sending three on their way this evening.’ The caretaker had finished with her cake and confined herself to sips of coffee. Mrs Mooshaber looked uneasily at the mousetraps and glanced from time to time at the clock above the stove.

‘The Faber man has a long journey home, after all,’ said the caretaker, ‘he’s at work till six, you know, he even works today when it’s a public holiday. It’ll be seven before he gets home.’

‘He takes the bus?’ asked Mrs Mooshaber with another uneasy glance at the clock.

‘Trolleybus,’ said the caretaker.

‘I’ve never been by trolley.’ Mrs Mooshaber turned her head to face the door to the next room. ‘I’ve only been on the underground once. When I got married, that’ll be fifty years ago now. We started here in Blauental and went to Anna Maria the Blessed Square, then to the Town Hall Station and then to Cemetery Central. In the square at the back of the town hall there used to be a pub, but now the space has been taken up by some modern apartment blocks.’

'Listen here, Mrs Mooshaber,' the caretaker said all of a sudden, rising from her seat, 'Listen, something's just occurred to me.' While Mrs Mooshaber glanced anxiously up at her, the caretaker went on:

'Mrs Mooshaber, do you know someone called Mary Capricorn?'

'Mary Capri....' Mrs Mooshaber looked taken aback so the caretaker repeated:

'Mary Capricorn.'

'Not someone I know,' said Mrs Mooshaber, 'No, I don't know her. And who might she be, this Mary Capri...'

'I've no idea, Mrs Mooshaber,' replied the caretaker as she once more took a seat; 'I don't know her at all.'

'But how can it be that you know about her?' Mrs Mooshaber went on.

'How can it be that I know about her,' echoed the caretaker with a laugh, 'the thing is that I've heard about her. I've heard that she's called Mary Capricorn. That's all I know about her. But if I get to know anything more about her,' she added quickly, 'I'll tell you about it straight away. Straight away, seeing that it interests you to know, I'll tell you straight away.'

There was a short period of silence while the caretaker sipped her coffee and Mrs Mooshaber stroked the mousetraps with her palm while she spent a while looking at the clock above the stove. Finally she spoke:

'All the same I don't get the thing about this Mary Capri. Is she someone special, or what...'

'I really do not know about this Mary Capricorn,' said the caretaker. 'Just like I've told you, don't think about it, Mrs Mooshaber. The world is full of people and it would addle our brains to think of each and every one of them. Then the caretaker uttered a sentence which surprised even her. She said: 'I just don't think that it would be possible to think about everyone in the world. It's enough to think about the people we know. I also think now and then about our princess from Thalia and sometimes I even give a thought to the old man. I mean that old man of mine who fled from me.'

The hands of the clock above the stove crept up on a quarter to seven and Mrs Mooshaber suddenly got to her feet.

'Where are you off to now?' asked the caretaker, 'still laying traps?'

'Only fetching the bucket from the other room,' said Mrs Mooshaber. 'Just sit down and have something to eat, you're not eating your cake. I'll be right back.'

Mrs Mooshaber went into the next room and shut the door gently behind her. She took a damp cloth from the bucket and went over to the window to look at the courtyard. And the very moment she looked into the courtyard she had the impression that something was out there waiting to be seen.

It was as if in the darkness of the courtyard, broken by the light from the upper floors, some kind of shadow was lying just a short distance from the window and the scaffolding. In the darkness of the courtyard, broken by the light from the upper floors, a shadow lay as if it had dropped down from the sky. 'It looks,' Mrs Mooshaber said to herself, 'like one of those nosebags they put under a horse's neck, and here it is, fallen from the sky.' Mrs Mooshaber remained standing at the window with the damp cloth in her hand and staring at the shadow, staring for one minute, for two, for three, for no one knew how long, even the caretaker had no idea, and no one knew what Mrs Mooshaber was thinking all that time. Then the clock in the kitchen struck quarter to seven and Mrs Mooshaber let the cloth drop onto the ground. It fell down with the long thud of a falling tree.

When Mrs Mooshaber stood at the door of the kitchen again the caretaker had a mouth full of cake while her eyes skirted the ottoman.

'Didn't you hear something?' asked Mrs Mooshaber as she stood in the doorway. 'You didn't hear anything?'

The caretaker was about to swallow and only silently shook her head.

'Yes, there was something,' said Mrs Mooshaber in a voice that sounded strange and unfamiliar, 'something came down with a splat. Into the courtyard beneath the scaffolding, just as the clock was striking quarter to.'

'Perhaps it's one of those rocketships flying back from the Moon,' said the caretaker with a smile, while she wiped her lips with her palm, 'there's one landing this evening at about this time.'

It was getting on for seven when steps could be heard at the entrance to the building.

The caretaker pricked up her ears. 'Hear that? It's Faber. He's coming home from work and he's likely had a skinful. It's sure to be him.'

It was him, for sure.

He was about to set foot on the first of the flight of steps when he threw a glance at the silent courtyard into which the darkness had now fallen, to be broken only by the lights from the upper floors, and his unsteady tread ceased. He went round the steps and into the courtyard. Once there he froze to the spot.

There in the darkness of the courtyard, broken only by the lights of the upper floors, a small boy was lying, young Faber, lying on his stomach with his face pressed against the paving and a chequered rag peeping out from under his forehead. Silent and unmoving, he lay like a knot of misery, like a beggar's bundle, a pitiful little ball. In fact he was lying there just like he had a quarter of an hour or even longer beforehand, except that the pool of blood underneath his face had now grown much bigger and was gleaming like a small lake in the night. And silence reigned everywhere.

'Can you hear it?' shouted the caretaker suddenly in the kitchen. 'Can you hear him in the courtyard?'

Mrs Mooshaber's heart missed a beat.

III

After the hearse had left the courtyard at eight in the evening, the inspector opened the door of the police car which had stayed on and said to Mr Faber:

'Come with us, Mr Faber. You'll have to make a statement down at the station. It's just a formality and you'll be back in no time. That empty jug of beer, Dan,' he went on, turning to a young man in uniform who was standing by the car holding the jug, 'kindly hand it over to the lady. Take it, Madam, we have no further use for it.'

'Take the jug, Elizabeth,' said Mr Faber as he got into the car with the inspector, 'take it and stop hanging around all the time in the courtyard. Go into the house, Elizabeth, I'll be back in no time.'

'Mrs Faber will come to me in the meantime,' said Mrs Mooshaber decidedly, 'it would do no good for her to be alone. I'll make some tea.'

'Off you go,' said the inspector from the police car as he opened the back door to the young man in uniform, who had been standing next to the car the whole time, although he'd managed to dispense with the jug. Then the inspector glanced at the surface of the courtyard gleaming in the headlights and said to the caretaker:

'And you, Madam, could do a little tidying up round here.'

The engine spluttered into life, the headlights flashed their beams around the courtyard and the police car went out through the passage. The courtyard was in darkness once again. A few distraught tenants were left standing there, along with Mrs Faber holding the empty jug and the Steinhägers who lived on the first floor. The blood on the surface of the courtyard, illuminated once again by the lights from the upper storeys of the house, continued to glisten. Then the Steinhägers took Mrs Faber, jug in hand, by the arm and slowly escorted her behind Mrs Mooshaber into the passage. Meanwhile the caretaker dragged herself off to fetch a pail of water, which she used to rinse the blood off the surface of the courtyard and went to wash her hands. Then she followed Mrs Faber and the Steinhägers to Mrs Mooshaber's apartment.

'How could a thing like that have happened?' She was terribly pale and upset when she entered Mrs Mooshaber's kitchen. 'Do you think the poor lad really clambered to the edge of the scaffolding and lost his balance? Did he really climb up there this very evening when he went for beer? The inspector said that he took a tumble. Took a tumble. When

I was with Mrs Mooshaber we did hear a banging sound at some point.'

Mrs Mooshaber was standing by the stove with her back towards the table while she made tea. Mrs Faber was sitting on a chair looking as though she had been frozen into the upright position. Her expression remained rigid as she held in her lap the jug which the police had found up on the shared balcony. Mr Steinhäger and his wife were sitting on the ottoman looking shattered, while the pale and distraught caretaker sat next to them. Then she said:

'It's terrible the way he fell like that. When he came to see you with that eye of his, you said he'd be as fit as a fiddle by evening. He'd be off to school next day with a spring in his step.'

'Fit as a fiddle, quick as a squirrel' whispered Mrs Mooshaber from the stove before turning round and bringing mugs of tea to the table. Then she moved to the sideboard, glanced at Mrs Faber and spoke quietly and hesitantly:

'You know, Mrs Faber,' she began in her quiet and hesitant manner, her hands resting on the sideboard, 'I do not believe in God. When I was still small and at school, the farm steward, or perhaps it was one of the farm hands, I cannot recollect any more, told me to stop praying. He said that there was no use in it, because there was no Lord God to hear. He said I'd do better tending my turnips, because it was at least something to live on, and if I had to believe in something I should believe in Fate. Because I could see the hand of Fate everywhere and there was no need to pray to it. Things happen the way they happen. If there's anything I believe in now, then it's Fate. It was Fate, Mrs Faber, so stop tormenting yourself,' Mrs Mooshaber went on addressing

Mrs Faber while she sat coldly upright in the chair with her features frozen, the jug in her lap. Then Mrs Mooshaber continued to talk, with her hands still resting on the sideboard:

'My own deal from Fate was much worse. What have I not suffered at the hands of my children, when have they ceased to be a source of worry to me, despite all that I did for their good? I even used to sing them a lullaby. The caretaker knows it, but what good did it do. Off they went to the school for troublemakers and then the house of correction, now my Wezr is behind bars for the third time and I tremble at the thought he could be out again any moment. And as for Nabule, she threw the kolaches I'd baked out of the window at her wedding and then she threw me out too, without giving me anything to drink, not a crust of bread or a drop of lemonade, and I'd worn my one and only best clothes for the occasion. And there are other things, many other things,' Mrs Mooshaber sighed, 'things which I do not want to tell you, Mrs Faber. However the caretaker knows what I'm talking about.'

'I do,' said the caretaker as the pallor retreated somewhat from her cheeks, 'some money was stolen, your savings in fact.'

'Money was stolen,' echoed Mrs Mooshaber, all the while leaning on the sideboard and looking at Mrs Faber, 'Wezr stole the few guineas I'd been keeping in a cupboard here. They came to the whole of my savings. Once I threw them into the stove and burned them right in front of him. Then I took to stashing the money in rat poison in the larder. Now that he's behind bars I keep it in the cupboard once again. But it's not just the stealing,' said Mrs Mooshaber with a sigh, 'Wezr knows some stonemasons who engrave tombstones in the cemetery. I think they may be from that workshop by the main gate. Who knows whether he doesn't get together with them and attack people, you know what they say, going round that cemetery at night scares the living daylights out of you. I don't mean the main gate by the square but on the other side from the Philipov area, where the park ends. Then there's Nabule on tour at night doing her various rounds. Oh if only I had not had... those children.' For a moment Mrs Mooshaber stopped speaking and silence fell over the group in her kitchen. Mrs Faber continued to sit coldly upright with frozen features, clasping the jug in her lap. The caretaker fingered the blouse below her throat and again went pale. The Steinhägers sat next to her on the sofa, still looking shattered. Then Mrs Mooshaber continued speaking with a shake of her head:

'But since I wanted children, that was that. In any case I had them late, when I was way past forty...I thought I might get some support for my old age. That Wezr would be a soldier or a gentleman of the chamber, that things might one day get a bit easier for me... well, you know...' Mrs Mooshaber suddenly lowered her voice, 'I'd wanted to be a housekeeper or a stallholder from when I was small, to be able to sell things...yes, and now you can see what I've ended up with...'

'But at least you have the Welfare,' said the caretaker, 'you have a card to prove it. You look after other people.'

'I look after other people,' agreed Mrs Mooshaber as she looked at the sideboard, 'I look after others but I can't look after my own family. That I can't do any more. I never could, really. From the time that he went to school Wezr was hitting the other pupils, playing truant and stealing, and it was the same with Nabule. They were always insolent and uncouth.

Wezr was even drinking from when he was a young lad...' Mrs Mooshaber stopped talking and looked at Mrs Faber, who was still sitting coldly upright with frozen features, clasping the jug in her lap, 'you are trembling, Mrs Faber, on the point of collapse, but who knows what might have happened to that lad had he lived? Maybe he would have ended up at the Mother and Child Support Serice with Mrs Knorring, he could have been off to the school for troublemakers and the house of correction and finally he'd have ended up a labourer, an unskilled pair of hands like as not hired for the day like my Wezr and he could have ended up, God forbid, behind bars too. It would have frayed your nerves or been the death of you. Oh...' Mrs Mooshaber shook her head and looked at Mrs Faber, who didn't so much as twitch a muscle in her face, 'do not torment yourself so. And take some tea.'

'Someone should press charges against the masons,' said Mr Steinhäger from the settee, 'for not taking the proper security precautions concerning their work on the balconies. They went off yesterday leaving everything as it was. They knew that it was a national holiday today and that they wouldn't be working, but they did nothing to make the place secure.'

'That's not the masons' fault,' said the caretaker, 'it's the responsibility of the building contractor. They're responsible for all the equipment outside Mrs Mooshaber's door and in the passage. If there's nothing in the way of a light out there at night, it could be the death of someone tripping on those bricks or that 'barrow. And that tub of lime, I mean if Mrs Mooshaber were to fall into it....charges should be pressed against the contractor.'

'And who would press these charges,' asked Mrs Steinhäger in an apprehensive whisper, 'the Fabers?'

'What good would that do?' asked Mrs Mooshaber, moving away from the sideboard and sitting down on a chair, 'if someone managed to kill themselves on the bricks outside my door or if I fell into that tub, they'd say that we should have paid more attention. They'll say this lad shouldn't have gone shinning up the scaffolding. If he hadn't climbed the scaffolding but had gone up via the balcony in the proper manner, he wouldn't have fallen down. A contractor will likely as not prove that the boy drank from the jug of beer on his way home and that it went to his head. Take some tea and have a piece of cake.'

The Steinhägers nodded and hung their heads, but the caretaker merely fiddled with her blouse and remained silent. Then everyone drank tea for a while.

Before long the clock by the stove struck nine. Steps could be heard near the passage and for a moment Mrs Mooshaber froze in her seat. But it was obviously only Mr Faber coming back from the police station. Mrs Faber, forever sitting straight as a board and frozen in position with the jug in her lap, rose to her feet without a word and the others rose with her.

'We will hang out the black flag, Mrs Mooshaber,' said the caretaker with a sigh, 'you've got it in a wardrobe in the corridor, haven't you, along with the pole?' Mrs Mooshaber replied with a nod.

'I have,' she agreed, 'and a spare one besides, I'll hang it out now for the night. I'm glad that Mrs Faber has relaxed and calmed down a bit. Do not torment yourself,' she said again as she went to open the door.

'Just a moment, Mrs Mooshaber,' said the caretaker when the others had all left and the two of them were alone in the kitchen, 'just a moment, I have to speak to you. There's something fishy about all this. The inspector said he took a tumble. Took a tumble - that's what he said, but the way he put it made it seem as if he was really trying to say something else. It seemed to me he almost wanted to suggest...well, I don't quite know what.' The caretaker shook her head and fiddled with her blouse before continuing:

'Perhaps it's nothing. I tend to get this funny feeling sometimes. Of course I could be barking up the wrong tree.'

When even the caretaker had taken her leave, Mrs Mooshaber cleared the table, emptied the bucket which had been left in the room, and went out into the corridor. She extracted a neatly folded black flag attached to a wooden dowel from the wardrobe before reaching behind it and taking hold of the pole. The pole was very long and reached as far as the ceiling. When Mrs Mooshaber went through the door into the passage she had to hold it at an angle. Once there she made her way with pole and flag around barrel, bricks and 'barrow, before going out in front of the house.

Ten paces or so in front of the gateway to the house a gas lamp cast its light onto the street. It was too weak to illuminate the area in front of the dilapidated house properly, but the area wasn't dark because light fell from the windows of the floors above, besides which the sky was bright from the many lights and neon signs in other better parts of the city and perhaps even from the fireworks being set off in the area of the airport and the palace in order to honour Albinus Rappelschlund on his name day. Pole and flag in hand, Mrs Mooshaber gave a quick glance down the poorly-lit street and suddenly had the feeling that she'd caught a glimpse of shadows at the corner. The shadows of two people standing there. Once again Mrs Mooshaber felt her heart miss a beat. She hurriedly attached the dowel to the end of the pole which she used to steer the flag onto a hook protruding above the gate to the house under the first-floor window. The flag unfurled and hung in the air. Again Mrs Mooshaber glanced at the corner of the street. Empty. There were no longer any shadows. Carrying the pole Mrs Mooshaber vanished into the gateway and then to her apartment. She took care to lock the door and returned the pole to its place in the corridor behind the wardrobe. Then she went to the kitchen and for a while was in no state to do anything else.

'In the morning I was getting ready to go to a wedding,' she said to herself, 'and in the evening I went to hang out the black flag. What am I to make of it all? And on top of all that wasn't this meant to be some kind of public holiday...'

Mrs Mooshaber looked at the sideboard and with her head in a whirl it suddenly struck her that she what she really needed was sleep.

IV

They placed the coffin on the right-hand side of the grave and laid a posy of flowers on a pile of earth behind it. Mr Faber stared at the hole in front of his feet. Mrs Faber, frozen upright, was looking vaguely into the beyond, where an endless line of gravestones met her eyes. Beside the Fabers stood a lowly church official and a few other people were behind him with the Steinhägers, Mrs Kralec the caretaker and Mrs Mooshaber with her big black bag. Pride of place

among the people there was assumed by a tallish thin woman with delicate, prim features and some sheets of music in her hand. This was Mrs Knorring from the Mother and Child Support Service.

But the people standing behind the Fabers and the wretched servant of the Church were not the only ones there. To the right of the grave, by the coffin and the pile of earth with the posy on top, was a small path on which three other people were standing. One was an oldish gentleman in a bowler hat and unbuttoned tail-coat, a gold chain with a watch hanging from the waistcoat beneath. Next to him stood an older lady, plump of figure and sporting a blue summer bonnet, behind which a restive hair of black curls peeked out. This was Mrs Eichenkranz, the owner of a small shop on the boundary between the cemetery and the park. Beside her a boy in a blue-and-white stripey top stood fidgeting. From time to time Mrs Eichenkranz threw a glance at Mrs Knorring from Mother and Child Support while giving the lad repeated tugs by the elbow.

'Behave yourself,' she whispered as she gave his elbow another tug, 'people are looking at us.'

But stripey little Eichenkranz kept fidgeting with one hand behind his back where it played with the posy on the pile of earth, while he slowly edged up behind his mother as if he was trying to hide himself.

'You're at a funeral, and that over there is Mrs Knorring from Welfare,' Mrs Eichenkranz hissed at the lad, 'stop your fidgeting and stop crawling up behind me...'

But the lad took no notice. He kept fidgeting all the time, playing with the posy of flowers behind his back and crowding up more and more to his mother.

'It's your friend they're burying,' said Mrs Eichenkranz, giving him a nudge, 'he did something foolish and you can see for yourself what came of it. In a short while the poor lad will be in that hole there.'

At this point the church official came to the end of his prayers and there was a moment's silence. Mr Faber was still gazing into the hole below his feet and Mrs Faber, still frozen in her upright pose, was staring ahead at the endless array of graves. Then the gravediggers took hold of the straps and began to lower the coffin. Little Eichenkranz was now standing behind his mother and as close to her as he could get. He had stopped playing with the posy and had a final fidget. At that moment even the old man in the bowler hat and the unbuttoned tailcoat, standing on the other side of Mrs Eichenkranz with the watch-chain in his waistcoat, began to fidget. When the coffin bumped on the bottom of the grave, the lad standing right behind his mother shrugged his shoulders, put his hand into his pocket and climbed the pile of earth. Before Mrs Eichenkranz could turn round and get hold of his arm there was a flash of blue-and-white stripey top behind the grave and then he vanished among the tombs as if he'd merged with them. Mrs Eichenkranz and the old man in the bowler hat had to move aside at this moment, because the gravediggers wanted to get to work with their shovels on the pile of earth with the posy behind them. That was when the old man in the bowler hat yelled out.

'Help me!' he shouted 'Help! Someone please help me, I've been....' While he spoke he was groping for his pocket and for the waistcoat in which the gold watch and chain were hanging, 'I've been robbed. I've been robbed.'

'Please sir, you are at a graveside, 'said somebody behind the Fabers, while one of the gravediggers remarked: 'Have some decency.'

'Nonsense,' said Mrs Eichenkranz, her plump cheeks colouring under the blue bonnet and curls. Soon the funeral was over and Mrs Knorring, Mrs Eichenkranz and a few other women stood alongside the old man in the bowler hat under a chestnut tree on a path near the grave. 'You can't have been robbed. There's your watch,' Mrs Eichenkranz went on as she turned to the old man and pointed to the waistcoat beneath his tails, 'it's hanging right there.'

'It's not the watch that's missing,' the old man yelled, 'it's my wallet. I keep it here behind the coat-tail.'

'Now then, sir,' said Mrs Eichenkranz as a certain sharpness crept into her voice, 'who knows where you might have lost your money. Perhaps you didn't bring the wallet with you.'

'Of course I did,' the old man shouted, 'I'd never go to the cemetery without some money. I couldn't even use the trolley-bus. I had all of two guineas.'

'Mrs Eichenkranz.' It was Mrs Knorring who was speaking now, the tallish thin woman with the elegantly prim features and sheets of music in her hand, 'it's certainly true that complaints to the Mother and Child Support Service about your son never stop these days. Things go missing at the school and everyone suspects him of taking them. He doesn't pay attention, he plays truant and goes wandering off.'

'I can't keep an eye on him all the time,' wailed Mrs Eichenkranz, her plump cheeks still red, 'I have a shop to keep going. I can't spend all my time in his wake, I can't watch his every step. How can I know where he goes? But stealing, that's not something he'd do. I was always a decent woman, always honest, where could he have got such habits from? Such things run in the genes, don't they?'

'What about the air-gun, Mrs Eichenkranz?' Mrs Knorring was shaking her head and clutching the score to her bosom. 'A week ago a policeman confiscated it from him. He was shooting birds here in the cemetery. Finches and tits. It is forbidden to shoot at any live target.'

'He'd never shoot finches and tits,' protested Mrs Eichenkranz, 'not even blackbirds. And not squirrels, never squirrels, he really likes them. He likes all living things and that includes birds. He just wanted to shoot some crows during the winter - after all, they're real vermin. But he didn't get any. Look for yourself, see how many there are right here in the cemetery...' Mrs Eichenkranz pointed at the endless rows of trees and tombstones around her, among which at that moment there wasn't a single crow to be seen, 'he's never shot a single crow. He couldn't hit one if he tried. He's never so much as touched a crow.'

'Mrs Eichenkranz,' said Mrs Knorring as she shifted her score from one hand to the other, 'you don't take enough care of him. You say you can't keep an eye on him because you have a shop to keep. That you can't follow him around and watch his every step. You don't take enough care of him. That means Mother and Child Support can remove him from your care.'

'Oh my God!' exclaimed Mrs Eichenkranz, feeling for the black curls under her bonnet, 'how can you say I don't take enough care of him? I always take the best care I can. I never take my eyes off him. I watch his every step. He has all the food and sleep he needs, everything he could possibly want. There are goldsmiths who don't provide so well for their children.'

'Mrs Mooshaber,' said Mrs Knorring, performing a slight about turn in order to face the woman standing behind her next to the caretaker, the big, black, bulging bag nestling in her hand, 'Mrs Mooshaber. Mrs Eichenkranz's twelve-year-old boy, that lad who was standing here a moment ago, plays truant from his school, goes wandering off and shoots birds. You know this cemetery well, better than Messrs Smirsch and Landl – you know who I'm referring to – oh no, you don't...' Mrs Knorring promptly corrected herself, 'you don't know them yet, they're new to our Service. Why don't you take the case, Mrs Mooshaber, and make a report for me at the office. I've got choir practice now.' And before you could blink an eyelid Mrs Knorring had made off in a rustle of sheet music as she transferred the score between her hands yet again.

For a moment silence reigned on the cemetery path beneath the chestnut tree.

Then Mrs Eichenkranz, her face still red beneath her black curls and blue bonnet, turned to Mrs Mooshaber and said almost in sobs:

'I'm a decent woman, a widow, I take care of my boy every way I can. I take care of him till I'm ready to drop. How could they take him away from me? You work for them at the Welfare?'

'My name is Natalia Mooshaber and I am not an employee of the Mother and Child Support Service. I just do some work there,' said Mrs Mooshaber, 'I have a card to prove it.'

'Mrs Mooshaber has a document to prove it,' the caretaker butted in, 'she's had one for the last twenty years. As for that poor Faber boy,' she went on, pointing to the lad's

grave, now some distance off and already filled in, 'she saved the poor fellow's eye. Were it not for her, the lad would have lost his sight in that eye.'

'I have a card,' Mrs Mooshaber repeated, taking one out of her bag, 'here's my licence, Madam. See for yourself. With an official stamp and the signature of Mrs Knorring herself.'

Mrs Eichenkranz looked at the card which made her recoil without thinking.

'But I do take enough care of him,' she repeated in a sharp tone of voice as she reached for the bonnet and curls, 'I'm a widow living a decent life and with a shop to manage. And now I am going to find my boy.'

'But what about me?' wheezed the old man in the bowler hat with the open tailcoat and the gold watch-chain in his waistcoat. He had remained standing there the whole time, shuffling from one foot to the other. 'What about me? Madam,' he went on, addressing Mrs Mooshaber, 'Will you investigate this?'

'Investigate I will,' agreed Mrs Mooshaber.

'Mrs Mooshaber will investigate,' put in the caretaker, 'she has experience of this sort of work. She's been doing Welfare jobs for the last twenty years.'

'For God's sake, Madam,' exclaimed Mrs Eichenkranz in a vehement new outburst, 'he never took anything from this gentleman. He doesn't know him. He's never seen him before in his life. Nor for that matter have I.'

'What does that have to do with it?' yelled the old man before turning to Mrs Mooshaber once again and saying, 'In any case, Madam, be sure to start investigating the matter.'

'One thing at a time,' said Mrs Mooshaber with a shake of her big black bag, 'first I must see the lad and ask him a thing or two. I must do some fact-finding work. Go home,' she said to the old man in the bowler hat, 'come in three days' time at two in the afternoon to see Mrs Knorring at Mother and Child Support. She'll tell you what my inquiries have revealed. Now I will join you, Madam,' she said to Mrs

Eichenkranz, 'You will go and find your boy, but you must come with me first.'

'For God's sake,' Mrs Eichenkranz cried out again, her eyes nearly popping out, 'are we going to the police? I'm a widow who lives a decent life and I've never had any dealings with the police. I look after my boy properly.'

'Not the police,' said Mrs Mooshaber, shaking that bag of hers, still big, black and bulging, 'we're going over there to a grave some way off. It's one of mine, and when I'm here in the cemetery I have to take a look at it. But when I've had a look, we'll get on straight away with tracking down the boy.'

'Good Grief!' exclaimed the caretaker as she scanned the endless rows of tombstones, 'it's a pity that I can't go with you. I could give you a hand. I suppose you'll ferret him out?' she wondered, addressing Mrs Eichenkranz.

A few of those who had been at young Faber's graveside had already left. Further off the grave had been filled in and the posy placed on top of it. From somewhere in the distance came the sound of horns, trumpets and sublime singing.

'That must be another funeral,' Mrs Mooshaber told the caretaker with a further shake of the big, black and bulging bag, before saying to Mrs Eichenkranz: 'Come along, then.'

'What about me?' persisted the old man in the bowler hat, left standing below the chestnut tree.

The women followed the path lined with chestnut trees and Mrs Eichenkranz, her plump cheeks still flushed, remarked:

'How can he possibly claim that the lad robbed him? How can he dare to say such a thing? Madam, I know this boy, I'm a widow and fifty years of age. He wouldn't steal a penny.'

'For all I know, you may be mistaken about him, Madam,' said Mrs Mooshaber. 'I know of one mother who was just as wrong about her children. She also thought that her children would turn out just fine, and then they ended up in the school for troublemakers and then the house of correction.'

'But there's nothing bad about my boy,' persisted Mrs Eichenkranz, 'I make an honest living with my shop and I take care of him. And he's never shot squirrels and tits, he loves them, he hasn't even shot the crows round here. He just pretended he was shooting them, but the truth is he never got one; he never so much as touched one. And he wouldn't so much as steal a bunch of flowers off a grave.'

'No shooting is allowed,' insisted Mrs Mooshaber, 'no shooting at any target. Madam, I know of one mother whose son is returning today from his third spell behind bars, and before long her daughter will be going the same way.'

'I look after him as best I can,' persisted Mrs Eichenkranz, 'I always know where he is and what he's up to. I know his every move. Night has scarcely fallen before he's back in the house. How could he ever go roaming around? He'd never steal so much as a candle from a church.'

'The Support Service can take him off you,' Mrs Mooshaber reminded her, 'children must obey and they are not allowed to miss school. I know a mother who even sang a lullaby to her children, and you should see what they're like now. Her daughter was getting married and she flung the kolaches which her mother had baked for the wedding ceremony out of the window at a horse in the courtyard.'

'Perhaps they'd gone hard,' said Mrs Eichenkranz

'Not at all,' insisted Mrs Mooshaber with a shake of her ever big, black and bulging bag. 'They were very good kolaches. She spent all day making them using butter, vanilla and raisins. Cream cheese into the bargain.'

'My boy would never throw away food,' said Mrs Eichenkranz, 'if anything, he'd give a horse a sugar lump. Why would the Welfare take him away from me? He'd never so much as steal a light off a grave.'

'A light off a grave,' repeated Mrs Mooshaber with a shake of the head, 'that's how it all begins, you know. School for troublemakers, the house of correction, a labourer, an unskilled pair of lands like as not hired for the day, few oddjobs and a career that ends behind bars... my dear lady, I know a mother, whose daughter was getting married and she threw her mother out of the wedding reception before the banquet was on the table. She didn't even get a crust. They had ham and salad, lemonade and wine too. And the mother had worn her one and only best outfit for the occasion.'

The two of them were silent for a while, Mrs Mooshaber in her long, black and ancient skirt, dark scarf and waistless jacket and bag big, black and bulging, Mrs Eichenkranz with her plump red cheeks in the blue bonnet underneath which the curls peeked out. It was a beautiful September afternoon, the sunlight bathing the tops of the trees and bouncing off the tombs and flowers. They took a long and larger path, lined by green chestnut trees, although it was not the main thoroughfare. Then they reached a fork in the road beyond which there was a section of cemetery containing big and beautiful tombs. 'We go in this direction,' said Mrs Mooshaber as she gave her bag a shake, 'my grave is over there. As soon as I've done my duty by it, you have to find the boy for me.'

'You can be sure that I'll find him,' said Mrs Eichenkranz, 'how could I not do so? I know his every move. He's somewhere here in the cemetery.'

They reached a large marble gravestone with a statue of an angel, a grave light inside a lantern and a small enclosure covered in luxuriant green grass.

'This is it,' said Mrs Mooshaber, 'you must wait for me here. First there are some things I need to do and after that I will do my duty by the lad.'

Mrs Eichenkranz stopped in front of the gravestone and read the inscription. Large gold lettering looked back at her:

THE FAMILY OF THE DIRECTOR OF EDUCATION
BARON DE SCHUBAUER

Beneath were the words:

Director of Education
Baron Joachim de Schubauer
Born 1854, Died 1914

Under this came a row of names and dates featuring a Mathurin, an Anna, a Leopold and a Rozalie.

'This is the grave you look after, Madam,' said Mrs Eichankranz in a choking voice.

'It is,' agreed Mrs Mooshaber, as she bent down and opened the big and bulging bag, 'none of the family has been spared to live and tend the grave, so there's only myself. Wait for me here.' Mrs Mooshaber removed a watering-can, a brush and some pruning shears from that bag of hers. 'Then, we'll go straight away to find your boy, Mrs....er, Mrs...'

‘Eichenkranz,’ said the other quickly, ’Klotilda Eichenkranz. I have a small shop between the park and the cemetery. Next to the Philipov area.’

Mrs Mooshaber extracted another bottle from her bag. It contained water which she now poured into the can. Then she used the brush to clean the marble headstone and around the lantern containing the grave light. Afterwards she took the pruning shears and gave the small patch of grass a neat trim. Then she reached for the watering-can.

‘Other times I don’t bother to bring water from home,’ she said without looking up at Mrs Eichenkranz, who was standing and silently watching behind her without so much as breathing a word, ‘I get the water from a barrel here. Today I brought it from home because I was going to the funeral and didn’t want to make a detour to the barrel and back. None of the family has been spared to live and tend the grave so there’s just myself,’ she repeated.

‘So, Madam,’ Mrs Eichenkranz continued in more tender and even shy tones, ‘you are a baroness?’

‘I am not a baroness,’ replied Mrs Mooshaber, ‘I am Natalia Mooshaber and work for the Mother and Child Support Service. I’m in charge of a few graves which I look after here in the cemetery.’

‘And may I ask,’ Mrs Eichenkranz inquired with a more cheerful countenance, ‘whether you are paid for this work?’

‘I am,’ confirmed Mrs Mooshaber, now extracting a rag from her bag, ‘for all the graves in my keep I receive two guineas per month. I have only a little by way of widow’s pension. My husband worked as a coachman in the brewery.’

‘Hang on a moment, Madam.’ Mrs Eichenkranz made a quick leap towards the grave, ‘let me give you a bit of help.

This rag is for cleaning the headstone? I'll give it a wipe myself.'

'Go ahead and give it a wipe,' said Mrs Mooshaber, 'but be careful of the angel. It's got a cracked wing.'

Mrs Eichenkranz wiped the angel and the tombstone, while Mrs Mooshaber used the brush to sweep the rest of the slab in front of it. Then everything was done.

'How well your patch of grass grows,' Mrs Eichenkranz remarked, 'I've never seen anything like it. Do you sow it in the spring?'

'I sow it in the spring, yes,' said Mrs Mooshaber as she put her implements back into the bag, 'I also do some tilling to loosen the earth. I've a trowel at home for that. I like a grave to be tidy and seemly. Now we'll continue on the path leading to Chapel Five.' Mrs Mooshaber rose from filling the bag and pointed the way. 'We'll look for the boy all right, but first I have to show you a couple more graves in these parts which belong to me.'

'We'll tend those too, shall we?' asked Mrs Eichenkranz quickly. Mrs Mooshaber shook her head. 'They were seen to yesterday,' she explained, 'I'm just going to check on them today. I'll just show you them and then we'll look for the lad.'

They left Baron de Schubauer's grave behind and slowly made their way along the path to Chapel Five. The section of cemetery featuring large and splendid graves gave way to others which were smaller and humbler.

'Take a look.' Mrs Mooshaber had stopped for a moment and was pointing at a round gravestone, 'See that grave there? That was a happy mother. She lived to be eighty,' she went on, pointing at the inscription, 'her son was very successful. He was a master builder.'

Mrs Eichenkranz stopped and read the gold lettering on the gravestone:

VINCENCIA CANCER

'He was a master builder and she was happy,' Mrs Mooshaber repeated with a shake of the bag, while Mrs Eichenkranz went on to read the second name underneath the first:

VINCENCIUS CANCER, MASTER BUILDER

'Now I'll show you something very different,' said Mrs Mooshaber as she moved on, 'we go back to the path here.' They walked on the grass, passing several graves and turned onto a small path, continuing on their way in silence for a while. Then Mrs Mooshaber stopped and pointed to a gravestone which tapered at the top beneath a birch tree.

'Take a look,' she said.

Mrs Eichenkranz stopped by the grave and read:

THEREZIA BEKENMOSCHT

'Who was she, this Mrs Bekenmoscht?' she asked.

'She was an unhappy mother,' said Mrs Mooshaber as she swept a couple of leaves that had fallen ahead of their time off the grave, 'she had children who went bad. Became labourers, unskilled pairs of hands like as not hired for the day. She thought that they'd turn out decent and help her in her old age. As it was, when old age crept up on her she hanged herself.' With a glance at a few thick bushes further off which hid from sight several of the neighbouring graves, she went on:

'One of the Bekenmoschts is perhaps still alive, he's a stonemason. He engraves the inscriptions on tombs here in the stonecutter's place by the main gate. My son Wezr probably knows him. All in all, he knows quite a few masons. Let's be getting along, Madam.'

They moved over the grass between several more graves before reaching a small path, after which they turned back onto the larger path.

'Where are we actually going?' asked Mrs Eichenkranz as she reached for the bonnet over her curls, 'it's such a big cemetery here.'

'Perhaps you know where we should be going,' replied Mrs Mooshaber, 'perhaps you know the place where a certain boy likes to squirrel himself away.'

'He doesn't squirrel himself away,' said Mrs Eichenkranz, 'he buzzes around. He's forever to-ing and fro-ing. He could have nipped across from the cemetery to the street and that would mean he isn't in the cemetery at all. Anyhow come this way, we'll probably come across him over there,' she said, pointing at Chapel Five.

'More likely there.' Mrs Mooshaber was pointing in another direction. 'That's where the water supply is. By the tomb of the Loch family.'

They skirted Section Sixteen of the cemetery by means of a larger path, which continued towards an avenue in the distance. They came across people in summer clothes, including a smattering of old ladies, it being a beautiful September afternoon.

'Graves have to be tidy and seemly,' Mrs Eichenkranz concurred. 'That's the mark of a good family. Your graves, Madam, are so spick and span that they are a pleasure to behold.' After a while she added: 'But it's no wonder they're like that, seeing as you take such good care of them, even to the point of tilling the ground in the spring. If you wanted, you could get a commission to look after a hundred. You know how to do it so well. You could even look after the Tomb of the Unknown Soldier.' Finally she went on:

'Those coachmen in the breweries, they were real gentlemen. Were it not for them, the beer would never have reached the guests. I am someone best placed to know that, Madam.'

They came to a smaller parting of the ways and Mrs Mooshaber said:

'We should do a bit more ferreting around. I thought we were looking for him.'

'But who's to say we aren't looking for him?' said Mrs Eichenkranz, 'hang on a minute...' She scurried off to a tombstone beyond the fork in the path, took a look behind it and said:

'He's not here. Where can he be?'

'We must look harder,' said Mrs Mooshaber with a shake of her big, black and bulging bag, 'we must go on looking so that I can make my report to Mrs Knorring. Perhaps over there behind that burial mound...' she was pointing at a tombstone with a tapered top. Mrs Eichenkranz ran off to the tombstone, peered behind it and shook her head.

'Not there either,' she said, 'but wait a moment. I know what. I'll ask someone.'

An old lady with a lace collar was sitting on a bench in front of one tombstone and Mrs Eichenkranz went up to her.

'Excuse me, Madam, but have you by any chance seen a boy in a stripey top round here?'

The old lady with the lace collar, who was blinking at a prayer book through the spectacles on her nose, responded to the question with a weak shake of the head.

'She's not seen him either,' Mrs Eichenkranz told Mrs Mooshaber, 'he'll be in the street somewhere.'

At last they arrived at the water supply by the Loch family grave. The supply amounted to a pipe with a tap fixed onto a huge barrel from which people ran water to use on the graves. Underneath a big chestnut tree beside the water supply stood a huge rubbish bin. This was full of withered flowers, paper and watermelon peel.

'No shortage of watermelons this year,' said Mrs Eichenkranz, 'there was a bumper crop. I ought to check the ones at home to make sure that they haven't gone off.'

'You know something,' began Mrs Mooshaber as she walked up to the barrel, 'I feel thirsty. I must drink something. I will pour some into my bottle,' she said as she opened her big black bag.

'You drink the water from here?' Mrs Eichenkranz exclaimed in surprise.

'Needs must,' said Mrs Mooshaber, 'but what of it? It comes from the city water supply. They have the same water in the Elizabethan district, where those new homes are being built at the moment.'

'You know what,' said Mrs Eichenkranz, 'let me make a suggestion. Don't get your bottle out here, but come to my place instead. You can have a drink there. It's only a short distance away, between the cemetery and the park, and at least you'll be able to see my shop and how I make a living. And you never know, the lad might even be there.'

'And where exactly do you have this shop?' Mrs Mooshaber inquired.

'Between the cemetery and the park in the Philipov area,' Mrs Eichenkranz repeated, 'just a short distance away. You'll be able to have something to drink there.'

'And what do you sell there?' asked Mrs Mooshaber, 'watermelons?'

'Not watermelons,' said Mrs Eichenkranz with a shake of the head, 'things for the cemetery. Flowers, candles, lamp oil, graveyard lights.' Then she went on: 'But I really have two shops in one. I also have a little off licence.'

'An off licence?' asked Mrs Mooshaber in surprise, 'do you sell beer on tap?'

'Not on tap,' said Mrs Eichenkranz, shaking her head, 'I sell it in bottles.'

'Lemonade too?'

'Naturally,' nodded Mrs Eichenkranz, 'lemonade, beer and a little something to eat.'

'Surely not ham and salad?' asked Mrs Mooshaber.

'Not that, no.' Mrs Eichenkranz shook her head. 'They have that in the kiosk. I don't have a kiosk, just a shop, even though it has a counter outside. But besides flowers, candles and lamps I have other things, as you will see. And you will at least see how I look after my boy. It's this way to Philipov,' she said, pointing the way.

They reached the end of the cemetery, where there was a wall and a large barred gate, behind which lay the park. By the wall, a few paces from the last row of graves, stood the back of some single-storey building, half-hidden by bushes.

'There they are,' said Mrs Eichenkranz as she reached for the bonnet above her curls, 'my apartment and my shop. The front of the building faces the park and that's where the front entrance is. But I have a door here in the cemetery too, a back door, can you see it?' She pointed it out and Mrs Mooshaber saw that there was a small door to the building from the cemetery, half-overgrown with shrubs.

'Don't you feel afraid here?' asked Mrs Mooshaber.

'You grow used to it, Madam,' said Mrs Eichankranz with a smile, 'I've been living among these tombs for years now and I've grown accustomed to the nightly goings-on in the cemetery. Besides, this back door,' she went on, pointing at the bushes, 'is shut for good and secured with nails. And rusted over as well. It can't be opened. And even if the door could be opened, it still wouldn't happen because there are no keys for it. Not even a ghost could get in using that route.'

'But aren't you afraid for other reasons,' asked Mrs Mooshaber, 'I mean about people getting in from the park side of the building? People say it's not advisable to walk around the outside of the cemetery in the park here, around Philipov... there being several mobsters in the area.'

'You know, Madam,' said Mrs Eichenkranz with a nod, 'sometimes there are all sorts of people loitering here of an evening, but what do you expect of a park? How could I tell which are mobsters and which aren't? My place has not been burgled yet.'

'The shop is shut at the moment?' asked Mrs Mooshaber. Mrs Eichenkranz nodded.

'I had to close in order to go to the funeral. I won't be opening today. Please come along.'

They went out of the cemetery through the barred gate and found themselves at the end of the park, right by the cemetery wall. Several paths led further into the park from underneath some tall trees surrounded by thick bushes. Skirting the wall they turned a corner, passed a large plane-tree and then they were right in front of the shop and residence of Mrs Eichenkranz. Above a broad window with a shutter was a sign saying:

KLOTILDA EICHENKRANZ, WIDOW

Caters for all your cemetery needs

Next to that was a metal sign sporting a coloured picture of a bottle and the inscription:

BEER AND LEMONADE!

Mrs Eichenkranz drew out a key and opened the door next to the closed window.

'The lad is probably not here, seeing as it's locked,' said Mrs Mooshaber as they went in, and Mrs Eichankranz nodded. 'Probably not,' she agreed, 'he's bound to be somewhere on the street or in some alley, the little rascal. Please come on in.'

Mrs Mooshaber found herself in a small kitchen with doors leading to the shop and to a living-room. The door to the shop was open. A special sweetish scent hung in the air all around them.

'This is my kitchen and you can see the shop through there,' said Mrs Eichenkranz. 'There are lots of items,' she said pointing to the shop, 'take a peek.'

Mrs Mooshaber's peek into the shop took her breath away. There was a heap of faded artificial flowers, together with candles and oil-lamps. The table was stacked with every sort of light or lantern for a grave. Bundles of tattered ribbons in rainbow colours and inscribed with gold and silver lettering were hanging from pegs.

'You sell all these things?' asked Mrs Mooshaber in surprise.

'All of them,' confirmed Mrs Eichenkranz as she reached for the bonnet atop the head of black curls, 'I sell at low prices. People buy from me when they're going to the cemetery from the park here in Philipov. The ones who go through the main gate also know me, as do those who use the gate from Anna Maria the Blessed Square, coming from the main station or from the Blauental area. Anyway, I sell other things too, take a look.' Mrs Eichenkranz stepped up to a curtain and drew it to one side. Behind the curtain was a pile of walking sticks and umbrellas, and a shelf on which hats, gloves and colourful scareves of every kind lay in abundance.

'You sell these too?' asked Mrs Mooshaber, still sounding surprised.

'These too,' Mrs Eichankranz confirmed, 'and at low prices too. The goods are pre-loved as they like to say. But some of them are nice and nearly-new. I doubt whether they've been used more than once. Like these umbrellas or this hat here. It's a hunter's hat. I've got bowlers over here, have a look. And nice gloves too. Deerskin for the autumn, fur for the winter and also odd gloves for just one hand, left or right, people buy them for cleaning. I sell everything here.

I must check the watermelon and see whether it's gone bad,' she went on and looked at something kept under a glass by the stove. 'No, it's not gone bad yet. But you said you were thirsty,' she added quickly, 'take the weight off your feet in the kitchen and put down that bag. I'll have something for you right away.'

'You say you've got lemonade,' Mrs Mooshaber remarked as she returned to the kitchen, sat down and set the bag at her feet.

'Oh my, Madam.' Mrs Eichenkranz was bending down beneath the counter in the shop, 'You know something, there's not a single lemonade left. Nothing but the empties which I keep under here,' she went on, pointing under the counter. 'Never mind, I'll give you something even better. Beer.' And she came into the kitchen bearing a bottle of beer and a glass which she set down on the table.

'Oh but Madam,' said Mrs Mooshaber suddenly from her chair with the bag at her feet, 'I hadn't reckoned on this. I mean I've only got small change with me.'

'Come now, Madam,' laughed Mrs Eichenkranz as she took off her bonnet to reveal an even lovelier harvest of rich black curls, 'You are my guest. Such an honoured guest, indeed, that I'm only too pleased that you permit me to be your host. Allow me to give you some cake,' Mrs Eichenkranz continued as she slipped out to the shop to reach under another glass and came back to the table bearing cake. Then she clipped off the metal cap of the bottle with a hook and poured the beer into a glass. 'Have something to eat and drink.'

'What a pleasant place you have here,' said Mrs Mooshaber as she took a drink and thanked her host, 'I've just noticed that you've got a window over there looking onto the park. The window in my kitchen is frosted glass and leads into the house corridor. Do you sleep here too?'

'Here on the sofa,' confirmed Mrs Eichenkranz, 'but you still haven't seen my other room. It's just over here...' Mrs Eichenkranz hurriedly opened another door and pointed to the room. 'Take a look', she said.

Mrs Mooshaber got up and examined the room. There was a wardrobe, a desk, a chair and another ottoman. Pictures hung on the walls.

'Very nice,' said Mrs Mooshaber, 'and that window looks onto some bushes.'

'The bushes in the cemetery', said Mrs Eichankranz with a smile, 'it's beside the rusty back door that doesn't open, the one for which there's no key. You can't even see the window from the cemetery, it's so overgrown now. But in the winter when the growth dies down you get a direct view of the graves through that window.'

Mrs Mooshaber gave a nod before returning to her seat in the kitchen.

'Splendid,' she repeated, 'splendid. And where does that aroma come from? It's everywhere. I could sense it from the moment I came in. Like marzipan or incense. Perhaps you have even...'

'Now then, Madam,' Mrs Eichenkranz put in quickly, 'now then, what could you be thinking? Perhaps that I'd been burning a little incense for the national holiday in honour of Rappelschlund. Not me. Who could do a thing like that? Mind you, if it was a a day in honour of the Princess, then I would burn incense all right, I would put flowers in the window, not to mention candles and cakes,

I would put wine right here in the window facing the park and in the other window too, yes I would. But not for that Rappelschlund, not a thing for him. It's those dried flowers that you can smell.'

'And you do your cooking here?' asked Mrs Mooshaber as she looked at the hob.

'Here in the kitchen,' Mrs Eichenkranz confirmed, 'it's a pity that I haven't done any today. If only I'd made crow soup, you'd have been able to taste some, Madam. Full of goodness it is. But it must be a young crow, the old ones are no good at all. It's better than chicken. Have you ever eaten crow soup?'

'Not yet,' Mrs Mooshaber confirmed with a shake of the head, 'though once I ate dog. But that was a long time ago. Where do you go for bread?' she asked.

'To Elizabeth Verdun,' said Mrs Eichenkranz, 'in the square by the station.'

'That's a bakery, is it?' asked Mrs Mooshaber. Mrs Eichenkranz shook her head. 'It's a grocer's, their bread's baked by a man called Moos.'

'I go to the co-op for it myself,' said Mrs Mooshaber, 'they have good bread at low prices. They have fresh bread every third day at three o'clock. In fact I'm going there tomorrow.'

'The co-op bakes good bread,' Mrs Eichenkranz agreed. 'I'd go there myself, but there's no co-op near the park and cemetery. You live in the Stadium district, don't you?'

'In Blauental,' said Mrs Mooshaber, 'by the crossroads near the *Sunflower* department store. But in the old part of Blauental, not the new part, if you know the area I mean. My daughter got married recently and will move to the Elizabeth district. She's saving up for an apartment there.'

'It's lovely in Elizabeth, she'll certainly like it there,' said Mrs Eichenkranz, 'and whom did your daughter marry, then? Perhaps an artist? An official from the Welfare?'

'A bricklayer,' said Mrs Mooshaber, 'a bricklayer called Laibach. He's well brought up and hard-working. In the meantime he has lodgings with Miss Klaudinger. No sign of the boy,' Mrs Mooshaber went on, and took another sip of beer.

'No there isn't,' sighed Mrs Eichenkranz, 'where can he be? Oh God, he's such a worry to me,' she suddenly exclaimed as she sat down on a chair opposite Mrs Mooshaber and buried her face in her palms, 'no one knows how much I worry about him. And now the Welfare's threatening to take him away from me. I look after him as best I can, I watch his every step. I already worry enough about him getting into trouble at school.'

'That's how it is,' said Mrs Mooshaber as she looked at the plump cheeks and dark curls in front of her, 'I know what it's like. My own children got into trouble at school. My Nabule has been in scraps since she was a tot and my Wezr was so uncouth, getting into fights and injuring his schoolmates. They sent him to Mother and Child Support when he got to Year Two and that was when I actually got to know Mrs Knorring. You'll realise how long I've known her when I tell you that Wezr is now twenty-five. When I met her Mrs Knorring had only just started there. They sent Wezr to a school for troublemakers and later the same thing happened to Nabule.'

'Is that the house of correction?' asked Mrs Eichenkranz

'No,' said Mrs Mooshaber, 'it's more a school for badly behaved kids, where they have rules they must obey and are kept under constant supervision. He didn't go to the house of correction until he'd finished at the one for the trouble-makers,' Mrs Mooshaber explained.

'What happened to him after that?' asked Mrs Eichenkranz.

'It's like this,' said Mrs Mooshaber, 'he threw in his lot with some stonemasons, probably the ones who have that workshop by the square, and as a result he's twice been behind bars. Now he's locked up for the third time. In fact he's just about served his time by now, and I'm afraid that he'll soon be back home. He'll come straight round to me, at least for starters. And Nabule flung the kolaches I'd baked for her wedding out of the window for the horse to eat and then she flung me out to boot. Before the banquet began – I didn't get a crust to eat. And I sang a lullaby to those two when they were little. And I wore my best outfit to the wedding banquet. Nothing like this one with the waistless jacket you see me in today.'

'But Madam,' began Mrs Eichenkranz with an expression of surprise, 'you mean that it was your own children that you were referring to in the cemetery just now?'

Mrs Mooshaber nodded. 'It was my own children,' she confirmed, 'I was indeed talking about them. 'Then she went on:

'I wouldn't wish what I've been through on anyone. You would need to see it to believe it. How many times have I said to myself that I wish I'd never had them. But I wanted to have them, and that's how they've turned out. It's the hand of Fate.'

'That's terrible,' said Mrs Eichenkranz after a while, 'really terrible.' Then she buried her head in her hands once more and sat for a while in silence.

'You know better than anyone else,' she continued after a while, removing her head from her hands, 'the worry I've been though. What else can I do? All this will wear me out in the end. I daresay it will be just like that woman...the one whose grave you pointed out to me, the one under the birch tree.'

'Mrs Bekenmoscht,' said Mrs Mooshaber with a nod, 'I can well believe you. And you still don't know what else you might have to put up with later. Look at the Fabers, I expect you knew them seeing that you were at the funeral....' And when Mrs Eichenkranz nodded Mrs Mooshaber went on:

'With their child it might well have been the same story. After all, Mrs Faber used to complain that he was rude and badly-behaved. She was at rock bottom from having to deal with him. It's possible the lad used to drink. Does your boy drink?'

'Oh yes,' said Mrs Eichenkranz with a wave of her hand, 'he drinks as well. He nicks one of these bottles of beer,' she said with another wave in the direction of the shop, 'and drinks it dry. I can't keep him under guard round the clock. I can't follow every step he takes. It's lucky that I don't sell any of the strong stuff. I wanted to, but I didn't get the licence.'

'There you are,' said Mrs Mooshaber with a nod. 'My Wezr was a drinker too from when he was eight years old. He'd started on the beer even earlier and then turned to spirits from the age of eight. And has your boy been coming home late in the evening?'

'That too,' agreed Mrs Eichenkranz, 'when they lock the cemetery gates he can still get into the house from that side. He uses the little door at the back, the one you saw behind the bushes. The thing is that he knows how to get in through it easily. He's got a key. But he never spends much time in the cemetery after closing, an hour at most, and less in winter when it goes dark early. He gets scared. But there's the park. He always goes there and stays until the light starts to fade. Then he comes home at dusk or after dark.'

'That's right,' nodded Mrs Mooshaber, 'it was the same with Wezr. From when he was seven he was always on the prowl. He hung around the river under the bridge and came home in the dark. And Madam, just one other thing about this lad of yours... does he go thieving...?'

'Oh,' sighed Mrs Eichenkranz as she passed her palm through the dark curls, 'a little, perhaps. Though as you know I can't say, not really, I can't keep watch over him all... but perhaps he does, yes...' Mrs Eichankranz glanced at the shop with its ancient artificial flowers, its candles and lanterns and ribbons, which could all be seen from the kitchen through the open door, 'I just don't know where he is or where he's off to at every single moment. I'd have to be with him all the time and never let him out of my sight.'

'That's the way it is, Madam,' agreed Mrs Mooshaber as she took a further sip of beer, 'my Wezr was a thief too. From when he was little. He stole whatever was there for the taking, even money. Even what was mine. He stole my only savings. So we're in the same boat. And there's no knowing what's in store for you when yours grows up. For all you know, he might drive you to distraction and you might even do away with yourself. You know something, I don't believe in God. When I was small, I used to say my prayers, but a servant working on the estates or maybe he was a farm steward, anyway he talked me out of praying and so I don't do it any more, I believe in Fate instead. Everything is a matter of Fate, even the fact that I had children, the fact that as luck would have it I wanted them in the first place, and now Fate is punishing me. But I know plenty of people...'

Suddenly Mrs Eichenkranz rose from her chair and said hurriedly: 'You know plenty of people, Madam, and something has just struck me. Please,' she began with a swipe of the hand across her black curls, 'you know plenty of people, perhaps you know a certain Mary Capricorn.'

'Mary Capri?' exclaimed Mrs Mooshaber in surprise, 'good God, that's a name I've heard before. The caretaker, Mrs Kralec, mentioned the name to me the other day. 'Who's that Mary Capri?' she said. 'Just who is she?'

'I don't know her,' said Mrs Eichenkranz, 'I can't tell you. Like you, I've only heard her name mentioned. I heard it mentioned here in the cemetery.'

'She died then?' asked Mrs Mooshaber with a glance at the room with the window and a view of the cemetery.

'She didn't die,' said Mrs Eichenkranz with a shake of the head, 'I just meant that it was in the cemetery that I heard about her. But if you'd like me to find something out about her, I can let you know. A person gets to know a lot of things in a cemetery. Once I even found out about that new shop selling butter. Well now, Madam, why don't you drink a bit more and have some cake.'

Mrs Mooshaber took some more beer and looked down at her legs where the big black bag was bulging. 'You've got a nice place here,' she said with a nod, 'when I was young I always wanted to have a little shop of my own. Did you know that I always wanted to have a kiosk and sell beer, salad, ham, lemonade...and I saved up my money for it, for that little shop or kiosk, but then...' Mrs Mooshaber sighed, 'then it never came to anything. The kiosk,' she went on in a sad and slow voice, 'I never had. Ever since I was little I've also wanted to be a housekeeper. To be a houskeeper like one of my friends from school who became one. She got married and then her husband died young so she became a housekeeper. Anyhow, I must be getting along...'

'And what will you do about that old man with the gold watch chain?' asked Mrs Eichenkranz. 'You invited him to the Welfare Office in three days' time. My boy never took anything from him, let alone some guineas. It wasn't even possible. He couldn't have picked that pocket behind the man's coat-tail at the graveside.'

'Perhaps the man lost it somewhere,' said Mrs Mooshaber with a sigh, 'even so we haven't yet found the boy.'

'But we did look for him,' said Mrs Eichenkranz, 'we spent the whole afternoon looking for him. My God it would be terrible if the Welfare took him. I just don't know what I'd do.'

Mrs Mooshaber paused suddenly, bit back her words and threw an uncertain glance at Mrs Eichenkranz. Then she spoke in a hesitant voice:

'But Madam, why are you so afraid of Mother and Child Support taking him? Indeed it would only make life easier for you without a badly-behaved boy around. At least you'd have some peace and quiet.'

'Peace and quiet,' said Mrs Eichenkranz with a sigh, 'peace and quiet perhaps. But you know what these houses of correction for young offenders are like...you know better than anyone what they're like...grisly places. Stocks for their legs and thumbscrews for their hands. They beat them with belts, sometimes one of them even goes blind...' Mrs Eichankranz looked a picture of desolation as she glanced at Mrs Mooshaber, and when Mrs Mooshaber said nothing but just looked at the table in front of her, Mrs Eichenkranz leaned over to her and continued:

'And you can see for yourself, Madam, how much I need him. He helps me here in the shop. How could I sell anything if I didn't have him with me? That's the point. Madam, it could make all the difference, the fact he helps me make an honest living...'

'You have a point there,' agreed Mrs Mooshaber. Then she rose to her feet, picked up her bag and glanced at the floor as she did so, 'don't distress yourself. Come to the Mother and Child Support Service, make it the day after tomorrow in the afternoon. Perhaps something can be done. You tell me,' Mrs Mooshaber went on with another quick examination of the floor and a further passing glance at the shop which could be glimpsed through the open door, 'you tell me that the lad goes wandering in the park of an evening?'

'In the park,' Mrs Eichenkranz confirmed. 'By the fountain where the statue of the poet is.' Then she looked at the table before continuing:

'You haven't touched the cake, Madam. At least take some home with you. Let me see...' and Mrs Eichenkranz proceeded to pick up the cake and put it into Mrs Mooshaber's bag. 'Will you not have something more to drink?'

'Not any more, and thank you for your hospitality,' replied Mrs Mooshaber, eyeing the floor yet again, 'so then, in the park by the fountain where the statue of the poet stands?' And when Mrs Eichenkranz nodded, Mrs Mooshaber moved

towards the door. But when she reached it she once again glanced around and suddenly remarked:

'You don't have mice, do you?'

'Yes,' said Mrs Eichenkranz with a laugh, 'of course we get the odd one. You can see that we live with a park on one side of us and a cemetery on the other. You're bound to find a mouse or two. But they can't get at the cake,' she added hurriedly, 'I keep that under glass'.

'You should lay some traps,' said Mrs Mooshaber as she passed in front of the shop, 'so they don't become rampant. Once you get hordes of them under your roof they'll be the ruin of you. The day after tomorrow at the office, then.'

And with a parting farewell Mrs Mooshaber was gone.

V

The next afternoon Mrs Mooshaber was returning home after shopping in the co-op. Some bread, a little sugar and a half kilo of barley could be found in her small black bag. As she was approaching her ramshackle house she met up with the masons, who were on their way from work. They were wearing only their whitewash-covered overalls – it was a sunny September afternoon – and singing as they went, while they scarcely threw a glance at Mrs Mooshaber. 'It's high time they finished,' she thought to herself, 'or we'll all end up falling to our deaths. I've just taken down the banner...' she was looking at the façade of the dilapidated house, 'but I need to wash it before I put it away. And in the evening...'

A visit to the fountain in the park was what Mrs Mooshaber wanted to make in the evening. A visit to the statue of the poet by the fountain where young Eichenkranz was wont to go roaming around. 'This evening I shall go to the fountain in the park,' she said, as she made her way home, 'I must track down that lad there. We didn't find him yesterday and tomorrow I have to make my report to Mrs Knorring. That old man who was robbed by the grave and poor Mrs Eichen will be there. In the evening I will go to the park and find the boy.' Thoughts of Mrs Eichenkranz, her own evening visit to the park and the report she'd have to make next day to Mrs Knorring absorbed Mrs Mooshaber as she made her way home.

As she opened the front door beside the bricks, the wheelbarrow and the barrel of lime she had the impression that there was someone inside her flat. When she went on to set foot in the corridor, she gave a terrible start. A gruesome voice of some kind was coming out of her kitchen, and before she could throw her bag onto the ground and perhaps even run out of the building for breath of fresh air, the kitchen door had opened and there was Wezr standing in the doorway.

'At Your Service,' he said.

'At Your Service,' came again after a while.

'At Your Service,' he offered for a third time and then turned his back on her.

She felt dizzy while, accompanied by her small black bag, she followed him into the kitchen. Even though she had expected him to come here to her flat and had prepared herself for it, now that it had actually happened she felt faint as she followed him in. She had the feeling that he had grown stronger and coarser during his time of confinement. He was broad-faced with a low forehead and cold pale eyes. So cold and pale that when he looked at someone, they shuddered with fear. Mrs Mooshaber touched her forehead and then all of a sudden the feeling came over her that she must be sitting on the settee next to the black banner which she wanted to wash and that the small black bag with her shopping was there at her feet. And the terrible Wezr was sitting at the table with Nabule right opposite him and another man besides. At first she took him for one of the witnesses from the wedding. Short and tousled hair, forehead dark and low, the corners of his mouth turned down. He looked like a droopy black dog.

'She thinks she's dreaming, but what of it?' said Wezr in a voice rougher than that of the worst gravedigger, 'that could be dealt with. I won't show you how or she'll have one of her fainting fits,' he went on, resting his fist between his eyes.

'She thinks she's dreaming,' came Nabule's echoing shriek. She gave an exaggerated, half-witted cackle to go with the swagger of one of her twirls. 'But she's not dreaming. If she'd kept away a bit longer,' she went on shrieking, 'she wouldn't have come back to all this on the table.'

'She would have,' said Wezr. He lit a cigarette which disappeared inside hands that were even bigger than those of the bridegroom Laibach. 'She would have, because there'll be something for her too today. To celebrate my arrival. So she can't call us Scrooges.' He suddenly reached across the table and started to count something. That was the moment when Mrs Mooshaber became aware from the sofa that there was a pile of money lying on the table and that Wezr was counting banknotes. It was also the moment when she noticed Nabule's garish green summer coat with a dark collar, while Wezr wore a black suit with a white shirt and tie. She had never seen either of them in such clothes before. And this was also the moment when she became aware of some kind of umbrella with a lovely gleaming handle beside the cupboard. Suddenly she felt as if her head was spinning, but Wezr was starting to speak again.

'This is for you.' He counted out some money and pushed it across to Nabule. 'And this is for you,' he said, counting out some more money and pushing it across at the third party, the black dog, who stayed ever silent but occasionally shot a glance at Mrs Mooshaber, 'and this, ladies and gentlemen, is mine. This...' he went on, indicating what was left over, 'we'll give to her. To celebrate my homecoming. So that she doesn't think we have tight fists.'

Mrs Mooshaber looked at the four piles of money on the table and her head was in a spin. Suddenly she felt as though she were fast asleep.

'She thinks she's nodded off,' shrieked Nabule as she eyed her pile of money in a strange manner.

'Her sleeping,' said Wezr in his gruesome gravedigger voice, 'could be dealt with. But I won't show you how,' he went on, thrashing himself between the eyes with the palm of his hand, 'anyway it's no longer done these days. You just need a strong will.' He flicked the ash from his cigarette and moved his head towards Nabule. 'What have you got to say?' he asked.

'What have I got to say?' shrieked Nabule as she threw the money onto the table, 'can't you do better than that? When I go to the salon with this, they'll think I got it from begging.'

'At the church no one would give you two pennies to rub together,' said Wezr with another flick of the fag, 'it's halfpennies in church and farthings in bed. Maybe some rich student would give you more for that,' he grinned, 'so get a move on.' At which point Nabule wriggled and swaggered and grabbed the money.

'This will get a light rinse in the beauty salon,' she said as she moved her hips and raised her eyes, 'and this will do for an evening gown. This is for jewels and a divan – not like that shitty sofa over there,' she went on as she jerked her head at the ottoman – 'you can see the springs coming out. And with this I'll buy a picture. The one of that woman with three eyes and the swan.' Then came another half-witted, exaggerated cackle as she snatched hold of the money and stuffed it into a pocket.

From the sofa Mrs Mooshaber stared at the scene in front of her. Her head was in a spin and she could barely breathe. Three piles of money were now lying on the table while the umbrella with the beautiful gleaming handle was hanging next to the cupboard. Suddenly Mrs Mooshaber felt thirsty. The third person, who had so far been sitting in silence and just throwing the odd glance at her, the black dog, now struck her as being a typical Wezr associate, one of the stonemasons, perhaps. Searching for breath she felt for the crumpled black banner beside her.

'This will pay for a motorbike', said Wezr with his hands on the banknotes, 'this will relieve the drudgery of daily toil and with this I'll ride off for a beach holiday. Hunting sperm whales.' Then he too snatched up his pile and pocketed it.

Now there were two piles left on the table and the umbrella with the gleaming handle hanging beside the cupboard.

Mrs Mooshaber was at the sofa staring in front of her with her head spinning and feeling thirsty. Suddenly she noticed the window with the frosted glass which gave onto the staircase and again felt the fainting fits coming. Two hares were hanging in the window, still in their skins with their back legs tied and their heads down.

That was the moment when the kitchen clock struck half four and it was as if Mrs Mooshaber suddenly came to.

'Good God,' she roused herself to say from the sofa, 'Good God, here you are dividing up every last penny. You're carving up a whole estate. With that sort of money you could buy a villa in the Stadium district. And how can you not know,' she went on, turning to Nabule, 'that Laibach wants to buy a flat in the Elizabethan district? You could at least pay something towards the flat, seeing that you've got such a fortune.'

They looked at her, Wezr with the cold gleam in his eyes, the black dog who turned his eye in her direction and Nabule who began to speak. Began to shriek.

'For the flat,' she shrieked, 'for the flat. As if Laibach wasn't working. As if he wasn't saving. As if I could go out in rags tonight like some street harlot. A picture and a divan,' she shrieked, 'is that too much to ask?'

'Quit the bawling,' said Wezr, his voice as gruesome as a gravedigger's, 'quit bawling. You're not talking to Laibach.' Then he flicked ash from his cigarette and turned to the person with the short black hair, the low dark forehead and the drooping mouth, the black dog. And the black dog smiled and began to speak:

'Madam,' he said with a smile and a voice that was as soft as velvet, 'Madam, would you want Nabule to provide Mr Laibach with clothes too? Should she take him his food? Should she pay for him to have his hair cut? Everyone, Madam, must earn their own living...' He gave one of his soft and silky smiles before grabbing his own pile of money and stashing it away in a pocket. The last pile of money was left lying on the table, alongside the umbrella next to the sideboard and the hares in the window. And seated on the sofa Mrs Mooshaber again had the impression that she must be dreaming or sleeping, while her eyes kept staring, her head kept spinning and her thirst kept raging. Now Wezr threw her a sudden glance with his cold, gleaming eyes and said: 'You look really out of sorts. As if you're asleep or have a fever. Look, here's a pile of money. Look, your money…' and he reached for the money lying on the table, flicked the ash from his fag and went on: 'It's all yours, and yet you go round telling people that I steal. This is your twopennyworth. There's guineas galore here. You could buy a kiosk for that,' he said with a smile and a flick of ash.

Mrs Mooshaber felt that she'd knocked over the bag by her legs, that her throat had gone dry and that she had chapped lips. There was no doubt that she had a fever. But at this moment the stranger, the black dog, began to speak all over again.

'Twenty guineas' he said in his silky voice, the velvet tones accompanied by a quiet smile, 'perhaps you've never had such a pile of money in your life. You could buy the kiosk and stuff it full of goods. You could go to the Moon and still have enough left over for ice cream. You could have a hot lava bath in the Borman crater and still be eating roast squid for dinner. And will you still tell everyone that Wezr steals your savings from you? Surely not, Madam', he smiled and the downturned corners of his mouth rose beatifically, 'you must be mistaken.' Nabule covered her own stupidly bloated mouth with her palm and Wezr remarked drily:

'She used to keep money in the cupboard, then in the top of the oven, and then in the mouse poison in the larder. Now she keeps it in the nightstand in her other room where she has her fancy outfits. Where she has her hat, her glasses and her sealing-stick. Probably put it there when she was expecting my return. From behind bars, as she keeps telling everyone.'

And while the other person, the black dog, was composing his look of amazement into a grin, Wezr went on: 'Yes, from gaol. From prison. Where I was doing time. And we haven't yet spoken about that window over there. What about those two hares,' he turned to the sofa and pointed at the frosted glass window, 'what do you say to them? Enough food for one person for one whole week.'

'Yes, Madam,' said the black dog, the stranger, in his silky tones as he looked at Mrs Mooshaber, 'they are freshly shot, the blood still dripping from them. Your son shot them a while ago in the forest. You should have seen how they toppled over, like acrobats they were.'

Mrs Mooshaber sat staring from the sofa, her head spinning and her lips dry. As she took note of the remaining pile of money on the table, the umbrella by the cupboard and the hares in the window it was as if she suddenly came to again. All at once she pointed at the hares and said:

'I'll cook them for you. And I'll roast part of them with butter. Or red pepper,' she went on as she reached across her legs to turn her bag the right side up again, 'I need to get some cream. I've only got barley in this bag here.'

'Would you make some for me too?' asked the strange black dog with a soft and silent look.

'My pleasure,' said Mrs Mooshaber in a state of some perplexity, 'if you are... are a friend of my children, then they'll surely invite you too.'

'Madam' the strange black dog went on with a silent smile, 'could you not make some coffee?'

'I'll make some,' said Mrs Mooshaber with a nod. She was just getting up from the sofa and going to the cupboard when Nabule burst out laughing:

'We'll be drinking too much coffee for our own good today,' she cackled as she did a twirl in her lurid green coat with the black collar, 'we're off to the Ritz, aren't we?'

For a moment silence reigned in the kitchen. Mrs Mooshaber was standing hesitantly by the cupboard, looking at Nabule, at Wezr and even at the black dog before she fixed her attention on the table. All of a sudden Wezr flicked the ash from his cigarette and looked at his sister.

'Spot on,' he said, fixing his gaze on his sister, 'we're off to the Ritz, aren't we. You'll even meet that student there, whatsisname... Baar, that's it, and maybe the other one will be there too. Hold off with your coffee,' he went on, turning to his mother, 'cook the hare, why not in seaweed. What's that black rag over there?' he continued, pointing at the ottoman.

'Can't you see it's a banner,' said Mrs Mooshaber, 'it was hanging from the house. The Faber lad has died.' Then she added:

'I must wash it and go to the fountain in the park.'

At this moment Wezr put out his cigarette and look at his mother. Then he looked at Nabule, who was covering her puffy mouth with her palm, and then at the other man, the black dog, before leaning against the back of the chair. He leaned against the back of the chair while putting his hand on the table, just as officials tend to do, before continuing:

'So she wants to wash the banner and go to the park. Wash the banner and go to the fountain in the park. Here I am back from being locked up, and her words tell you that...' here came the gravedigger laugh '...she doesn't give a fig. That I was working these fingers to the bone...' here the gravedigger laugh joined up with the weighing of an enormous fist in his other hand... 'that's all the same to her. Here we are off to celebrate and we'd like her to come with us. But no, she's not interested. She's going to wash her banner and have a walk in the park.'

Mrs Mooshaber was suddenly rooted to the spot by the cupboard as if she'd been turned to stone, unable to believe her own ears. If it had earlier seemed to her that everything was a dream, she was now afraid that she had gone mad. She wasn't able to speak a single word.

'What are you doing just standing and staring?' asked Wezr.

'What are you doing just standing and staring?' he repeated.

'Come on, what are you doing?' he exclaimed for the third time...

'For God's sake,' said Mrs Mooshaber in a whisper as she leaned against the cupboard for support, 'for God's sake, I didn't know anything about your being off to celebrate. Or that you wanted to invite me. It's just not possible.'

'Everything's possible,' said Wezr drily while fixing his cold, gleaming eyes on his mother, 'everything's possible for someone who's done time.'

'Madam,' began the black dog, his smile returning with the silky voice that was soft as velvet, 'for someone who's done time everything is possible. We are off to celebrate and we would like to invite you. But do you really think that Wezr has come back from prison? Madam,' he said smiling, 'you couldn't be thinking that this money, these hares and the umbrella have been stolen, could you. That they are swag of some kind. Really, Madam, you just don't know anything about what Wezr's really like.'

'Of course I'll go with you,' Mrs Mooshaber eventually blurted out, as she kept supporting herself against the sideboard, 'I'll wash the banner and go to the fountain in the park tomorrow...'

'Look here,' said Wezr, interrupting her firmly while his cold eyes fixed themselves on the floor next to her feet, 'go and get yourself ready. In a moment's time we'll be going. But do it properly, because you never know who you might meet at the Ritz.' He glanced at Nabule, at the black dog and at what was left of the money on the table.

Mrs Mooshaber wrenched herself away from the sideboard and went to her room as if she was lost in a fog.

'For God's sake,' she said at the door, 'of course you never know who you might meet there. The young gentlemen from the wedding might be there. Those two students, Mr Baar and the other one. Am I right?' Wezr nodded.

A short while later Mrs Mooshaber presented herself in the kitchen in her long,black shiny skirt, waistless jacket with sleeves and flat shoes. She was in the old outfit which she had worn to the wedding. The black-and-gold scarf was in her hand.

'So here I am,' she said, still feeling dizzy.

'She's back already,' Nabule blurted out, wiggling her hips.

Wezr looked at his mother for a while without speaking, once again leaning against the back of his chair and tapping lightly on the table with his hand. Then he remarked drily:

'The students will be there and goodness knows who else. You cannot go in that scarf. It makes you look like an undertaker. Haven't you got something light?'

While Nabule's foolishly puffy face was plumping itself up and twisting itself into a laugh, and the strange black dog was silently casting a critical eye over the black-and-gold scarf, Mrs Mooshaber blurted out:

'I know what. I know exactly what. The caretaker has a light-coloured scarf which she'll lend to me. I'll nip off to see her and be back in a jiffy.'

'So get nipping,' said Wezr, still leaning on the chair and tapping on the table with his hands, 'get nipping and don't be long. In any case we must go by taxi. And there's something else,' he went on. 'When you find the caretaker, tell her...that you could do with...a bit of a makeover.' Then he rapped on the table, stood up and laughed his gravedigger laugh.

Mrs Mooshaber let go of the black-and-gold scarf and ran out of the kitchen. She ran through the front door and through the passage and then burst in on the caretaker.

'Goodness gracious, Mrs Mooshaber,' exclaimed the caretaker who was in her bath-robe and in the act of sewing on a button, 'what on earth has happened? Your Wezr's here, isn't he...'

'He's here,' cried Mrs Mooshaber, 'he's here and imagine this – I just can't believe my ears. I'm beside myself. It's all so unexpected...'

'What's going on?' asked the caretaker, 'has prison aged him?'

'Not aged him, no. It's made him stronger. But perhaps he's changed too,' said Mrs Mooshaber, 'he invited me to a celebration. A celebration of his return. Nabule will be there and some other fellow I didn't know, a stonemason of some sort, I expect. It's being held at the Rit, no the Riz... Well in any case I don't know where, but just imagine, there might even be those two young men there, Mr Baar and the other one who were the students at the wedding ceremony. I was with them when Nabule threw me out, it made me so ashamed and now I'm going to meet them again. But this black-and-gold scarf of mine does not seem right to him. Apparently I look like an undertaker in it, and he wants me to find something in light colours. Mrs Kralec, you have a silk one...' But before she could finish the caretaker had already put down her sewing and was dashing to the wardrobe.

'Heavens above,' she exclaimed, 'there are things would make the heavenly powers turn in their graves if they had them. Your Nabule threw you out of her wedding reception and then Wezr comes out of jail and invites you to celebrate. But it always seemed to me...' the caretaker went on as she pulled a scarf of some kind out of the wardrobe, 'it always seemed to me that Wezr was a better person than she, I didn't want to say too much about it to you but now I'm going to. If it was the other way round and your Nabule was coming back from jail, she'd never dream of inviting you, not a bitch like her. Look, here it is, take it,' said the caretaker as she gave Mrs Mooshaber a pretty white scarf.

'Listen here, Mrs Mooshaber,' the caretaker went on speaking rapidly while she fastened her dressing-gown around her, 'where exactly is it you're going? Rit-something, Riz-something? Heavens above,' she suddenly cried out, 'you don't mean the Ritz, do you?'

'That's it, the Ritz,' agreed Mrs Mooshaber with a nod, 'Yes, the Ritz, that's what he called the place. What exactly is this "Ritz"? A student dive of some kind?'

'Student dive!' The caretaker was in such stitches that it was a wonder she could stay upright, 'it's a hotel. To be precise,' she went on, throwing her hands into the air as she spoke, 'it's the swankiest hotel in the city. It's in the Stadium district. When some government delegation arrives to see Prime Minister Rappelschlund, that's where it's put up. Rappelschlund arranges banquets there for distinguished visitors that he doesn't want to have in the royal palace. It has a first-class restaurant frequented only by society's crème de la crème. Professors, engineers and rich business types. Military officers, councillors, gentlemen of the royal chamber. You know what I mean. Rich students too, for sure, can be found there, born with silver spoons in their mouths. You'll be eating from silver plates there.'

'Eating from silver plates?' exclaimed Mrs Mooshaber as she sat down in a chair. 'Good God, do you think that means they have things like ham, Italian salad and lemonade...'

The list made the caretaker laugh and wave her hands about all the more. 'Ham and salad, I ask you!' she went on, continuing with the cackles and the semaphore, 'pheasant and oysters more like. Escallops and squish. So hurry up and wrap that scarf around you so I can see if it suits you. Mrs Mooshaber quickly wrapped the scarf around her neck and said:

'I must just say one thing to you, Madam Caretaker. Imagine that Wezr had left some money on the table for me. I don't even want to tell you how much or what I could buy with it. He gave me a couple of hares as well, they're in the window and I need to cook them in seaweed. And hanging beside the cupboard there's an umbrella with a beautiful handle, but I don't suppose that's for me, at least he didn't mention anything to that effect. And he said something to me besides. He said that when I was going to a restaurant like the one he was taking me to, and God knows who might be there, I should do a little to make myself up. Add a few touches here and there, that's probably what he meant,' Mrs Mooshaber continued with a laugh, 'I've never so much as touched make-up, not when I was young, not even when I was getting married. But what do you think, seeing that the students and God knows who else are going to be there... Wezr said that you know best about these things.'

'Well if he thinks so,' the caretaker blurted out, her cheeks burning bright red, 'then for sure, that's how it must be. And if you know that, then do as I tell you. The Ritz is where the real ladies go, so I'll give you some rouge.' The caretaker ran off and hurried back with the rouge which she applied to Mrs Mooshaber by the window. Then with a sudden 'Just a jiffy' she got hold of a black pencil and gave Mrs Mooshaber some eyebrow treatment. Then with yet another 'Just a jiffy' she took some ointment and gave Mrs Mooshaber rosy cheeks. And then to top it all she added a dusting of white powder.

'God in Heaven!' exclaimed Mrs Mooshaber as she stood in front of the mirror unable to believe her own eyes. What she saw took her breath away and made her head spin. 'I'd never have believed it. You know, Mrs Kralec, this is a day when I had so much work to do. I wanted to wash the banner and a bit later - with evening coming on - I have to go to the fountain in the park.'

'Wash the banner and go to the fountain.' The caretaker spat the words out and her cheeks burned bright red. 'I ask you, how can you think of such a thing when you have the Ritz to go to? What complete and utter nonsense. And one more thing,' the caretaker exclaimed with her cheeks still burning bright red, 'I'll lend you something else to go round your neck. It'll go with the waistless jacket. I've got a necklace. Look at yourself in the mirror for a while. I'll be back in a jiffy.' Once more the caretaker scurried off before coming back a moment later with the necklace. It was a string of large black, green and gold beads.

'They're made of bamboo,' said the caretaker with a smile, 'I used to have earrings to go with the beads but I lost them. At a masked ball. Let's take a look at you, Mrs Mooshaber, I'll slip it on for you.' She proceeded to slip the necklace around Mrs Mooshaber's neck and then jumped to one side in order to take in her work.

'Good God,' gasped Mrs Mooshaber, gasping for breath in front of the mirror once more while she both did a turn and had one, 'and I was supposed to be heading for the fountain today, because that's where Mrs Eichen's boy goes. Indeed I've got to go to the Mother and Child Support tomorrow with a report. The old man who was robbed at the graveside is going to be there too.'

'The old man who was robbed at the graveside.' The caretaker spat the words out as she repeated them. 'Do me a favour, Mrs Mooshaber, and stop thinking such nonsense. You'd be foolish if you went to the park instead of the Ritz. Such an opportunity doesn't come twice. You say that even the students will be there. Wezr is making amends for what happened at the wedding. Perhaps you know all this and yet you still want....' When Mrs Mooshaber did no more than give a sigh and a nod she added: 'Simply tell Mrs Knorring you haven't found anything yet. I wonder at the fuss you're making. After all, it isn't as if they pay you to do this. But Mrs Mooshaber,' the caretaker went on with a sudden shake of the head, 'I can see from looking at you that we still haven't got everything right. Only if you're dressed to perfection can you visit the Ritz, especially when the students will be there. The light scarf – I don't think it goes so well with the rest, it looks a bit too countrified. You shouldn't have a scarf round your head at all – it's a hat you need. If you put this hat on, I can comb your hair behind your ears – that way they can be seen.'

'What's the point of that?' Mrs Mooshaber blurted the words out in amazement.

'What's the point of that,' echoed the caretaker with a chuckle, 'just this, that I'm going to lend you some earrings.' Then she added: 'I've got a pair of glass ones here. And you must have white gloves on your hands, Mrs Mooshaber. I've got a pair for you. For the students' sake alone you must be far more fetching at the Ritz than at that miserable wedding.'

The caretaker proceeded to comb Mrs Mooshaber's hair, brought her the earrings, red ones hanging from long shiny wires, attached them to her ears, gave her the white gloves with lace and pulled them tight over her hands. Then she ran out of the room and came back with the hat.

'Where did you get that?' asked Mrs Mooshaber in amazement, 'where on earth did it come from? I've never seen the like of it. Is it from Paraguay? I'm sure I've never seen you wearing anything like it.'

'I don't wear any of these things,' laughed the caretaker, 'the gloves were for my wedding, bought for me by my old man to wear at the altar, and the hat did indeed come from Paraguay, it was something I got for masked balls. To go with the bamboo necklace and some earrings which I've since lost. Here – try it on.'

Mrs Mooshaber tried on the hat and for the third time she found her breath taken away and her head in a whirl. She couldn't believe her eyes. The hat was black and wide-brimmed, with a violet bow and feathers at the back. The long and delicate green and red tail feathers trembled when the hat was still, let alone when you moved your head, however slight the movement.

'Mrs Mooshaber,' cried the caretaker with a chuckle, 'I can't believe it. Your Wezr won't know who you are. Not even the students will recognise you. I have to say that you look like an actress or the wife of a trader from those Parrot Islands. They won't half stare at the Ritz when they set eyes on you.' And while she pulled the dressing-gown closer round her neck she started laughing all over again. 'Mrs Mooshaber,' she cried in amusement, 'you look like the lady of a gentleman's gentleman or the wife of a general. Indeed you could be married to a minister. You know what, seeing that it suits you so well, keep the necklace and the earrings and the gloves for the moment – the hat too – and take the rouge, some powder and cream, and this eyebrow liner too, I've got quite enough to go round.'

And while Mrs Mooshaber collected up the creams and powders, her head still swimming and still gasping for breath, the caretaker laughed and said:

'As for the hares...they might last you a week, and then there's the money, goodness knows how much, but in any case, off you go now to the Ritz. The finest fillets, oysters and squish. Sea cradles too, they're molluscs that you eat with sea-weed. And do you know what jollyfish are? Or octopus? And have you ever had turtle salad?'

'We're going by taxi', said Mrs Mooshaber on her way out, 'I've never been in one of those. We went by underground when I got married. And I didn't even have a hat for my wedding, though I think I sometimes had some kind of tiara on my head. And I'll say to Mrs Knorring that I've found out Mrs Eichen is a decent widow and that Mother and Child Support should let her son stay with her.'

Decked out in the hat with long coloured feathers, her cheeks powdered and rouged, her lips and eyebrows painted, with her necklace of bamboo beads, earrings hanging from their wires and powders and creams in her white gloves, Mrs Mooshaber ran back to her kitchen as if she was in a trance. She was ready to surprise the others. A surprise they might not wish to show but which would be there all the same. Nabule especially, in her lurid green raincoat with the black collar, might screech and even clutch her midriff, squirm and twist, while Wezr would clench his fist and heave his chest and as for that strange fellow, the black dog, he would raise the corners of his mouth into a twisted smile that wouldn't go away – yes, it could all happen like that. But that wasn't important. What mattered was that Wezr – for the first time in his life – had given her something and had invited her, Mrs Mooshaber, somewhere, and it might be that those students would see her there...

But when Mrs Mooshaber ran into the kitchen there was no trace of anyone to be found. The door to her other room was wide open. So that was obviously where they were, waiting for her to come back. Mrs Mooshaber hurried in and saw that they weren't in that room either. Not a trace of them. She ran quickly back into the kitchen, put the creams and powders onto the table while she tried to catch her breath and at that moment noticed that the money had gone from the table, the umbrella had gone from the cupboard and the hares had disappeared from the window with the frosted glass. Their things were gone and the flat was bare.

And then Mrs Mooshaber suddenly noticed a piece of paper on the table. She picked it up in her white gloves and read:

We're off. Why don't you hire yourself a horse?

Under this was written:

The money and hares are for the Klaudinger woman and that goes for the umbrella too. She is the one going to the Ritz with us. Madam, your field of expertise is apparently tombs, children and mice. Tombs and children have I none, but mice I have in my flat in abundance. If you are prepared to assist me, I will cross your palm with silver. But you need to bring your own traps. You know neither who Wezr is nor what he does – and that's a fact.

VI

It is impossible to say how long it took Mrs Mooshaber to come round, though it was still light outside. She felt under her throat and touched the bamboo globes, reached for her ears and touched the earrings, put her hand above her head and made contact with the hat. Then she went into her bedroom. She opened the little bedside table and extracted a terrible bonnet of some kind with a bow, together with spectacles and a sort of sealing stick. Then she pulled out a threadbare old bag. There were some guinea pieces, a few shillings and a handful of coppers inside it. She returned the bag to the bedside table and then looked at the window facing the courtyard. Twilight was slowly falling over the courtyard, especially beneath the scaffolding, but lights had yet to appear in the windows on the upper floors with the shared balconies. Silence still reigned supreme there. Mrs Mooshaber gazed at the courtyard for a while...as if she was gazing at the silence and feeling it... and then ran into the kitchen. She glanced at the black banner, which was lying on the settee like a monstrous apparition, and then looked at the clock. 'I must get to the fountain in the park,' she said, 'tomorrow I'm due at Mother and Child Support.' She made a quick lunge at the bag on the ottoman for her key and then ran out of the flat.

With her long green and red feathers, cheeks powdered white, lips reddened and eyebrows lined, with her necklace of bamboo globes, earrings hanging on the end of their wires and white gloves over her hands...in her long, black shiny skirt, her waistless jacket and flat shoes, she skirted round the 'barrow, bricks and barrel of lime in the passage and went away from the building. She navigated the three drab streets without meeting a soul, and found herself at the asphalt crossroads by the *Sunflower* department store. She went over the white stripes of the crossing and looked at the wide avenue in the middle of which – although it was still daylight – the neon sign of the editorial offices of *Our Blooming Homeland* was already shining. She looked along the avenue to Albinus Rappelschlund Square in the distance, the erect statue of its namesake facing the avenue, and although it was far away you could see that it was still beribboned on account of the recent festivities...but that was not what Mrs Mooshaber made for now. She ran towards the street kiosks with their glass and laminate. Many of them were already bathed in neon and people were drinking lemonade and eating ice cream in front of them, it being September and still warm, with the trees still green and the flowers still in bloom in those places where it was still possible for flowers to grow. Mrs Mooshaber went especially quickly past the people by the kiosks, but she knew that many of them were watching her behind her back. She'd known that many eyes had been turning to look at her when she came out of the three run-down streets a little earlier and found herself at the crossroads by the *Sunflower* department store...and she was saying to herself: 'I look like an actress or like the lady of a gentleman's gentleman, I must keep going.' On she ran while the feathers in her hat went on fluttering, the beads of her necklace went on jangling and the rings under her ears went on quivering, while she felt the blood coming to her cheeks beneath the layer of white powder. At last she arrived in the Philipov area, by a wood of some sort with greenery and trees. She'd finally reached the park. Then she found herself in an open space next to the fountain and the statue of the poet.

Water from a reservoir was splashing out of the four upward-pointing beaks of some stone birds, after which it fell back in an arc – this was the 'fountain'. A man was standing on a cube leaning against a column with a book held in one hand and a rose in the other – this was the 'poet'. A bed of white flowers edged the area. Mrs Mooshaber slowed her step.

She slowed down to walking pace...and unlike during her journey past the crossroads and the streets she began to notice people. She saw mothers and nannies sitting on benches, gazing at the fountain and the poet. But what she mostly took note of was the children playing beside them... yes, they were sitting and enjoying the view as the twilight was falling and night coming on, for it was September and it was warm and the flowers were still blooming and the trees still green...but some mothers and nannies were already starting to stir themselves as they prepared for the journey home. Mrs Mooshaber saw the fountain and the poet, whom she did not know, seeing that she wasn't very likely to read poetry, although she remembered one poem, God knows from when, perhaps while she was still at school. She still remembered it and while she looked at the poet, she recalled the words. 'Leaving church the blind old lady', she recalled, 'feels her way with stick unsteady. Forward with her stick she fumbles, blind old lady often tumbles.' She turned away from the fountain and the statue of the poet and once again saw the mothers and nannies still on their benches in the half-light, as well as those who were starting to stir themselves to prepare for the journey home, and again she eyed the children in the half-light and nodded in approval. 'These will surely grow up to be good people,' she said to herself as she looked at them in the growing darkness, 'they are well looked after and will grow up to be students or colonels or traders, I dare say.' But now she noticed another thing – many of the mothers and the nannies, not to mention the children, were staring at her. They were looking at her in the same way that she'd earlier been scrutinised by people in the street, and she knew perfectly well why. They were looking at the hat, the earrings, the beads around her neck, they were looking at the red and white cheeks, the white gloves, and perhaps the long black skirt into the bargain...and she said to herself: 'I look like an actress or the lady of a gentleman's gentleman. Or maybe the wife of a trader from those Parrot Islands...' Now it almost seemed to Mrs Mooshaber as if some of the mothers and nannies were nodding at her, even bowing slightly and smiling. Mrs Mooshaber didn't know for sure whether that was really what she was seeing but it could have been so, it could have been that they took her for an actress or the wife of a trader from the Parrot Islands. She walked on slowly, scanning, searching, surveying the surroundings, the trees nearby, the lawns and bushes, and already she wanted to leave the vicinity of the fountain and the statue and move onto one of the wider paths and take herself hither and thither or somewhere close to the wall of the cemetery and Klotilda Eichenkranz's little shop, but all of a sudden she came to a halt.

On the edge of the fountain area next to the bed of white flowers she had spotted a boy sporting a stripey blue-and-white top.

It was as if he'd dropped down from the skies or had stepped out of those white flowers – if this were the cemetery, one could have supposed he'd emerged from somewhere among the huge forest of graves. He stood facing the floral display with his back to the path, his eyes evidently fixed on the white flowers. All of a sudden he jumped to the very edge of the flowerbed and then, before you could say Jack Robinson, he'd picked one of the white flowers, and in another twinkling of the eye had scampered back onto the path and had fixed the flower onto his top. For another few moments he stood still by the flower bed. Then he turned his back to the flowers and faced the path, his chest swollen with floral pride as he took in the benches, the nannies, the mothers and the children. He was looking around and surveying them all, perhaps in the hope of winning their attention. Finally he leaped up, ran past the fountain and scurried onto one of the wider paths. And Mrs Mooshaber set off in his wake.

Every now and then little Eichenkranz moved to the edge of the path, slowing his pace and then quickening it again. At times he stopped and simply gazed at the trees and bushes or else at the people on the benches, who were slowly getting ready to go home. He stopped for a while at a bench on a path with a cypress tree. An elderly lady with a long, black shiny skirt, a waistless jacket and simple shoes was sitting on it. She was folding up a piece of paper in her lap, carefully sprinkling the few remaining crumbs it still held onto the ground for birds that had not yet gone for the night. A few steps away from her the lad silently watched as she fed the birds, until she suddenly looked up from her

feeding and had him in her sights with his white flower and stripey top. The lad puffed out his chest as he turned around so that the old lady could get a better view of his flower. Then he suddenly jumped up and ran a few steps with arms outstretched, imitating a bird in flight. Once again, Mrs Mooshaber was taking no notice of the people around her. She wasn't paying attention to anyone likely to be staring at her because she looked like an actress or the wife of a trader from the Parrot Islands. Instead all her attention was focused on the boy. She stayed all the time in his wake, walking to the edge of the path, slowing or stopping or quickening her pace and never for a single moment letting him out of her sight. When he came to a fork in the path he stopped once again and looked at someone sitting on a bench with an umbrella propped beside him. But the person didn't pay much attention to him, or even to his flower, because he was looking in another direction. In fact he was turning round to look at Mrs Mooshaber as she came to a standstill. The lad nodded and moved on until he found a bench that was entirely empty, and at that very moment several black birds, black birds cawing, flew out of a nearby hedge. The lad lifted his head and gazed after them until he could no longer see them. And that was the moment when Mrs Mooshaber suddenly lost sight of him.

It was impossible to say how it had happened, but it had. It had happened behind an enormous plane tree with a trunk that had split. The lad had simply gone behind this split trunk and disappeared before Mrs Mooshaber managed to make him out. The thought flashed through her mind that now there would be trouble. 'This is a real how-do-you-do, I must find him come what may....' She quickened her pace and found herself in an area with more grass, but still there was no sign of the boy. She looked along several side-paths, but it was as if the lad had vanished without trace. She returned to the bench where the black birds had been flying and cawing, and even went back to the fork in the path where the person with the leaning umbrella had been sitting, but not a dickeybird. Had this been the cemetery, it could have seemed that the boy had become one with the endless ranks of the entombed. Then suddenly, while she was scanning and searching, some middle-aged man in a hat turned up, bowed to her and said: 'Is the lady looking for her glasses? Or perhaps for some lost lacework?' She turned abruptly to face him but did no more than startle a few birds. The darkness was now really falling and to Mrs Mooshaber it was more and more as if she was losing her eyesight.

Suddenly she heard a soughing sound like a bird flying at ground level, and when she turned round she saw the lad in the stripey blue-and-white top just a few steps away from her, the white flower on his chest and his arms outstretched like wings as he flew across the path. He ran across part of the lawn and then found himself on the path again. Mrs Mooshaber sighed with relief and quickened her pace until she was once more in his wake. After a while, when it had grown even darker and even more of Mrs Mooshaber's eyesight had faded away, the lad ran onto a smaller path lined by trees overgrown with lush creepers. From this he ran onto an even narrower path bordered by dense shrubbery. And it was on this track that he came to a halt and remained standing in front of a bush.

He was standing there with his hands in his pockets staring at something. Something that was possibly underneath the bush. Something that was perhaps on the ground. Something that couldn't be seen from a distance. Slowly Mrs Mooshaber began to close in on him. She could see the path disappearing into the darkness and that apart from the lad there wasn't another living soul upon it. When she was six paces away from the lad she noticed that there was, after all, another living creature in the vicinty, on the ground under the bush. This was what he had been looking at, a small squirrel sitting on its hind legs and examining the boy while the boy examined the squirrel. At that very moment the lad raised his head, looked around and spotted Mrs Mooshaber for the first time. That is to say, he saw some old lady in a hat with long coloured feathers, a long, black shiny skirt and a waistless jacket. He saw a woman with white cheeks, red lips and black eyebrows. He saw glass earrings hanging from wires, he saw the red, green and yellow beads around

her neck and the white gloves on her hands. The lad saw that the old lady was looking and looking and looking at him, perhaps even with a bit of a smile as she did so. He stared at her with a half-open mouth, as if he couldn't believe his eyes, and then, perhaps in order to show that he was not doing anything wrong, he puffed out his chest, touched the white flower and turned back again to the squirrel. He stretched out his hand towards it and began to call out loud so that he could be heard from six paces away. It was as if he was giving a calling cluck to chickens.

That was the moment when some church tower behind the park chimed the hour. Perhaps it chimed six, or perhaps it chimed the hour a resounding seven times, and Mrs Mooshaber with her white face and her vision impeded – night had really fallen now – went up closer to the lad. As she did so he jerked his head round and fixed his attention on her cheeks, her hat and her string of beads which made him more startled than ever. That was when Mrs Mooshaber had a sudden recollection. Perhaps she had it a second before the sound of the chimes in the tower, or perhaps a little later, when the chiming had begun and the boy gave her a startled look before retreating slowly towards the bushes – it is really impossible to say, just as it is impossible to say exactly what it was that went through her mind. Mrs Mooshaber now took a further step forward and the boy disappeared further towards the bushes. Mrs Mooshaber advanced another step and raised her hands. Hands in long white gloves, which gleamed in the darkness...that was when the squirrel under the bush squealed and was gone, while with Mrs Mooshaber it was as if she'd suddenly come to herself. She spoke saying:

'So you must be Eichenkranz.'

The lad went on staring at her in open-mouthed dismay, and it seemed as if he'd been struck dumb. He took another small step backwards towards the bushes.

'Look out for that thicket,' Mrs Mooshaber pointed behind his back with her white glove, 'what if somebody grabbed hold of you here? What if somebody did away with you right here? What if someone flung you into the undergrowth? It's late and you are still out and about. You must now go home with me, I will walk you back.'

The lad was starting to recover from shock and found room for speech:

'We live a little way from here.'

'A little way,' agreed Mrs Mooshaber, 'but you must go that little way with me. So I can see that you really do go home.'

Mrs Mooshaber gave another nod, turned around and started walking slowly. And strange as it may seem, the boy started moving as well, turning around and joining in the dawdle. He walked even more slowly than Mrs Mooshaber, keeping a step or half a step behind her, keeping his eyes on her the whole time but no longer looking so startled. They moved along the track until they came to a wider pathway.

'You were watching that squirrel,' said Mrs Mooshaber, 'it was a late one that hadn't yet gone to sleep. Squirrels tend to go to sleep early, like chickens. You wouldn't have wanted to kill that squirrel, by any chance?'

'Kill it?' said the boy in surprise. 'Kill it? No one does a thing like that. You're supposed to feed squirrels. I was talking to that one.'

'And what about tits and finches,' asked Mrs Mooshaber, 'don't you shoot them?'

'Why should I shoot them,' the boy answered, 'what harm do they do?'

'What about crows then,' Mrs Mooshaber asked, 'is there enough reason to shoot them?'

'There's more than enough of them,' said the boy, 'they do a lot of damage.'

'They took away your rifle, didn't they?'

'An air-rifle,' said the lad, 'only soldiers have real rifles.'

'But you know that you're not allowed to shoot anything that's living. You're not even allowed to shoot crows,' said Mrs Mooshaber.

'But I don't shoot them,' the boy answered, 'I couldn't even aim well enough.' They found themselves on the path with trees taken over by creepers and then on the larger path beside the lawn.

'And you're not allowed to drink,' said Mrs Mooshaber, 'you're still too small for that sort of thing.'

'People have to drink,' said the boy, 'or they can't live. They have to eat as well.'

'They don't have to drink spirits' said Mrs Mooshaber.

'I never drink those,' said the boy with a shake of the head, 'At most I just drink beer. I drink beer,' he went on, 'when I've got a thirst. But mostly I drink water.'

'And you're not allowed to take anything from the cemetery,' added Mrs Moosehaber, 'I have to admit that I don't believe in God, I believe in Fate, but to take the candles or ribbons, the bunches of flowers or the graveyard lights, that is a sin. How can people do a thing like that?'

'They do such things,' agreed the boy, 'but I don't. I only take a flower when it's withered. Those flowers get thrown in the bin in any case. I'm just giving a helping hand to the cleaners.'

They reached the huge plane-tree with the split trunk and Mrs Mooshaber stopped for a moment. 'Here', she pointed a white glove at the split in the plane-tree, 'this is where you lost me a while ago. It was as if you'd fallen through a trapdoor in the ground. By the time I'd made it past the tree and could look around again, you'd flown away like a bird.'

'No flying bird,' said the boy, now with the ghost of a smile on his face, 'more a burrowing mole. I disappeared into this hole here.' He pointed at a cleft in the trunk.

'Into this hideyhole here,' Mrs Mooshaber looked at the split in the trunk in wonder, 'I understand now. Well, let's be going.'

They went to the fork in the paths where the person with the umbrella had been sitting not long before, although he was gone by now. They reached the path with the cypress tree, where the old lady with the long black skirt had been sitting feeding the birds, and she too had now gone. Then they came to the fountain and the statue of the poet. He was on his cube leaning against the column, book in one hand and rose in the other. From the beaks of the stone birds the water came gushing out before falling back in an arc. A bit further off, the bed of white flowers could be seen. Everything was in darkness now, and the little gas lamps were already blazing. The benches nearby were already empty, the mothers and nannies having left with the children. Only a handful of people were walking there, strolling to and fro, and Mrs Mooshaber had the feeling once again that they were looking at her, and once again she knew just why they were doing so.

'That flower,' she said, pointing to the lad's stripey chest and to the other white flowers in their bed, 'came from here.'

'From here,' the boy agreed, puffing out his chest, 'it's allowed.'

'And you don't pay attention in school. You get up to mischief.'

'No, I don't' said the boy.

'You don't do your studies', said Mrs Mooshaber.

'Yes I do', the lad protested.

'Tell me what you've been studying,' said Mrs Mooshaber, shaking her head so that the feathers in her hat fluttered wildly, 'tell me what you've learnt.'

'We're learning about Prime Minister Rappelschlund at the moment,' said the boy, 'there was a national holiday just recently in his honour.'

'So tell me what you learned about him,' said Mrs Mooshaber as they left the fountain behind and headed towards the cemetery.

'Albinus Rappelschlund worked in a tannery,' the lad began, 'and then went to military college and then to study how to be a waiter. He learned how to carry up to ten plates at once in his hands. When he was twenty he entered the service of the sovereign Dowager Princess Augusta as her valet and then as a colonel…I live over there,' he added, pointing in another direction.

'At the end of the park,' agreed Mrs Mooshaber. 'Where the cemetery is. Come on now. What happened next….'

'Next he became a minister,' the boy went on, 'and brought order. And he flew to the Moon five times. When he got back his blood never grew heavy as lead in response to gravity. He founded a museum and built a spaceport for rockets and he unmasked the traitors who were planning to overthrow the sovereign Dowager Princess. But they say…'

here the lad paused for a moment before continuing, 'they say that the princess had already been squirrelled away somewhere and was no longer in power. In fact she might have already been dead. But she...' here the lad paused once again and a smile crept across his features... 'are you a nurse or a police officer?' he asked, looking up at her.

'I am neither a nurse nor a police officer,' said Mrs Mooshaber with a shake of the head that sent the feathers of her hat trembling and a rattle through the bamboo necklace, 'now go on with your story. You haven't told me the rest. I suppose they don't teach you that in school.'

'They don't teach that,' agreed the boy, 'it's not something we're allowed to talk about'

'What are you not allowed to talk about?' asked Mrs Mooshaber.

'The fact that the sovereign Dowager Princess might still be alive,' said the lad laughing, 'among the people, but who knows where. If anyone knew about her and didn't say, Rappelschlund would have him shot. He'd be tortured till he spilled the beans about where the princess was and then his whole family would be shot. Still it may be that he himself knows about her. He could be keeping her in a prison in the royal palace here in the city.'

They were approaching the wall dividing the cemetery from the park. They were in a small clearing from which they could see a few thick bushes and some tall trees in the distance. By the wall next to the barred gate that led to the cemetery a lamp had been lit and there was a large plane-tree, while next to them stood a single-storey building which functioned both as living-quarters and as shop for Klotilda Eichenkranz.

‘I’m nearly home now,’ said the lad.

‘You are indeed,’ agreed Mrs Mooshaber, ‘I take it you have brothers and sisters?’

‘No, I don’t.’ The boy shook his head and puffed out his chest. ‘Not at all. I’m the only one.’

‘What about your Dad?’ asked Mrs Mooshaber.

‘He’s dead and buried here in the central cemetery.’

‘And your Mum too?’ inquired Mrs Mooshaber

‘No, not at all,’ said the boy shaking his head, ‘of course she’s not dead. She runs the shop over there.’

‘And that is where she sells candles, ribbons, flowers and graveyard lights, isn’t it,’ said Mrs Mooshaber, nodding the feathers on her head into a tremble, ‘hats too, and gloves and brollies. Do you give her a hand in the shop?’ The lad looked up and puffed out his chest with its white flower once again.

‘Now then, there’s something I have to tell you,’ said Mrs Mooshaber as the feathers on her hat trembled and the necklace round her throat went clickety-clack, ‘I’m going to recite a short poem which I have never forgotten since my schooldays. I’m telling it to you so that you will be a better student and will not play truant from school and go roaming around.’ Then Mrs Mooshaber recited the poem:

Leaving church the blind old lady
Feels her way with stick unsteady
Forward with her stick she fumbles
Blind Old Lady often tumbles

‘That’s it,’ she concluded with a nod, ‘now run off home.’ They had already reached the thick trees and bushes at the edge of the clearing, and the cemetery gate with Mrs

Eichenkranz' home and shop was just ahead of them. 'Off you go, let me see you go straight home. And no getting into mischief,' she added, 'no taking things that aren't yours, no shooting and no drinking, or you'll upset your mother, and you know where that will lead you. First the school for troublemakers, then the house of correction, then an unskilled pair of lands like as not hired for the day, a few oddjobs and a career that ends behind bars. I'll stand here for a while and keep an eye on you until you've reached the front door.

The lad took a last look at Mrs Mooshaber, at her white face, her earrings, her hat, her necklace and her white-gloved hands and with a hesitant smile went up to the front door of the building. He glanced back three times as he went. Mrs Mooshaber stood under a tree by the bushes and watched him go. She kept an eye on that door, on the window with its blind pulled down, on the sign above it and the colourful metal sign with a bottle next to it.

A moment later the lad arrived, made a grab for the door and in a flash the stripey blue-and-white top disappeared inside. Mrs Mooshaber stood under the tree by the bushes a little while longer, eyeing the door, the building, the window with its blind, the sign above it ...and then she suddenly leaped behind a bush.

The door of the building had burst open to reveal Mrs Eichenkranz herself.

'Mrs Mooshaber! Mrs Mooshaber...' From behind a bush Mrs Mooshaber heard the voice calling her and then she caught sight of Mrs Eichenkranz rushing off towards the park.

'Mrs Mooshaber, is that you there?' Mrs Eichenkranz called out, 'Mrs Mooshaber, if it's you there can you wait a minute. Wait there, Mrs Mooshaber.' But it was already dark in the park and the light from the gas lamps couldn't penetrate the thick bushes beneath the trees and reveal Mrs Mooshaber as she stood there. So Mrs Eichenkranz saw nobody and went back inside.

When she had shut the door of the building behind her, Mrs Mooshaber, standing behind the thicket, felt for her hat, for her earrings and finally for her bamboo beads, while she became aware of a dull aching in her leg.

VII

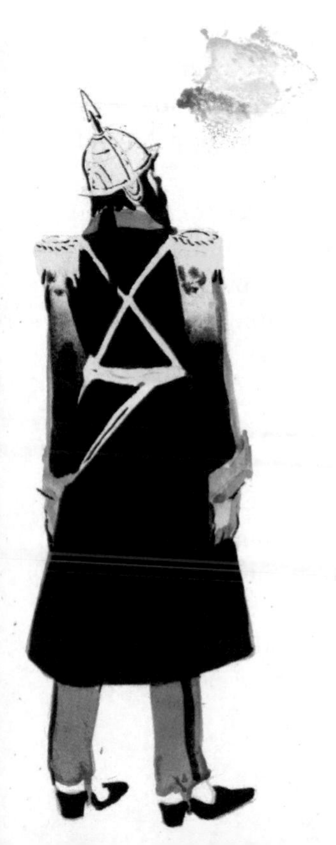

She went home through the park, but took a short cut owing to her aching leg. As she left the park she caught sight of a policeman on the pavement beneath a street light. He had stripes on his shoulders, a black helmet edged with silver and his hands were behind his back as he gazed up at the sky, where the red and green lights of a spaceship were just about to disappear from sight. When the spaceship was no longer visible, the policeman lowered his head and slowly moved in the direction of Mrs Mooshaber. She hurriedly crossed to the other side of the street and then slowed her pace in response to her aching leg.

She went over the crossroads by the *Sunflower* department store, which was a blaze of neon, and threw a glance at the stalls nearby, in front of which a few people were still eating and drinking. This was when she started to feel that someone was following her. The feeling struck her while she was looking from the crossroads down the great avenue in which the editorial offices of *Our Blooming Homeland* were situated and which ended some way off in Albinus Rappelschlund Square with its bunting-beribboned statue. As she made her way into the three forlorn streets leading towards her home, she swung round and looked back, but there was no one to be seen.

The first thing that Mrs Mooshaber did when she was back in her kitchen was to switch on the light. Then she took off her hat, gloves, beads and earrings, while she found a little corner of the room in which to put them for the time being. She saw the caretaker's rouge, cream, powder and eyebrow-liner lying on the table and put them in the same corner. Her leg still ached and she glanced at the stove wondering whether there was still some heat in it. 'I'll give my leg a warm bath in vinegar,' she thought, 'and then put a compress on it for the night.' She poured some water into a basin and washed the make-up from her lips, cheeks and eyebrows before drying them and slipping into her nightdress. Then she applied a comb to her old grey locks before taking several pieces of string from the sideboard in order to tie her hair. Bedlinen, bolster and blanket she brought from the other room and set down on the sofa. She placed a saucepan of water on the stove and fetched vinegar from the larder. Later she would examine the traps underneath the sofa and the sideboard and behind the stove, not to mention the corridor and her other room, to see whether she had caught any mice, and would fetch some new pieces of streaky bacon from the larder. At just that moment the clock above the stove began to strike the hour and there was a knock on the door into the passage. 'That'll be the caretaker,' she said to herself, 'she thinks I've just got back from the Glitz, and she wants to know what it was like. Oh dear, won't she be surprised to hear that I never went there, but went to the park instead.' She went out of the kitchen into the corridor, her hair tied up for the night and opened the door with a sigh. But it wasn't the caretaker standing there. It was two men.

'Mrs Natalia Mooshaber?' asked one of them.

'We're the police,' said the other, showing some identification.

Mrs Mooshaber stared at them and took a step backwards.

'I had no idea,' she began as they advanced into the kitchen, 'that you were coming. I'm ready for bed, as you can see. You've come here about the Faber boy, I suppose, but your colleagues have already been and gone. He fell down just before seven, that clock was striking at the time, the funeral was yesterday.'

The policemen sat down in chairs at the table and began to examine the kitchen. Their eyes even examined Mrs Mooshaber in her nightclothes, her old hair combed straight and tied with the pieces of string. It brought them out in smiles.

'We're not here on account of the Faber lad,' one of them said.

'Well then, I expect you're here on account of the Eichen boy,' Mrs Mooshaber said from the sideboard, 'he's suspected of taking things from the cemetery and shooting crows.

Indeed I've just taken him home from the park. Someone could have killed him while he was out and about in the evening and then dumped the body in bushes.'

'We're not here about any Eichen boy,' said the police while they continued to look around and to smile.

'So I suppose it's about Wezr,' said Mrs Mooshaber as she went with a sigh towards the sofa, 'I might have guessed.'

'That will be your son...' said one of the policemen.

'It is indeed,' said Mrs Mooshaber, 'he spent three months behind bars but now he's back out. He doesn't live here, I'm glad to say. I don't even know where he's living now. He just visits from time to time. Even Nabule doesn't stay here much now. She's just got married.'

'And what was it that landed your son in jail?' asked one of the policeman. For a moment they both wiped the grins off their faces and stopped looking around the kitchen.

'I've no idea,' said Mrs Mooshaber with a shake of the head as she parked herself on the sofa, 'certainly it will have been something bad. Probably an assault of some kind. From when he was a small boy he was always in scraps. He went to the school for troublemakers and the house of correction. And then,' she added from the sofa with a shake of the head, 'what could come of him but to be an unskilled pair of lands like as not hired for the day, a few oddjobs and a career that ends behind bars.'

'And what did he want from you when he came to se you, Mrs Mooshaber?' asked one of the policemen.

'He was just visiting,' said Mrs Mooshaber as she reached for her leg, 'Nabule came with him and so did some stranger who might have been one of the witnesses at her wedding. A stonemason.'

'Did your son bring you anything, Mrs Mooshaber?' the policeman continued.

Mrs Mooshaber looked around hesitantly and visited her old grey hair with her hands.

'Yes,' she said after a while, still looking around, 'he brought an umbrella and some hares. They were hanging by the legs in that window...' she went on, pointing at the window of frosted glass.

'Did he bring you anything else?' asked the policeman.

'Some money,' Mrs Mooshaber confessed after a while.

The policemen looked at the sideboard, at the stove, at the clock and then nodded to each other. Finally one of them said:

'Did he want to give you some of what he brought?'

Mrs Mooshaber nodded.

'He wanted,' she said, 'to give me the hares and some money. He said that it was enough for me to be a stallholder. I've always wanted a kiosk and to sell things, you see. Like I've always wanted to be a housekeeper. And the stranger, the stonemason, he said that I could go as far as the Moon with money like that and bathe in lava and still have enough for an ice cream.'

'Did you know that your son was out of jail, Mrs Mooshaber?' asked one of the policemen.

'I knew he'd done his time,' she agreed. 'He'd done three months. It was his third time behind bars. He's twenty-five now. I had children late in life.'

'We didn't come here on account of your son,' the policemen now said as they began a new round of smiling, scanning the kitchen and staring at Mrs Mooshaber seated on the sofa. 'We came on account of something completely different. To tell you the truth, we came – to have a look round. To see how you live.'

'How I live?' exclaimed Mrs Mooshaber in surprise. 'How I live? You mean – how I live?'

The policemen nodded. 'That's right. How you live.'

'Well you can see for yourself. I live right here.' Still in a state of astonishment she pointed at everything around her. 'That window of frosted glass over there faces the corridor under the staircase, while in front of it there's a corridor with a larder. There's a wardrobe in the corridor where I keep two black flags and a pole in one corner. And I have another room over there, come and see for yourselves.' Mrs Mooshaber got up from the sofa and the policemen rose with her.

'This is it, my other room' said Mrs Mooshaber, showing them through the door, 'take a peek...as you can see I've got a small table, quite a large mirror and two beds. The window faces the courtyard. There's scaffolding outside at present. The children used to sleep there, my Wezr and Nabule, but as I said they hardly do so at all now. Wezr never. Nabule lives here even if she doesn't sleep here. Her husband Laibach still has lodgings with Miss Klaudinger. He's saving for an apartment in the Elizabethan district. When they were small I'd sing to them. A lullaby.'

The policemen nodded and went back to the kitchen table. Then they said:

'Mrs Mooshaber, since you live with a window onto the courtyard and a front door leading into the passage, that must mean you have mice...'

'Oh yes,' said Mrs Mooshaber, leaning on the sideboard, 'I'm the one to know about that. The caretaker says that the rat-catcher should be sent for. She says even a cat won't do the trick. But I don't think there's anyone like that in the whole city.'

'I think there is,' said one of the policemen hesitantly, 'I think there's a rat-catcher at the Bureau for Street Cleaning.'

'I think not,' chimed in the other policeman, 'Mrs Mooshaber is correct. So you haven't got a cat?' he inquired.

'I haven't,' Mrs Mooshaber replied, 'but someone in the house has. I put down traps. Right here...' Mrs Mooshaber opened a drawer in the sideboard and took out three empty traps. 'I have some right here. The rest are set under the sideboard and the sofa. And over there behind the stove. Also in my other room and in the corridor. I keep some streaky bacon on a plate in the larder and sprinkle it with poison. It's a white powder. *Moroccan*. I keep that in the larder too.'

The policemen examined the traps. They tried to open the little doors and even to poke a finger through onto the little board behind the tiny bars. Then they nodded.

'These are well-made traps,' they agreed, 'the mouse is trapped and poisoned at the same time. After that you take them outside...'

'After that I take them outside,' repeated Mrs Mooshaber as she comforted her leg, 'and put them in the dustbin with the rubbish. It's behind that frosted glass window.'

The policemen nodded and once again scrutinised Mrs Mooshaber. Their eyes examined her from head to toe in her night attire, her old grey hair combed out and tied up for sleep, and now they stopped trying to wipe the grins off their faces.

'Well then,' they said as they rose from their chairs, 'well then, everything seems to be in order. Please excuse the fact that we came so late in the evening, Madam, when you wanted to get some sleep. We wish you good night.'

Mrs Mooshaber accompanied the officers as far as the door into the passage, where they shot fleeting glances at the wheelbarrow, the bricks and the barrel of lime before leaving.

Once more Mrs Mooshaber locked the door. Then she examined the traps she'd placed in the kitchen, but there wasn't a mouse to be found. She put them back as they were and prepared a footbath. She poured some water from the saucepan into a bucket, added some vinegar and bathed what she could of her leg in it. 'That was a strange thing to happen,' she said to herself as she bathed the leg, 'they came to see how I lived. What are we to make of that? Nothing, I suppose. They didn't nose around that much, they were hardly in before they were out again. The whole thing makes not the slightest bit of sense.' She removed her leg from the bucket, bandaged it with a rag and then switched off the light before lying down on the ottoman. She lay for a while looking at the dark ceiling above her, while various thoughts and imaginings chased each other through the interstices of her brain. Then she closed her eyes.

VIII

A day later two men in plain clothes led the way for Mrs Natalia Mooshaber as she headed to the first floor of a grey building with bars on the windows. They deposited her in the appropriate office on a bench in front of a desk. There was a telephone on the desk and above the table were portraits of the Prime Minister, Albinus Rappelschlund, and the sovereign, the Dowager Princess Augusta.

A small table with a typewriter lay to the right of the desk, while to the left was a window, barred and grey. The door to some kind of waiting-room covered Mrs Mooshaber's rear, while there was another door behind the desk covering her front. This latter door led to yet another office and was open.

'We know everything,' someone was saying from behind this open door, 'the perpetrator has been found. There's just one thing which you haven't realised so far, my dear daft Kefr. It's a woman.'

'I'm aware of that,' replied the said Kefr in a huffish tone of voice, 'I know as well as you do that the police arrested her this morning at half past seven in Central Cemetery underground station. She is the criminal party.'

The first voice came back with 'You always have a quick answer, dear daft Kefr. Whether she is indeed the criminal party cannot yet be known. The facts have not yet been properly ascertained. Incidentally, what you say happens to be true where this unpleasant affair is concerned, but to make such a presumption where other cases are concerned would be a mistake. Everything must always be investigated first and the evidence weighed in the proper manner. But it simply won't do to pass judgment, even when that judgment is motivated by personal distaste. It's unbelievable how evil people can be.'

From her bench in front of the desk Mrs Mooshaber could catch what the voices were saying and pricked up her ears. Despite listening intently she didn't fail to notice the two plain-clothes men entering the office through the door behind her.

'Right then, you are Natalia Mooshaber?' asked one of them. Mrs Mooshaber had the impression that the question was shouted rather than spoken. Before she could begin to remember the answer, the plain-clothes man had seated himself at the typewriter on the right hand side, had fed it with a sheet of paper and was saying in severe tones:

'How old are you and where do you live?'

Mrs Mooshaber started to rouse herself and snapped back:

'Old enough. And I live in a house that's on its last legs.'

'In Blauental in the old part of town?' asked the other plain-clothes official, who had positioned himself on the left, next to a barred window.

'Just so,' said Mrs Mooshaber.

At this moment a voice could again be heard from the open door in front of Mrs Mooshaber.

'Indeed I'm not saying that people are all that good. God knows how that could be,' the voice was saying, evidently this Kefr, 'on the contrary, I am in favour of malefactors being put away. Where would we end up if malefactors were left free to roam among upright citizens like ourselves? Surely it must never come to that. In next to no time this woman would have a horde of followers.'

'There again,' chuckled the second voice, 'among upright citizens like ourselves, you say, but you shouldn't jump to conclusions on that front. From your point of view, dear daft Kefr, an upright citizen is someone who adores their ruler. And if that citizen isn't in cahoots with the government, then they can't be upright - isn't that what you think? Such a citizen can only be a criminal, right? But I have something else to say to you, dear daft Kefr, something you certainly don't know. Just imagine that when the policeman was arresting that woman in the metro station this morning at half past seven, he got quite a scare to start with.'

Mrs Mooshaber was all ears and made an involuntary movement forward, bending over and touching her leg.

'It is interesting to note, Mrs Mooshaber,' began the plain-clothes official from behind his typewriter, 'that your son has returned from jail, as you say.'

'He's back from behind bars,' agreed Mrs Mooshaber, 'but that's already known. The police paid me a visit on that account yesterday.'

'And you're quite certain that he is back from jail?' asked the plain-clothes official, his finger hovering over the keys of the typewriter.

'From behind bars, quite so' repeated Mrs Mooshaber, 'but they already asked me that yesterday.'

'Very well,' said the officer. 'So your leg started troubling you in front of the house?'

'Not in front of the house,' said Mrs Mooshaber crisply, 'it happened yesterday evening as I was coming back from the park. After the police left I put it into a bucket with vinegar at home.'

'You used a compress of some sort?' asked the plain-clothes official, but Mrs Mooshaber did no more than raise her head. Once again a voice could be heard from the door in front of her.

'Why was the policeman so scared when he arrested her? Why?' The voice sounded irritated. 'Do you really think that our police forces are afraid, Mr Rott?'

'My dear daft Kefr,' replied the other, evidently the Mr Rott in question, 'one can see that you really understand very little and know even less. You know that there is water and life on Mars, but you don't know what sort of time we are living in. Did you arrive here from the Moon the day before yesterday? All I can say is that even up there you should know. The policeman was afraid because he was up against trouble. Even our police get into trouble these days. You are not clever, the penny rarely drops with you, and you want evil-doers to be put away. But you don't even know who the evil-doers are. You mix them up with those upright citizens. And yet you would have them put away. If I were you, I'd feel that I'd be putting my time to better use paving courtyards. Be that as it may,' he went on in a casual tone of voice, 'everything was quickly cleared up. It was a mistake for the policeman to be frightened. Incidentally, she really was a criminal. And there's something else you should know...'

'Put the door to so that we're not disturbed by Rott,' cried the plain-clothes officer at the typrewriter to the other one standing by the barred windows, 'I can't bear rantings on matters like these at home, let alone in the office. Then he got up from the chair himself and put the door to. 'Well then, Mrs Mooshaber,' he went on in a voice which had some of the severity removed from it as it travelled in her direction, 'how strange that we're not yet acquainted. You and me and my colleague,' here he pointed towards the barred windows, 'That's Mr Landl, Mrs Mooshaber, and I am Mr Smirsch. We have both been playing the French horn for a long time.' Mrs Mooshaber responded with a nod and a proffered hand. 'Natalia Mooshaber,' she said, 'Mrs Knorring told me all about you in the cemetery. But what about this Mr Rott,' she went on with a glance at the half-closed door in front of her, 'what was he speaking about to that Mr Kefr? About some woman at Central Cemetery....' Mrs Mooshaber had something to add, but said no more.

That was because the door behind her back, the one leading to the waiting-room, had suddenly opened and in had come Mrs Knorring. She had high-heeled shoes, a face delicately prim and a head held high. In her hands she carried her musical score. Mr Smirsch quickly got up from behind his typewriter and Mr Landl was similarly quick to bow from the barred windows, while Mrs Mooshaber turned on her bench and offered a greeting.

Mrs Knorring nodded, sat down behind her desk facing Mrs Mooshaber and laid the sheets of music out in front of her.

'There's always something going on,' she said, 'this morning at half seven they arrested a woman at Central Cemetery metro. She is suspected of leading a gang of parcel thieves. However, what's even worse is the fact that the policeman who was about to arrest her took fright himself at first. The police find themselves in an awkward situation these days, one that seems to be getting worse all the time. But you don't like speeches of this kind, Mr Smirsch, do you,' added Mrs Knorring with a glance towards the typrewriter. 'By the way,' she added turning her attention to the bench in front of her, 'what have you managed to find out, Mrs Mooshaber?'

'A great deal,' said Mrs Mooshaber. 'I spoke to him yesterday in the park. I found him in the evening by the fountain. He'd picked a flower and was tucking it into that stripey top of his. I went behind him like the evening star while it was getting dark and I saw him watching the birds which were still around feeding, and he had his eye on the crows and some chap with an umbrella. Then in a flash he'd vanished, next to a tree. The ground swallowed him up. It was as if he'd joined the tombs in the graveyard.'

'The ground swallowed him up?' Mr Smirsch looked up from his typewriter as he spoke.

'Swallowed him up – but I found out about that. He'd hidden inside a hole in the tree. I found him again. Flying across the path behind me like a bird. Then he turned off onto another route and on one path he started talking to a squirrel. He didn't do anything to it. He said he didn't want to kill it, as squirrels were just there to be fed. Then I took him home and found a thing or two out on the way back.'

'And how did it turn out,' asked Mrs Knorring, now fairly deep in thought...'is it true about him stealing at the cemetery and shooting birds?'

Mrs Mooshaber shook her head. 'He says that he only takes old flowers from the cemetery, the ones that would be thrown into the bins anyway, so in fact he's helping the people who clean up there. He says that the crows cause damage, but that he could never hit one even if he tried. He's got no brothers or sisters, his father's dead and buried in the cemetery. But not his mother, she's still alive...'

'I know that,' said Mrs Knorring with a nod, 'what else?'

'What else,' said Mrs Mooshaber with a nod, 'he has a place to sleep, Mrs Eichen cooks for him and he helps her out in the shop. If he wasn't helping her she couldn't keep her shop, she couldn't make a living without him. She gave me beer and a cake, the day before yesterday it was, the lad hadn't taken the money from that man's coat-tail pocket, he must have lost it somewhere. Mrs Eichen has the odd mouse in that home of hers in the cemetery. But the mice can't lift the covers and get at the cakes or the watermelons. When

I took the lad home yesterday I recited a poem to him, one that I've known ever since my schooldays.'

'Good evening, good night, may the angels hold thee tight?' asked Mrs Knorring as she raised her head.

Mrs Mooshaber shook her head. 'Not the lullaby, the poem about an old blind woman.'

'A pretty poem,' said Mr Smirsch from his typewriter, while Mr Landl nodded from over by the barred windows. 'A pretty poem,' he agreed.

'I've an idea,' said Mrs Knorring with a glance at the sheets spread out in front of her on the desk, 'that it's been put to music, but I'm not sure. But to return to the matter in hand, Mrs Mooshaber,' said Mrs Knorring while she offered another glance, this one pensive and questioning, at the bench in front of her, 'what is your opinion of the matter, all things considered?'

'All things considered,' began Mrs Mooshaber with a nod, 'what I think is that it could end up badly for him and that he gives his mother a lot to worry about. He must really be a lot of trouble, if Mrs Eichen says so, because otherwise she wouldn't say so. But perhaps it's worth trying persuasion once more. Mrs Eichen needs him by her side in the shop.'

For a moment silence held court in the office. Mr Smirsch and Mr Landl looked at Mrs Mooshaber and Mrs Knorring in turn, while Mrs Knorring looked pensively and inquiringly at Mrs Mooshaber from behind her desk. 'Very well,' she said in a strangely hesitant voice, 'Mrs Mooshaber, just one last question. When you took the lad home from the park yesterday evening, did you accompany him to the flat and speak with Mrs Eichenkranz?'

'No, I didn't go and speak with her,' explained Mrs Mooshaber shaking her head, 'I waited in the bushes until the lad had gone into the flat and then went away. My leg was hurting.' At this moment the telephone rang on Mrs Knorring's desk, and when she had finished speaking she said to the men stationed at the typewriter and the barred windows:

'Gentlemen, I have to go to the second floor for a while. They're expecting me. Regarding the Central Cemetery metro case. Wait here and after a short while summon Mrs Eichenkranz. She is in the waiting-room and quite overcome by this misfortune.' Mrs Knorring rose to her feet, glanced at the musical score on her desk and went out through the half-closed door at the front.

Now Mrs Mooshaber spoke up from her bench. 'Mr Smirsch, you left the door to, as did Mrs Knorring. Couldn't you open it a little again? I wonder whether those gentlemen are still talking in there.'

Mr Smirsch laughed and said:

'But Mrs Mooshaber, they are talking about the Central Cemetery affair, on account of which Madam went upstairs. If the case interests you, Madam will tell you about it. As for me, I really have no time for Mr Rott's political rantings and ravings which have no business being aired in public, least of all by a person vested with public authority. They could be the occasion of a splendid suspension for Mr Rott one day. But to get back to the point....' he turned to Mr Landl by the barred windows, 'Mrs Eichenkranz is quite overcome by this misfortune. If there has been any misfortune. For all I know nothing may have happened at all. One naughty boy does not make the world go round. We'll call her in.'

From behind Mrs Mooshaber, Mrs Eichenkranz entered the office through the door from the waiting-room. She wore black. Black locks peeped out from beneath a black cap. There wasn't a hint of pink on her plump cheeks. She was deathly pale. When she recognised Mrs Mooshaber's back on the bench, she cried out.

'Calm down, Madam,' said Mr Smirsch from his typewriter, 'nothing bad has happened, has it?'

'Calm down,' repeated Mr Landl from the barred windows, 'I'm sure that nothing bad has happened.' But Mrs Eichenkranz in her black clothes and hat remained deathly pale, far from calm and possibly even close to fainting.

'Pray tell me,' said Mr Smirsch from the typewriter, 'why you are so filled with alarm by Mrs Mooshaber. You are indeed already acquainted with her, you walked around the cemetery with her the day before yesterday and you invited her to visit you. Indeed Mrs Mooshaber was in your home where you gave her cake and beer. And now she frightens you, as if you had a bad conscience about something. What is it all about, Mrs Eichenkranz?'

Finally the lady in the black cap and clothes came out with it.

'It's not as if I'm frightened,' she said, the words tripping over one another in the haste of her speaking, 'I'm not alarmed. I know Mrs Mooshaber well, how could I have a bad conscience? I've done nothing bad to Mrs Mooshaber. And she likewise has done nothing bad to me. On the contrary, Madam promised to speak up for me here at the Welfare.'

'There you are then,' said Mr Smirsch,'so there's no reason to be so pale and agitated. Why don't you take a seat?'

Mrs Eichenkranz sat down but without ceasing to look terribly pale and disquieted. She cast looks full of uncertainty at Mr Smirsch by his typewriter, Mr Landl by the barred windows and most of all at Mrs Mooshaber on the bench. Then Mr Smirsch suddenly remarked:

'It seems to me that Madam will have to see the lad again.'

'For God's sake,' shrieked Mrs Eichenkranz and clasped her hands over her black cap.

'Yes.' Mr Smirsch was nodding agreement. 'It's very unfortunate, but there's nothing can be done about it. After all Madam can put up with quite a lot. She has even seen decomposing corpses, a stage that your lad has not yet reached.' Mr Smirsch got up from his typewriter, went to the door of the waiting-room and opened it. He called something to an assistant and into the office walked Eichenkranz junior.

He arrived in his stripey blue-and-white top with a flower on his breast and a smile on his face. He threw one quick glance around the room and went to stand beside his mother's chair.

'It is really beyond me what is the matter with you, Mrs Eichenkranz,' said Mr Smirsch, when he was seated once again behind his typewriter, 'just tell me what has happened. If anything at all has happened. Of course there's no denying....' he went on, looking at the lad on the chair, 'that he looks a picture of innocence, a little stripey angel who has only to spread his wings. But appearances are deceptive.'

Mrs Eichenkranz, still parked on the chair in her black clothes and bonnet, suddenly became a shade calmer. She became a shade calmer, but this still left her far from relaxed and she remained white of pallor. Then she spoke up:

'Mr Counsellor, I really am doing what I can. Mrs Mooshaber knows this very well, don't you, Madam.....' here she turned to the bench and Mrs Mooshaber responded with a nod...'he doesn't steal, he hasn't even taken a candle out of the church or a stick from the forest. He hasn't even shot anything. Indeed....' Mrs Eichenkranz turned suddenly towards the little lad and said in agitated tones: 'It's just like you said to this lady who brought you home from the park yesterday, isn't that so?'

'That has got nothing to do with our current business,' said Mr Smirsch from behind his machine, 'do not repeat what has nothing to do with our current business.'

'Thank Heavens for that,' said Mrs Eichenkranz, a little calmer though still pale and far from being at ease, 'Thank Heavens for that, Mr Counsellor. But he never took anything from that old man by the tomb either. I tell you that man cannot have been in his right mind. How could anyone pick someone's pocket at a graveside? And from a coat-tail, when the victim is standing sideways on? Mrs Mooshaber knows best that you can't steal things in such a manner, don't you, Madam...' When Mrs Mooshaber responded with a nod, Mrs Eichenkranz again turned suddenly towards the lad and repeated in agitated tones: 'It's just like you said to this lady who brought you home from the park yesterday, isn't that so?'

'That's nothing to do with our business either,' said Mr Smirsch from behind his typewriter, 'and Mrs Mooshaber does not know that things cannot be stolen in such a manner. It's not as if she is a pickpocket. This Mr Klevenhütter has already been to see us and the case is now closed.'

'Mr Counsellor,' exclaimed Mrs Eichenkranz, who was still calming down in stages but remained pale and with trembling voice, 'Mr Counsellor, I thank God that it is so. But the lad has everything he wants at home, so why would he want more? He even has his own drawer. And yesterday evening he said the same thing to Mrs Mooshaber when she brought him home from the park...you said it to this lady here, didn't you...' she turned quickly and emphatically again to the little lad. 'Mrs Mooshaber knows everything. She went through it all the day before yesterday and carried out her investigation. We were looking for the lad all afternoon, weren't we...' and from her bench Mrs Mooshaber vouchsafed a third nod.

'Except for one fact, Madam,' said Mr Smirsch from behind the typewriter, 'this is not what matters. What matters is something completely different.'

'God in Heaven!' exclaimed Mrs Eichenkranz and she became agitated all over again and turned a deathly pale hue. 'Lord Jesus, I guessed as much. I guessed as much. Oh Lord Jesus, what is this about?'

'About this,' said Mr Smirsch, 'About the fact that I am not a counsellor, but a pensioner, and all I do here at the Mother and Child Support Service is to help out.'

The pallor suddenly receded from the face of Mrs Eichenkranz, while her eyes seemed to pop out in surprise. She was again somewhat calmer. She looked at Mrs Mooshaber on her bench and Mrs Mooshaber gave her a nod.

'Yes,' Mrs Mooshaber confirmed, 'Mr Smirsch is a pensioner and used to play the French horn. In fact he still plays it. And the other gentleman here....' Mrs Mooshaber pointed at Mr Landl by the barred windows, 'he is Mr Landl and is also a pensioner and was another player of the French horn – indeed he too still plays. My leg started giving me trouble in front of the building and these gentlemen helped me to get here. Until then we didn't know each other.'

'I play that coiled brass wind instrument that goes by the name of a French horn,' said Mr Smirsch, 'just like Mr Landl, my colleague. At the same time this is our place of work. We are rehearsing a performance of the great *Requiem*,' he added quickly with a glance above the desk, namely at the portraits of the Prime Minister, Albinus Rappelschlund, and the sovereign, the Dowager Princess Augusta, 'we will perform jointly with the greatest orchestras. We have a lot of rehearsals and the conductor is Mr Scarone from Bosnia. And so...' now he turned again to Mrs Eichenkranz 'so do not call me Counsellor. Have you calmed down? Are you becoming less pale? Are you not so frightened now of Mrs Mooshaber? It is indeed very peculiar that you should have been so pale and agitated and in such a state of alarm to begin with. Now it is perhaps a litle better for you. And how about you...' now Mr Smirsch turned to the lad, 'you haven't spoken a word to us.'

'He lost his voice in the night, sir,' said Mrs Eichenkranz who had surprisingly enough become rather agitated and pale all over again, 'it was yesterday evening in the park, when Mrs Mooshaber was bringing him home. He got a bit of a chill and today he can hardly speak a word.'

'Allow me to point out that it is still September and the weather is warm,' said Mr Smirsch, 'so how could he have caught a chill? The trees are still green, the flowers are still blooming – I see that he has a white one in his top which has faded somewhat. Wherever did he get it?'

'I found it,' said the lad with a smile.

'He found it on a path somewhere in the park, Mr Counsellor,' said Mrs Eichenkranz quickly, 'someone must have dropped it there yesterday and now he's wearing it. He's been wearing it since yesterday, since the time when Mrs Mooshaber brought him home in the evening. It's not as if he'd ever pick one.'

At that very moment the front door opened and in came Mrs Knorring. She nodded at Mrs Eichenkranz, who quickly stood up from her chair, and proceeded to her desk where she sat down and glanced at the score in front of her. 'This case at Central Cemetery Metro,' she said, 'is most intriguing. The woman arrested this morning at half past seven on the platform is actually suspected of having led a band of parcel thieves. The fact that the policeman about to arrest her took fright himself is of course an error. The police have a really difficult job to do these days and it's only going to get more difficult for them. It's a bad situation and we don't know what will come of...' she glanced at Mr Smirsch behind his typewriter...'Mr Smirsch does not like to hear such things. But there is something else...' Mrs Knorring glanced across at Mrs Mooshaber on the bench in front of her, 'it appears to me, Mrs Mooshaber, that this woman on the metro who was arrested this morning bears some resemblance to yourself.'

'Good God!' Mrs Mooshaber shook her head and looked taken aback, 'Good God, Mrs Knorring, it was definitely not me. I have never led any parcel thieves anywhere. And I wasn't at Central Cemetery any time this morning. Really, it wasn't me,' she repeated, though now in a way that made a joke of the matter.

'Of course it wasn't you,' laughed Mrs Knorring, 'how could it have been you, when they arrested a woman and you are here. I am simply saying that she resembles you. But we have other important matters to deal with. This...' Mrs

Knorring pointed at the score in front of her and glanced up at Mr Smirsch behind his typewriter and at Mr Landl by the barred window, 'this part here is very demanding. The French horns play while the choir sings and the choir has to sing while the French horns play. It's extremely demanding and can only come off if the utmost effort is put into it. Now, Mrs Eichenkranz, to the matter I was referring to.'

Mrs Eichenkranz was still on her feet and was again deathly pale and almost as agitated as when she'd first arrived. Holding the boy's arm with one hand she stared at Mrs Knorring as if she'd seen a ghost. 'Mrs Knorring,' she said in a voice full of perturbation, 'I am so miserable. Mrs Mooshaber can certainly verify the fact of my unhappiness. Mrs Mooshaber brought the lad home from the park yesterday evening.'

'It's true, Mrs Eichenkranz is certainly not happy,' agreed Mrs Mooshaber.

'Madam, please be seated again,' said Mrs Knorring with a nod, 'we already know all about the lad. Mrs Mooshaber has presented her report and I am now going to give you my conclusion.' And with head erect and eyes focused on the ceiling, as if she wanted to look up at the portraits of Albinus Rappelschlund and the sovereign, the Dowager Princess Augusta, although they were not within range, Mrs Knorring spoke:

'We will have another try. We will let him stay at home, on the understanding that he helps you make an honest living. Look here,' she fixed her attention on the lad who remained glued to his mother's side, 'we will give you one more chance, but this is the last. If you continue to misbehave, if you don't go to school but instead lounge around, if you take things and shoot birds, then it will be off to join the remedials without so much as a by your leave. Mrs Mooshaber is a regular at the cemetery and so she can keep an eye on what goes on. Now then, Mrs Mooshaber, have your say.'

'If you are naughty once again,' said Mrs Mooshaber turning to face the lad and nodding, 'you'll be off to the school for troublemakers, then the house of correction, then you'll be an unskilled pair of lands like as not hired for the day, a few oddjobs and a career that ends behind bars. And you will worry your mother to death – you heard how she's not at all happy. She has a lovely shop and anyone else would be happy to be in your shoes but no, you just make your mother miserable. He drives you to distraction, doesn't he, Madam?'

'He does,' agreed Mrs Eichenkranz hastily and again became somewhat calmer while her chubby cheeks became less pale, although even after this happy conclusion she still remained somewhat pale and ill at ease... 'he does indeed drive me to distraction. You are not to go wandering or go stealing', she said to the lad, 'I can't think where you got such behaviour from, seeing that I am such a decent person and a widow and these things are supposed to run in your genes. And this airgun which they confiscated from you, you won't ever lay a finger on it again. Mrs Mooshaber will supervise all this and you know what that means. Mrs Mooshaber is strict and she won't give you an inch. That way you'll be kept out of the house of correction and won't worry me to death. Mrs Knorring, I would like to thank you for your wise decision. And I would also like to thank you, Mrs Mooshaber, for taking on this case. I knew that you were a great expert who knew everything there was to know and could even work cures. And as for you,' she said to the lad, 'you will now thank these ladies in a very nice manner. Mrs Knorring first of all. Kneel gracefully and say: 'Madam, I thank you for the fact that you are giving me another chance. So that I can go home and help out in the shop.'

The young lad gave a smirk and held back for a moment before kneeling in front of the desk and repeating the words his mother wanted to hear. When he had finished he sprang quickly to his feet again.

'All right, now thank Mrs Mooshaber,' said Mrs Eichenkranz. 'Say: Mrs Mooshaber, I would like to thank you for putting in a good word for me and for taking me home from the park yesterday evening. Off you go.' All of a sudden Mrs Eichenkranz was almost calm and the colour began to drift back into her plump cheeks. But at that very moment a blow was struck. The boy did not get down on his knees.

The lad suddenly thrust out the chest with the withered white flower on it, while he smirked and shook his head.

'That lady,' he said with a smirk and a shake of the head, 'did not take me home. It was a completely different lady who did that.'

The deathly pallor returned to Mrs Eichenkranz who proceeded to collapse onto the chair. Mrs Knorring and Messrs Smirsch and Landl looked as if they'd been turned to stone as they fixed frozen glances on Mrs Eichenkranz. And Mrs Mooshaber loked at Eichenkranz junior, while curiously enough not a muscle moved in her face. It was Mrs Knorring who found words to speak.

'How could it not have been this lady who brought you home from the park yesterday evening? It must have been she.'

But the lad went on smirking and shaking his head.

'Heavens above,' declared Mrs Eichenkranz as she started pulling herself together, 'of course it was this lady, for God's sake. It was Mrs Mooshaber who found you in the park and brought you home.'

Once again the lad smirked and shook his head.

'Oh God,' exclaimed Mrs Eichenkranz, her pallor deathly again while she wrung her hands over her black bonnet, 'I thought something bad like this would happen. I thought so. The poor lad is not at all well...' she wailed, 'when Mrs Mooshaber brought him home yesterday evening he caught a cold and lost his voice during the night...'

'But he does seem to be speaking now,' chipped in Mr Smirsch.

'Yes, but he's hallucinating,' insisted Mrs Eichenkranz and then looked across at Mrs Mooshaber on the bench while she clasped her hands together and blurted out:

'Mrs Mooshaber, I beseech you, after all you are such an expert in these matters, save me once more, poor wretch that I am. Say that it was you who took him home. Indeed it was you, wasn't it? Explain to Mrs Knorring and the gentlemen here that the lad doesn't know what he's talking about, he must have a fever. And I spent the whole morning telling you...' Mrs Eichenkranz was now in a state of great agitation as she turned to her son, '...the whole morning and the evening before, telling you what you have to say here at the Welfare, and now you go and do this to me...'

'I was the one there,' said Mrs Mooshaber.

'There you are!' Mrs Eichenkranz shouted at her son, 'you see, it was this lady here and it was your fever speaking just now. Tell them that you caught a cold and lost your voice.'

'I didn't lose it,' the lad said with another shake of the head, 'and I didn't catch any cold. It was some other lady.'

'Wait a minute,' Mrs Knorring intervened from behind her desk all of a sudden, her head held very high and her face severe, 'wait a minute. Keep calm while the matter is sorted out. Now look here,' she turned to the lad at this point, 'when the lady took you home from the park yesterday evening, did she recite a poem to you?'

The lad thrust his chest forward, smirked and nodded.

'Mrs Mooshaber,' said Mrs Knorring, 'recite the poem about the blind old lady. You will recite and the lad will listen.'

Mrs Mooshaber nodded, turned towards the lad and recited the poem about the blind old lady.

Leaving church the blind old lady
Feels her way with stick unsteady
Forward with her stick she fumbles
Blind Old Lady often tumbles

'What a beautiful poem!' exclaimed Mrs Eichenkranz.

'Beautiful,' echoed Mrs Knorring. 'Now then, did the lady who took you home recite this poem to you?' The lad nodded.

'Very well then,' said Mrs Knorring, 'that clears everything up. It clears everything up and there let us leave the matter. Now so that we can finish with this business, I will repeat that we are giving you one more chance. And if you do not listen to what we're telling you, you'll be off to the house of correction.' At which point Mrs Klotilda Eichenkranz leaped out of her seat, the deathly pallor disappearing all at once from her plump cheeks as they reddened for good this time.

Eyes blazing, with her black clothes and black bonnet she suddenly looked like a merry widow. 'I don't know how I can ever repay you, Mrs Knorring,' she blurted out cheerfully.

'We do not charge any fees,' said Mrs Knorring from behind the desk, 'at least you can recognise that the Mother and Child Support Service is human, injures no one and bullies no one, despite the rumous that go round at times. We don't sit in judgment on people here the way it might perhaps be done elsewhere. First we gather the evidence, then we weigh it and the one thing that you will always find spoken here is the truth. I have no idea,' here she looked at Messrs Smirsch and Landl before glancing at her score, 'I have no idea whether producing such difficult music in so short a time will not prove to be beyond us. There will be thirty French horns and a chorus of about a hundred. It will be the biggest *Requiem* ever performed in this country. The only thing is that we do not yet have a date for the première. Very well, Mrs Eichenkranz, you may now go and as for you, young lad, be a very good boy.'

Mrs Eichenkranz and the boy left with a chorus of effusive thanking and heartfelt leavetakings. Mrs Knorring spent a moment in silence and then glanced around the office.

'Strange things have been happening,' she remarked as she fixed her gaze on some point in the blue beyond, 'I have some peculiar feelings of foreboding. You are not one for political speeches, Mr Smirsch,' she went on, turning her attention to the typewriter, 'not even at home, let alone in a public office. But what's the good of your disliking such speeches when there's no avoiding them. If I hadn't known that it was really Mrs Mooshaber in the park yesterday evening, I would certainly have thought that this lad in the stripes was telling the truth. But there's no doubt that he had a fever, because it was indeed Mrs Mooshaber who was in the park yesterday evening, and to be sure she has made her report. It is a pity, Mrs Mooshaber...' here Mrs Knorring looked at the bench in front of her, 'it is a pity that you did not go right up to the house with the lad, but stayed by the bushes. We would have spared Mrs Eichenkranz unnecessary anxiety. However, the matter has fortunately been cleared up.' Mrs Knorring fell silent and Mr Smirsch spoke up from behind the typewriter:

'The only political speeches that I don't like to hear, Madam, are those spoken by Mr Rott. Mr Rott's speeches are always full of ambiguity and that, in my view, is not something fit for public consumption. It causes bad blood and stirs things up unnecessarily. To this day we are not clear whether there are changes to the rings of Saturn and how the said rings came into existence, even when searching from satellites, or whether Pluto is a former Moon of Neptune. And yet we waste our time here on matters of politics.'

'I don't know that these things haven't been known for a long time,' said Mrs Knorring, now sounding quite severe, 'in fact it seems to me that they *have* been known. What is *not* clear to me is what you mean by 'full of ambiguity'. It seems to me that what he says has one clear and definite meaning, and moreover it makes sense, so why wouldn't his words be fit for public consumption? Where else should such speeches be made, if not in public? On Neptune, perhaps? Or do you think that our country is inhabited by animals? Nor is it clear to me,' Mrs Knorring went on with a shake of the head, 'why such speaking should cause bad blood. Why 'bad'? Because it's aimed against the government? But must the government always be good? Where you see a flaw, Mr Smirsch, I see a virtue and I thank God for it.'

'Madam,' began Mr Smirsch from his typewriter, poised with his finger on a key and in a somewhat confused manner, 'Mrs Mooshaber here only wanted to know exactly what Mr Rott said from behind half-closed doors about the Metro Case. I said that if she was interested you would certainly let her know about it yourself.'

'I will let you know all about it, Mrs Mooshaber,' confirmed Mrs Knorring with a nod, 'I will let you know about it right away. The point is that I would like you to take a look at this case. Well then, the parcels in the post office in the metro at Central Cemetery have been going missing for some time. There must have been a whole gang behind it, familiar with the way the post office on the station platform worked. Yesterday they discovered who was the leader of the gang, a woman. She was arrested on the platform at half seven this morning. Her name is Klaudinger.'

'Klaudinger,' blurted out Mrs Mooshaber from her bench.

'Not the Klaudinger where your son-in-law lives,' explained Mrs Knorring with a shake of the head, 'it's just someone who happens to have the same name. This Klaudinger, as I've already said, happens to look like you – a mere coincidence as well. She must be pushing seventy.'

'And what do I have to find out, Mrs Knorring?' asked Mrs Mooshaber with interest, 'is Mother and Child Support involved in all this too?'

'It is involved,' confirmed Mrs Knorring, 'it is involved because there's a suspicion that a boy called Linpeck was part of this gang of thieves. Linpeck,' added Mrs Knorring as she lifted her head, 'is maybe thirteen years of age and is the son of Mrs Linpeck, who is claiming maintenance from her first husband and who runs a kiosk on a platform in the metro at Central Cemetery. The lad goes up and down this platform after school selling his wares from a trolley.'

'A kiosk,' said Mrs Mooshaber in surprise, 'she has a stall in the underground at Central Cemetery Station, does she? And what does she sell there?'

'The usual things, just like at any station,' said Mrs Knorring, 'sweet pastries, drinks, maybe cigarettes, perhaps even postcards and stamps. But it's her son who interests us most, the one who takes his trolley up and down the platform. He sells what you would expect people to buy from a trolley on a platform. Can you go there and have a chat with the lad and with Mrs Linpeck?' When Mrs Mooshaber gave a quick nod, Mrs Knorring went on:

'Find a way of asking them what they think of the parcel robbery and see from their faces how they react. Ask how Mrs Linpeck gets on with her son and what the lad's like. Judging from what we have here in Mother and Child Support, and from what I heard a while ago from upstairs, there's the germ of a criminal career in that lad. It will do if you can let me have some information within a week. The police will not have finished interrogating the arrested woman before then, as she is deaf.'

With Mrs Knorring looking at her desk and score, it seemed to Mrs Mooshaber that this was the moment for her visit to come to an end. Slowly she touched her leg and then just as slowly rose to her feet. Mr Smirsch at the typewriter and Mr Landl by the barred window were silent, seemingly also under the impression that the visit was over. But Mrs

Knorring suddenly tore herself away from her notes once more, looked at Mrs Mooshaber and said:

'I realise that you don't receive a penny for the work you do here at Mother and Child Support. But there is a means by which I can repay you in a small way. I may have some work for you in the near future, Mrs Mooshaber, something you will be paid for. It's not yet certain, but it's a possibility. It involves a few hours of minding every week for a wealthy family in a villa. The man is a widower who tends to be away from home and his housekeeper cannot keep an eye on the young son all the time. He needs supervision so that he doesn't go loitering after school and get up to mischief, but that's all he needs. He's a model pupil, perhaps the best in the whole school, but he lacks one thing – discipline. The man would pay you.'

'I'd accept it,' said Mrs Mooshaber, 'I could arrange things so that I managed to fulfil my duties at the cemetery too.'

'I'll let you know then,' agreed Mrs Knorring, 'now go to the platform and drop in on Mrs Linpeck.'

Mrs Mooshaber could at last make her farewells.

When she was out of the door and passing through the waiting-room, she heard Mrs Knorring saying to the gentlemen: 'Let's get down to this score.'

And when she had left the waiting-room and was in the corridor, she had the distinct impression that she could make out singing of some kind coming from the office.

IX

It was half past two by the time the women passed the main gate of the cemetery and found themselves in Anna Maria the Blessed Square. Sunlight coming from the west was reflected in the glass rooves of Central Cemetery Station, which stood at the end of the square. It was a huge and high building, a junction of the underground and street-level transport services by bus and trolleybus. Mrs Mooshaber came to a stop on the edge of the square. She was in her long black skirt, waistless jacket with sleeves, scarf and flat shoes. While she eyed the huge station building she shook her big black bag and it might have been thought that she was trying to gather her strength. In truth, however, she had stopped, looked at the station building and shaken her bag only in order to draw the caretaker's attention to some modern buildings in the distance.

'Over there,' she pointed out, 'there used to be a public house. That's where I had my wedding reception. *The Golden Carriage* it was called, and there's not a single brick of it left standing now. Now there are blocks of flats in its place. And over here is Central Cemetery Station and right behind that is the town hall where we were married. And over there where those kiosks are...' Mrs Mooshaber pointed at some stalls made of glass and laminate, which stood next to the modern buildings in the distance, '...over there you can't see a living soul right now.'

'Mrs Mooshaber,' the caretaker blurted out. She was in her flowery summer blouse and short skirt and her cheeks were aglow. 'What good eyesight you have, to be able to see there's no one there from such a distance. But I can hardly wait now! Mrs Mooshaber,' she blurted out again while her

PIVO
DORTY
Limo
Kiosk
KIOSK

cheeks glowed, 'I have never really seen you in action. In all the twenty years that you've been at the Welfare, I've never once seen you at work. You can't imagine the way I still regret it that I had to go home after the funeral of the Faber lad, when you were running after young Eichenkranz in the cemetery. But today I shall see you on the job. We should be going right now.'

They set off walking towards the huge and high station building, whose glass rooves reflected the sun in the western sky and by which stood the statue of Anna Maria the Blessed, and Mrs Mooshaber shook that bag of hers as she said:

'It's as I've already said to you, Madam Caretaker. When Mrs Eichen saw me, she took real fright and stayed frightened almost right up to the end. But then she thanked me heartily for things turning out well. And as for the lad,' Mrs Mooshaber continued with a nod of the head, 'he didn't get onto his knees at all. He just didn't believe that I was the one who was there. He said that it wasn't the lady in front of him who took him home, but someone else entirely.'

'Someone else entirely', laughed the caretaker and quickened her step, 'to be sure. Of course he wouldn't have recognised you, seeing that you appeared in the park looking like an actress or the wife of a Parrot Island trader. Were it not for the fact that I was the one who did your make-up, I wouldn't have recognised you either. You might as well keep those things for now, 'said the caretaker, her step quickening all the time, 'did you put them in the wradrobe?'

'Indeed, in the wardrobe,' Mrs Mooshaber affirmed, 'I hung up the hat, so that the feathers didn't get broken, the necklace and earrings I put into a box and the gloves into a bag. As for the powder, the red ointment and the pencils,

I put them away in the sideboard so that a mouse couldn't get at them.'

'So Mickey couldn't get at them,' laughed the caretaker, 'it would be a right laugh if one somehow managed to creep into the ointment and powder. Just imagine a mouse in make-up. None of the others would recognise it. They'd think that it was a cat of some kind.' And the caretaker picked up even more speed before continuing:

'But Mrs Mooshaber, you know how you can disguise yourself if you have to. People were certain to stare at you walking down the street, they were sure to look you over seeing that you looked like some grand actress, but as you said to me yourself you paid no attention to all this....'

'None at all, as I told you,' confirmed Mrs Mooshaber, 'even the mothers and the teachers by the fountain had a good look, even the policeman when I walked out of the park, even the people behind my back, but it was all the same to me. I know why they were staring. I'm getting on a bit now. If I'd been walking around like that fifty years ago, when I was having my reception in *The Golden Carriage*, that would have been quite another thing. But there's one more thing,' Mrs Mooshaber continued while she performed another bagshake, 'Mrs Knorring told me what a shame it was that I didn't take the lad all the way back to his home, but stayed behind the bushes. I should have taken him right up to the front door. The thing was that I was all made up like someone on the stage or like a rich trader's wife, you know how it was. I would have had to explain to Mrs Eichen about this Ritz business.'

Having reached the statue of Anna Maria the Blessed, which stood in the shadows of the huge glass station, Mrs

Mooshaber slowed her pace and the caretaker had to do the same, whether she wanted to or not. Some elderly guide was holding forth about the statue to a group of foreigners. 'The blessed Anna Maria', he was saying in a lisping voice while he kept fondling his waistcoat from which some kind of gold chain was hanging, 'was the mother of our present-day sovereign the Dowager Princess Augusta. She died sixty years ago at the age of one hundred. She was well-known for mingling with ordinary people. She sang in the choir in St Adalbert's Chapel and it was even whispered that she secretly sold candles in churches. It is said of our contemporary sovereign the Dowager Princess Augusta,' the elderly guide explained lispingly as he fondled some more of his chain, 'that she takes after Anna Maria. Said it may be, but true it is not. Our sovereign the Dowager Princess Augusta does not go walkabout. She sits in the royal palace and rules.'

'Why was the statue built here right next to a huge skyscraper of a station?' asked one of the foreign visitors in a lively tone from beneath a little yellow hat, 'why didn't they build it further away or right in the middle of the square? The statue gets lost next to such a towering giant of a station.'

'The statue was here before they erected the towering giant,' lisped the aged guide, 'that's the way it was and not the other way round. Prime Minister Albinus Rappelschlund had this station built...'

At that very moment Mrs Mooshaber was standing stock still looking at the statue, the strangers milling about the station, the kiosks in the distance and the modern houses where the hostelry in which she had her wedding reception used to stand. '*The Golden Carriage* it was called,' she repeated to the caretaker, but the caretaker who was standing next to her was transfixed by the foreigners at the statue, especially the one with the little yellow hat, and was listening to the guide.

'There's another thing,' the little-hatted foreigner piped up again, 'is it not the case that your sovereign the Dowager Princess Augusta isn't really in power at all? That she's in prison or in hiding somewhere?'

'No, that's not true,' said the guide shaking his head and throwing round a furtive glance or two, 'our sovereign the Dowager Princess is in residence in the royal palace on the other side of the city and from there she governs us.'

'One other thing,' persisted the foreigner in the little hat, 'is it not the case that your sovereign Princess has in actual fact been dead for a long time?'

'That's also not true,' said the guide with a few more furtive glances as he clutched the gold chain in his waistcoat, 'it's just a rumour that goes round on the quiet. People used to say that when I was still in my pram or when I was still driving waggons for the brewery.'

'There's not a living soul at those kiosks,' said Mrs Mooshaber, staring into the distance, 'of course it's afternoon now, the lunch break is over.'

'The lunch break is over,' repeated the caretaker as she wrested her attention away from the foreigner, 'my God, Mrs Mooshaber, it will soon be three o'clock. We must be going. Come along, Mrs Mooshaber.' And so they set off once again.

'There's something else I must tell you,' said Mrs Mooshaber as they walked along, 'Yesterday Mrs Knorring said that she had some strange premonitions.'

'What sort of premonitions,' asked the caretaker as she quickened her pace, 'perhaps that we might be invaded by

Martians? Or perhaps,' she added with a smile, 'she had a feeling that the world was about to end?'

'Not that the world was about to end,' said Mrs Mooshaber with a shake of the head. 'It was something else. I didn't really understand what she was saying and I didn't want to ask.'

'All sorts of people have these feelings in their bones,' laughed the caretaker as she quickened her pace even more, 'I had them too, just before my old man did a bunk. Mrs Knorring's premonitions probably had something to do with politics – anything's possible. But let me ask you something, Mrs Mooshaber,' said the caretaker as her cheeks started to colour with exertion – they had nearly reached the station – 'I want to know how you will begin your work with this Mrs Linpeck. Will you just go to her kiosk and ask her things?'

'The first thing I have to do – before I go up to her - is be sure that it is really she,' said Mrs Mooshaber, 'so that I don't end up speaking to someone else. I must know that it is she and that it is her kiosk. Then I show her my licence and explain who I am. I'll then put down this bag of mine and fish around with some questions.'

'You fish around,' said the caretaker, 'why is that? Is it because you're investigating?'

'Investigating,' agreed Mrs Mooshaber, 'and because this time I'm under instructions from Mrs Knorring. "Do some skirting around," she said to me, "see what she thinks about the pilfering of parcels. See how she gets on with the lad."'

'See how she gets on,' repeated the caretaker with a smile and a further quickening of step, 'I can't wait to see all this for myself. Tell me, Mrs Mooshaber, does Mrs Knorring always give you instructions before she puts you on a case?'

'She does,' Mrs Mooshaber agreed, 'she always must, if I am to conduct an investigation. But in this case I even knew half an hour before she told me. I was there in the office, just me and Messrs Smirsch and Landl, while Messrs Rott and Kefr were discussing the case in the next room, and Mr Smirsch then proceeded to put the door to. But Mrs Knorring then explained everything to me herself. That's the way it must be, when there's a case to be investigated.'

At that moment Mrs Mooshaber and the caretaker reached the tall giant of a station and went into the entrance hall.

It was a glass hall with buses and trolleybuses in one part and an array of little shops selling tobacco, fruit and soap in the other. Notices and coloured ads were everywhere. The sunlight had made its way in from the western sky but with a golden tint, for the huge glass roof of the hall was a yellowish colour. Surprisingly enough the place was quite empty.

'Not many people about,' said the caretaker, 'that'll be because it's after the lunch break. It's nice in here, isn't it.'

'Yes, it's nice,' said Mrs Mooshaber as she gave her big black bag a shake and took in the shops with all their variety of goods. She even glanced at the notices and the adverts. 'It's really just like a market. The only thing is that they don't sell butter or poultry here. I've only been here a few times, but then you know that I've only been on the underground twice in my whole life, both on the day I got married, once to go to the town hall and from there to the reception in the inn, and once to go back again. But at that time this glass station wasn't around. At that time there was just a low-lying chapel. I wonder which is the way to the underground.'

'Over there, Mrs Mooshaber.' The caretaker hurriedly pointed it out and quickened her step, 'where those steps are and where there's a notice saying: *To the Metro*. Come on, Mrs Mooshaber, let's move. I just can't wait.'

They hurried through the large hall to the steps leading underground, as if they were afraid of missing a train. The caretaker kept speeding up while Mrs Mooshaber was shaking the bag in her hand. She kept looking around as they made their rapid way. Then the caretaker said:

'Let me ask you something, Mrs Mooshaber. Once you are on the job, will you ask Mrs Linpeck about that Klaudinger woman, the gang leader? Could that be the Klaudinger your son-in-law rents from after all?'

'It can't be' said Mrs Mooshaber with a shake of the head, 'that's been proven. The Klaudinger he rents from is a young woman, whereas the one who's been taken into custody is seventy years old and deaf. Besides, Mrs Knorring said that they have nothing in common but their names.'

'And another thing, Mrs Mooshaber', said the caretaker as her cheeks kept reddening with excitement, 'will you take the job at the villa working for that rich fellow?' When Mrs Mooshaber nodded the caretaker went on, 'It would be foolish not to take it, seeing that they'll pay you to go there, seeing that you do everything else for free. You can always find a couple of hours in every day for it. What does this wealthy man do for a living?' she asked.

'I don't know,' said Mrs Mooshaber with another headshake, 'Mrs Knorring hasn't told me yet. All I know is that he has a housekeeper and that she is not enough when it comes to managing the boy.'

'A housekeeper,' exclaimed the caretaker, 'that's a rich man all right. Only the wealthy have housekeepers. How could he be anything else, seeing that he lives in a villa? What about this lad of his, is he like young Eichenkranz?'

'Not at all,' said Mrs Mooshaber, shaking her head. 'If anything he's quite the opposite. He's very good at his studies. The only problem is that he goes off roaming after his classes and isn't very obedient. He needs supervision.'

They reached the steps leading underground and joined a small stream of people going down them. The caretaker, sporting her flowery summer blouse and short skirt, took the steps in leaps and bounds, while Mrs Mooshaber, with one hand holding onto her long black skirt, watched her feet at every step. When they were at the bottom they found themselves in a huge corridor which suddenly divided.

'It forks here,' said the caretaker enjoying herself, 'Now what? This way! Look, Mrs Mooshaber, it's over here!' she called out while she pointed at an arrow marked *Central Cemetery*, 'that other fork goes somewhere else. It goes to City Hall. That's where you went to get married.' They followed the arrow with an even smaller stream of people after the parting of the ways, and soon arrived at a bridge arched over the underground railway tracks. The way down from the bridge led even deeper underground, either to one platform on the right or to another on the left. Only the front part of the platforms was visible from the bridge, and Mrs Mooshaber didn't know which of them to go down to. 'I just don't know,' she said coming to a halt, 'whether Mrs Linpeck's kiosk is on the right or the left platform. Mrs Knorring didn't tell me. It will all have to be part of the investigation.'

'Then let's investigate', exclaimed the caretaker, 'I'll ask someone.'

The caretaker stopped a young man who was passing them at that very moment.

'Can you tell me which platform has the kiosk, sir?' she asked.

'They both have kiosks,' said the young man as he glanced at a train roaring into the station under the bridge, 'both right and left.' He wanted to go on, but then looked at the caretaker and added with a wink: 'there is a kiosk on the right one and a kiosk on the left one, but a different one on each.'

'A different one on each,' repeated the caretaker laughing, 'let's start with the one on the right. If it's not the one, Mrs Mooshaber, well then we'll have to go back onto this bridge and try the left one.' So they descended from the bridge onto the right-hand platform. The huge platform was half empty and the underground restaurant was similarly half patronised. Only a few people could be seen through the huge glass windows sitting at the tables, reading the papers, biding their time with their drinks, perusing the sparsely populated platform and the railway tracks on which, at regular intervals, trains grey and green came to a stop and then resumed their journey. Groups of people from the bifurcating corridor were reduced in number still further by the separate routes from the bridge, and those that still remained on the great platform after these two divisions understandably looked almost lost. But then it was three o'clock, and there are always only a few people using the metro at that time. Those who work a six-hour day are already back at home, while those who work eight, ten or even twelve hours have not yet set out for home. Mrs Mooshaber and the caretaker went past the ticket machines and headed for the front where the kiosk shone in the distance in a blaze of reflected glory from the neon lights and various lamps. It was made from glass and laminate like the kiosks up above and some of its wares could be seen hanging inside it. Someone was sitting in the kiosk, but from a distance it wasn't possible to identify who.

'It could be her,' said the caretaker as she continued to quicken her step, 'we must get closer. I just can't wait. Mrs Mooshaber,' the caretaker went on as she went faster and faster and tapped her forehead, as she was rarely wont to do, 'wouldn't you like me to take your bag and look after it? It might be better if your hands were free for when you present your credentials.'

'Not at all,' responded Mrs Mooshaber with a shake of the head, 'I must have my bag with me. I have to get my licence out of it. Otherwise I can't introduce myself. Then I'll put it down at my feet. But I can see about that later.'

'Of course,' said the caretaker, 'but shouldn't I walk a pace or two behind you, as if we're not together? So that she doesn't get frightened by the thought that there's two of us?'

'She won't get frightened,' said Mrs Mooshaber, 'just come with me. I'll present my credentials at once and I'll introduce you at the same time. As the caretaker.'

'Splendid,' enthused the caretaker, 'I'll come with you then. But I've got a feeling that...' The caretaker's gaze was fixed on the kiosk which was getting closer now and she eased her pace, 'I've got a feeling that this is not Mrs Linpeck's place. There's some grandpa in this one.'

'You're right,' said Mrs Mooshaber who also eased down a gear when she recognised that it was an old man inside the kiosk, 'Mrs Linpeck must have the kiosk on the other platform. And so far as I can see there's no post office here, so it will be the kiosk on the left-hand side.'

So they turned round and retraced their steps past the half-empty restaurant and then up the steps onto the bridge over the tracks. The sound of a train roaring by came from under the bridge and Mrs Mooshaber said:

'I don't even remember what taking one of those things feels like. It's such an age since my wedding. I don't think that there were so many trains running then.' And down they went onto the platform on the left.

The platform on the left side was much bigger than the one on the right and perhaps even more decorous, because the trains running into this platform of Central Cemetery were not grey and green but green, red and yellow, and then went to those parts of the town which you couldn't reach by one of the trains on the right-hand side. Because there was a connection on this side with the nearby City Hall station, the restaurant here was both much bigger and more dazzling than the one on the other side. Through the large glass window-panes crystal chandeliers could be seen shedding their light onto a scene which included, hanging on a column, a portrait of Prime Minister Rappelschlund and the sovereign Dowager Princess Augusta. However, many tables were only half-occupied. Even here there were just a few people reading newspapers, biding their time with their drinks and perusing the sparsely populated platform. Mrs Mooshaber and the caretaker made their way around the restaurant to the front part of the platform, where they saw a kiosk bathed in neon and lamplight gleaming in the distance.

'I'm sure this is it,' said the caretaker, 'it cannot be anywhere else if this is really Central Cemetery station. And look,

there's a post office. See that neon sign saying *Postal Service, Central Cemetery Station*. This is where they were stealing, it must have been here.'

And indeed as they drew near to the post office they spotted another sign saying *Parcel Post*, with an arrow below it pointing at some kind of metal lift further away. The kiosk came closer while the caretaker quickened her stride and her cheeks burned with excitement. Inside the kiosk stood an array of delicacies, bottles of beer and lemonade and cartons of cigarettes, while in front of the window there stood a young lad in an orange sweater who was talking to someone behind the window. When he moved his head a little Mrs Mooshaber and the caretaker could see that the someone on the other side of the window was a woman.

'That's her,' said Mrs Mooshaber, 'we're there. But slow down a little, caretaker, you don't have to be in such a hurry...' the caretaker had been speeding up and reddening her cheeks even more... 'we must wait until this customer leaves. Let's hover about for a bit. And so they slowed down until they were beginning to hover.

'I am curious about how you'll introduce yourself,' said the caretaker with a smile as she scrutinised the young man in the sweater in front of the kiosk, 'and about how you'll do your investigating and what the upshot will be. Whatever will she say about that lad of hers? Do you think she might even tell us about those parcels?'

'If she doesn't I will touch upon the subject myself,' said Mrs Mooshaber with a shake of her big black bag, 'it is peculiar to have a parcel post here at the end of the platform by a tunnel next to that lift. That time when I was going to my wedding at the City Hall and then at *The Golden Carriage*, things were different even here in the underground. There definitely wasn't a post office here.'

'I expect at that time they didn't take parcels on the metro,' said the caretaker, 'they still used a coach and horses to move them about then. I say, Mrs Mooshaber,' the caretaker hurriedly put in, 'are you saying that the lad might have criminal tendencies? Criminal tendencies, why that's terrible! Will you touch upon that subject too?'

Mrs Mooshaber dismissed the idea with a shake of the head. 'Most likely not. About things like that probably not. I might just skirt round the edges. I must distinguish the things to be investigated from everything else. There can be no investigation without doing that.'

The caretaker laughed and glanced at the tracks. Green, red and yellow trains were coming into the station and as they were now hovering about and waiting for the young man with the orange sweater to be gone from the kiosk, even Mrs Mooshaber was drawn into watching the trains a little and saying:

'There's people sitting and people standing in those carriages. I can remember that when we came here that time for the wedding we were sitting. We bought tickets in an enclosed area over there. But only when we were returning. When we were coming here, we bought the tickets in Blauental.'

At last the gestures of the young man in the kiosk made clear that he was beginning to take his leave. A short distance away, the caretaker and Mrs Mooshaber interrupted their hovering.

'He's going, he's going,' cried the caretaker, her cheeks now flush with excitement, 'this is it now. Oh just look!' the caretaker exclaimed, 'just look, oh my God! Or am I seeing things?' The young man had moved his head just enough to give a good view of the woman behind the window and the caretaker was astonished. 'I must be seeing things,' she repeated, 'she's there in the kiosk and she's laughing. She's laughing, Mrs Mooshaber, she doesn't look driven to distraction at all.'

The woman behind the window had lips painted red, a tidal wave of permed hair held back by a black clasp and was indeed laughing.

'She could be masking her worries,' Mrs Mooshaber responded with a shake of the black bag, 'I also sometimes laugh.'

The young man's farewells had almost finished, his legs were already leading him out through the door and his head was bound to follow. The caretaker seized at her last chance for a glance at the platform and remarked:

'But I can't see the lad anywhere, Mrs Mooshaber. He's nowhere round here, is he? He must be around with his trolley only in the evenings. Oh look, that young man's gone.'

The caretaker took another look at the young man as he left the shop, and said with flushed cheeks:

'Mrs Mooshaber, I think that I am about to see something today that I've never seen before. Yes, I'm certain that I've never seen anything to compare with what I'm about to see now.'

They approached the kiosk just as a green train roared into the platform. Mrs Mooshaber took her licence out of her bag and opened the conversation:

'You're Mrs Linpeck, Madam?'

The woman was still all smiles beneath that permanent wave held back by a clasp. Her expression didn't change as the colourful face gave Mrs Mooshaber a colourful look.

'How may I help you,' the face said, 'Gingerbread?'

'My name is Natalia Mooshaber,' Mrs Mooshaber began as she showed the licence, 'Mooshaber from the Mother and Child Support Service. Take a look for yourself.'

All at once Mrs Linpeck's features froze, her eyes opened wide and both Mrs Mooshaber and the caretaker behind her had to jerk back their heads as that of Mrs Linpeck suddenly went crashing down onto the counter.

'Heavens above,' Mrs Linpeck shrieked while her head was still on the counter, 'God in heaven, what's happening to me now? What does it all mean? Are the phantoms coming back to haunt me? No way,' at this point she lifted her head, raising made-up eyes full of terror to look in fear at the platform outside the window, 'no way. This evening I am going to throw myself under a train. I'm going to throw myself under this very train right here...' she jerked her head to face the tracks at the very moment when a red train rolled in, 'you must be here on account of that hyena doing all the stealing around here, what else would you have come about? But my boy had nothing to do with that, he didn't take so much as this from a single parcel,' Mrs Linpeck put a crooked finger through the window to indicate next to nothing. That was when Mrs Mooshaber noticed that her fingernails were long and painted. 'As if we were thieves! No one in our family steals, except for my first husband and his alimony payments that never were. And you know what, lady,' Mrs Linpeck gave her head a sudden jerk behind the window, allowing the great permanent wave on her head to leap upwards, 'I just don't want to hear any more about this. I will not talk to anyone about this. I have a shop to run, I have things to sell. See...' She moved her hand from the window and threw it in the direction of the platform, which was still almost devoid of people, and sized up Mrs Mooshaber with a stern expression, 'take a look at the people here. I will fling myself under a train and that will be an end to it all.' And Mrs Linpeck turned resolutely to face the railway track along which a red train was speeding away at that very moment.

The caretaker was standing a step behind Mrs Mooshaber and looked taken aback.

'Madam,' she declared with flushed cheeks, 'you must be mistaken. Mrs Mooshaber certainly didn't come here to make you jump under a train. Mrs Mooshaber is a great expert in her field, with a lot of work experience. She was put on the case and that's why she's here now.'

Mrs Linpeck turned her head away from the rails and threw a curt glance at the caretaker.

'As for you, Madam' she exclaimed, 'just what do you want here? Are you her courtroom witness? Have the two of you come to slaughter me like a sheep? Just like the one on that carton of cheese over there....' she flung a hand somewhere behind the glass '...have you come to do away with me?'

'No, we're not here to slaughter or for a sheep,' Mrs Mooshaber finally put in as she shook the black bag, 'this is Mrs Kralec. She is the caretaker of the house in which I live and she happened to have a free moment so she came here with me. She knows that I have been working for the Mother and Child Support Service for twenty years.'

'Mrs Mooshaber has indeed been working for the Welfare for twenty years,' the caretaker piped up, still looking taken aback, 'I am the caretaker for the house, as Mrs Mooshaber explained to you. I am not any kind of courtroom witness. You see what I meant, Mrs Mooshaber,' the caretaker went on with a reproachful nod of the head, 'you see why I said I could walk a step or two behind you, the lady has been given a fright by seeing the two of us together and at once.'

Mrs Mooshaber shook her head. 'She's not had a fright. There's no reason for the lady to be afraid of us. There's no need for it.'

At that moment some middle-aged man who was completely bald approached the kiosk and asked for a lemonade. As if someone had waved a magic wand, the face of Mrs Linpeck lit up all of a sudden, her eyes sparkled and a smile could be seen on her blood-red lips. 'Lemonade,' she said with a smile from behind the window, while she reached somewhere and then flipped the top off the bottle. She poured the lemonade into one of the small cups she seemed to keep behind the counter while the bald man handed over a small coin, took the cup, stepped aside and began to drink. Mrs Mooshaber glanced at him enough to see him holding the cup and drinking from it, but then she turned back quickly so that she could look at Mrs Linpeck.

'Yes, Madam' said Mrs Linpeck whose face had now become rigid and whose voice had changed into something quiet and strangely deep, as if she were speaking from the bottom of a well, 'it's three o'clock and I don't have many customers at that time. If you and this other lady (she pointed at the caretaker) were to visit me in an hour and a half's time, you'd be surprised. That's when some people start to leave work and others are going to work, the ones doing night shifts, and at that time the platform's like an anthill. At that time I can't even think straight. One lemonade after another, beer, sweets, postcards, my right hand doesn't know what the left hand's doing, it's like being in a rocket outside the field of gravity. Even the station restaurant over there will be heaving at that time.'

'Can you please tell me why people go there, Madam?' asked the caretaker, her cheeks burning once again, 'are they waiting for the train? The trains run so often,' she went on, looking at the track along which a yellow train was just arriving at the platform, 'that no one ever has to wait for one.'

'People get off or change trains here,' said Mrs Linpeck in the quiet and deep from-the-bottom-of-a-well voice that came from her stiffened face, 'and so they simply let a few trains pass while they sit in the restaurant. They'd rather be there than in another restaurant above ground. The one here has crystal chandeliers and if you go inside you will see that it even has mirrors. It's twice as big as some others. People use it as a meeting-place or they simply look out onto the platform and watch the trains. My postcards are in great demand, because people like to write in there. They have a coffee or a beer and they write. And people who've been to a funeral go there in order to have a snack.'

Meanwhile the bald man finished his drink a short way off, put the cup into the bin standing next to the kiosk and went away. Mrs Mooshaber watched him go and then looked at the bin full of discarded cups before once more focussing her attention on Mrs Linpeck. But Mrs Linpeck had undergone another metamorphosis.

'I'm not going to get through this.' There she was in the window shaking her head and speaking in an unhappy – even a desperate – voice, now high like that of a thrush, 'it's easy for you to say you haven't come here to make me jump under a train but how can I *not* jump under one? How can I *not* jump? Mrs Linpeck lowered her head into her hands. 'Oh heavens above, why do the phantoms haunt me all the time ? It's not as if I'm on the stage, I'm just someone in a kiosk selling their wares like any other stallholder. It's all because of that hyena,' Mrs Linpeck's head rose abruptly from her palms and she looked fiercely ahead, 'it's all that old Klaudinger woman, the boy never took so much as piece of string from one of those parcels. We are none of us thieves, save for my husband. As for Mother and Child Support,' here Mrs Linpeck gave a sharp look at Mrs Mooshaber, 'Mother and Child Support have not been any help to me from that day to this when it comes to my getting my alimony. Don't you realise how expensive life is and how the boy costs me money? He doesn't even have a coat for the winter.' Suddenly Mrs Linpeck sighed and sorrow usurped the place of coldness in her lined eyes, 'he grew out of the old one and he hasn't got another, seeing as he's no thief. He has to go round all the time in that green sweater, Madam....' at this moment Mrs Linpeck was looking at the caretaker, who was standing next to Mrs Mooshaber and for once was being quiet as a mouse, 'and I have to buy a hat for him too, how can he go out in the frozen weather without a hat? You, other lady, can you tell me how he can go out without freezing to death ? And how can I get him some skis for Christmas ? No one knows the answer to my questions. People are strange, and in any case the same phantoms appear all the time as if I was on stage, and this evening I really will....' here Mrs Linpeck gave her eyes a wipe, 'fling myself under a train.'

At that moment Mrs Mooshaber observed that a couple of tears were trickling through Mrs Linpeck's eye-liner. The caretaker noticed it too and her mouth opened in amazement.

'Madam,' began Mrs Mooshaber with a shake of her bag, 'I really did not come here in order to make you jump under a train. However, you've already heard as much from Mrs Kralec, the caretaker here. I know better than any what it is like to have difficulties with children. My dear woman,' she went on with another bag shake, 'I know a mother whose son was behind bars three times over and whose daughter will find herself in the same place before long. I know a mother who sang a lullaby to her children and you should see them now. The daughter got married and didn't give her mother a crumb at the wedding feast. They had ham and salad, wine and lemonade, it was almost as good as the things you have. And that mother baked kolaches for her daughter's wedding and the daughter threw them out of the window for the horse to eat. And then she threw her own mother out.'

'Just a minute,' began Mrs Linpeck with a sudden shake of the head and a few signs of rejuvenation in her unhappy, desperate features while the flow of tears had slowed to a trickle, 'from where did she throw the mother out? From her apartment?'

'Not from her apartment,' said Mrs Mooshaber shaking her head, 'from the very local where they were holding the reception. The wedding banquet. Right in front of all the guests.'

'In front of all the guests, Madam,' put in the caretaker quickly with a new flushing of the face, 'and even in front of two students, which was the most humiliating thing of all for this mother. Unless you'd seen it, Madam, you could not have believed it. But Mrs Mooshaber knows about this all too well. She's worked for the Welfare for twenty years and recently saved a boy's eye.'

'One-eyed Jack – was he playing cards?' Mrs Linpeck asked the caretaker, before quickly turning away because another customer had shown up. It was an oldish woman with a floral design to her clothes. 'I'll have a lemonade, if I may,' she said as she handed over a small coin.

Mrs Mooshaber and the caretaker stood aside for a little, while behind the window of the kiosk Mrs Linpeck's face quickly lit up once again and the smile appeared on the blood-red lips. 'Lemonade it is,' she beamed from behind the window, before reaching for the bottle and clipping off the top. She poured the lemonade into a cup, which the woman in the flowery attire took hold of, carried to one side and began to drink from. Mrs Mooshaber gave her a passing glance, saw her drinking and then turned back to Mrs Linpeck. A red train had just arrived at the platform.

'You can see how they're always coming and going,' said Mrs Linpeck as her features went rigid once again and her voice resumed its quiet and deep bottom-of-the-well aspect, 'at this moment there are not many customers so it's as deserted as the Sahara. But the rush hour begins in an hour's time and then the customers will flock in like the crowds at the *Tetrabiblos* Theatre. That'll be the time when my right hand won't know what the left hand is doing. It'll be like being in a rocket beyond gravity.'

'They come and go quickly,' agreed Mrs Mooshaber as she looked at the red train which was already moving out of the station, 'the people standing must make sure they hold on to something. They'll be tossed about by the turns in the tunnels. I can still remember that. But we were sitting down at that time, I know it for sure.'

'Just so you understand,' the caretaker hastily explained to Mrs Linpeck, 'Mrs Mooshaber came here on the underground for her wedding reception. She had it in *The Golden Carriage* behind the square. Indeed Mrs Mooshaber, there are only blocks of flats there now and not a brick left of the inn. And the ceremony was in the city hall.'

'In the city hall,' confirmed Mrs Mooshaber, 'here behind the station. That's a long time ago now. The station wasn't built at that time. There was just a chapel there.'

'Why in the city hall ? asked Mrs Linpeck. Her face had come to life a little and her voice was quiet, no longer deep but high like a twittering thrush, 'why not in church ?'

Mrs Mooshaber shook her head. 'I wouldn't get married in church,' she said, 'I don't believe in God.'

'Mrs Mooshaber doesn't believe in God,' confirmed the caretaker with a smile, 'she believes in Fate.'

The woman in the floral outfit finished her drink, put her cup in the bin and left. Mrs Linpeck peeked out from the window a little before saying :

'They really didn't give the mother a drop to drink at the wedding reception ? They really flung her out of the inn? It was really the daughter who did that ?'

'From the inn, yes, and yes, it was the daughter,' said Mrs Mooshaber while she watched the flower woman disappear, 'not a drop to wet her lips with. But that's not all. When her son got out from behind bars, he went to her flat with his sister and some stonemason where the three of them divided up their loot. A pile of money, an umbrella and two hares, which were still fresh. When he was small he beat up his fellow pupils at school and the daughter brawled with boys. Then they ended up in the school for troublemakers.'

'The school for troublemakers?' Mrs Linpeck sounded horrified. 'You mean the one for young offenders?'

There was a Mooshaber shake of the head. 'Not that one. They did go to the house of correction, but only after they'd finished at the school for the troublemakers.'

'And wait till you hear this,' put in the caretaker, her cheeks forever flushed, 'Mrs Mooshaber, you haven't told the lady what happened next. These children, Madam,' she went on as she glanced at Mrs Linpeck, 'invited their mother to the Ritz when the one called Wezr got out of jail.'

'The Ritz?' Mrs Linpeck's lined eyes blinked in surprise, 'you mean to say, Madam, that they really invited you to that place ?'

'To that very place,' the caretaker put in quickly, 'right to the Ritz. And when the mother had put her glad rags and make-up on, in fact I helped her with the make-up myself, she looked just like the wife of a gentleman of the bedchamber or that of a trader in the Parrot Islands, these children ridiculed her and never took her anywhere. They left a note saying she should go to the cemetery and look after her mice, or something to that effect. You should have seen what a beautiful hat she had with coloured feathers and earrings hanging from wires and a necklace with beads the colour of these trains that are forever passing here in their green, red and yellow livery... and gloves too !'

'She even wore her best clothes, the ones she wore for the wedding,' added Mrs Mooshaber with a shake of her bag, 'and they didn't even leave her the hares.'

'That's really terrible,' said Mrs Linpeck in thoughtful tones, her painted fingernails reaching for her head and shifting the position of the clasp in her hair, 'really terrible. It's like one of those Chinese dramas. ' A moment later her eyes were fixed on the platform again and there was a tremor in her voice. 'But am I any better off?' The tremor was still in her voice and there was a look of terror in her eyes now. 'My husband doesn't pay his alimony, Mother and Child Support can do nothing to make him, I must have a winter coat for my boy, he can't be going round in that green sweater the whole time and he needs a winter hat and a pair of skis. What you have to understand,' she went on, looking at the caretaker, 'is that the poor lad himself already has to earn money, there's no other way I can manage, my husband being a thief who doesn't pay any alimony. I don't know whether you heard that the poor lad has to sell things from his trolley, and do you know how much he earns ?' Suddenly Mrs Linpeck's voice broke again and her head went back into her palms. 'Hardly enough for salty water. He's lucky if he gets a guinea a month,' she groaned from inside her hands.

'That's not much,' agreed the caretaker, 'you get more for your graves, don't you Mrs Mooshaber ?'

'Yes, two guineas a month,' confirmed Mrs Mooshaber with a glance at the lemonade bottles lined up behind the shop window.

'There you are, then.' Mrs Linpeck raised her head from her hands and said in a voice full of reproaches and sorrows, 'there you are. Don't I have a terrible time too? And having the school on my back all the time, is that supposed to be nothing? I sometimes wonder why it hasn't all driven me mad.' There were new tremors in the voice and a look of horror in the eyes, 'I'm surprised that I am still sitting here in this little store and that I didn't throw myself long ago under the wheels of a train.'

And what is the problem with the school,' asked Mrs Mooshaber, shaking her bag, 'why is the school harrassing you? Is it about his bad behaviour?'

'He doesn't behave well,' sighed Mrs Linpeck as the sound and look of reproach disappeared from her voice and eyes, leaving only the sorrow, 'he took some honey cake from one lad and beat him up. His teacher wrote to me about it. And my first husband doesn't pay me anything. He says that I let the boy go wild, as if it was my fault and I was letting him run to rack and ruin. And now every Tom, Dick or Harry wants to pin the blame on him for the postal theft. It goes without saying it's him, they say, he's always getting into trouble and his mother's letting him take the broad path to perdition, you can be sure that he's got the parcel business on his conscience along with everything else. But he hasn't, Madam, the theft really didn't have anything to do with him. Have you seen that play about Three-Eyed Philip or you, the other lady, have you ever seen it? When Mrs Mooshaber and the caretaker both proceeded to shake their heads, Mrs Linpeck went on:

'It's just like in the play. They pinned everything on Erwin too, because he once stole a window and roughed up the glazier. But it was that hyena who did everything,' said Mrs Linpeck in a voice suddenly firm and eyes at once grown hard, 'anyway, a policeman arrested her this morning, right over there in front of the restaurant. I saw the whole performance as if I was in the first row in the theatre.'

'They stole the parcels?' asked Mrs Mooshaber gently as she looked at a red train coming into the platform.

'They opened the parcels and stole things from them,' said Mrs Linpeck in a voice once again quiet and deep as if coming from a well, 'sometimes they took the whole parcel. But always before it arrived here by the lift at the back.' Mrs Linpeck pointed behind her with one hand. 'They only took the parcels that were being sent from here, not the ones arriving. That would be a more difficult enterprise, because they'd be in the postmaster's records. And they preferred smaller parcels to larger ones, because the larger ones don't usually have anything worth having in them. They went for clothes, coats, caps, sweaters and jewels. The hyena had an accomplice, someone inside the post office, because without an insider she wouldn't have been able to pull it off, not even for parcels that were being sent from here. The parcels go by metro early in the morning, at noon and at midnight, when there aren't many passengers. It all has to be done very quickly. Before people get on and off, the parcel carrier has one minute to take the parcels from the postman and place them by the engine in the front carriage, because the parcel post is up there at the end where the lift is and where the engine of the train comes to a halt. And there must be some other people who have their fingers in this pie, people the police don't know about, probably there are several intermediaries involved, perhaps even the deaf hyena herself doesn't know who they all are. I wouldn't swear by it,' Mrs Linpeck went on with her voice once again firm and her eyes hardening, 'I wouldn't swear by it but I reckon that old man in the kiosk on the other platform has a finger in the pie.'

This was the moment when another customer appeared, a youngish man with a woman, both of them in glasses and in beige-coloured clothes that had seen better days. The man panted a few times, pretended to swallow something, held up two fingers with his palm curled over and touched his lips with his head leaning slightly back. Once again Mrs Linpeck's features lit up quickly behind the window as she got the message and her lips composed themselves into a smile. She took hold of a bottle of lemonade, held it up and the man nodded. She then opened two bottles, poured them into cups, raked in a couple of coins and the man and woman took the cups, stood to one side and drank from them.

'They're deaf and dumb,' said Mrs Linpeck as she stroked the huge wave above her temple, 'they don't speak and they don't hear. And I....' suddenly Mrs Linpeck's voice broke and she sounded unhappy and desperate and a look of horror was to be seen above the eye-liner, 'Really and truly I'm going to get myself run over. How could my boy have anything to do with the parcel business? That hyena herself is deaf, mark you, so how could my lad have talked about anything with her? I'm going to throw myself onto the rails this evening when the train's coming in and it can go ahead and tear me to pieces. Even if they don't bother to collect my bits and bury me,' she said, her head in her hands and her voice sounding tearful, 'it will be a better thing for me than this suffering...'

'Suffering comes to everyone in this life, Madam,' said Mrs Mooshaber, shaking her bag, 'perhaps we can't do without it. If you knew what I've been through myself, you'd be mightily surprised.'

'That's right,' the caretaker put in quickly with a nod, 'you'd be mightily surprised. Mrs Mooshaber has been through worse things and she hasn't thrown herself under any train. Look at her. She's standing here. She's not under any train.'

'Still standing,' agreed Mrs Mooshaber, 'my son came back from behind bars to see me, my daughter flung the kolaches I'd made for her reception at a horse and threw me out of her reception, they divided up their ill-gotten gains in my own apartment...'

'And worse still there was some stonemason there,' put in the caretaker, 'and when the children were small Mrs Mooshaber sang them a lullaby. And the children invited her to the Ritz, and when she'd put on her glad rags and looked the very wife of a gentleman of the bedchamber, they made fun of her and left her at home. They didn't even leave her the hares.'

'But how is that?' Mrs Linpeck lifted her head out of her hands and her lined eyes opened in surprise. 'What do you mean? You mean it was *your* children you were telling me about?' Mrs Mooshaber and the caretaker nodded.

'They were mine all right,' said Mrs Mooshaber, 'Wezr is twenty-five and Nabule twenty.'

'Heavens above,' was the immediate response from Mrs Linpeck as she leaned forward from behind the window, 'why were you so late into the game? Couldn't you have them before or was it your husband who....'

'I could have,' explained Mrs Mooshaber, 'but I didn't want any. I was afraid. I didn't want children who might turn out badly. But later I badly wanted some. I wanted them so that I'd have someone to support me when I grew old. So I had them. That was my fate.'

'What about your husband?' said Mrs Linpeck quickly, still with her head leaning forward, 'is he another one who left his wife and refused to pay alimony?'

'I'm a widow,' said Mrs Mooshaber, 'my husband was a coachman for a brewery.'

The man and woman with the glasses and beige-coloured outfits finished their drinks a little way off, while they talked through finger gestures in front of each other's eyes. Then they put their cups into the bin. Mrs Mooshaber watched them for a bit, then glanced at the bin full of cups and said:

'When I was young I wanted to have a kiosk like yours and sell things. I'd sell....' She watched a green train come into the platform, 'I'd sell salad, ham, perhaps a drop of wine, ice cream and more than anything lemonade.'

'When Mrs Mooshaber was young,' the caretaker put in, 'she wanted to be a housekeeper, didn't you, Mrs Mooshaber?'

'That too,' said Mrs Mooshaber, 'one of my friends at school became a housekeeper. Maria was her name, she was quite small, frail and bent, the poor sickly slip of a girl, but children loved her. Then she got married and took the name of her husband. He died before his time and from that point on she became a housekeeper again. It must be fifty years now since I saw her last. Well there it is, I don't have a kiosk and I'm not a housekeeper. I've been helping out at Mother and Child Support for the last twenty years and looking after some of the graves in the cemetery.'

'And now you'll be helping out in a family, won't you, Mrs Mooshaber,' said the caretaker, 'Mrs Mooshaber will be looking after a boy from a rich family, one with a villa and a housekeeper. But the housekeeper cannot manage the lad on her own. Mrs Mooshaber will be a kind of governess.'

'Fifty years ago,' said Mrs Mooshaber as she looked up and down the platform, 'we passed here on the way to our wedding at the city hall and then the reception at *The Golden Carriage*. It was all very different here then. Not even your beautiful kiosk was around then, Madam. I think that at that time pretzel sellers used to walk the platform here. And now I have children who've turned out badly. As you were saying, Madam, your husband doesn't pay any alimony and that is bad,' Mrs Mooshaber suddenly added with a shake of her head, 'that is bad and something should be done about it. But explain something to me first, will you...'

Mrs Linpeck's features brightened again at this moment, her eyes blazed and she started speaking quickly:

'I assure you, Madam, I'll tell you whatever you want to know. Just tell me what it is. You, the other lady, you know that she only has to ask...' she said to the caretaker who quickly agreed and said: 'Ask away, Mrs Mooshaber, and the lady will tell you.'

'How does this lad of yours misbehave,' Mrs Mooshaber asked, 'does he go wandering off?'

'His wandering off,' laughed Mrs Linpeck while she adjusted the clasp in her nail with her painted fingernails, 'is something else that concerns me. Wait and see how I give him what for when he comes back from the refuge today. Do not think, Madam, that I don't keep discipline, which is what my husband claims. Of course I cannot discipline him here. I can't go chasing him up and down the platform, can I? And don't forget that he's pushing a trolley along as he goes. He'd hide from me in the toilet or in the post office and there'd be trouble. Besides I have my hands full working here. Wait a while and it'll be the rush hour, when you'll see how my right hand doesn't know what the left hand's doing, it's worse than being in a spaceship. But when I get him home I'll give him what for.'

'What did he do?' the caretaker put in quickly, 'did he break a jug?'

'A lift,' said Mrs Linpeck, now very willing to talk but with a voice that once again sounded as if it was trapped inside a well, 'it was yesterday, Madam, he'd come back and was fooling around in the lift in the house and destroyed it.

He caused so much damage that it stopped working. And he broke one of the glass panels in it which I shall probably have to pay for.'

'You live in a house with a lift?' asked Mrs Mooshaber in surprise. Mrs Linpeck nodded.

'I'm on the fifth floor,' she said quite impassively with a smile on her lips. 'How could I cope with that without a lift? I've got three rooms.'

'Another question, Madam,' Mrs Mooshaber continued with a shake of the bag, 'how else does he misbehave? Does he get into trouble in other ways?'

'Yes, he does,' said Mrs Linpeck, again very ready to talk but no longer from deep in the well but having risen to her high-as-a-thrush tone of voice, 'he is something special. Just imagine how he sometimes talks to himself as if he was speaking to someone else. It's just as if he was rehearsing a part in the house, if you understand what I mean. And he has dreams from time to time during the night. He dreams that he's flying through the air or levitating or riding in a lift – he likes that. But what he likes best of all,' said Mrs Linpeck as a mournful smile crept across her lips and invaded her face, 'what he likes best of all is fire.'

Mrs Mooshaber looked at Mrs Linpeck and kept her peace while the caretaker next to her gaped with her mouth half-open. She was all ears but there hadn't been a squeak out of her before she blurted out: 'Fire?'

'Fire,' said Mrs Linpeck, smiling at the caretaker, 'Fire. He likes looking at it. But he likes making a fire even more. When he was small he wasn't allowed access to matches. He'd have burnt the ottoman to a cinder, and not only the ottoman. Or he'd have gone down into the cellar and set light to the firewood. In summertime he makes fires in the meadow. Once he was at the *Tetrabiblos* theatre to see *The Heretics*, with a free ticket in the front row of the balcony. He liked that very much. When he got home I had to hose half of the flat down with water.'

This was the moment when another customer arrived at the kiosk, a better class of gentleman accompanied by a small girl. 'I will have one beer and one lemonade, if I may,' he began, and put two small coins onto the counter. Once more Mrs Mooshaber and the caretaker stepped back a little, Mrs Linpeck's features lit up from behind the window and the smile found its way back onto her face. She reached somewhere inside the kiosk, brought out a beer and opened it, did the same with a bottle of lemonade and then poured them into cups. The man and the little girl stepped aside and drank while the watchful glance of Mrs Mooshaber passed over them. She eyed them drinking before stepping back up to the kiosk with the caretaker. Then she said:

'The lad's not here at the moment, is he. Will he be pushing his trolley around later on?'

'Yes, later' said Mrs Linpeck, 'during the evening rush hour. But today he arrives a bit later, tomorrow also. Today and tomorrow he spends his afternoons at St Joseph's refuge.'

'St Joseph's refuge,' said the caretaker in surprise, 'what's he doing there? Is he learning to be a carpenter like St Joseph?' Mrs Linpeck shook her head.

'They take him there for two afternoons a week,' she answered readily in a high voice, 'Thursdays and Fridays. He goes there for lunch and he's back around five. I only pay a few pence for his food. The place is run by the bishop's consistory for supporting children in need, for some it's all free. They get soup, lunch and a cake or a bun. He likes that, seeing as he's got a sweet tooth. He likes sweet things, he takes after his father in that regard. He was another one who'd wolf down whatever was set before him provided it was sweet, but he's not one for paying alimony. You know, ladies...' Mrs Linpeck was laughing now, because Mrs Mooshaber and the caretaker couldn't help looking at the kiosk as she spoke, eyeing up the many delicacies on display inside it, 'can you begin to imagine the many things that sweet tooth takes from my kiosk? Chocolates, nuts, sweets... luckily I keep a watchful eye and I don't sell any honey cake. You know how it is, it would be real trouble if I had it here because he just likes it too much.'

'What does he sell from his trolley?' asked Mrs Mooshaber with a shake of her bag and a glance at the platform, which was now playing host to a yellow train.

'What does he sell?' repeated Mrs Linpeck with a smile and a glance at the train, 'he sells what people will buy in a hurry when they're changing trains or waiting for someone on the platform. Things they can wolf down when they haven't time to sit in a restaurant. Chocolate, oranges, bananas, wafers or cakes. Cigarettes too.'

'What about Italian salad or ham,' asked Mrs Mooshaber, 'or perhaps ice cream?'

Mrs Linpeck shook her head. 'No Italian salad and no ham, that sort of thing is only served at a counter. As for ice cream, there is a fellow called Lupl selling that. But we'll soon be branching out and making sandwiches.'

'What about lemonade?' asked Mrs Mooshaber

'He sells that too,' replied Mrs Linpeck.

'But Madam,' now it was the caretaker who was smiling

at Mrs Linpeck, 'I just can't understand how you make sure that the lad doesn't eat the things on the trolley, given his sweet tooth. You keep an eye on him so that he doesn't take anything from the kiosk, but he could clean the trolley out, you simply can't keep an eye on him there, when he's going up and down the platform, now by the lift, now behind the restaurant heading for the bridge, and so on. And you say he has chocolate and cakes on this trolley. If I was selling from that trolley,' said the caretaker with a smile, 'I'd scoff the lot.'

'You're quite right,' agreed Mrs Linpeck, who seemed to appreciate the question and was ready with her answer, 'but the trolley is another matter. What's on the trolley is his own merchandise and he must keep an account of what happens to it. If he took something from the trolley, then he'd be out of pocket and he wouldn't earn a penny. It's a different matter when it's his own stuff.'

The member of the upper crust and the little girl finished their drinks a little way off, put the cups in the bin and left. Mrs Mooshaber glanced at the bin, now full to overflowing with cups, then at the receding gentleman with the girl, before her eyes were drawn back to the lemonade bottles behind the glass in the kiosk. At that moment a red train arrived at the platform and another sudden sigh came from Mrs Linpeck behind her window.

'It's all so terrible,' she sighed, the look of horror returning to her lined eyes, 'You have never been pushed to the point of jumping, have you, Madam. But as for me, I don't know, I really don't know...' She was shaking her head, speaking in a desperately unhappy voice, 'I really don't know. You, my other lady visitor, what do you think?' she went on, turning to the caretaker, 'do you think there's some hope? Do you think I could recover the alimony? Do you think they'd recognise that the lad needs a winter coat so that he doesn't have to spend the entire winter in his green sweater and without a hat and a pair of skis? Do you think they might?'

'Mrs Mooshaber is a great expert,' the caretaker said quickly, 'she has a lot of experience. She even dabbles in healing. She saved a boy's eye, as I've already told you, and then there's the lady with a shop where the park meets the cemetery. Mrs Mooshaber ensured that the Welfare didn't take her son into custody. And let me tell you, Madam, that this son of hers shot crows, went prowling around and even did some stealing.'

'That can't be so,' said a shocked Mrs Linpeck, her eyes bulging slightly while she looked at the caretaker, 'surely it can't. Of course, lady, I believe, I really do, that Mrs Mooshaber is a great expert,' she went on in a considerate and persuasive voice, 'I knew it the moment she came up to the counter, she didn't even need to present her licence to me, and I also know that you are no mere courtoom witness. You are too refined for such a role and you have such a beautiful flowery blouse and couldn't possibly be one of those poor and shabby witnesses. Do you think, Madam, that it is at all possible that the lady expert here might be able to put a word in for....?' she asked. The caretaker smiled and looked at Mrs Mooshaber before replying:

'You can be sure that Mrs Mooshaber will put a word in. Yes, you can be sure of it. Mrs Mooshaber knows the Welfare inside out. She knows all the ins and outs of who does what and where, and now she's taking up the position of supervisor in a rich family with a villa and a housekeeper.'

'I say, Madam!' exclaimed Mrs Linpeck in a suddern burst of liveliness... but at just that moment a pale woman in a black outfit approached the kiosk wanting lemonade and Mrs Linpeck's features lit up and the smile flew onto her blood-red lips. Mrs Linpeck rummaged around in the depths of the kiosk, uncapped a bottle and poured the contents into a cup. Then she grabbed the small coin left by the woman as she took the lemonade and stepped aside. 'I say, Madam' Mrs Linpeck exclaimed again full of enthusiasm, 'if, as the other lady here says, and I can believe it, you know so many people, Madam, there's something that has just occurred to me. If you know so many people, do you perhaps know a certain Mary Capricorn?'

Mrs Mooshaber and the caretaker exchanged glances.

'Mary Capri,' said Mrs Mooshaber, 'Mary Capri, you say? You know her too, then, Mrs Linpeck?'

'I don't know her,' explained Mrs Linpeck, shaking her head and sending her permanent wave into a spin, 'it's just that I've heard of her. She was a housekeeper in some family. Isn't that right, Madam?'

'I don't know,' said Mrs Mooshaber, taken aback, 'I really don't know anything about her.'

'But you definitely told me you knew her,' said Mrs Linpeck in surprise.

'I didn't say that,' said Mrs Mooshaber with a shake of her head, 'all I know is that there is a Mary Capricorn. Mrs Kralec the caretaker who is here with me now told me about her, as did Mrs Eichen from the cemetery. But Mrs Eichen and the caretaker promised that when they found something out about her they'd tell me, isn't that right Mrs Kralec...?' At this point the caretaker's face flushed and she almost shouted out:

'When I find something out I will tell Mrs Mooshaber straight away, we only live a stone's throw away from one another, with nothing between us but the passage. And you, Madam,' she went on, turning quickly to Mrs Linpeck, 'do you also want me to tell you if I find something out?' Mrs Linpeck's eyes brightened up again and the smile crept back onto her lips. 'That would be nice of you,' she said to the caretaker with a smile, 'you can find me here any day. Right here in the kiosk. Look at that...' Mrs Linpeck leaned forward and looked at the pale woman in the black outfit who had just finished her drink a little way off and was putting her cup into the bin. 'Look. That woman is so tired and pale that she must have come from the cemetery. From a burial.'

'She was taking her time over her drink,' Mrs Mooshaber agreed with a shake of her head, just as a yellow train arrived at the platform, 'was she drinking that lemonade of yours which you keep behind the glass in brown bottles?'

'This one here,' Mrs Linpeck readily agreed, 'it's the best. At least that's what Beetle says – he has a new orange sweater, you know. But Madam...' here Mrs Linpeck suddenly cried out and jerked her head sending a great shock wave through her perm, 'but Madam, how unlucky I am. One of life's unfortunates,' she shouted, 'I sit here, reciting lines like a stage prompter in her cue box, but did I ever so much as ask you what you'd like to drink? I'd clean forgotten to. What will it be, Ladies?' she shouted, 'it's pretty sweltering, it's September, the flowers are still blooming in the park. Hang on a moment, I'll pour something out for you.'

'But I haven't got so much as a penny with me,' said Mrs Mooshaber with a hint of thirst in her voice, 'I just didn't think about it.'

'Oh I wouldn't take anything from you,' Mrs Linpeck replied, now laughing openly and at the same time clutching her temples in her palms, 'hang on, I'll pour out something really nice for you.' Mrs Mooshaber and the caretaker looked intently on while the hand of Mrs Linpeck reached for a bottle of delicious lemonade behind the glass of her kiosk, before suddenly withdrawing her hand and reaching instead for beer.

'Beer's a better idea, don't you think?' she said, 'That at least has some strength. Beetle swears by the dark beers, did I tell you he had a new orange sweater?' Mrs Linpeck proceeded to clip open two bottles covered in chilly moisture and poured the contents into two cups.

'Thank you very much,' said Mrs Mooshaber, taking a sip.

'Thank you too,' said the caretaker and took a drink herself before saying:

'This is a good beer, your Mr Beetle is right there. And it's cold too – you must have some fridge in there, Madam. Goodness me,' the caretaker went on, cup in hand while she looked along the platform, 'Goodness, it seems to me that numbers are growing. There are more and more people. The post-lunch lull is coming to a close, isn't it, Madam...'

'It's coming to a close,' agreed Mrs Linpeck with a kind smile, 'in a moment they'll be going home from work, buying snacks and coming here to meet up. In a while it'll be like being at the theatre for the première of *Bridges in the City of Copper Towers* and my right hand won't know what the left is doing, just like in that express spaceship that will be flying to Mars. Then the lad will come back in the evening, at around six. The refuge closes at five.'

'Is that the refuge in Blauental?' Mrs Mooshaber now asked.

‘In Linde,’ said Mrs Linpeck, shaking her head, ‘the St Joseph’s refuge. It’s the St Catherine’s refuge that’s in Blau-ental, and that one is for young girls.’

‘I should also see the boy at some point,’ said Mrs Moos-haber as she took another sip of her beer, ‘given the fact that I will have something to say about alimony. What does he look like? Is he a strapping lad?’

‘Fit as a fiddle,’ said Mrs Linpeck as her palms restored the clasp to its proper position on her permed head, ‘he’s a healthy blond-haired thirteen-year-old. But he’s too fond of sweet things and honey cake most of all. He’s fair-haired and forever wearing that green sweater. But when he’s here with his trolley he wears a white jacket like an apprentice waiter. They appreciate seeing him like that. And he needs a coat for the winter, so that he doesn’t keep wearing that sweater. And he needs a hat and some skis.’

‘Very well, then’ said Mrs Mooshaber as she put down the cup on the counter, ‘I’ll look into this at Mother and Child Support. I will report to Mrs Knorring. In the meantime, Madam, hold off from jumping under a train. You mustn’t let this business drive you to distraction. I’m not a believ-er in God, I believe in Fate, but such an action would be a sin.’

‘It would be a sinful thing to do.’ The echo burst out of the caretaker while her features looked all fired up. ‘It would be a sin for which Heaven would punish you. So young and fresh and beautiful and then under the wheels, how horrible, look at that, the grating sound,’ and she proceeded to wave a hand in the direction of the platform where a green train was just at that moment grinding to a halt. Then she gripped the cup again and sipped her beer to a finish.

'Heavens above, Madam,' exclaimed Mrs Linpeck as her whole face lit up, 'I will never forget your kindness. Oh goodness me!' she shouted from the window, 'wait a moment, this won't do at all. I have something to give you. You may not know it, it's rather a novelty.'

Mrs Linpeck made a quick rummage behind the glass and then handed some beautiful little boxes over to Mrs Mooshaber and the caretaker, each of them decorated with a sheep on the lid.

'It's a new sheep's cheese,' said Mrs Linpeck, 'delicious with bread. And here's something from the cooperative bakery.' At which point Mrs Linpeck proceeded to hand over a couple of cakes.

Mrs Mooshaber and the caretaker each took the sheep's cheese and the cake with thanks and then Mrs Mooshaber looked at her cup on the counter and said: 'This cup which I had my drink in, do you think I could take it home with me?'

'Help yourself,' said Mrs Linpeck with a smile, 'I'm sure it can be put to good use.'

Mrs Mooshaber squirrelled away the cup in her big black bag and then at the last moment – as a yellow train arrived at the platform – she glanced around and said;

'You will perhaps think what I want to ask is strange, but it's about mice. Mrs Linpeck, are there mice around here?'

'Well really,' laughed Mrs Linpeck, 'you know that there are. You always have mice in the underground. But there are pesticides to deal with them and they don't come here onto the platform or to the post office or restaurant. They die in the tunnels. In any case,' Mrs Linpeck went on, her blood-red lips forming a smile and her lined eyes looking upwards, 'if they came here I would have to take them on. I would have to keep myself under control round here. Ladies, I am one who used to play in the *Tetrabiblos*. Make no mistake, I am an actress.'

'I am quite astonished,' the caretaker blurted out when she and Mrs Mooshaber had taken their leave of Mrs Linpeck, each wishing the other well, and had taken a few steps away from her, 'astonished at the way you introduced yourself, made progress in the discussion, pursued your investigation and separated wheat from chaff. You didn't touch upon the criminal tendencies, mind you. I really think, Mrs Mooshaber, that you could be a minister of state. And we even got beer, sheep's cheese and cakes. Not that you didn't deserve it. As for my right to such things, it stands at the same level as the chance of a one-legged man walking to Mars on one foot. And how you skirted around the subject of the parcels, you know what I mean, but then the lady touched upon it hereself...' they had already passed the restaurant with its chandeliers and mirrors and were heading towards the bridge over the tracks...'and that Mary Capricorn, that was quite a shock, perhaps we should hunt for her seeing that everybody's asking after her. My God, the moment I know even the least thing about that Mary I'll come running here to tell Mrs Linpeck. And fancy Mrs Linpeck being an actress. And this Beetle she spoke of, that won't be his real name, Mrs Mooshaber, it's a nickname of some kind, that will have been the lad in the orange sweater, you might remember him, from when we were just coming to the place. And you know something, Mrs Mooshaber, that Mrs Linpeck resembles Mrs Eichenkranz in some way. I really can't tell you how, but there's just a little something that reminds me of her. Mind you there was one thing you didn't do, Mrs Mooshaber. I expect you didn't need to. At the station you said you'd put your bag on the ground by your legs.'

They went onto the bridge and were met by a rumble and rattle of trains below them, coloured green and grey on the right platform and green, red and yellow on the left. Then the caretaker stopped, looked down and laughed.

'You know something,' she laughed, 'the colours of these trains at the station here, these greens and reds and yellows, they're just like the colours of that necklace you got from me. Let's be going, then.'

They went down from the bridge to the passageway and soon arrived at the place where the two passages met – the number of people was clearly already growing, the post-luncheon lull was at an end – and then they took the steps to the top. The caretaker in her summer blouse and short skirt took them at a hop and a skip, while Mrs Mooshaber held on to her long black skirt. They came out into the glass entrance hall of the station with its many little shops and signs and adverts – even there you could see lots of people now – and then they emerged into Anna Maria the Blessed Square. What a beautiful early September evening it was.

X

The clock above the stove was on the point of striking one when someone knocked. In fact the door to the front entrance wasn't so much knocked upon as hammered into submission with knuckles. Immediately afterwards a key could be heard unlocking the door.

Mrs Mooshaber caught her breath in a sigh and put the traps down on the ottoman. 'It must be Nabule. Oh my God!' she exclaimed, sounding appalled. 'It's Wezr!'

The door to the kitchen flew open and there he was. Behind him stood Nabule and someone else. Short but shambolic hair, forehead dark and low, the corners of his mouth turned down. There was no doubt about it. It was the same stranger, the black dog. Mrs Mooshaber nearly fainted at the sight of them. Then she heard his voice.

'At your service.'

Then she heard Nabule's laughter.

'She's cooking.'

'She wouldn't be running a canteen here, would she?' Wezr again.

'When she's not working in the mousetrap business.' Nabule.

All of a sudden Mrs Mooshaber found herself by the stove on which she had a saucepan and some bowls. She saw the mousetraps, which she'd had in her hands a short while before, lying on the sofa. Then she set eyes on the little bag of *Moroccan* poison, which a moment earlier had been in the larder, lying on the sideboard. She saw that Nabule had yet another summer coat, light-coloured this time but with a lurid red buckle, while Wezr sported a new grey overcoat. Number three, the black dog who'd arrived with them, was in nothing more than a jacket, though underneath it was a beautiful white turtleneck sweater. And now Mrs Mooshaber also noticed something else – their arms were full of some white packages and there was also a pile of newspapers, tied together with thick cord. 'Her eyes are popping out,' said Wezr in a voice so coarse and cold that it could have been the sound of a snowslide, 'there's one way of dealing with that. Blindfold them.' Wezr threw the packages and the pile of papers onto the table.

'She thinks we're postmen,' cackled Nabule, with the foolish exaggerated laughter of a halfwit, while she undid the red buckle of her raincoat and sat down on a chair. 'She probably thinks it's Christmas and Santa Claus has just arrived.'

'She probably thinks he's brought some Christmas presents for her,' said Wezr, keeping his coat on as he sat down, 'and she wouldn't be wrong today, because there really is something for her this time. But exactly what that might be,' he went on in a voice like a roaring avalanche of snow, 'I don't know yet. Let's see what's inside the parcels.'

Mrs Mooshaber stood by the stove, her eyes transfixed by the sight of the white packages on the table. She saw everyone sitting at the table and Wezr cutting the string on one parcel and unwrapping it.

'This always reminds me of those "win a fortune" envelopes at the fairground,' he laughed. 'What will this one contain? Gold sovereigns? A guinea or two? Or will it be cotton wool or a mouse?' Then he dug into the parcel and cellophane crackled in his huge hands. 'It's got shirts in it,' he announced in his roaring avalanche of a voice, 'white silk shirts.' And there were really three white silk shirts inside.

'Those are not convicts' clothes,' shrieked Nabule. 'Convicts don't wear white silk shirts.'

'You're right there,' said Wezr, 'convicts wear stripey t-shirts. These must be for bribing the screws. Anyway they're small,' he went on looking at the collars, 'they're no good for us. They wouldn't even fit any rich student, let alone her over there....' he nodded his head towards the stove 'besides, she doesn't wear men's shirts, she's not off to a carnival. Leave them in the cellophane, wrap them up and we'll flog them' he said to the strange black dog before grabbing hold of another parcel. But before cutting the string he took a look at the address.

'There was some other address here originally,' he said, 'B. Klaudinger, District of Pinetreestal, Blossom Street. Someone's crossed it out and written a new one, our address. Whoever sent it doesn't even know that the lady has moved house.' He cut the cord while Nabule burst out laughing and even the strange black dog managed a smile as he glanced at the stove.

Inside the parcel was an old cap, an old pair of small shoes, a belt for a pair of trousers and a schoolbook with familiar school-blue paper. There was also an envelope.

'It's from a child,' screeched Nabule, when she saw the writing on the envelope, 'read what the child says to the Klaudinger woman.'

Wezr ripped open the envelope and read:

Dear Auntie, I am doing fine and I'm sending you some things which I don't need any more. I got the cake, I let Henry have some of it too, he gave me his as well, he got a parcel from his stepfather. I got the chewing gum too. I found it inside my tights. I will be coming to visit on the national holiday and for Christmas, otherwise we're not allowed out. We get up at six and at ten we have to go to bed. We go hauling coal. I haven't had my legs in the stocks yet but Henry has. He says he's going to kill the person who did this to him some day. He's had his palms caned many times now, I've had it done to me only twice so far and I'd kill that person too if I could. On Sunday we have tea for breakfast. Send me the knife you keep at the back, and the caps for my pistol and a bit of a comb. I don't know what more to write so I'll stop. Write to me soon. All the best, Ali.

'The poor thing,' spluttered Nabule as she grabbed hold of the red buckle of her raincoat, 'he must have written it from the house of correction.'

'From the house of correction to his auntie,' said Wezr. 'What he doesn't know is that Auntie's also behind bars now. She won't be sending the dear little boy any caps for his pistol now. Over here...' he called to his mother by the stove, 'take a look at this trash and see whether any of it's of use to you. Hat, belt, shoes, they're not for you. You wouldn't go round in a cap and belt as if you were off to a carnival. But perhaps this book...' Wezr opened it and flicked through some of the pages, 'It's a reform school primer,' he said drily, the cold light of his eyes locked into a stony-faced expression of contempt, 'there's a poem about Prime Minister Albinus Rappelschlund. And there's something here about the old whore, that serial gravedodger....do you want any of it?'

From by the stove Mrs Mooshaber understood none of this. She just stared and struggled for breath.

'Take some of this trash or leave it,' Wezr repeated in a voice of thunder that crushed her like an avalanche.

'But it really must be Mrs Klaudinger,' began Mrs Mooshaber, finally managing to find some words, 'the Klaudinger where Laibach lives. Or the other Klaudinger, the one who led the gang of thieves at the underground post office inside Cemetery metro station.' At this both Wezr and Nabule burst out laughing and even the black dog managed a smile.

'Madam...' At last he began to speak in a smooth voice that was soft as velvet, 'how could it be the Klaudinger from where Laibach lives? She doesn't have a nephew in reform school. Indeed she doesn't have a nephew at all. And she doesn't live in the Pinetreestal district, which is at the other end of the city, but here in Blauental. And furthermore,' the black dog went on, as did his soft smile, 'they haven't arrested the Klaudinger where Laibach lives. She's still out and about and Nabule's husband is living at her place. And how could this be the Klaudinger who led the gang in the metro? That one's seventy years old and doesn't have a thirteen-year-old nephew. Do you think, Madam, that there are only two people called Klaudinger?'

'Wrap this lot up,' said Wezr, throwing the letter onto the parcel, 'wrap it up and we'll open another one.' He reached for a small parcel in dazzling white.

Mrs Mooshaber was now leaning on the edge of the kitchen range where it was cool, even though the stove was lit. She was still staring and struggling for breath. She watched while Wezr opened a third parcel and then spotted something gleaming inside his huge palm.

'Gosh,' spluttered Nabule as she gouged it out of Wezr's palm, 'a necklace fit for a ball. And this must be the jeweller,' she went on as she reached for his card, 'at the *Sunflower* department store. Blow me! What's this here...' Nabule snatched out of the parcel a beautiful white-and-gold scarf.

'It's not something for you, you know that perfectly well,' said Wezr as he looked at his sister and took the things out of her hands, 'it's for someone older, such as her. And it wasn't destined for a jailbird either,' he laughed as he looked at the jewellery and the scarf, 'jailbirds go round in t-shirts and tight-fitting jackets, not necklaces or white-and-gold scarves. They sent it to a jailbird to be used as a bribe for the wife of a screw. Come here and take a look,' he called out in the direction of the kitchen range.

Mrs Mooshaber remained staring and struggling to breathe beside the kitchen range and now she felt her head spinning too. She could see the glittering necklace and the gold-and-white scarf and her head span while she felt a sudden thirst.

'Come and have a look, I say,' repeated Wezr with a look at Nabule and the black dog stranger, 'have a good look. That's a silk scarf and that necklace will be costume jewellery.'

Her eyes riveted by the sight of the necklace and the scarf, Mrs Mooshaber took a few steps forward towards the table. Her head still span and she still felt a thirst. Nabule used her palm to cover her bloated gob, the mouth of a half-wit, with her hand, the black dog stranger kept a tracker's eye on Mrs Mooshaber and Wezr felt in his pocket for his cigarettes, one of which he duly lit.

'So tell us whether you want it,' he said, expelling a cloud of smoke, 'but first of all tell us what it is and what it's worth.'

Mrs Mooshaber took another small step towards the table, head still spinning, throat still parched, still struggling to breathe. She felt the necklace and the scarf, then she felt them once again and then she looked at Wezr, Nabule and the black dog.

'Tell me what I'd get for it, for Christ's sake,' Wezr exclaimed in a voice that crushed like an avalanche, as he flicked ash off the end of his cigarette, 'are we in the land of the deaf and dumb, or what?'

At just that moment the clock by the stove struck half past one and Mrs Mooshaber felt a little better.

'It's embroidered satin,' she felt the words come out of her.

'Which is worth what?' asked Wezr with another look at Nabule, 'a guinea, would you say?'

'I'd say more than that,' commented Mrs Mooshaber as she felt the scarf and necklace for a third time.

'Well do you want it, then?' shouted Wezr, fixing his cold, pale eyes on Mrs Mooshaber.

Mrs Mooshaber threw an unsettled glance at Wezr, Nabule and the black dog, who continued to fix a tracker's eye on her. Then all of a sudden she turned her attention to the corner of the sideboard and the handle of the frosted-glass kitchen window.

At that moment Nabule exploded into giggles and Wezr said:

'All right then. You're as silent as one of your graves and you're right to be. It's not the sort of thing to be worn to a cemetery or to the Welfare. This can only be worn to the Ritz and that's not where you're off to. You'd rather run off to the caretaker and hide yourself away. You'd rather wash a banner and go off to the park. So,' he went on with a laugh, his voice cold and rough like the crush of an avalanche, 'you won't be getting this.'

Mrs Mooshaber retreated a step closer to the kitchen range, her eyes still running across the frosted-glass window and the corner of the sideboard, and then her attention turned to the sofa. To the mousetraps on top of it. And at that moment she seemed to have come back to life.

'So I'd rather run off to the caretaker and hide myself away, would I? I'd rather wash a banner and go off to the park? You left without me. You were making fun of me. It was all in the note you left, wasn't it. And where did you get these things,' she exclaimed, stretching out a hand at the parcels, just where did you get them? You stole them.'

For that she received the quizzical looks of Wezr's cold, pale eyes, a glance from the black dog's tracker's eye and Nabule's laugh which amounted to a shriek.

'Yes, stole them,' cried Mrs Mooshaber as she retreated further towards the kitchen range, 'you stole them just as last time, when you brought money and other things, they were stolen too. You divided up the spoils here. Only this time the spoils have come from the post office...'

'Madam,' began the black dog stranger in his smooth voice, soft as velvet, 'what post office are you talking about? Perhaps this is all a figment of your imagination. What's more, you know every detail, as if you were part of the police investigation yourself. Or perhaps you're a fortune-teller?'

'I'm no fortune-teller,' Mrs Mooshaber shouted, 'but I know that these are stolen goods. Taken from the post office inside Cemetery metro station.'

'From the post office inside Cemetery metro station,' repeated Wezr with a flick of ash.

'Yes, from the metro,' shouted Mrs Mooshaber from back by the kitchen range, 'from the metro. You're handling stolen goods. But the police are on your trail. They've already arrested the hyena, as you yourselves know, and now they'll arrest you. And God knows who else they'll lock up with you. I know all about this.'

'Well, well,' said Wezr with a look at Nabule and the black dog, who had relapsed into silence again and kept quietly holding Mrs Mooshaber in his tracker's eye, 'and where on earth did you get that idea from? That all these things are from the post office at Cemetery metro station – and who is this hyena? All I know is that it's an animal in a zoo. Kept in a cage in a zoo, like a lion. Who is this hyena, please? Would you care to tell us?'

'Madam,' smiled the black dog again, his voice soft and velvety while the drooping corners of his mouth rose, 'what is all this about a hyena and God knows who else and about the post office at Cemetery station? That is indeed a post office and people send parcels from it to various addresses. But how can you not see that all these parcels went to one and the same address? How can you not see that the one and the same address of all these parcels is the state prison? The largest prison in our land.'

Mrs Mooshaber was lost for words for a moment over by the kitchen range and looked uneasily at the table.

'So they're for the prison,' she said, 'that's not the point, the point is that they're from the post office. And you'll be going back behind bars in two shakes of a lamb's tail. No sooner have the gates closed on your leaving,' she said to Wezr, 'and they're opening to receive you back in again.'

'You see what she wants for you,' spluttered Nabule as she nudged her brother.

'Madam,' the black dog stranger was making another soft beginning, 'you always say such very strange things. I explained to you only the last time we were here that you have no understanding of who Wezr is or of what he does. You always make so much of his having been in prison and now you even claim that he'll be sent back,' he went on with his quiet smile, his eyes on Mrs Mooshaber all the time , 'and yet you have no idea who Wezr is. If you knew who Wezr was,' he quietly repeated, the smile and the look remaining in place, 'you would be proud of him. But where these parcels are concerned, I can see that you'd be willing to go to the police and turn us in, isn't that so? Would you denounce me too,' the black dog asked with a smile that made the drooping corners of his mouth jerk madly upwards, 'when you don't even know me?'

'She'd turn in the lot of us, if she could,' Nabule shrieked as she swaggered, 'the lot of us. But she,' Nabule cried out, 'had better take care. She,' shouted Nabule as she reached for the dark red buckle on her coat, 'will think better of it.' Then she laughed once again in her foolish, exaggerated manner and screamed: 'She knows that she'd be at the receiving end of something very nasty, she knows that it wouldn't be worth her while.'

'Stop shrieking.' Wezr suddenly stubbed out his cigarette on the table, 'there's no time for this now, there's still the well and the papers to deal with. Now look,' he went on, fixing his cold pale eyes on his mother, 'these things are nothing to do with you, all you have to do is find somewhere nice to stash them away. Stick them under that sofa with the traps on it and I'll come back for them.'

'This is just the place for them, Madam,' said the black dog with a smile, 'we'll stow them away under the sofa but they shouldn't get damp and the mice mustn't nibble at them. Put traps all around the parcels,' he went on, smiling and pointing at the sofa, 'it's not as if you're short of them. And Wezr will be back to collect everything.'

'Good God!' exclaimed Mrs Mooshaber as she moved once more from the stove to the table, 'I'm not putting anything anywhere. These things which you're asking me to hide are not yours. It's clear now that you're what they call fences and I won't have any stolen goods in my place.'

'Look here,' began Wezr as he rose from his seat. 'I won't have any stolen goods in my place,' he echoed. 'As if it wasn't our place too. She's throwing us out. But that may be because she doesn't know anything about the pile of newspapers...' he pointed to the pile on the table wrapped in a thick piece of cord, 'and because she doesn't know anything about the well. I really don't know what to do,' he laughed and his voice again came across like a crushing avalanche of cold snow, 'I really don't. Should we leave this pile of papers here for her, when she's about to throw us out? Should we tell her anything about the well or not?'

'I wouldn't go on about the well to her,' said Nabule as she fiddled with the bright red buckle of her coat, 'she'll blab about it to that bragging caretaker and that will be an end to our plans. She doesn't deserve to be told.'

'Madam,' the black dog stranger began again, 'you are making difficulties about the safekeeping of our parcels. You are claiming that they are not ours and that we are receivers of stolen goods and at the same time Wezr wants to tell you about the well and to leave this pile of newspapers for you. That is the way you show your gratitude,' the smooth, soft monotone continued, 'the way you show your gratitude for all his good efforts. There is something else, Madam, which I would like to check with you first. What if these parcels were not everything? What if they were just a beginning,' he said quietly, smiling and looking straight at Mrs Mooshaber, 'perhaps there will be other parcels from the post office inside Cemetery station, if that is where they have come from, as you claim they have. There could be silver and gold inside them. Gold and silver,' he repeated in his quiet voice, the smile locked in place and the attention fixed on Mrs Mooshaber, 'and you must stow it all away so that no one can find it, and you must keep mum. If you speak a word about this,' he went on in his quiet voice and with his perpetual smile, 'then you will have betrayed us. And you know that could have some very nasty consequences, don't you.'

Meanwhile Wezr lit another cigarette, took the parcels and shoved them under the sofa. The black dog stranger got up from his chair and helped him. Nabule stood up as well. She looked at the traps on the sofa and cackled.

‘That should do it,’ said Wezr, ‘packed away just like in a warehouse at the airport. Somewhere dry and warm.’ Then he flicked the ash off his cigarette, went up to his mother and said:

‘I’m now going to tell you something. So that you realise there’s something for you in all this, though you don’t deserve it. These newspapers here. See this pile of papers,’ he went on, taking the bundle by the cord, ‘there’s a profit to be made and you won’t have to wait for it. It’s the lunchtime edition of *Our Blooming Homeland*. It’ll be two o’clock…’ he glanced at the clock by the stove, ‘in a short while it’ll be time for you to go out and sell this little lot. There’s two hundred copies here, for every hundred you sell you get a tanner for yourself, and you can sell two hundred within a quarter of an hour. People fight to get the lunchtime edition, because what’s written there can’t be found in the morning or the evening editions. And when you’ve sold them, you take all the lolly you’ve raked in and with this card…’ Wezr dug into his grey coat and pulled out a card bearing the address of *Our Blooming Homeland* and a number, ‘with this card here you go to the editor’s office and hand over the loot and then you get your palm crossed with silver. That’s money in your hand for a quarter of an hour’s work. Compare that to what you get for a month’s work hanging round tombs. Very few people get the chance of a bargain like this. What is more I’ll give you some advice about where you should stand and what you should shout to make all those copies disappear inside fifteen minutes. So that people fight to get hold of them. Position yourself by the crossroads at the *Sunflower* department store on the corner near the kiosks, by the avenue leading to the square named after our Prime Minister Rappelschlund.

That's the one containing the editorial office of *Our Blooming Homeland*. And shout out one of the headlines on the front page...' Wezr pointed at the top copy on the pile of newspapers, 'you know how to read, don't you? Shout out this headline about the old tart who's always cheating the grim reaper. And don't forget the card,' he added, throwing the card onto the pile of papers.

Mrs Mooshaber was now standing close to the table and staring at the pile of papers. Her head was spinning once again and she felt thirsty once more. Then all of a sudden she heard a voice coming from the stove behind her back.

'I see you're cooking something nice, Madam,' the black dog was saying next to the stove, where he was taking frequent peeks at the saucepan and the bowls, 'I see you're cooking lunch, and yet you haven't even offered us a spoonful. It's not as if we visit you all the time.' Mrs Mooshaber wanted to say something, but at that moment Nabule piped up.

'What about the well,' she shrieked as she showed off her curves, 'we still have to tell her about the well. Of course it's a tall order for her. Might be the sort of thing to send her over the edge. Best tell her half the story today and the rest some other time,' she shrieked and swaggered some more, 'at least she'll get to appreciate us and then the next time we come she'll have lunch ready for us.'

'The well,' sniggered Wezr as he flicked ash onto the floor. 'The well. Do you know what this is all about?'

Mrs Mooshaber had been looking at the black dog stranger while he in turn kept his eyes on the potato soup and the corn mash on the stove, but now she turned and looked at Wezr.

'What well?' she asked.

'The well,' began Wezr as he walked around the kitchen, 'is to be found not far from here in a courtyard and it seems that you don't know a blind thing about it. You've been living here for well on half a century and when it comes to a well on your doorstep your mind's a blank. But why should you know anything about it when no one else has a clue? And whoever knows that there is a well,' he went on as he flicked some more ash onto the floor and glanced suddenly at the sideboard where the *Moroccan* poison lay, 'whoever knows that doesn't know the first thing about it. The point is that inside this particular well there's treasure.'

With a toss of the head Mrs Mooshaber looked at Wezr, at Nabule and at the black dog stranger who had moved away from the stove and was quietly looking at her. Then she said:

'I expect that's untrue. It's a swindle of some kind.'

'What did I tell you,' shouted Wezr, 'now we're telling lies and trying to swindle her.'

'I always knew she was potty,' Nabule blurted out as she snatched at her red buckle.

'Madam,' began the black dog in a smooth and soft tone of voice while he seated himself once again, 'how can you say such a thing? You have already made one false accusation today, namely that the parcels were stolen from Central Cemetery station on the metro, and that we were handling stolen goods. Now you claim that the story of the well is a lie and a swindle. And at the same time you admit that you are neither a police officer nor a fortune teller. But perhaps you can read the stars? How can you say something like that? Not to mention the fact,' the black dog continued, as did his quiet smile, 'not to mention the fact that you're always saying that Wezr was in prison and will soon be on his way back inside...'

'Why don't you tell me what well this is?' asked Mrs Mooshaber as she looked at the pile of newspapers on the table.

'What well this is,' echoed Wezr as he went and stood by the sideboard next to the little bag of *Moroccan*, 'I've already told you. It's in a house not far from here, and it contains treasure. No one knows that, other people only know there's a well. As for you, you don't even know that there's a well, and you've been here for half a century. You can have some of the treasure too, if you're prepared to give us a hand. There's gold and silver and a sackful of money.'

'She doesn't need money,' said Nabule, cackling like a half-wit, 'she's rich enough. She's a moneybags already,' she went on, with more foolish laughter, 'she keeps it in the bedside table in her room with all her fancy disguises. You shouldn't have told her about the well,' she cackled, 'I bet she'll pass the news on to that braggard bitch the caretaker.'

'I'm not telling her any more about it,' said Wezr, throwing his cigarette onto the floor, 'we'll see how things are when we come back. We'll see how she's looked after the parcels, which she's made such a fuss about taking. We'll see whether they've got damp under the sofa or been gnawed at by mice. And whether we're going to get any lunch,' he went on, with an eye on the stove.

Mrs Mooshaber had been keeping a constant eye on the pile of papers and the editor's card on the table. Now at last she spoke:

'I can give you some lunch right now if you like. But I've only got potato soup and corn mash. I can't keep a good table, not when all I can afford to buy is bread. And I'll need coal for the winter.'

'Would you also put a little something on a plate for me?' asked the man who looked like a black dog.

'I'll give you some too,' agreed Mrs Mooshaber.

'Good,' said the black dog, and now even he had his attention caught by the little bag of *Moroccan* poison on the sideboard, 'that is good. What have you got in that little bag there, Madam? Is that sugar? For icing a cake?'

'That's not sugar,' said Mrs Mooshaber, 'it's *Moroccan* mouse poison. I sprinkle a few morsels inside those traps,' she explained, pointing at the ottoman.

'*Moroccan*,' said the black dog with a smile, 'mouse poison. You sprinkle morsels. Madam,' he continued, smile in tow, 'I take it that you have forgotten me completely. You are aware of the fact that on the occasion of my last visit I made you an offer in writing. I offered you a guinea or two if you could rid me of my mice. But I expect you just ripped the piece of paper up. You didn't even bother to reply.'

'I don't even know your name,' explained Mrs Mooshaber.

'You know that I'm a stonemason,' said the black dog with a smile, 'since you're well aware of that, you can go to the masons' workshop. It's by the main gate of the cemetery. I believe you'll still be able to find a mason there by the name of Bekenmoscht.'

'Right, we're off,' said Wezr with another glance around the kitchen, at the sofa on which the traps lay, at the sideboard with the *Moroccan* poison on it, and at the stove on top of which lay the saucepan of soup and bowl of corn mash, 'we're going. So take the papers out with you and look sharp about it, it's already two o'clock. At the crossroads by the *Sunflower* department store , shout out the story about the old tart,' he went on, tapping a headline on the top copy, 'and then hop it to the editor's office with the takings and this card. They'll cross your palm with a tanner or two. And there's something else,' he continued, 'make sure about the cord around the papers. Keep hold of it when you sell them and bring it back home with you. It would be a shame to lose it, it's good and strong, you could hold a hundred kilos in it. Right, we're off...'

Nabule cackled and twirled and wiggled her hips while she fastened the bright red buckle of her coat and all three went out of the kitchen into the corridor.

'I wonder if she still has the pole and those black rags,' Nabule spluttered in the corridor and Mrs Mooshaber said as she followed her out:

'You can see yourself that I've got the pole, you can see it poking out there in the corner. I've got the banners too. They're washed and put away in the cupboard, as is right and proper.'

Then Wezr opened the door and they went out into the passage.

'Look after yourself, Madam,' said the black dog quietly as they passed the tub of lime, his low forehead looking a little furrowed beneath his black hair. 'Take the newspapers, keep hold of the cord and think about the well. And remember my offer about the mice, I'll pay you well. This tub of lime is becoming a fixture.'

Before long the sound of their footsteps had died away outside the house, until they might have been parting ghosts.

Mrs Mooshaber looked at the pile of newspapers bound in thick cord on the table and then ran her hand over them, as if she could not quite trust the evidence of her eyes. She could not believe her eyes even though the pile was really there on the table, the copies still perfectly smooth and in position, as if they had come there straight from the press, with *Our Blooming Homeland* , the heading in printer's ink, blazing up at her in black. Never mind selling a newspaper, Mrs Mooshaber had never ever bought a newspaper and rarely read them – someone from the house, like the caretaker or the Steinhägers, sometimes gave her a newspaper for lighting the fire, but that was it. The fact that now she should be going out into the streets and selling papers made her feel as if it was all a dream. What is more, she couldn't believe that they'd leave her two hundred copies for which she'd get a bob or two when she'd sold them. She looked at the headlines on the top copy under the cord and slowly

began, cord permitting, to read them. The headline at the top read: *Interior Minister Scarcola Summoned to Prime Minister Albinus Rappelschlund. Is Trouble Brewing in our Lovely Land?* Underneath this article were two others: *Compound for Killers Complete in Crater Einstein: 500 to be Deported, Sentenced to Life in a Space Suit*. And next to this was another headline: *Requiem Preparations: 1,000 Musicians and 1,000 Singers Working on it. Opening Date still Open Question.* Underneath this article came a fourth, but only half of it could be seen, because this was the place where the newspapers were folded over. The headline ran: *The People Want to See their Princess.*

Mrs Mooshaber briefly wondered whether this might be the article which Wezr had advised her to broadcast in the street so that people would fight to get their hands on the papers, and shook her head. As for the article on the 1,000 singers and 1,000 musicians rehearsing, that was probably also about Mrs Knorring and Messrs Smirsch and Landl from the Mother and Child Support Service. 'That's surely about them playing the French horn and singing,' she said to herself. 'The one about the modern prison for five hundred killers in some crater...' again Mrs Mooshaber shook her head, 'that's just another mod con on the Moon.' As for the first article about the arrival of the Minister for the Police and the trouble brewing in the land, she somehow skipped it altogether.

Mrs Mooshaber glanced quickly at the clock. It was a quarter past two. She remembered that when she was out on the street at this time of day, for instance when going to the cooperative for bread, she really did often see newspaper sellers announcing the lunchtime edition of *Our Blooming Homeland*. She also remembered actually seeing people snatch the papers out of the hands of the sellers, meaning that they really must sell like hot cakes. And that decided Mrs Mooshaber.

Quickly she put on her old scarf, waistcoat and flat shoes, put her key and the *Our Blooming Homeland* card into a pocket of her long black skirt and threw no more than a fleeting glance at the little bag on the sideboard as she took hold of the bundle of papers by the cord. Then out she went.

The weather had stayed pleasant and it was a bright and beautiful September afternoon, still warm with the sun shining. Mrs Mooshaber bore her bundle of papers through the three drab streets which ended up close to the crossroads by the *Sunflower* department store. This was where the modern Blauental district began and here she stopped for a while. The pile of papers was quite heavy, the sun was shining and it was a warm day. She put the pile down on the ground for a while. Then she was struck by something she'd all but forgotten: the well. 'There's a well somewhere near here and no one even knows that there's treasure inside it. I'm not supposed to say anothing about it,' she told herself, 'but I could perhaps mention it to the caretaker. See if she's got anything to say about it. Whether she thinks it's another swindle like the Ritz was.' She picked the papers up from the ground and continued on her way. She took the crossing, passing over the stripey white lines of the asphalt when the light was green, and came to the corner of the main avenue, in the middle of which lay the offices of *Our Blooming Homeland* and at the end of which, in the distance, was to be found Albinus Rappelschlund Square and his statue. She looked at the kiosks of glass and laminate which were not far away from her, where a few people were standing drinking lemonade, perhaps even eating ice cream. There were only a few people there, however, as it was the post-lunch period...and Mrs Mooshaber came to a stop on the corner of the avenue. She put the pile of papers on the ground against a wall and began to untie the cord.

'I wonder how I'm going to sell these,' she said to herself, 'I'll have to shout out. I've never ever sold newspapers, and when I tell the caretaker about this she'll be really surprised. I could have told her straight away and then she could have come with me.' While she was thinking this Mrs Mooshaber went on untying the cord. It was a really strong one and had been wound round the papers several times over. Meanwhile people were passing by behind her but no one took much notice of her. However, a few people did somehow register the fact that an elderly lady in an old scarf and waistcoat, a long black skirt and flat shoes was untying a bundle of papers lying on the ground next to a wall. When from time to time she lifted her head and glanced around a little, she had the impression that such people deliberately slowed their pace as they walked past her. Suddenly she got the feeling that there were people hiding near the corner where she was standing and untying the bundles. They were in some entrance or passage nearby and secretly observing her. She looked in that direction and also towards the kiosks, but saw nothing to confirm her intuition. There were just a few people standing by the kiosks drinking lemonade, perhaps a few of them enjoying an ice cream. She bent down once again to tackle the last knot. And at that moment it occurred to her that many of the people behind her might already be lurking, waiting for the street cries and the selling to begin. 'It's a strange thing,' she thought to herself, 'I've always wanted to be a vendor, to set out my own stall, to sell salad, ham and lemonade. I never got my stall but I'll be selling stuff anyway. When I tell the caretaker about this, she'll be amazed.' At last she managed to untie the bundle, gather up the strong cord and put it away in a pocket of her skirt, though there was hardly enough room for it. Then she took hold of a few copies, leaving the rest by the wall behind her back, straightened her shoulders and opened her mouth to speak.

'*Our Blooming Homeland,* lunchtime edition,' she cried out and didn't even recognise the sound of her own voice, so strange did it sound here on the street, on the corner where the crossroads met the main thoroughfare. Mrs Mooshaber had never in her life shouted anything out in the street on her own like that... '*Our Blooming Homeland,* lunchtime edition,' she cried out, 'New prison on the Moon, minister for the police, rift in the government, people want the princess, read all about it...' And passers-by began to stop.

First of all some bald-headed gent ran up and held money out to Mrs Mooshaber. She recognised that it was a piece of silver and she didn't have any coppers to provide change.

'I don't have any change, sir,' she said and the bald-headed man withdrew his hand and went off without a word. But others were already there. Mrs Mooshaber gave them papers and they put coppers into her hand. One had silver but by then Mrs Mooshaber had enough coppers to give him change. And at moments when no one was buying she cried out: '*Our Blooming Homeland,* lunchtime edition, Many for princess, Minister for police, Moon for prison, read all about it...' and more punters rushed up. Soon Mrs Mooshaber had to bend down in order to take more copies from the pile while the coppers flowed into her palm and she thought to herself, 'So I'm a vendor, a vendor. I'm not selling salad, ham and lemonade and I don't have my own stall but I'm selling. I'm a newspaper vendor.' And she really felt very happy about it. What happened next, happened perhaps inside a minute, though who can measure time in such a moment of horror, for what happened then was really terrible...

Suddenly someone else was shouting, just a few steps from Mrs Mooshaber along the pavement. He was shouting to her, to Mrs Mooshaber, as she stood there by the wall, the pile of papers lying behind her and as she was thinking to herself, 'At last I'm a vendor'. He was shouting at her, Mrs Mooshaber, but also to the crowd of people flocking round her. He was shouting into the open air, as they do when they sound the alarm in the streets of lands more blessed than ours.

All of a sudden Mrs Mooshaber spotted that people were stopping in front of her, but not stopping as they had been before, when they were buying newspapers. She saw that many of them already had the paper she was selling, *Our Blooming Homeland,* in their hands. She heard some more shouting, and then suddenly raised fists flashed in front of her eyes amidst the noise and commotion. She didn't understand what was happening. She thought perhaps she'd suddenly dozed off on the street corner and this was all part of a dream. Or perhaps a building had collapsed somewhere nearby. She gripped hold of a few copies as if they were the straws a drowning man clutches at. At that moment some man or other presented himself in front of her and shouted at her in a terrible voice:

'What do you think you're selling, you old nursemaid? Are you trying to pull my leg? This edition of *Our Blooming Homeland* you've been selling is a week old.'

Mrs Mooshaber staggered back, lost for words.

'Get away from here, Madam,' someone hissed at her, 'Quickly, get away before you get a thrashing.'

'Scarper and be quick about it, get out of here now,' hissed another, 'get away before they lynch you.'

'Swindler,' yelled a third, 'Thief.' Then one of the crowd shouted: 'Get me a stone.'

But Mrs Mooshaber didn't even register these words. She felt someone's hands pulling her away from the circle of people who seemed to have her in a vice-like grip. She could still see the raised fists and then, behind the main body of people she saw the faces of some people who were laughing horribly. She had the feeling that these could be the faces of those who had been hiding in some passage nearby and perhaps she knew them from somewhere...and then she didn't know what was happening any more. Someone threw the pile of papers that had been lying behind her at her head, but it half missed the target. She was already running away with a few copies of the paper still in her hands. She fled to the crossroads while someone behind her was shouting; 'Move it, move it, make yourself scarce,' and another was shouting: 'Police, police' and yet another: 'Throw away the money you swindled out of us, chuck it on the ground.' But she was already escaping over the crossing, the stripey white lines in the asphalt passing beneath her as she took the crossing at red, just as the cars were starting to move. She ran past the *Sunflower* department store. Her flat shoes were slipping off her feet and the long black skirt got under her feet and something else got in her way too. Then she glimpsed a policeman in a black helmet with a silver stripe and with a tassel on his shoulder and she ran and ran and then suddenly…

Suddenly, when her strength was on the point of giving out, everything went quiet inside her. It was the moment when she ran into the first of the three drab streets near her home and when she just couldn't go any further. The moment when the blood was rushing through her head and chest so fiercely that the pounding of her heart might knock her to the ground. Why everything behind her suddenly went quiet, she could not imagine, perhaps it was a miracle or perhaps it was the fact that she'd taken the big crossing when the light was red, leaving her pursuers to face the oncoming traffic. God alone knew what had happened. All she knew was that when she stopped in the first of those drab streets, perspiring and almost expiring, the blood pounding in her head and her chest, there was not a living soul following her. She saw some people passing by opposite her, who took no notice of her, who were unaware and unsuspecting of what had happened, who were coming from somewhere else, and a little further on from them she saw some people in overalls stained with whitewash, perhaps the masons from where she lived, who were returning home from work… Mrs Mooshaber was soon on the move again and finally reached home. She ran into the entrance area, hurried past the bricks, the 'barrow and the barrel of lime, unlocked the door and disappeared inside her apartment. In the kitchen she dropped down onto the sofa like a withered old tree that had just been felled. The only movement she made was to open a hand, from which a few copies of *Our Blooming Homeland* fell onto the ground at her feet, where one end of the strong cord also lay, while the other was still inside her pocket.

XI

No one knows what happened next in Mrs Mooshaber's apartment. To know what was running through her mind at the time is quite impossible. Perhaps she was looking at the one or two copies of *Our Blooming Homeland* lying at her feet while she thought of the way she'd shouted out the headlines on the street corner. Perhaps she looked at the thick cord lying at her feet and ideas ran through her mind that are beyond description. Perhaps she glanced for a moment at the sideboard and saw the bag of *Moroccan* mouse poison, a white powder looking like sugar, which was still in its place... no one knows what was going on in Mrs Mooshaber's flat or in her head at those moments. The only thing that can be known for sure is that when the clock by the stove struck three, Mrs Mooshaber pulled herself together.

Suddenly Mrs Mooshaber stood up from the sofa and ran into her bedroom. She went over to the bedside table. She opened it, took out a few rags, some old stick of sealing-wax and a threadbare old bag containing two golden guineas, a tanner or two and a few farthings...then she began to rummage deeper in the bedside table with one hand. She pulled out a terrible bonnet with a bow and a pair of spectacles, the spectacles of her late husband, the brewery coachman. Then she rummaged around some more and pulled out a small box. Inside it were the bamboo beads in red, green and yellow, the earrings and a bag containing the pair of gloves. Finally she fished out the face powder, rouge and an eyebrow pencil. Then everything happened quite fast. Mrs Mooshaber looked at herself in the mirror and it's possible her heart missed a beat. Perhaps she was surprised that she didn't have the hat with its long, fluttering feathers on her head instead of the bonnet with the bow and the spectacles on her nose, and that she didn't look like an actress or the wife of a gentleman's gentleman – but more like the rich widow of an Old Baptist Missionary or one of those Salvation Army widows. Or perhaps she didn't even register what she saw in the mirror but just gave herself the quick perfunctory glance of someone in a hurry, or maybe she didn't look in the mirror at all before she hurried back into the kitchen. For a while she fiddled around on the sideboard where the little bag containing the icing sugar lookalike that was really mouse poison lay. Perhaps she took hold of the bag or perhaps she pushed it away or perhaps she moved it nearer to her – no one knows. What she definitely did was to grasp hold of the small black bag – not the big one, the one she took to the cemetery – and felt in her dress for a handful of coppers left over from selling newpapers and a card of some kind...and then she went out of the flat. She met no one, not in the passage, not in front of the house and perhaps not even in the three drab streets. It was four o'clock in the afternoon.

So wearing the terrible bonnet with the bow tied under her neck, the big round glasses in their black frames, with her cheeks powdered white with a layer of blush and much evidence of lipstick and eyebrow pencil, wearing the string of coloured, bamboo beads, the earrings on ear wires and the white lace gloves...and her long black skirt – but the old one, not the shiny Sunday-best one – in her waistless jacket with sleeves and her flat shoes – all this was Mrs Mooshaber as she suddenly found herself at the asphalt crossroads by the *Sunflower* department store. She took the stripey white lines of the zebra crossing at a run and reached the corner of the avenue, in the middle of which the editorial offices of *Our Blooming Homeland* were to be found and at the end of which lay Albinus Rappelschlund Square...hardly a moment had gone by since she'd been on this very corner as a street crier drawing attention to those wretched papers. Of the horror she had been through and of the papers that had been scattered about the place there was now not a single trace. Perhaps people had grabbed them to use as kindling, or perhaps they'd been cleared away by the road sweeper. But a small group of people was standing near the corner, a few men, women and students, talking about something. Mrs Mooshaber quickly passed them by. She had a feeling that they were talking about something to do with an approaching national holiday of some sort, but she didn't really hear what they were saying. She adjusted her glasses and headed for the glass and laminate stalls where a few people were eating and drinking. Then she started down a bigger avenue which also ran from this fateful corner and she went down and down this other avenue until she finally came to another corner where she found herself in front of St Joseph's refuge.

St Joseph's refuge was located in a quiet side street in an old but meticulously well-kept house. There was a niche in the façade of the house at first-floor level which contained a statue of the Lord's foster father in a brown Franciscan habit. The ground-floor windows were barred, though this was not on account of the inmates within but of thieves without. Thanks to the bishop's consistory the refuge opened its doors on the two afternoons each week during which it offered charity to needy children.

The pavement on the opposite side of the quiet side street was lined with trees and these trees, unlike several of those in the park or the cemetery, were already noticeably yellow in hue. Though it was still warm and pleasant in the second half of September, this was perhaps one of those species that faded early. Every now and then, a leaf circled in the air on its way to the ground. One such leaf fell onto a horse standing with its cart under one of the trees, evidently waiting for the coachman. There was a sheet metalmaking business with a clock above it on the same side of the street, not directly opposite the refuge but on the corner.

Mrs Natalia Mooshaber, she of the long black skirt, waistless jacket and flat shoes...of the bow-accompanied bonnet which was tied under the neck, of the big round glasses with the black frames, of the layer of blush and the white-powdered cheeks, of the lipstick and the pencilled eyebrows, of the coloured bamboo beads and the rings in her ears, she also of the small black bag held in her white-gloved hands, went to and fro along this other pavement, from the horse and cart to the metalmakers at the corner and then back again. She spent quite a long time walking and from time to time a leaf from one of the trees landed on her too, though with her layer of protective blush they did not disturb her. She never took her eyes off the refuge on the other side of the road. When someone came out of it, she quickened her step, but then at once slowed down again, since it was no one she knew. She took no notice of the people who passed her by on this pavement with the trees either, though she knew that they were looking at her and she knew why they were doing so. She did not look like an actress that day, not even perhaps like the wife of a gentleman's gentleman or of a colonel, but only like one of the rich widows of an Old Baptist missionary or a Salvation Army general...she never took her eyes off the refuge. When she saw from the clock above the toolmakers that it was getting close to five, she stopped by the cart and without taking her eyes off the refuge looked at the horse. It had a shabby collar in which its bent head was looking calmly at the cobbles below its neck. The neck had a bag of oats hung round it. A whip with green and red knots rose up from a sheath in the coachman's box. The clock above the metalmakers now showed five minutes to five and footsteps could be heard from behind Mrs Mooshaber on the pavement where the horse stood. Mrs Mooshaber looked round and saw a sturdy older fellow in a green smock and high rubber boots approaching. First of all he took a look at the horse and then he took a look at her, Mrs Mooshaber, and at that moment he stopped and opened his mouth.

'I'm waiting for one of the youngsters from the refuge,' explained Mrs Mooshaber as she gave her little bag a shake.

The sturdy fellow's eyes narrowed as he looked at the eyes behind the big round spectacles and then his head gave a little jerk.

'My husband used to be a coachman too,' said Mrs Mooshaber as she continued to keep an eye on the refuge opposite, 'a coachman for a brewery. But he's no longer with me. Died in the war.'

Suddenly the coachman spat, climbed onto his seat, took hold of the whip and the reins and shouted: 'Tally ho!' And at that very moment the entrance to the refuge on the other side of the street opened and its charges began to swarm out. Mrs Mooshaber stood behind a tree and kept her eyes peeled. They emerged in twos or in small groups, with the odd one coming out alone, and Mrs Mooshaber had the feeling that they could be people coming out of church or clerks leaving a bank. And then finally she had a piece of luck. All of a sudden she spotted the fair-haired boy in the green sweater among a small group of the same age.

For a moment he stood still with the rest of the group in front of the gate and then all of them, the rest of the group and he, headed across the street towards the metalmakers at the corner. Mrs Mooshaber moved away from the tree behind which she'd been standing and set off walking at a slow pace, heading for the corner where the metalmakers lay. This was where the fair-haired boy in the green sweater again stopped for a moment with the other members of their little group and then they all turned the corner. They turned into the bigger avenue and Mrs Mooshaber quickened her pace. Around the corner of this avenue she caught up with them and then stayed a suitable distance behind them. Now and then she shook her bag and adjusted her glasses and felt under her neck for the bow of her bonnet...she knew that people noticed her, knew they were looking at her, perhaps even turning to look at her, she knew why and she didn't care. She just kept an eye on the green sweater in front, going along with the rest of the group some way ahead of her. As the group moved on it started thinning out, its numbers gradually diminishing. One boy would disengage himself and go left and then another would do the same and hive off to the right. Mrs Mooshaber knew that there would come a point when the boy in the green sweater would be all on his own. As it was he was heading towards Central Cemetery station and from this part of the Linde district he would have to go over the crossroads by the *Sunflower* deparment store. And indeed by the time he approached the crossroads by the *Sunflower* department store the boy in the green sweater was already making his way entirely alone. Mrs Mooshaber quickened her step and let the boy get as far as the crossroads. He stopped there for a moment, because the light was red. And that was the moment, while the light was red and car drivers were speeding over the crossroads, when with a shake of her black bag Mrs Mooshaber went right up to the boy.

'Young man,' she began as she shook her black bag, 'I'd like you to escort me across the street. I am an old lady who doesn't see well and if you take me across I'll give you something tasty.'

The lad looked up and stiffened for a moment. He took in the old lady in the bonnet with a bow under the neck, big round glasses, necklace, earrings, red and white cheeks, red lips and black eyebrows, and he took in the white gloves and the small black bag in her hand...and for a moment he stiffened. Mrs Mooshaber smiled a little and then, curiously enough, the smile was returned.

'I'll help you across,' he agreed.

The light was already green and they could go. Mrs Mooshaber took the lad by the arm in its green cotton sweater and over the white stripes of the crossing they went.

'The other day I went on the underground,' said Mrs Mooshaber while they were still on the white lines of the crossing, 'I got out at the cemetery. You wouldn't be the one who sells things from a platform trolley at Cemetery station, would you?'

'At Central Cemetery station,' the boy corrected her, 'in the underground or the metro as they say.'

'So you really must be Linpeck,' said Mrs Mooshaber and the lad nodded with a strange smile on his face.

'And you're going there now, aren't you,' said Mrs Mooshaber and the boy smiled his strange smile and gently shrugged his shoulders.

'I go there as a rule,' he said. 'I start selling at six.'

Once over the crossing they found themselves on the pavement right next to the *Sunflower* department store. Its large window displays contained a plentiful supply of all kinds of products, lit up by garish neon lighting. It was almost half five, it was mid-September. Mrs Mooshaber looked at the big window displays and said:

'You were kind enough to take me across and I'm going to give you something tasty. But I don't have it right now,' she explained, 'I have to go and buy it. I would have bought it on the way to the refuge,' she went on, 'but I was afraid of being late. I must buy it now.'

'What will it be?' asked the lad. 'Can it be a chocolate cream puff?'

'Chocolate cream.' Mrs Mooshaber considered the request with a shake of the bag she was holding in her white gloved hand. 'Chocolate cream puff. But if you tell me about all the mischief you get up to in school, I'll buy you something better. Honey cake.'

'Honey cake,' echoed the fair-haired lad in the green sweater with a smile, 'why wouldn't I tell you about all the mischief I get up to at school when I don't get up to any? Why should I? I'm already working and earning my keep. And how come,' he asked, still wearing his strange smile, 'how come you would have bought a cake already on the way to the refuge but didn't want to be late...'

'I would have had it all ready in this,' said Mrs Mooshaber as she shook her bag, 'but I was afraid of being late and so I haven't got it ready for you in the bag. I must buy it first right now. But you must tell me about your bad behaviour at school. You get into scraps.'

They turned into the street behind the *Sunflower* department store, which if you allowed it a bit of leeway would lead you right up to the cemetery, and the lad said:

'Scraps? Oh yes, I know what you mean. You're thinking about what the teacher wrote to my mother. That I got stuck into Billy. But he started it. He was poking fun at me.'

'How did he poke fun at you?' asked Mrs Mooshaber as she adjusted the glasses on her nose.

'He got out this honey cake,' said the fair-haired lad, 'and waved it in front of my face. You'd like to eat this, you'd like to eat this, but you haven't got any cakes on your trolley. You've only got hay on your trolley.'

'Hay?' asked Mrs Mooshaber in surprise as she reached for the bow under her neck, 'why hay?'

'Yes, hay,' said the lad, tossing his head, 'like I was selling hay for horses. Hay and oats. Like I was a dealer in horse products. That's when I got stuck into him.'

'You stuck something into him?' Mrs Mooshaber jerked her head. 'Stuck something into him? A knife?'

'Not a knife,' laughed the fair-haired boy. 'I got stuck into him with my shoulder.'

Mrs Mooshaber fiddled a bit more under her neck, then nodded and said:

'Well, that's not everything, I'm sure. Don't you sometimes talk to yourself?'

'Talk to myself?' The boy laughed. 'That's what people do. It means nothing. The teacher talks to herself too. She says things like 'I'll see about that' or 'I'd better get started.' When Mum was working in the *Tetrabiblos* theatre, she used to talk to herself too. When she was rehearsing a part. And what about the newspaper sellers', said the lad with a smile, 'they talk to themselves when they shout in the avenue: 'Read all about it! Read all about it...'

Mrs Mooshaber jerked her head and made another adjustment to her spectacles. They continued along the street behind the department store which led to the cemetery. All the shops were now lit up. Mrs Mooshaber said:

'What about dreams? Don't you also have dreams? For instance, dreams that you're flying?'

'Yes, I do,' said the fair-haired lad in the green sweater, 'I do have dreams like that. I like those dreams.'

'And you like going in lifts, isn't that right?' she inquired.

'That too,' laughed the boy. 'How do you know that? Or did you find out that I broke a pane of glass in one?'

'Nothing like that,' said Mrs Mooshaber, shaking her head, 'I worked it out. Everyone who likes to fly goes in lifts. Come on,' she continued, 'let's cross the road. It's easier to get to the gate of the cemetery from the other side.' And while they were crossing the road and were right in the middle of the street, Mrs Mooshaber went on:

'What about fire?'

'Fire?' The lad looked surprised. 'What about fire? I don't follow you.'

'Fire,' Mrs Mooshaber explained as she shook her bag and as they reached the pavement on the opposite side of the road, 'I was wondering whether you might like it. Whether you might perhaps set fire to something now and again.'

'I don't set fire to things,' the lad replied, shaking his head, 'I build little fires in a meadow. During the holidays, when I'm in the countryside. And also in the field with stubble, if you know what I mean. Are you going to Central Cemetery Station with me or what?' he asked with a glance into the distance, 'I thought we were going somewhere else...'

'We are,' said Mrs Mooshaber as she adjusted her big round glasses, 'we're going to the sweetshop so we can buy that honey cake.'

'To the sweet shop for a cake,' said the lad with his strange smile, 'that's all right. Normally I'm on the platform by six but I can be a bit late for that. I can even get there at nine, if I have to...And how come,' he continued, 'you went to the refuge and were afraid that you'd be late? It's not as if you know me, is it?'

'I don't know you,' said Mrs Mooshaber, shaking her head, 'all I know is that you sell things from a trolley on the platform at Cemetery. How would I know you when I've never in my life seen you?' Then she went on:

'You still haven't told me about all the mischief you get up to in school. I suppose you don't do your schoolwork properly either.'

'I do do it,' insisted the boy.

'Tell me what you learn at school,' said Mrs Mooshaber with a shake of the head and a tweak of her glasses, 'do you learn any poetry?'

'We read poems about Prime Minister Rappelschlund,' said the lad, 'there's been a national holiday in his honour. There was bunting on his statue in the square.'

'And what else do you learn?' Mrs Mooshaber asked with another tweak, this time to the bow under her neck, 'tell me.'

The boy smiled his strange smile and replied:

'Albinus Rappelschlund exposed the traitors and had them punished. He started ruling with the dowager princess our sovereign Augusta and will continue ruling with her until the end of time.'

'Well that can't be all,' said Mrs Mooshaber, 'don't they teach you any more than that?'

'He gave people more work to do,' said the boy, 'he restored law and order, he built a launch-pad for space rockets, he's been to the Moon five times and he never suffered from any thickening of the blood during touchdown. Also he's finishing a modern prison next to the Einstein Crater for five hundred killers, it was in last week's papers...' And Mrs Mooshaber again jerked her head a little and added quickly:

'Tell me what else.'

'He's also founded a museum,' said the fair-haired lad in the green sweater, 'we went there once from school. It's called the Albinus Rappelschlund Museum of Peace.'

'And since you've been there you can tell me what's in the museum,' said Mrs Mooshaber. 'Stuffed birds?'

'Stuffed birds,' echoed the fair-haired boy with a laugh, 'why on earth would you get stuffed birds there? They're somewhere else. This is the Albinus Rappelschlund Museum of Peace, there are no birds there. There are rifles, machine guns, sub-machine guns, howitzers, cannon and tanks. Also cutlasses, pistols and revolvers. And all sorts of daggers. And lots of notices in various colours. Our teacher told us that Albinus Rappelschlund is a peacemaker and a most charitable ruler who is loved by all the people and she recited a poem to us: *Fly away, blue-grey bird, fly into the blue beyond, Albinus Rappelschlund is there, protecting you from every wrong.* But she read all this from those notices there, including the one about how he won the short war that once took place, if you can still remember it...she certainly knows other things too, she can't be stupid since she's a teacher. Only she's not allowed to say them.'

'What does she know?' asked Mrs Mooshaber, shaking her head and, with the distinct impression that her bonnet was moving on it, felt under her neck, 'what does she know...'

'She knows what people say,' said the lad with his strange smile, 'you know, the rumours about the dowager princess our sovereign Augusta. Like the one about the princess having already been long in her grave, perhaps from when she was a small girl, and so she isn't the one ruling us. Or the one about her being alive and imprisoned in the royal palace. Or the one about her hiding somewhere in the city. Rappelschlund secretly removed her so that he could govern alone. And now he's getting afraid that news is getting out and the people will rise up in rebellion. Perhaps that's why he's looking for her, you can never be sure, don't you think so? The people still want their princess. Don't you know that?' asked the boy with his strange smile. 'But if anyone said anything about it, they'd be shot. The people are afraid,' the fair-haired boy in the green sweater continued with a smile, 'they are afraid, really scared. But now and again a little gets written about it in the papers. For example a week ago in the lunchtime edition of *Our Blooming Homeland...*'

This produced a third jerk of the head from Mrs Mooshaber. She reached quickly for her spectacles and shot a glance at the lad as she did so. The lad shot back a glance and an inscrutable smile at her. Suddenly Mrs Mooshaber was struck by the idea that this fair-haired boy in the green sweater might have seen her earlier that day on the corner of the crossroads, witnessed the scene with the newspapers and now recognised her.

'There's a big sweetshop over there,' said Mrs Mooshaber hurriedly, 'I'll go in and buy you a cake there. Honey cake, and you...' she shook her bag a little and glanced quickly inside it, 'in the meantime you should wait for me in front of the shop.'

They went towards the confectioner's, which on the outside was decorated in pink marble and was called *When Lightning Strikes* or *At the Severed Sky*. The bright neon with the name above the door was split into two parts by an image of forked lightning. Behind the shop window, which was divided into two parts, there were many delicacies of various kinds lit up by yellow lights. Mrs Mooshaber threw a quick glance over them and suddenly thought she could see some bottles of lemonade there. All at once she felt thirsty.

'*At the Severed Sky*,' laughed the fair-haired lad, 'doesn't that seem like a strange name to you?'

'Wait here, then' Mrs Mooshaber told the lad, 'I'll be back in a jiffy. I'm going to get the honey cake.'

And Mrs Mooshaber proceeded into the confectioner's.

Even the confectionery interior was beautiful. After all, it was located on a big avenue which led to the main gate of the cemetery and Anna Maria the Blessed Square. It sported mirrors and two crystal chandeliers hanging from the ceiling. The chandeliers were lit up just like the window displays, since it was getting on for six in the evening. A shop assistant in a black lace bonnet with a white headband was standing behind the counter. When she saw Mrs Mooshaber, she went a little goggle-eyed.

'There's something I would like,' said Mrs Mooshaber in what sounded like a parched voice. Then she shifted her specs, fiddled under her throat and opened her bag.

'And what would that be?' asked the assistant obligingly, still goggle-eyed as she took in the bonnet with the bow, the big round glasses and the made-up face, 'How can I be of service to you, Madam? Perhaps...' The assistant continued as she turned to the shelves behind her and pointed out some beautiful bottles of lemonade in an uncertain manner...but then all at once her hand moved to one side and she was indicating something else...'perhaps a very select box of sweets, perhaps this one with the gold markings or that one with the chrysanthemum...or this very select item with a picture of the royal palace and a golden carriage on the box, it weighs a kilo and each chocolate inside is stately...'

'Cake,' said Mrs Mooshaber, 'honey cake'.

'Ah yes,' said the assistant with a rapid smile, 'we have some excellent ones. How many would Madam wish for? A plateful of Severed Sky Specials?'

Meanwhile other people were coming into the sweetshop and two other shop assistants emerged in black lace bonnets and white headbands. Then a small package appeared in front of Mrs Mooshaber on the counter. Honey cake wrapped inside delicate blue tissue paper with a flash of lightning.

'How much do I have to pay?' asked Mrs Mooshaber as she shook her opened bag and took another glance at the open shelves containing beautiful lemonade bottles, 'sixpence?'

'One shilling and sixpence,' said the assistant with a smile. Mrs Mooshaber quickly rummaged in the pocket of her long black skirt, extracted a handful of sixpences and handed three over to the assistant. Then she took the package, the cake wrapped in the delicate blue paper with the flash of lightning, and turned away from the counter.

'*Au revoir*, Madam,' the shop assistant called after her. Mrs Mooshaber nodded as she headed for the exit with her bag still open and with the small parcel made up of honey cake wrapped in delicate tissue paper. She had the feeling that all the shop assistants and the customers who had just gone in were looking at her, but the feeling evoked no response inside her. She knew perfectly well why they were looking at her. Not on this occasion because she looked like an actress or the wife of a gentleman's gentleman, but rather because she looked like one of the rich widows of a Salvation Army general or an Old Baptist missionary. After all she was wearing a bonnet. She moved slowly to the door with her open bag and the small parcel of honey cake wrapped in tissue paper, and as she went out she parted the tissue paper slightly and glanced into the open bag...but by the time she opened the door of the sweetshop she'd already shut the bag.

She went out onto the pavement and looked up. The fair-haired lad in the green sweater was standing there looking up at the display and at the sign above it.

'So here you are,' said Mrs Mooshaber as she gave the lad the cake in its delicate tissue with the lightning design.

'*When Lightning Strikes*', said the boy, 'and the paper looks like it's been split by lightning too.' He unwrapped the paper and looked at the honey cake.

'That's strange,' he said, looking at the honey cake, 'I've never seen anything like this.'

'Never seen anything like this?' asked Mrs Mooshaber with a shake of the bag, 'whatever do you mean?'

'The surface is all white and sprinkled.'

'That's a sugar coating,' said Mrs Mooshaber as she adjusted her glasses.

'But you don't put sugar on honey cake,' laughed the fair-haired boy in the green sweater, 'the honey alone is enough to make it sweet. This is like adding sugar to chocolate or sprinkling salt onto a gherkin.'

'Well it comes from a very good confectioner's, the one here,' Mrs Mooshaber pointed behind her with her gloved hand, for they were still right in front of the shop, 'just look at the marble, and inside there are mirrors and chandeliers. In a confectioner's like this they even take the trouble to sweeten honey cakes. Come on now, we should be getting going.'

The lad repeated his strange smile and took a bite out of the cake. Then off they went.

'There's no need for scrapping,' said Mrs Mooshaber while they were going along, 'I expect he didn't bait you that much. You just went and took his cake. And talking to yourself isn't the right thing to do either. A person can think to himself quietly and not say anything out loud. And you shouldn't go running in lifts, lifts can break and stop working. But the main thing is that you must never start fires. You could burn a house down that way. You mustn't get up to such mischief,' Mrs Mooshaber went on while she looked at the lad dawdling along and eating the cake, 'or you'll drive your mother to distraction. You'll be no end of worry to her and what will become of you then? You'll end up an unskilled pair of hands, like as not hired for the day. You'll be the death of your mother, she might even jump under a train. You know how the trains go in and out of the platforms.'

'She won't jump,' laughed the boy as he ate the cake, 'why should she jump under a train? She's more likely to go back to acting. She'll go back into theatre at the *Tetrabiblos*.'

'What about your father?' asked Mrs Mooshaber, 'your father doesn't live with you, does he?'

'He's gone,' said the boy. 'He's left. And he doesn't pay anything for my keep. He says that we've got more than he has. That we run a stall and he's just a poor diver.'

'Diver?' asked Mrs Mooshaber in amazement while she fiddled under her neck. 'He's a diver? Where does he dive? Into puddles?'

'Into rivers,' the fair-haired boy in the green sweater laughed as he swallowed a mouthful of honey cake, 'he dives for sunken boats, or he does dredging. He goes searching for people's things when they fall into the water. He's got a diving-suit.'

'Like the space suits they wear on the Moon,' remarked Mrs Mooshaber.

'Except that on the Moon,' the boy said, 'they wear their space suits all the time, whereas he is only in his diving suit in the water. There's a difference there.'

'And I would like to ask you,' Mrs Mooshaber continued as she shook her bag, 'about those parcels from the post office. It's been said that you had a hand in all that.'

'That's a barefaced lie,' said the lad as he slowly munched his cake, 'only people who know nothing about it think that. That was a gang led by a deaf old jailbird who's done time over and over. She was called the Hyena.'

'Mrs Klaudinger,' said Mrs Mooshaber and the lad nodded. 'Klaudinger the Hyena,' he confirmed. 'The parcel thief was her, not me. They checked out the post office and the lift, which is at the back behind the platform. I go up and down the platform with my trolley selling.'

They moved on slowly down the avenue, which led to the cemetery by Anna Maria the Blessed Square next to the station. The stores were lit up, for it was now already evening. Past six o'clock. They went slowly along the avenue which led to the cemetery, and Mrs Mooshaber looked at the boy as he slowly ate his cake.

'Do you like it?' she asked.

'I like it,' the lad said, 'I like it, but there's something special about it. It has a special smell,' the boy went on as he sniffed the cake, 'a bit like bitter almonds. There must be bitter almonds in it, I think.'

'Could be,' said Mrs Mooshaber as she fiddled under her neck.

'But they don't put those in honey cakes,' laughed the boy.

'In the upmarket sweetshops they might,' said Mrs Mooshaber. 'I wouldn't know. It's the first time I've heard of such a thing. That was a very good confectioner's. You saw the marble for yourself and there's mirrors and chandeliers inside. *At the Split Sky* - it was almost like being in the Ritz in there...'

'*At the Severed Sky*', the fair-haired boy in the green sweater corrected her and then all of a sudden he looked up and said:

'I say, Madam, just what sort of glasses are those? They're glasses without any glass in them. They don't have any lenses. Surely you can't see anything through them?'

'What do you mean?' said Mrs Mooshaber with a shake of the head, perhaps for the first time becoming properly aware of the fact that the spectacles of her late husband, which she had long kept stowed away in her room, really didn't have any glass in them...'it's true that they don't have lenses. But that's precisely why I can see through them. I'd never be able to see through the spectacles if they still had lenses in them.'

The fair-haired lad swallowed another mouthful, laughed and went on:

'That's something special. And they're so big and round. People don't wear things like that any more. They're from before the Flood.'

'They are a bit before Noah, aren't they,' agreed Mrs Mooshaber as she reached out to adjust the bow at her throat, 'I'm sure you must have divinity lessons at the refuge, so do you know when the Flood was?'

'A long time ago,' said the lad as he munched slowly on through the cake, 'there's no one who lives to tell the tale any more. There haven't been any survivors around for four thousand years.'

'Come off it,' said Mrs Mooshaber, 'there hasn't even been a world to flood for that long.'

They were still slowly making their way to Central Cemetery Station while Mrs Mooshaber watched the lad eat his cake. Then the boy looked up and spoke once again:

'And what about that hat you're wearing? And what's that ribbon for? They're also things you don't see around any more. They must be from before the Flood too.'

'They are,' Mrs Mooshaber agreed. 'They're out of fashion now but one day they'll be all the rage again.'

'And what's that necklace made of?' the boy started suddenly while another mouthful went down inside him. 'Those big coloured things, are they made from wood?'

'Not from wood,' said Mrs Mooshaber, shaking her head and shifting her glasses, 'from bamboo. Do you know what bamboo is?'

'I do,' replied the fair-haired lad in the green sweater with a laugh, 'how could I not know? Bamboo. That's what they make ski sticks from.'

They continued on their way while the boy gradually finished off the cake. Mrs Mooshaber watched his slow progress intently, and then the lad said:

'That was a really special cake. I've never eaten one like it. Sugar-coated with almonds. And Madam...' the lad continued hurriedly with a strange smile on his face, 'might the cake come from a castle by any chance?'

'From a castle?' Mrs Mooshaber asked in surprise, 'why from a castle?'

'From a palace, then' said the boy, still with a curious smile on his face.

'It comes from a confectioner's,' said Mrs Mooshaber shaking her bag, 'from the sweetshop *At the Severed Sky*, which is all covered in marble. You saw me buy it there.'

The lad went quiet for a while, wearing a half smile as if he were smiling just to himself. Then he said:

'I say, Madam...do they also sell things from trolleys in castles?'

'What trolleys would they drive around?' asked Mrs Mooshaber as she adjusted something under her neck.

'Well if they have guests there, do they drive a trolley around and serve food from it? Like the way I go up and down the platform at Central Cemetery station.'

'Probably not,' said Mrs Mooshaber with a shake of the head. 'If they want to eat something I expect they sit down for it.'

Then Mrs Mooshaber saw that the fair-haired lad had polished off the last morsel of cake. He swallowed the last piece and wiped his hand on his sweater. Mrs Mooshaber nodded and said:

'You needed that winter coat and hat, didn't you. You needed skis too.'

'Skis...' said the fair-haired boy in the green sweater, 'skis. I needed them, yes, but I still need them. And I will get them.'

'You will get them,' said Mrs Mooshaber with a smile, 'you will get them all right.' Then she suddenly stopped. The lad stopped too and said:

'I will get them because Mum will buy them for me. But there's something I have to tell you about her. She knows all about how to deliver a speech and one day she'll deliver a speech from the balcony. From the balcony of the *Tetrabiblos* theatre and then you'll really hear something... why exactly have we stopped here?'

'Why have we stopped?' repeated Mrs Mooshaber in surprise, 'because you've finished eating and I'll leave you here.'

And when in turn the boy looked surprised and shook his head, she went on:

'It must already be half six. You must surely go to your platform on Cemetery station and sell things from your trolley. And I must hurry to church for evening mass. Even though I don't believe in God. If I believe in anything I believe in Fate, but you won't understand that. Now I must be off to church.'

'And just why are going there when you're not a believer?' The fair-haired lad in the green sweater gave an amused laugh while he kept an eye on the street, his attention drawn towards a slow-moving cart which was keeping close to the kerb in order to avoid getting in the way of the cars. 'What reason can you have? Is it the Cathedral of Saint Quido of Fontgolland you're heading for, or is it some chapel? Are you going there to pray even though you don't believe in God? Or is it perhaps…' (here the fellow smiled inwardly at the thought)…'is it perhaps that you have candles to sell?'

'I've nothing to sell and never in any cathedral or chapel,' said Mrs Mooshaber with a shake of the head as she too looked along the street, watching the slow-moving cart close to the pavement, 'It was always something I wanted to do, but I never got round to it. Only once did I do some selling and it was a terrible experience.' And Mrs Mooshaber shot another glance at the kerb-crawling cart. It was drawn by a horse and she could see a sturdy-looking coachman wearing high rubber boots and a green tunic in the driver's seat. He had a whip with knots in his hand and was saying something to himself. 'Get a move on then,' she said to the lad as she groped for her glasses and bow while her bag shook in her hand, 'get going now. You're a good'un to have helped me over.' And once again she looked at the cart beside the pavement and at the horse in its harness, head bowed, slowly making its way, while the coachman said to it: 'Run along, little mouse, run along, I've got a nice white sugar lump in my pocket...' And Mrs Mooshaber turned once more to the fair-haired lad in the sweater and said: 'Off you go, it's half six, don't let your mum start worrying about you. Get yourself off, nice of you to have helped me across. Now run along to the Cemetery underground.' And then she went back in the direction from which they'd come before quickening her step and disappearing into a side street which, with some effort, could convey her to the gloomy place that was home to her.

XII

Mrs Mooshaber was back at home.

The first thing she did was to switch on the kitchen light. Then she unfastened the bow beneath her throat and removed her bonnet. Gloves, necklace and ear-rings came next, all of them tidied away in a corner of the room. Then she looked at the stove. 'My foot didn't hurt today as it did the other day' she said, 'not today, even though I had to run so fast in the afternoon.' She ran water into the basin and washed her lips, face and eyebrows. Then she ran a comb through her old grey hair. But she did not go to the sideboard for new pieces of string in order to tie her hair and she did not even change into her nightdress. What she still wanted to do today was to make a thorough inspection of the mousetraps and replace any morsels that had gone stale. She went to the larder and fetched some slices of bacon on a plate. She put them on the table and then took a bag of white powder out of the sideboard. This was her *Moroccan* poison, and it went onto the table next to the plate. She was on the point of picking up all the traps in the kitchen, her other room and the corridor when someone knocked on the front door. 'That'll be the caretaker,' she said to herself, 'I'm glad she's come. She'll be stunned to know I've been selling and what a disaster it all was. And Mrs Mooshaber went into the corridor with her hair loose and opened the door.

But it wasn't the caretaker. It was two men.

'Mrs Natalia Mooshaber?' inquired one of them.

'Police,' said the second, showing some identification.

Mrs Mooshaber gawped and took a step backwards.

It was when they were entering the kitchen that Mrs Mooshaber noticed they were not the two who'd been there

before. These two had never been to see her. 'Do sit down,' she said to them and moved some chairs up to the table.

'Right then, Mrs Mooshaber' they began when they'd seated themselves and taken a look at the plate with the pieces of streaky bacon and the bag on the table, 'here we are, Mrs Mooshaber. I wonder whether you know why we're here', they said as they glanced around the kitchen and a smile began to dance around their faces.

'It's probably about those newspapers from this afternoon,' sighed Mrs Mooshaber as she looked at the floor next to the sofa, where a few copies of *Our Blooming Homeland* were still lying next to the cord which had bound them, 'I've got some sixpences for the editor and this card which they gave me. I'll go there tomorrow. I haven't got round to it today, you see. But I'll give everything back to him tomorrow.'

'We're not here on account of any newspapers' they replied with a smile while they fixed their eyes on the bacon and the bag, 'we're not journalists and writing's not our business. We've come here on account of something else.'

'You've come on account of the things Wezr stashed away here,' Mrs Mooshaber said with a sigh and a shake of the head, 'I thought as much. He put them here under the sofa. I'll fetch them right away. Also some shoes and a textbook. There's nothing I could do with them. I didn't want him to leave them here at all.'

'Wezr's your son, isn't he?' asked one of the policemen, 'and you've also got a daughter called Nabule.' When Mrs Mooshaber reacted with another sigh, the policeman grinned, looked around the kitchen and went on:

'We're not here about that either. There's no need to drag any things out from under the sofa, Madam. We're not here to go shopping.'

'Heavens above!' Mrs Mooshaber gave a start and grabbed hold of some of her freshly combed hair. 'You're here about that chap Linpeck.' When this response met a wall of silence she went on: 'Yes, it's about that fair-haired boy in the green sweater, the one who sells things from a trolley at Cemetery station.'

'Madam,' began the policeman while he eyed the clock above the stove, 'we're not here on account of any Linpeck. We don't know any Linpeck from Cemetery station. We know an Ulrich Linpeck from the Eden area, that's true,' he said while he looked at his colleague, 'he's a criminologist who wrote a book all about amnesia. But he'll have been dead for a hundred and twenty years by now. We're here for something completely different. We're here to take a look at the way you're living.'

Silence reigned awhile in the kitchen.

'The way I'm living?' said Mrs Mooshaber with another lunge at her hair, 'the way I'm living?' The policemen nodded and repeated 'The way you're living.' There was a further period of silence while the policemen scanned the kitchen, looked at the frosted glass of the window, at the sofa and the stove and the sideboard, until they went back to looking at the table, at the plate with streaky bacon and at the white bag.

'Well then, the way I'm living.' Mrs Mooshaber finally spoke up and even she had to sit down in a chair. 'I've always lived here. But two colleagues of yours were here not long ago to see how I was living. My daughter and son-in-law are saving up for a flat in the Elizabethan district and that's where they'll be living.'

'We know all about that,' said one of the policemen with a nod, 'but tell us exactly how long you've been here.'

'It'll be for more than half a century by now,' said Mrs Mooshaber from the chair, 'I don't even remember any more. Everyone in the building knows how long I've been living here. Kralec the caretaker, Steinhäger, Faber, that's the one whose boy fell to his death, they've also been living here a long time or at least the parents have. We've all known each other for fifty years.'

'And where did you live before you came here, Mrs Mooshaber?' asked the policemen, whose eyes stopped roaming for a while.

'Before here I'd have been living somewhere else,' said Mrs Mooshaber, 'where exactly I don't even know any more. I suppose I've already lived everywhere.'

'Perhaps you could put things into some order for us,' said the policemen, looking straight at Mrs Mooshaber, 'at the moment we seem to be putting the cart before the horse. You're country-born, aren't you?'

'I was born in the countryside, yes,' said Mrs Mooshaber. 'In Fettgolding. That's a village.'

'Fettgolding. Fettgolding,' said one of the policemen to himself, 'isn't that somewhere in the lower reaches of the Black Forest? Somewhere near Cat's Castle? Where the Lords of Thalia hand down their estates from one generation to the next?'

'It is.' Mrs Mooshaber nodded in agreement and looked at the plate of streaky bacon. 'That's exactly where it is. Fettgolding is a village and Cat's Castle is a day's journey away from it.'

'Have you ever been to that castle?' asked one of the policemen.

'Once I went there on a school trip. I was still at primary school then. They took us there from Fettgolding in a waggon drawn by horses. I went there once again after school. I went on foot from Fettgolding. I was fifteen at the time.'

'On foot?' The policemen were astonished. 'You went all the way from Fettgolding on foot? From Fettgolding all the way to Cat's Castle? You couldn't have managed it there and back inside a day.'

'I didn't manage it,' said Mrs Mooshaber, 'I had some bread and some ears of corn with me. I took a day to get there and slept over in fields, perhaps in a haystack or a barn next to some farmhouse. It was summertime, just after the harvesting. The next day I made my way back to Fettgolding.'

'So you looked over the castle,' they observed, 'do you recall what you saw and what impression it made on you?'

'I don't think they let me into the castle,' said Mrs Mooshaber with another glance at the streaky bacon on the table, 'someone was actually living there, and when one of the owners was in residence they didn't allow visits. But when we went there as a school party there was no one in the place at the time so they let us see one corridor of it. I saw antlers, some of them were even from a stag. But when I went on my own I just walked in the park and looked at the windows. I didn't see in, but I remember there was a fellow at one of the windows and he was looking at me. He had a green jacket. I expect he was the gamekeeper or one of the servants.'

'And what about your father?' asked the policemen, 'Tell us something about your parents.'

'My father had a cottage in Fettgolding', said Mrs Mooshaber, 'he had rabbits and hens and also a bit of land behind the cottage, about the size of this flat. We grew potatoes and cabbages there. And turnips, I think. A little maize as well.'

'Not enough to live on,' observed one of the policemen. 'Your father must have done something else. He worked on the railways or in a factory...'

'He did what work he could on one of those estates,' said Mrs Mooshaber.

'One of those local estates belonging to the Lords of Thalia?' they inquired, and when Mrs Mooshaber nodded they went on:

'And what sort of work was this? He rode around the estate supervising...'

'He didn't ride around and he didn't supervise anything', said Mrs Mooshaber with a glance at the bacon, 'he cut the rye with his scythe and stacked the sheaves. He also repaired wheels.'

'A worker by hand?' they asked

'He used his hands, yes.'

'And you went to school in Fettgolding?'

'Yes, I went to school there,' said Mrs Mooshaber, 'I still remember one poem. I recited it to someone the other day. It was about an old blind woman. I also had one good friend there, called Maria. She was a bit on the small side, sickly and crooked, but she was clever and the children loved her. She was from a rich family. They lived just next to the school, I think. Her father was a steward on the estate and had a gold watch and he used to ride regularly to Cat's Castle. Then she got married, but her husband died soon afterwards. She kept his name and took up work as a housekeeper. She always held the same position somewhere here in the city. I haven't seen her in fifty years. There was also someone on the estate – a steward or a servant, I don't remember which – who told me once that there wasn't a Lord God so I shouldn't pray. He'd rather I worked with my hoe on the turnips, because then I'd at least have something to eat.'

'And what about your mother, Mrs Mooshaber, and your brothers and sisters?' they asked.

'My mother used to go to the edge of the Black Forest for brushwood and I'd go along with her. But we didn't go very far into the forest, no one went far into that forest. People were simply afraid to go further. My mother wore herself out and then she took ill and died. But she isn't in the cemetery in Fettgolding any longer. The lease on the grave ran out and so someone else is in there now.'

'And your brothers and sisters?' they asked.

'There weren't any,' said Mrs Mooshaber, 'I never had a brother or a sister. I just had one relative, an uncle, the brother of my father, but he also died long ago. He'd have been over a hundred by now. There was also a cousin and a nephew, but I never got to know them. They're all dead now. The lease on their graves has expired and I don't even know where they are.'

'And what did you do when you left school?' the police inquired.

'I wanted to be a housekeeper just like my friend Maria and as a matter of fact... matter of fact...' Mrs Mooshaber suddenly clammed up, blinked up at the ceiling and then shook her head. 'In point of fact I became a housekeeper after all. Yes, I was a housekeeper,' she said with a shake of the head, 'I remember it now, I wonder if I've ever mentioned it to the caretaker, perhaps I never really told her about it in the right way, yes I was a housekeeper. But only for a short while. It was hard work with that family. I went to feed the goats, fetching grass for the livestock, carrying pails of water. I wore myself out and had to leave.'

'Tell us about this family where you worked as a housekeeper. What was their name and where did they live?' the policemen asked.

'I don't know any longer what they were called, but they were here in the city.'

'And where in the city would that have been?' asked the policemen. 'It must have been somewhere outside the city if they kept goats and you fetched grass for them. Don't you remember the house or at least where it was?'

'The house isn't there any longer', said Mrs Mooshaber with a shake of the head, 'it was outside the city in the Stadium area, and when they were building the spaceport they knocked down the house. Not a single brick was left standing. Perhaps the family died out. At least I once heard something to that effect.'

The policemen were quiet for a moment before continuing:

'The houses in Stadium were knocked down at the time Rappelschlund built his launchpad for rocketships there. That was over twenty years ago. They did some demolition before then, but that would have been at least half a century ago.'

'This was about fifty years ago,' said Mrs Mooshaber with a nod.

After a period of silence the policemen went on, keeping an eye on the plate and the bag on the table. 'And what did you do after you left the family?'

''When I left the family I returned to Fettgolding for a time. I was about twenty-five by then, my father was still alive but my mother was no more. I can remember helping him around the house. I used to go to the forest to plant trees and I used to cook for the children of the farmers who had to work in the fields all day.'

'You didn't make any trips to Cat's Castle at that time?' they asked.

'Not at that time,' said Mrs Mooshaber with a shake of the head and a glance at the streaky bacon on the table, 'I'd already been there twice and by then I didn't have the time to make any trips like that. I had hens and rabbits to look after, trees to plant and cooking to do in the canteen. I didn't even have a free Sunday.'

'And later on?'

'Later on, I had a husband. A coachman for the brewery, you see. He drove dray horses delivering barrels.'

'Where did you get married? Was it in Fettgolding or was it somewhere else? And which church was it? Would you still know that?'

'It wasn't in Fettgolding. It was here in the city. And it wasn't in a church, I don't believe in the Lord God. We had our wedding in the town hall behind Cemetery station. But there wasn't any station there at that time, just some kind of small chapel. We went there on the underground. That was how we got back too, sitting all the way. We had our reception in *The Golden Carriage*, that's the name of a pub in the square. It's another thing that's gone, it was knocked down a long time back, ages ago. Blocks of flats have taken its place.'

'And you took the name of your husband, Mrs Mooshaber?' they inquired.

'I kept my own name,' said Mrs Mooshaber with a shake of the head. 'My husband took my name. He was called Mooshaber then, Medard Mooshaber. He was a coachman. I had the same name when I was a singleton.'

'Your husband is dead?' asked the policeman.

'Dead. He died a long time ago, right after my daughter Nabule was born. He was a casualty of war, that short war which at one time was...'

'Mrs Mooshaber,' said one of the policemen, 'you tend some of the graves in the Central Cemetery. You water the plants, cut the grass, keep things trim. Do you never visit your husband's grave?'

'I do visit it,' said Mrs Mooshaber quietly, 'though not so often these days. My husband's grave isn't in the Central Cemetery. In fact he doesn't have a grave anywhere in the city. He came from Drozdov and that's where he's buried. Drozdov by Etlichy, it's a long way from here.'

'There are buses and trains which go to Etlichy,' said the policemen, 'it's barely an hour's journey.'

'That's true,' said Mrs Mooshaber, 'but when I go there it's on foot. It takes half a day there and half a day back. When I was younger I used to walk there every week. Now I go twice a year. In the springtime and in autumn for All Souls. I'll be going there this year for All Souls as well.'

A shroud of silence hung over the kitchen once more. The policemen kept looking around, eyeing the window, the sideboard, the stove and the sofa, before suddenly piping up:

'You're quite sure about your husband being buried in Drozdov by Etlichy?' After a moment's silence they followed this up: 'You never had any reason to suppose that he might be buried somewhere else?'

Mrs Mooshaber looked at the policemen in some surprise. Looked and stayed silent. Then she shook her head and said:

'There's no doubt about it. He's buried in Drozdov by Etlichy. That's where his grave is. Why would I have any reason to suppose otherwise?'

'Why indeed,' agreed the policemen after a pause. Then they asked:

'Were you already living here when your husband died?'

'Yes, quite definitely,' insisted Mrs Mooshaber, 'the caretaker hung a black flag from the house to mark the occasion. I don't mean the ones I've got in the wardrobe in the corridor. They're new ones. The one which hung from the house then fell to pieces long ago, when even she was still a slip of a girl.'

'You were already getting on when you had the children,' said the policemen, 'and they caused you some trouble.'

'I was and they did,' agreed Mrs Mooshaber, her eyes fixed on the ground beside the sofa where the piece of cord lay next to the copies of *Our Blooming Homeland*, 'they went to the school for troublemakers and then to the house of correction. Then Nabule became a salesgirl in various shops. She ended up selling tape recorders and wirelesses.'

'What does she do now?'

'I don't know. She's a married woman now. She's hardly ever to be seen here. She's saving up for a flat. She and Laibach are buying one in the Elizabethan district.'

'And Wezr?' asked the policemen, looking straight at Mrs Mooshaber.

'He's back from prison, now. He was behind bars for three months.'

'The policemen were silent and didn't inquire any further about Wezr.

'Just one further question,' they said, looking at the table, 'apart from housekeeping there was something else you longed to do. You wanted to sell things.'

'Yes, sell things' agreed Mrs Mooshaber with another look at the floor next to the sofa, 'I wanted to have a kiosk and sell ham and salad – lemonade too. But it didn't work out...'

'I see that you don't own a cat and that the mice won't go away,' said the policemen with a grin as they looked round the kitchen.

'They won't, so I set traps. I have them under the sofa and the sideboard, under the stove too. They're also in the room next door and the corridor.'

'Do they ever catch a mouse?'

'Sometimes yes, sometimes no. It depends on whether any mice come and whether they take the bait. Do you want to look at one?'

'That won't be necessary, Mrs Mooshaber' said the policemen with another grin. They took another look around the kitchen and fixed their attention on the table – with the plate of streaky bacon and the white bag. Then one of them said:

'You were just about to have dinner and we disturbed you. You don't have sugar on your bacon, do you?' He pointed at the bag. 'Or is it perhaps salt?'

'It's not salt and it's not sugar', said Mrs Mooshaber, 'you couldn't guess what it is.' The policeman opened the bag and sniffed.

'There's an almondy aroma,' he said, 'it's definitely not sugar or salt. In any case, Mrs Mooshaber, you mustn't let us trouble you any longer. Eat up and we'll be on our way.'

'It's not my food,' said Mrs Mooshaber with a laugh, 'the bacon's not for me, it's for the mice. As for this powder,' she said glancing at the white bag, 'it's poison, *Moroccan*. I sprinkle it over the bacon.'

The policemen rose from their seats with a laugh and explained that they were going.

'You were having a wash just before we arrived, isn't that so?' they asked from the doorway with their eyes on the stove, 'had you been out for a walk?'

'For a walk, yes.' Mrs Mooshaber nodded and looked at the clock, 'It helps me sleep better. But didn't you want to see the other room?' she asked all of a sudden. 'It's right nearby.'

'We didn't', they replied from the doorway. 'Our colleagues have already taken a look at it. You have a bed, a small table and a largeish mirror. Still, there is one other thing. Yes, one other thing,' they'd suddenly remembered it, 'you'll soon have something to celebrate, Mrs Mooshaber, your name-day...'

'Name-day, name-day...' Mrs Mooshaber came out with another laugh, 'I don't even know that I have a name-day. I might, but I never celebrate it. Never have done. I doubt whether even the caretaker knows anything about it.'

From the doorway the policemen took a last look at the kitchen, at the sideboard, at the frosted glass window, the stove and the ottoman, before finally departing. Out they went from the kitchen to the corridor and from the corridor into the entrance passage. They looked at the pile of bricks, at the wheelbarrow and the tub of lime, they smiled at Mrs Mooshaber with a doleful look on their faces, and there was a sigh in Mrs Mooshaber's smile too as she waved farewell at them. Then she went back to her kitchen.

XIII

A few days later Mrs Mooshaber was wearing her usual long black skirt and shoes without heels. When she entered Mrs Knorring's office she found the place full of people. Mrs Knorring was ensconced behind a desk beneath a portrait of Albinus Rappelschlund and the sovereign Dowager Princess Augusta. Mrs Knorring had a delicate and prim face, held her head high and kept her right hand on the telephone. To the right of her Mr Smirsch sat at a small table with a typrewriter on top. Mr Landl was standing on her left beside some barred windows. Two men were standing behind Mrs Knorring and her desk right in the doorway, probably Mr Rott and the famous Mr Kefr. And there was some woman sitting in a chair by the wall. She was the human equivalent of a dilapidated ruin, shaking as if in the throes of some strange fever and as pale as death. She wore the black clothes of mourning, including a black hat, black stockings and black shoes. When Mrs Mooshaber entered the office from a waiting-room at the rear, a pall of silence fell over the room. Mrs Mooshaber passed through the deep silence to a bench in front of Mrs Knorring's desk and took a pew in the way that elderly ladies in long black skirts seat themselves in crematoria or chapels. It was only when she sat down that the sickly-pale and washed-out woman in mourning on the chair by the wall gave herself over to a fit of weeping.

'Madam,' said Mrs Knorring as she spoke out of the deep silence, her right hand on the receiver and her head held high, 'these lamentations must cease. Stop your moaning and groaning. It won't make anything better. You must come to terms with what has happened, for such is the life we all have. Death and misfortune do not confine themselves to the mountains. They come for all of us.'

Mrs Mooshaber looked across from her bench at the wailing woman in mourning but kept her calm. She had obviously arrived before the Linpeck case could be considered. She neither knew who the wailing woman at the chair by the wall was nor what had happened to her. 'It's probably a mother,' she thought, 'why else would she be at the Mother and Child Support Service? Probably the mourning clothes mean the death of someone close to her. A child, I expect.' Mrs Mooshaber was on the point of turning to face Mrs Knorring when the weeping wreck in the chair by the wall suddenly cried out.

'For God's sake,' she shouted in a voice full of despair while her arms shot up above her head. 'For Gods's sake,' the cry was repeated in an even more desperate voice while she started to pull herself to her feet.

'Calm yourself, Madam,' said Mr Smirsch from behind his typewriter.

'Calm down,' said Mr Landl from the barred windows.

'Look here.' Mrs Knorring weighed in again with more words while her hand took off from the telephone, 'it might be better for you to have some rest. You should go to the doctor and get a sedative prescribed. Perhaps recreanum. You can't go on like this.'

'I can't go on at all,' the woman resumed her wailing in the chair by the wall, 'I can't. Heaven knows I can't.' Another sudden shriek came out of her before her strong voice, full of despair and horror, broke down and she fell to more weeping with her head in her hands.

'Now I will never buy him a winter coat so that he needn't freeze in his sweater,' she cried out with her head in her hands, 'Now I will never buy him a hat so that he doesn't freeze in winter. I will never buy him the skis he was looking forward to so much. I will never buy anything for him again. It's all over. Tomorrow I will go to the funeral parlour where I will buy a coffin and a wreath. That's what I'll be buying. And in two days there'll be the funeral.' At these words Mrs Mooshaber stiffened on her bench.

'Mrs Linpeck,' said Mrs Knorring from behind her desk, 'in the hope that it might calm you down I can tell you that we have had hundreds of unhappy mothers like you in our time. And we know very well what human life is and what death is.'

'But such a horrible death,' shouted Mrs Linpeck as she lifted her head out of her hands, 'so horrible. Such a horrible way to go,' she cried out and her eyes bulged as she looked at Mrs Mooshaber who could hardly manage to breathe, 'such a horrible death must come to very few. Not even Becket met with such a horrible death as that.'

'Mrs Linpeck.' Now it was the voice of Mr Smirsch behind his typewriter. At the same time he shot a glance at Mrs Mooshaber. 'What has happened has happened, and what will be will be. It is the essential property of poison to be toxic, it has been so from time immemorial and it is why poison is called poison. You must simply come to terms with this fact.'

'Come to terms with it!' screamed Mrs Linpeck from her chair by the wall, while she shook as if death had just brushed against her, 'come to terms with it. With a horrible death like that. If I imagine it, if I so much as think of it, it makes me feel faint…' and all of a sudden Mrs Linpeck slid down in her mourning clothes from the chair by the wall and ended up lying on the ground.

Messrs Rott and Kefr, who had been standing all this time in the doorway behind Mrs Knorring's desk, ran to get water. Mr Smirsch stood up from his typewriter and with the help of Mr Landl stationed by the barred window lifted Mrs Linpeck off the ground. When they had seated her back in the chair, Messrs Rott and Kefr arrived with a jug of water and began to bring Mrs Linpeck round with a wet handkerchief. Mrs Mooshaber could scarcely breathe as she stared at Mrs Linpeck from her bench.

'Look here, Mrs Linpeck.' It was Mr Rott who now started to speak, Mrs Linpeck having been brought round and the jug of water having been deposited on the windowsill in front of the bars, 'you must pull yourself together. As the lady said to you, there are other families which are hit by tragedy, you are not the first in our country and you will not be the last. Just take a look around you at the time we're living in. Consider the agonies of other people as they suffer the prejudice of their fellows or their own unbalanced judgments…' Mr Rott was looking at Mr Kefr at this point. 'Consider all the evil and lies, all the trickery and villainy around. There are people who would love to wield the axe and what they would like best is to see as many people as possible in chains. There are people who yearn to make the world into one great prison, not only here but everywhere else too. Just look at what they're about to finish in the Einstein crater. And it's interesting to note that it's not the police who think like this but rather the military. I am aware of the fact that you do not like to hear such things, Mr Smirsch,' Mr Rott went on while looking across at Mr Smirsch behind his typewriter, 'particularly when they are spoken in the office, but that's too bad. People will say these things and you can't stop them. There are people from whom God took much more than he has taken from you, Mrs Linpeck, and yet their lives go on.'

'But I'm not up to it.' Mrs Linpeck, in her mourning clothes on the chair by the wall, once again put her head in her hands and now her black hat started to slide down her face, 'I cannot do it anymore, the fact is that I have weak nerves. Now that I've lost everything,' she wept with her head in her hands, 'I will buy a coffin with a wreath, just like I said, and then I will throw myself under a train. When I think about such a death,' now she wept again, 'about the screech of brakes as the train grinds to a halt...I feel faint all over again.'

'Right, Mrs Linpeck'. Mrs Knorring spoke quite firmly now and detached herself from her desk, 'Mrs Mooshaber is here. She went to see you, she has made her own inquiries and now she can tell us what she thinks.' Mrs Knorring glanced across at Mrs Mooshaber and nodded.

'I went there,' said Mrs Mooshaber returning the nod and still barely able to manage her own breathing, though she spoke in a fairly calm manner, 'I went there, I made my inquiries and I can tell you about them. But do not throw yourself under a train,' she said to Mrs Linpeck, 'you know how I talked you out of it on the platform, and so did Mrs Kralec. You know about the sound of a train coming to a sudden stop, you've said as much yourself.'

'Mrs Linpeck' said Mr Rott, addressing her from the front door, 'do not throw yourself under a train. Perhaps you already feel a little better. The faintness brought on by the idea of making that jump, buying a coffin and in two days' time having a funeral has already left you. We will leave the jug right here on the windowsill, and if you feel unwell again, Mr Landl will wipe your head with a cloth. Madam,' he went on, addressing Mrs Knorring behind her desk, 'if possible, I would like to take my leave with our dear and daft Mr Kefr. In the meantime I will prepare a report for you concerning Oberon Felsach.

'Good idea,' agreed Mrs Knorring, 'prepare the report on Oberon Felsach and bring it here.' Messrs Rott and Kefr bowed and went out through the front door, which closed behind them.

'I have something to say too.' Mr Smirsch could be heard from in front of his typewriter, 'Madam, when you say that Mrs Mooshaber can explain things to us, shouldn't we be summoning...'

'Speaking of which,' said Mrs Knorring with a nod as she reached for a drawer of her desk, 'go right ahead.'

Mr Landl opened the door to the waiting-room and the summons was made.

A while later a fair-haired boy in a green sweater appeared in the office.

'Good day to you,' he said and remained standing in the doorway.

'Let us proceed then' said Mrs Knorring after a moment's silence. She reached into the drawer and some sheets of music appeared on the desk. 'We may proceed. The substance of Mrs Linpeck's complaint,' began Mrs Knorring with a glance at her score, 'is that she cannot buy this fellow a winter coat, a cap and skis, that her ex-husband pays nothing in the way of maintenance, that he is full of poison, with toxic effects on both herself and the child. Mrs Mooshaber,' she went on, lifting her gaze away from the music, 'you may give us your professional opinion. Please deliver it in the presence of both Mrs Linpeck and the boy, so that justice may not only be done but be seen to be done.'

'Mrs Mooshaber is a great expert' Mrs Linpeck suddenly chipped in, using her well-manicured nails to adjust her hat which had gone somewhat awry, while her voice sounded a little less desperate and the colour was creeping back into the face that had begun so pale - if it still seemed very pale, this was more because it was surrounded by the black mourning clothes - 'Mrs Mooshaber is well-informed about everything. She knows that I cannot buy the lad a winter coat, a hat and skis, that I get no child support from my ex-husband, that he is toxic and is poisoning both myself and the lad and that my son goes up and down the platform with a trolley selling goods. And that he had nothing to do with any stolen parcels. That's just the Klaudinger woman and her gang who now want to drag the lad into the affair. He got mixed up with this through behaving badly at school, because they think that if he gets up to no good at school then he must be a parcel thief. And Mrs Mooshaber knows another thing too, that I am genuinely distressed to the point of wanting to jump under a train and buy a coffin with a wreath.'

'That's true.' Mrs Mooshaber nodded in agreement from her bench. 'Mrs Linpeck is a woman in distress. The lad is a constant worry to her and she wants to throw herself under a train. I tried to talk her out of it and so did our caretaker, as Mr Rott has done just now. The one thing I didn't know was that she wants to buy a coffin with a wreath and that her husband is poisoning her. It seems that Mrs Linpeck didn't say anything about that to me. None of my inquiries has turned up anything about the lad helping with the parcel theft.'

'You see,' shouted Mrs Linpeck in a voice as high as a tweeting thrush, while her palm travelled across her face, 'you see. Mrs Mooshaber, thank you for your judgment,' she exclaimed with a gleam in her eyes, 'I knew you were an expert from the very first moment, and also that lady who was with you, Madam Caretaker. But you are the lead expert, whereas she is the associate. There is a clear difference of roles.'

'Very well,' said Mrs Knorring with a nod and a glance at her score, 'but Mrs Mooshaber still has to tell us what more she has been able to ascertain.'

'What's more,' said Mrs Mooshaber in response, 'What's more, Mrs Linpeck has a nice kiosk in the underground on a platform at Cemetery Central, and she works hard at it. People buy beer and lemonade from her in the main, but they also buy postcards to write in the underground restaurants where they feel much better than they do in some of the ones above ground. As for the young lad...' Mrs Mooshaber turned round on her bench to face the back door, since the fair-haired boy in the green sweater appeared to be rooted to the spot there, 'he slips up and down the platform selling from his trolley after six in the evening and his favourite food is honey cake. Madam gets no alimony payments from her ex-husband, who's a diver. He drags things up from the riverbed – people, sand and other sunken treasure. And Mrs Linpeck...' Mrs Mooshaber turned back to face Mrs Linpeck, who was listening carefully from her chair by the wall as if in a state of mental rapture, 'is an actress. She used to perform in the theatre...the theatre...what is it called...'

'*Tetrabiblos*,' said Mrs Linpeck with a kindly smile. '*Tetrabiblos*'.

'That's right,' chipped in Mrs Knorring with another glance at her sheets of music, '*Tetrabiblos* is close to the Academy of Music. Both modern and classical works can be found in their repertory.'

'I saw *The Downfall of Lupel the Clown* there not so long ago,' said Mr Smirsch from his typewriter, 'they have dances too.'

'Yes, dances', agreed Mrs Knorring, 'but right now why don't we let Mrs Mooshaber tell us how the lad has turned out.'

'How the lad has turned out', repeated Mrs Mooshaber with a nod from her bench and another swivel to face the back door, where the fair-haired boy in the green sweater remained motionless at his post, 'he's turned out all right. He often talks to himself as if he was addressing another person, but there are many such people, I dare say. He dreams that he's flying, and he loves this. That's why he keeps going up and down in the lift. Oh, and there's another thing. He loves fire.'

'He loves fire?' Mr Smirsch glanced up at these words.

'Yes, fire,' said Mrs Mooshaber, 'but he only lights fires in fields during the summer.'

'You see,' exclaimed Mrs Linpeck as she used a neat little finger to straighten the hat on her head, 'you see. Mrs Mooshaber speaks nothing but the unvarnished truth. Why can't I just be left to live in peace?' She made another adjustment to the hat. 'Why must someone always come and take it away from me? The first time it was my husband who ruined my life, because he is full of poison. The second time was my husband again because he pays me no alimony. And now comes the third stroke of fate. The lad is suspected of stealing parcels and I don't know what else. This hat,' said Mrs Linpeck with a shake of the head, 'keeps slipping off my head for some reason.'

'Very well', repeated Mrs Knorring with a nod from her chair. She glanced at Mr Smirsch at his typewriter and at Mr Landl by the barred windows. 'Very well. We will now proceed to a second matter. Mrs Mooshaber does not yet know about this, because it was discussed prior to her arrival. Concerning this other matter, Mrs Linpeck, you say that this boy of yours escorted a lady across the road and was rewarded for his good deed.'

'He helped the lady across and was rewarded with a honey cake from the confectioner's.' All of a sudden Mrs Linpeck removed the black hat from her head and started adjusting her permed hair instead, 'Let him explain. Tell them!' She turned to face the lad in the doorway and in a somewhat strange voice continued: 'Tell it like it was.'

'An old lady stopped me at the crossroads by the *Sunflower* department store,' said the fair-haired boy in the doorway, wearing his mysterious half smile. 'She wanted me to help her across the road, saying that she didn't see very well. She said that if I helped her there'd be a titbit coming my way. So I escorted her over and asked her what she'd give me. She said that she must first buy it. I asked whether it was going to be a chocolate cream puff, and she said that if I'd tell her all the mischief I'd been involved in she'd buy me something better. Honey cake.'

'And that's what she bought him' said Mrs Linpeck with a smile while she stroked the black hat, now held in her lap, with the palm of her hand, 'you see, there are still some nice people around. Who give a boy honey cake for a helping hand across the highway. And she bought it for him in the very best conectioner's. Somewhere on General Darlinger Avenue, and judging by what the lad says, it was a confectioner's with partitions of some sort, all in marble. And tell us,' Mrs Linpeck turned to face the door again, 'tell us what it tasted like, how it was a really special cake.'

'It was a honey cake,' said the boy in the doorway with a strange smile, 'but it was still iced with sugar.'

'Though honey cakes don't tend to be like that,' Mrs Linpeck quickly chipped in with a laugh.

'And it smelled really nice', the boy continued, 'like almonds.'

'Though honey cakes don't tend to be like that either,' Mrs Linpeck once again chipped in, 'there are no almonds in them.'

'Very well,' said Mrs Knorring as she nodded and looked at the lad in the doorway, 'and now let us move on to the name of the lady whom you assisted across the road.'

'Madam, I think...' began Mr Smirsch with his finger on a key of the typewriter, 'I think that we shouldn't speak about that.'

'We shouldn't,' interjected Mrs Knorring in a voice that suddenly sounded quite dry, 'you're quite right that we shouldn't , but we will all the same. Mr Smirsch, I am aware of the fact that you don't like talk of a certain kind, especially when it is heard in the office, but I do not see why we cannot touch upon anything here at the Mother and Child support Service which pertains to the cases with which we are dealing. We are an office of the state and we have the right to do so. If Mr Rott were here...' Mrs Knorring turned slightly towards the closed front door, but at the same time raised her head a little, making it seem as though she wanted to get a close look at the portraits above her, even though it was impossible to do so. 'Mr Rott would say that to discuss this matter is nothing less than our duty. The point is that if we do not speak about this here and now, someone may raise the matter elsewhere. And that, Mr Smirsch...' at this point Mrs Knorring raised her head 'is something that I cannot allow. Did you know the lady?'

'I did not' said the boy in the doorway with another mysterious smile.

'He did not know her and he has no idea who she was,' said Mrs Linpeck and her voice again sounded strange, as if it was resonating from inside a well, 'this was the first and last time that he saw the lady. She was a complete stranger to him.'

'Of course,' said Mrs Knorring with a grin and a wink at Mrs Mooshaber, who was listening intently, 'of course you were seeing her for the first time. And did she speak with you? What did she say?'

'She inquired about the sort of mischief I got up to,' said the fair-haired boy in the green sweater, still smiling and standing in the doorway, 'that was the condition of her buying me a cake. Then she asked me about my mum and dad, then about the theft of the parcels in the metro, and then about what we learned in school...she asked me about everything...'

'And what about a short poem?' Mrs Knorring raised her head and smiled, 'did she recite a poem for you? A poem about an old blind woman, for instance?'

The lad shook his head. 'She didn't recite any poem to me. All she said was that she was going to the cathedral.'

'To the cathedral?' Mrs Knorring was suddenly taken aback and the lad gave a nod.

'To the cathedral', he confirmed, 'but she said that she didn't believe in God. She just believed in some kind of, kind of...'

'Destiny,' said Mrs Knorring with a smile, 'so that's it. So you see, Mr Smirsch,' Mrs Knorring went on with a glance at the typewriter, 'there we have it. At least everything that could have come out of this has now been made clear. The lady, the one you helped across the road,' Mrs Knorring now addressed the lad in the doorway, 'was none other than Mrs Mooshaber who is right here.'

The fair-haired lad in the green sweater in the doorway gave another mysterious smile and stayed silent. Mrs Linpeck and the two gentlemen kept their own counsel and Mrs Mooshaber did likewise. When the silence had reigned for too long and the lad was still wearing his strange grin, Mrs Knorring spoke up:

'Well then, move closer and have a good look. Mrs Mooshaber is sitting on the bench right here.'

The lad moved slowly away from his position in the doorway, approached the bench and glanced at Mrs Mooshaber. Then he looked at Mrs Knorring behind the desk before producing a puzzled grin. 'But Madam, there's been a mistake', he said, 'that's not the lady.'

'It wasn't Mrs Mooshaber,' said Mrs Linpeck in a quiet voice, her voice still sounding peculiar but without a trace of fear or anxiety in it now.

'Don't you mean to say...' Mrs Knorring shook her head, keeping her calm, 'are you sure that it wasn't Mrs Mooshaber? It surely was.'

'It was not,' said the lad with a smile as he looked at Mrs Mooshaber, 'the lady whom I helped across the road and who bought me a cake afterwards wore a bonnet with a bow, a necklace of bamboo beads, some earrings, strange spectacles and make-up.'

'A necklace and earrings,' said Mrs Knorring who was taken by surprise, 'and spectacles? Mrs Mooshaber doesn't wear spectacles. But then,' Mrs Knorring laughed all of a sudden and went on 'but then who else has spectacles? So far as I know, Mr Smirsch,' she smiled at the typewriter and all but recovered her calm, 'no one wears spectacles...'

'But she really was wearing spectacles,' the boy laughed, 'only they didn't have any glass in them. She had these really ancient frames but they had nothing in them.'

'Spectacles without glass,' Mrs Knorring sounded amazed, 'I ask you, who would wear a pair of glasses with no lenses in them? You must have made this up.'

'I have not made it up,' insisted the lad with a shake of the head, 'I really did see it. I saw it and I asked about it. I asked her why she wore spectacles with no glass in them, what was the point of doing something like that. She told me that *was* the point. She said that if there'd been glass in her specs, she wouldn't have been able to wear them. She wouldn't have been able to see anything through them.'

'This is all very strange,' said Mr Smirsch. 'You can see, Madam, how if we'd all kept quiet about this...'

'It is strange indeed,' chipped in Mr Landl, 'so someone was wearing a disguise. And without any reason to do so.

Indeed, as far as we know, there wasn't any reason,' he added quickly. 'Madam is quite correct. Mrs Mooshaber does not wear spectacles. And Madam is correct in one further respect too. So far as we know,' he added quickly, 'no one wears spectacles...'

'I was the one who was there,' said Mrs Mooshaber from her bench and she nodded at the boy who had fixed his gaze on her, 'yes, I was the one. The glasses belonged to my late husband, who was a coachman for the brewery, and I took them because there was no glass in them. How else could I have asked for help crossing a road? I've got good eyesight, even the caretaker can tell you that...'

'Right then,' said Mrs Knorring in resolute tones and casting a glance at Mr Smirsch, 'there we have it. It was Mrs Mooshaber and that's the end of the matter. Nothing happened, the lad did a good deed and that's it. I had a duty to speak about this matter and it was good that I did so. In order that someone else,' she went on looking at Mr Smirsch, 'would not bring it up at some other time and in some other place, a point that I have already made. In order that nothing is hidden and that what has to be said is said.' At this point Mrs Knorring smiled at Mrs Linpeck who smiled back and said in a perfectly calm voice:

'Mrs Knorring, you are a great artist. I have no great anxieties about such matters, but your greatness, Mrs Knorring, is that of an artist.'

'To get back to the point, Mrs Mooshaber' said Mrs Knorring with a nod and smile from behind her desk, 'could you now tell us your thoughts and conclusions concerning the Linpeck case? What is your overall opinion?'

'My conclusion, my overall opinion,' said Mrs Mooshaber, nodding, 'is that as nothing can be known for certain where the parcels are concerned, nothing can be done about the matter. Furthermore, Mrs Linpeck should get her alimony.'

'So be it,' Mrs Knorring nodded agreement, 'so be it. Seeing that Mrs Mooshaber sees fit to put in a word for you.'

'Thank God!' exclaimed Mrs Linpeck from her chair by the wall, raising her voice while her eyes lit up, looking now more like a merry widow in her black mourning clothes with the hat in her lap, 'Thank Heaven! Words fail me, Mrs Knorring, I don't know how I can thank both you and Mrs Mooshaber. Perhaps I can only thank you with the words of the poet Virgilius Sickle, the one with a statue in the park: *My thanks no longer come to you from this world, for I have already flown up to Heaven*. You should get down on your knees,' Mrs Linpeck had now turned to the boy, 'get down on your knees and straight away give thanks to the lady, right over here in front of the lady's desk, for the kindness and consideration which have been shown to you. Do so. Kneel.'

The fair-haired lad in the green sweater nodded and came forward to Mrs Knorring's desk. As he did so he threw another glance in the direction of Mrs Mooshaber on her bench and followed it up with a weak smile. Then he knelt before Mrs Knorring's desk and said:

'Thank you for your kindness and consideration, Madam.'

'You may get up now,' said Mrs Knorring, 'thank Mrs Mooshaber too on the bench over there, for her investigating and fact-finding work.'

The fair-haired lad in the green sweater went over to Mrs Mooshaber's bench and kneeled once again.

'Thank you, Madam,' he said with his weak smile, 'thank you for your investigating and fact-finding work.'

'You may get up now,' said Mrs Mooshaber with a nod, 'and go to your mother.'

'Mrs Linpeck, you threatened to buy a coffin with a wreath and to throw yourself under a train,' said Mrs Knorring to Mrs Linpeck, who was radiant now, 'if everyone was to act in this way, buy a coffin and jump under a train at the slightest provocation, who would be left in the land of the living? Mr Kugler is of the opinion,' here Mrs Knorring glanced at Mr Smirsch, 'that Pluto used to be a Moon of Neptune. But Pluto resembles planets like the earth, and is also much smaller than Uranus and Neptune. So perhaps Mr Kugler is mistaken. That at least is the rumour nowadays. That's something I've been able to check out,' she went on with a glance at Mr Smirsch. 'But you, Mrs Linpeck' she went on, turning to the chair by the wall, 'you have a kiosk selling things underground at Central Cemetery metro stop. And for as long as you sell things from that kiosk, for as long as you

have a son and a husband from whom you're divorced, for as long as you need to go on making a living, you cannot have peace and quiet all the time. Mr Rott was quite right, look at the time we are living in. Everything goes from bad...' here Mrs Knorring once again glanced at Mr Smirsch, 'everything goes from bad to worse and who knows what lies in wait for us round the next corner. I have a strange presentiment from time to time. In fact I have such a presentiment all the time now. It's not as if saying a thing like this causes bad blood and stirs things up unnecessarily, because people know it already, they have known about this for a long time. We here at the Mother and Child Support Service...' Mrs Knorring glanced at the sheets of music in front of her, 'we do what it is within our power to do in order to protect the young and to make sure that any mother gets what she is entitled to. But look...' now Mrs Knorring turned to the fair-haired lad in the green sweater, who was standing by his mother next to the chair, 'if we find out that you were involved with these parcels, then it's all over for you. And the same applies if you don't behave in school. You should be aware of the fact that everything decided here is only on a trial basis. Mrs Mooshaber, tell him what you have to say about this matter.'

'If you don't behave,' agreed Mrs Mooshaber, 'then you know what will be coming to you. First the school for troublemakers and then the house of correction. You'll end up an unskilled pair of hands, like as not hired for the day. And you'll worry your mother to death. Look here, she's already been wanting to buy a coffin and a wreath and throw herself under a train. And she has such a nice kiosk, anyone else in your position would feel themselves fortunate. And you should consider yourself even more fortunate as you are already doing some selling yourself and not everyone of your age is so lucky. So remember that and behave yourself, or you really will drive your mother under that train. Isn't that so, Madam,' Mrs Mooshaber went on as she turned towards Mrs Linpeck, who was nodding and smiling graciously 'if he won't behave he'll be the death of you, won't he? You'll be jumping under that train.'

'I will jump,' said Mrs Linpeck with a smile, her eyes and face all aglow, 'I will jump and that'll be the end of me. You won't have any winter coat or skis or the benefit of my alimony. So remember what the lady and Mrs Mooshaber have been saying to you here.'

'It is a real challenge for one's memory,' said Mrs Knorring with a glance at the table where the sheets of music were lying, 'you have to know everything by heart. Obviously it is more of a challenge for the sopranos than it is for the tenors and of all the musical instruments the French horn is the worst. Have you yet rehearsed,' now Mrs Knorring was looking at Mr Smirsch at his typewriter and Mr Landl by the barred window, 'have you yet rehearsed the *Dies irae*?'

'Yesterday,' said Mr Smirsch with a nod, 'Monsieur Scarone objected to our fortissimos. He thought them too weak.'

'Even though we stretched our neck muscles to breaking point,' said Mr Landl.

'It's about the *Requiem*,' Mr Smirsch explained to Mrs Linpeck, who was hanging on every word from her seat by the wall, 'five hundred singers and a thousand musicians are working at it. The largest number that we have ever had for a performance in this country.'

'But the date for the première has not been set yet,' added Mr Landl.

'It was in the papers the other day,' said Mrs Knorring raising her head, 'in a midday edition of *Our Blooming Homeland*. That was more than a week ago...and that's it for the moment. So, Mrs Linpeck,' said Mrs Knorring with a nod, 'you may go now. The alimony you will receive by post. And you make sure you behave yourself...' Mrs Knorring wagged a finger at the boy.

With outpourings of gratitude and the warmest of farewells, Mrs Linpeck made for the door with the fair-haired boy in the green sweater, her eyes and face radiant. She didn't even return the black hat to her head, but held it on her tidy little finger, retiring hatless beneath a great wave of hair held in place by a dark clasp. At the door she stopped in order cordially to invite both the ladies, Mrs Knorring and Mrs Mooshaber, as well as the gentlemen, to visit her kiosk in the metro at Central Cemetery station.

'Really, even if the facts hadn't been so neatly ascertained here and now,' she continued in the doorway, her voice and appearance suffused with a remarkable calm, while Mrs Knorring and the men were aware of what she meant, 'I should still have had no great anxieties.'

'Mrs Linpeck was an actress at the *Tetrabiblos*', said Mrs Knorring when the doors had shut behing them, 'now she runs a kiosk in the metro, but it seems that in all likelihood she will return to the theatre. And now we will speak no more about it, the case is closed. We have one more outstanding item of business, which concerns Mrs Mooshaber. Mr Landl, summon Mr Rott.'

Mr Landl summoned Mr Rott from the next office and Mr Rott arrived bearing a sheet of paper.

'You must have wanted the information about Oberon Felsach, Madam,' he said, 'you'll find it right here.' He proceeded to place his sheet of paper on top of the musical score on the desk.

Mrs Knorring raised her head. 'Mrs Mooshaber, I said to you last time that I might have something for you. Supervising a child in a family for three afternoons a week. I also said that you should be paid for this. Well then, will you accept?' When Mrs Mooshaber nodded from her bench, Mrs Knorring took hold of Mr Rott's paper and said:

'It's one Oberon Felsach, widower, wholesale trader, lives in one of the villas in the Blauental villa colony not far from where you live, 6, Spring Street. Being a wholesaler, Mr Oberon Felsach tends to be very occupied with his trading.'

'To be precise, Mr Felsach deals in radios, tape recorders, televisions, lamps and electric heaters,' said Mr Smirsch from behind his own machine.

'But if Madam will permit me to say, the main thing,' said Mr Landl from the barred windows, 'the main reason why Mr Felsach is so busy is because his trading activity takes place neither here nor abroad but on the Moon. Sometimes he spends a whole month trading on the Moon.'

'Just so,' agreed Mrs Knorring, 'and that is the reason why he is seldom at home and cannot look after the lad as he would like to. He has a housekeeper but that is not enough. As I have already explained to you, Mrs Mooshaber, the housekeeper has to look after the villa and do the cooking. The boy needs supervision for three afternoons a week, so that he doesn't go wandering off and learns discipline.'

'What is his name?' inquired Mrs Mooshaber.

'The same as his father's,' said Mrs Knorring with a glance at Mr Rott's sheet of paper, 'Oberon Felsach.'

'The report,' Mr Rott now began from a position which appeared frozen next to Mrs Knorring's desk, 'the report which I have just provided you with contains a few other details about the lad. Perhaps it would be a good thing if Mrs Mooshaber knew about them.'

'Right,' agreed Mrs Knorring, 'I'll just take a look at them...here we are, he's named after his father, he's fourteen years of age, is the best in his school, excellent grades, in conversation like an adult, on the page practically a writer, in short a genius. Discipline and supervision are all that he needs. He reads voraciously and loves music. He likes good food – and here it also says he likes sweets. Doesn't drink, doesn't smoke, that's good, but here we have...'

'I don't think that's such an important matter,' put in Mr Rott.

'Not so important, perhaps' said Mrs Knorring with a degree of hesitation, 'it is mentioned here that he has a certain partiality for long hair, long black hair just like his own. Secondly, he likes to dress up in a long black cloak. The last point is that he also has piercing black eyes.'

'It sounds important enough.' The words came in a strange voice from Mr Smirsch behind his typewriter, but no one paid much attention to what he was saying. Mr Rott smiled and said:

'There's something even more interesting, Madam, but it's not important either. It's the item on the next page, Madam...'

Mrs Knorring turned the page and said:

'Yes, here it is. He lets his nails grow long and has a penchant for the occult sciences. And there is something else that is underlined here: he should not go wandering, he should stay at home. There we are, Mrs Mooshaber,' Mrs Knorring glanced up at the bench, 'go and introduce yourself to them in a week's time. Oberon Felsach Senior will be home within the week. He's flying back from the Moon.'

'He will make all the necessary arrangements with you, 'said Mr Smirsch from his typewriter, 'he wants to pay you all told the grand sum of four guineas.'

'He'll tell you what you should do, ' said Mr Landl from the barred windows, 'which in fact means hardly anything, just sitting in his villa for three afternoons a week. So that the lad knows you're there in his home and watching over him.'

Now Mr Rott weighed in. 'You'll go there in a week's time. Felsach Senior flies back to the Moon almost at once. He should introduce you to the lad and to the housekeeper.'

'I'll take the job, I'll go there,' agreed Mrs Mooshaber. Her head was turning. She had the feeling that there was something wrong with her hearing.

'There's something else,' said Mrs Knorring with a glance at her score, 'please come to see us and let us know how you got on. But Mrs Mooshaber,' Mrs Knorring continued with another look at her score, 'there's something else I must tell you about. You shouldn't come here. The Mother and Child Support Service has had to find new premises.' Mrs Mooshaber opened her eyes a little wider and once again had the impression that she wasn't hearing properly. Mrs Knorring nodded and continued:

'Yes, I'm afraid so. The organisation is on the move. Up and away after twenty years. Here on this slip of paper you'll find our sorry new location.' And Mrs Knorring passed the slip over to Mrs Mooshaber.

'But why is that?' asked Mrs Mooshaber, feeling herself to be coming round with the slip in her hand, 'this building is perfectly adequate.'

'Indeed it was,' agreed Mrs Knorring, 'but it has bars on the windows. Bars on the windows,' she repeated, pointing at Mr Landl, 'not only here but on the ground floor and upstairs too, and that's all very suitable. Suitable so far as those officals are concerned who've decided that a building in the Kerke district with one storey only is enough for the Mother and Child Support Service, whereas our existing building will be turned into a prison.'

'That reminds me,' said Mrs Knorring a moment later as she reached for the telephone, 'to thank you for your report, Mr Rott. As for this jug of water which was left on the window sill, you can take it away. Now I will join the gentlemen in studying this lamentation, that is to say one of those psalms which are full of despair and death.' And hand on telephone Mrs Knorring became absorbed in her score.

XIV

It was no longer a beautiful September afternoon.

The leaves on the trees were shrivelling, turning yellow, every now and then even falling and not only in that quiet side street in front of St. Joseph's refuge. Indeed they were already shrivelling, turning yellow and from time to time falling even in the park and indeed in the cemetery. The flowers in the parks and elsewhere, where there were flowers to think about, were no longer in full bloom but either past their prime or going to seed. The sun itself was far from providing the warmth and light it had given earlier in the year. The people at the glass and laminate kiosks were less often eating ice cream and more likely consumed only lemonade. Already they stopped going about without an overcoat or at any rate a raincoat. October, herald of the coat season, had arrived.

And on one of these October days the caretaker, Mrs Kralec, went to visit Mrs Mooshaber at half past two in the afternoon. She arrived in a short woollen skirt through which she'd stuck some needles and was in a state of some excitement. Her features had a festive flush to them and her arms were full of a lot of strong stripey fabric of some kind. It was so strong and there was so much of it her arms might have been carrying the entire contents of a drapery. Mrs Mooshaber was already expecting her. She was in her long shiny black skirt and flat shoes, and nodded as she opened the door and the caretaker came flying into the corridor.

'Here already,' she said as the caretaker flew into the kitchen, taking special care about the way she put all that stripey material onto the ottoman while exclaiming excitedly: 'Yes, it's me.'

'I'll give you some coffee to begin with,' said Mrs Mooshaber as she glanced at the stripey mass on the ottoman, 'I bought it yesterday when I was at the co-op. I even got myself a little corn. We've got nearly two hours,' she went on as she pointed at the clock by the stove.

'A good two hours,' said the caretaker who had already taken a seat, 'if you take the short cut you can get there in a matter of minutes. You'll be there in no time.'

'Here's the coffee.' Mrs Mooshaber put a mug onto the table and took another look at the stripey draper's shop on the ottoman. 'I wanted to clean the kitchen, you know, but in the end I never got round to it.'

'Of course you didn't,' laughed the caretaker as she took hold of the mug, 'it's just like you to want to clean the kitchen right now. Today of all days! I'm going to have a drink of your coffee after all.' The caretaker raised her mug and drank quickly. Mrs Mooshaber took yet another look at the stripey material on the sofa before she said:

'Listen here, Madam Caretaker, what have you brought with you? Just what is it?'

'Mrs Mooshaber,' the caretaker began with a laugh and a shake of the head, 'it's not something that I can show you right now. I'll tell you when we've finished. It's a surprise.' The caretaker leaned across from her seat to the ottoman and laughed as she rolled all the stripey fabric on the sofa up into the tightest bundle she could so that as little of it as possible stayed in sight. Then she said:

'Let's get started.'

Mrs Mooshaber went into her other room and brought back a box containing the necklace and earrings, ointment and powder for her face, rouge and eyeliner, not to mention the small bag with the pair of white gloves in it. Then she took out of a wardrobe the waistless jacket she'd worn at the wedding. She proceeded with special care to take out a black hat with a mauve ribbon around it and some long colourful feathers. That was when the caretaker intervened:

'Look here, Mrs Mooshaber, I know that you've got the hang of it by now, but today you have to take their breath away. Put that hat and jacket down on the table and sit down on this chair here.'

When Mrs Mooshaber had done as she was told the caretaker took another swig of coffee and reached for a comb:

'Now let's get down to business,' she declared as she bent over Mrs Mooshaber and went to work with the comb, 'I went there yesterday to have a look. To number 6 Spring Street. It's in our neighbourhood, and as I told you if you take the back street you're there in no time, you don't even need to go to the crossroads by the department store. Just imagine,' the caretaker went on while she was combing hair, 'it's the tallest villa there, even though it's only single-storey. The thing is that it's wide and I expect it has high ceilings and big rooms. It has a grand entrance with two columns just like a ministry building,' she went on while she was combing Mrs Mooshaber's hair, 'and there's a path through the garden from the entrance to the gate leading to the street. There are heavy curtains in the windows and inside there'll be carpets and crystal chandeliers, just like in that restaurant inside the metro on the platform at Central Cemetery. But what am I going on about,' the caretaker went on, correcting herself as she finished combing, 'it'll be like the Ritz itself in that place. Right then,' she went on as she put down the comb, 'I'll put the earrings on once I've done your face. Now I'll get the cream.' She took the ointment and began to rub it into Mrs Mooshaber's cheeks.

'You know, Mrs Mooshaber,' she began again while she applied make-up, 'it's no wonder that they have such a big place. After all he's a magnate and goes to the Moon on business, so he must be rich. Did you say that he sells radios?' she asked as she worked on Mrs Mooshaber's cheeks.

‘Radios, heaters, lights and tape recorders,’ confirmed Mrs Mooshaber, ‘do you think that business is good on the Moon?’

‘Rather!’ The caretaker laughed as she put down the cream and reached for the eyebrow-liner. ‘Up there on the Moon people still listen to what’s happening back on Earth and for that they need radios. And they must have light, because it’s been proved that they have night there too. And during the night it gets cold,’ the caretaker continued as she applied the black eye-liner, ‘as cold as the inside of a fridge. When the sun sets it gets freezing and by morning anyone without a heater is frozen. And people need tape recorders there too. They take tapes to the Moon and play them there. The widower even sells televisions there. People like looking at the Earth, at our forests, meadows and rivers, while the landscape up there just strikes fear into them. So we’re talking big business, Mrs Mooshaber. I’ll put my head on the block and say that the rooms inside that widower-magnate’s villa are lined with gold.’

The caretaker put down the eye-liner, took a drink and reached for the lipstick.

‘The housekeeper simply can’t do what it takes,’ said Mrs Mooshaber.

‘Of course she can’t,’ laughed the caretaker, ‘now you mustn’t speak for a moment while I do your lips. Not even Mrs Linpeck had lips like these when she was acting in the theatre. That housekeeper is goodness knows how old, and she has to take care of the villa and cook into the bargain. She can’t deal with that lad... whatsisname...’ For a moment the caretaker stopped work on the make-up and when Mrs Mooshaber said ‘Oberon’ she laughed and said ‘she can’t watch that lad Oberon’s every step. In any case perhaps the housekeeper just isn't up to the job. Did you say that the lad was some kind of prodigy?'

'Just so,' confirmed Mrs Mooshaber with a nod while the caretaker again stopped working on her for a while, 'the best pupil in the whole school. And he's studying some kind of occult science.'

'Ooh my,' laughed the caretaker as she quickly resumed work with the lipstick, 'who knows what you might learn from him. You could learn to practise magic. I'd go with you like a shot if I could, but on this occasion it's just not possible. You see, Mrs Mooshaber,' the caretaker went on as she quickly applied more lipstick, 'this is not like it was with Mrs Linpeck. On that occasion you went as an investigator, whereas today you're going to introduce yourself.' The caretaker stood back from the chair a little, looked at Mrs Mooshaber's face and laughed. 'That's just great,' she said with an enthusiastic chuckle, 'now I just have to powder your face and then fetch the jewellery.' She reached for the powder.

'You will be like a governess there and you know what that means, Mrs Mooshaber,' she went on while she zealously powdered the lady's face, 'a governess in a family like that, the family of a widowed Moon magnate. Certainly you'll get something to eat while you're looking after the lad in that villa of his, and you can be sure that it will be good food.'

'Do you think there'll be ham and salad,' asked Mrs Mooshaber, 'do you think there might even be lemonade?'

'You can count on it,' said the caretaker with a nod as she went on with the powdering, 'wine too... now you're all done and dusted!' she cried out.

'I'm curious about this housekeeper,' said Mrs Mooshaber as she took a look in her pocket mirror, 'I'm a little concerned about her too. I fear it might ruffle her feathers that I'm coming to look after the lad.'

'Come off it,' said the caretaker with a wave of her hand, 'why should you ruffle any feathers? She's not up to the job, the lad needs proper supervision, that's the way it is.' And then the caretaker came out with a sentence that seemed to frighten even her. 'Mrs Mooshaber,' she said, 'as a governess you will be more than she is, because she's in charge of a house, whereas you're in charge of a human being.'

There was a period of silence in the kitchen before Mrs Mooshaber turned to the huge mass of stripey fabric lying on the sofa. The caretaker drank her coffee and then added a few touches here and there to Mrs Mooshaber's cheeks, eyebrows and lips. Then she took a step back once again and gave a nod. Her own cheeks were flushed with satisfaction. Mrs Mooshaber got out of the chair and said:

'Then there's the question of how things are likely to turn out with the lad. I expect he's very disobedient. And he has this black hair, these dark eyes and long nails. And he likes best to wear a black coat. When you hear something like that,' she went on as she looked at the clock by the stove, 'it's almost enough to put the wind up you.'

'What wind?' laughed the caretaker. 'You wouldn't be scared of the boy, would you, Mrs Mooshaber?' asked the caretaker. 'You're bound to be able to deal with him. Given your experience, you'd be able to deal with the Devil himself. Did you say that he was rather finicky about his food?'

'He's got a sweet tooth,' confirmed Mrs Mooshaber with another glance at the fabric on the sofa while she began to put on her best jacket, 'just like the Linpeck boy.'

'Tell me something, Mrs Mooshaber' said the caretaker with a laugh and another sip of coffee. 'How will you go about it today when you get there? It won't be the same as going to Mrs Linpeck's kiosk, will it? Will you introduce yourself and show your credentials like you did with Mrs Linpeck?'

'I will do both right on the doorstep,' confirmed Mrs Mooshaber as she looked at the clock above the stove, 'that way they'll see that I'm the person they're expecting rather than someone else. And when I've introduced myself I'll probably sit down somewhere, probably with the father, and I'll explain that I'm taking the job. Three afternoons each week.'

'Mrs Mooshaber,' began the caretaker, going up to her and starting to slip the earrings into her ears, 'How will you get paid? Will he make you an offer?'

'He will,' confirmed Mrs Mooshaber, 'I couldn't possibly state my price myself. Mr Smirsch said four guineas, but that's surely out of the question. Not even a typist gets four guineas.'

'It sounds like a fortune,' exclaimed the caretaker, 'you'll be rich. If only Wezr and Nabule knew about it.'

'I expect they'll find out,' said Mrs Mooshaber with a sigh and a glance at the clock above the stove, 'I just hope they won't rob me again.'

'You shouldn't ever let them in here again,' said the caretaker firmly, while she went on attaching Mrs Mooshaber's earrings, 'those things of theirs under your sofa had better be collected and thrown into the bin by the steps. And they shouldn't be able to come here again. But those two have got keys and can get in, that's the problem. You would have to change the lock. One of the masons working here is also a locksmith, did you know that? What if I tell him that you want your locks changed?'

'How much longer will they be here?' asked Mrs Mooshaber with a sigh, 'that barrow, those bricks and the barrel of lime are always right in front of my door. They never take them away and I'm really going to fall into that barrel one of these days.'

'They will be clearing up soon,' said the caretaker, now taking hold of the bamboo beads, 'they are nearly finished here now. They've repaired the balcony by the Fabers' apartment and in about a week's time they'll start removing the pillars from the courtyard. They've already begun dismantling some of the scaffolding, but they have to start from the top when they're doing that, so at first you don't notice the difference here below. So, Mrs Mooshaber, let's see now...' The caretaker put the coloured bamboo beads around the neck of Mrs Mooshaber and then came out with an excited:

'Perfect. Mrs Mooshaber, it looks just perfect. Now for the hat. You don't need to take the hat off when you get there. Hats are not even removed in the Ritz, except by the gentlemen. Let's take a look...' The caretaker took the hat with the long coloured feathers and carefully set it down on Mrs Mooshaber's head. 'There we are,' she said, 'and now I just need to use a pin, because heaven knows if there's a wind in the street outside it could carry it off. September's away and autumn is here.' The caretaker took hold of the needles which had been pricked through her woollen skirt and pinned Mrs Mooshaber's hat to her hair. 'There we are,' she said, 'that should do it. Now the wind couldn't go off with your hat, even if it wanted to. Now there's just the gloves, which you put on last of all. And so we can now proceed to deal with the stripes.'

'At last,' said Mrs Mooshaber with a shake of the head as she looked at the striped fabric on the ottoman, 'at last. I've never actually seen those beautiful stripes on you.'

'You've certainly never seen them on me,' laughed the caretaker. 'I haven't had this out in thirty years. It belonged to my ancestors. To the sister of my old man, who ran out on me ages ago. I've never really worn it,' laughed the caretaker, 'I just put it on for fancy-dress balls. I went as a lion. The thing is that you can't see it properly when it's rolled up on the sofa over there,' she laughed, 'I carried it like that on purpose just so that you'd see the stripes and nothing else. But the main thing about it is still hidden. Hidden inside it.' The caretaker quickly finished her coffee, scurried to the sofa and took hold of the striped material. 'Mrs Mooshaber,' she blurted out with cheeks aglow, 'shut your eyes for a moment, I'm going to put it on you while you can't see. Afterwards I'll lead you into your other room where you have a bigger mirror and you can look at yourself for the first time in there.'

Mrs Mooshaber laughed and shut her eyes while the caretaker put the huge stripey fabric onto her. Then the caretaker walked round her and did up some buttons.

'If you ask me,' said Mrs Mooshaber with her eyes still shut while she shook her head a little, 'if you ask me there's something tickling my ears. Just what can it be?' The caretaker just laughed and escorted Mrs Mooshaber into her other room. When she reached the room and opened her eyes in front of the mirror, Mrs Mooshaber almost screamed.

She found herself wrapped in a black-and-brown striped fur, but that wasn't the main thing. The main thing was the unbelievable mane of hair around her throat.

'I told you so,' laughed the caretaker with cheeks aglow, 'I told you that I wore it a couple of times when I went to a fancy-dress ball as a lion. It belonged to the sister of my old man.'

The bamboo beads of Mrs Mooshaber's necklace, not to mention the neck itself and the earrings, had disappeared inside the long brownish hair of the rampant fur. Indeed the whole lower part of her face had disappeared. It was a huge shaggy mane.

'Lo and behold, this time you really do look a miracle,' announced the caretaker, a proud glow in her cheeks, 'not just like the wife of some trader from the Parrot Islands or the wife of a gentleman's gentleman, a minister of state or even like that famous actress Melissa Nedo. When you enter that villa,' she went on, laughing and cheeks glowing, 'that lad...that lad whatsisname...that Oberon,' she went on laughing as she grasped hold of her skirt, 'will be struck dumb the moment he sets eyes on you. I'll stick my neck out and say that however much of a mischief-maker he is, when he catches sight of you he'll be struck dumb.'

The clock by the stove struck four and Mrs Mooshaber put on her white lace gloves and took her smaller black bag. She looked to see that she had her licence and her keys and nodded. And then she left the apartment together with the caretaker.

'These gloves, Mrs Mooshaber,' the caretaker continued as she glowed with enthusiasm while Mrs Mooshaber was standing in the passage and locking her apartment, 'don't take the gloves off when you're there either. Ladies remain gloved sitting in the Ritz and in some cafés too. I'll wait for you to come back so that you can tell me all about it. About the widowed Moon magnate, the housekeeper and this Oberon.' Mrs Mooshaber nodded while she carefully negotiated the 'barrow, the bricks and the barrel of lime. The caretaker accompanied her to the front gate leading to the street where she came to a stop.

'Oberon', she said with a laugh as she came to a halt, 'Oberon, it's not a name I've ever heard before. And the widower is called the same? Mrs Mooshaber,' she went on laughing as they went into the street, 'the villa district is near to these streets here, you don't actually need to go over the crossroads, just take the back streets and you're right there.' Mrs Mooshaber nodded and went off.

She went off in the black and brown stripes, the huge hairy mane, the hat with coloured feathers trembling and fluttering and with the caretaker behind her watching her go, staring and staring until she was round the corner and out of sight.

In the hat with long coloured feathers, cheeks white and red, eyebrows lined and lips rouged and the stripey brown-and-black fur with its huge hairy mane – this was how Mrs Mooshaber followed the back streets to 6, Spring Street while it was still daytime. But the ground floor of the villa was already bathed in light. It really was a high single-storey building with two columns at the entrance, which indeed was just like the entrance to a ministry, and there was actually a

path leading from the entrance across the garden to the gate leading to the street. Mrs Mooshaber took hold of the gate from the side of the street and felt it give way.

She made her way along the path to the entrance with its twin columns. While she walked she took a look at the garden. The trees were already quite lifeless and bare, but their fallen leaves were nowhere to be seen on the ground. 'Probably some servant or other picks them up at once,' Mrs Mooshaber told herself, 'in all likelihood they have a gardener.' There were no flowers in the garden, just various circular flower beds which would certainly have been full of flowers a month earlier, but which were now dark, damp and desolate. Mrs Mooshaber reached the columned entrance and rang the bell. A moment later the door opened and a man stood in the doorway.

He was of medium height, about fifty years old and with a choice of clothing that ran to a blue suit, white shirt and yellow tie. He looked tanned, like someone who'd just taken a break from days lounging by the sea. His eyes were dark but his hair had gone its own way and was light, in places with a touch of grey. As the door opened he appeared with a fleeting smile on his face. But it was a smile that didn't stay. It packed up quickly so that the eyes could widen and the mouth open.

'My name is Natalia Mooshaber from the Mother and Child Support Service,' began Mrs Mooshaber, taking her licence out of her smallish black bag and passing it over. The man didn't so much look at it as take an involuntary step backwards. The mouth stayed half open and the eyes stayed wide. He didn't start to recover until he'd shut the door behind Mrs Mooshaber, who found herself on the threshold of a giant hallway.

'Oberon Felsach,' he began, coming to with a bow, 'Come this way, Madam, to remove your things.' He went up to Mrs Mooshaber and while she managed to keep the smallish black bag in her hands as she undid some buttons, he cautiously took hold of the back of her fur coat beneath its mane. Then he helped her out of the coat. He hung it up on the hall stand which stood guard on the edge of the massive hall. Now Mrs Mooshaber found herself in just a hat with feathers, her best waistless jacket and white gloves, not forgetting the smallish black bag and bamboo beads and the earrings, which were now open for viewing. Mr Felsach's eyes opened wide all over again as he said, 'Come this way, please...' He led Mrs Mooshaber to a three-piece suite – more specifically, a sofa, three armchairs and a little table – and pointing towards one of the armchairs said: 'Please be seated. What may I offer you? Will it be coffee, cognac or curacao?'

Mrs Moshaber sat down in an armchair, her hat still in place and the bag held in the white-gloved hands. In fact she all but sank into the armchair. Her feathers fluttered, her beads rattled, her earrings swung to and fro. She had the feeling that she was sitting on feathers or foam. From the armchair she began to look around and spotted Mr Felsach who was standing a short way off waiting for her to order a drink. A feeling of embarrassment suddenly came over her. She chose the last thing he had mentioned, pronouncing it 'cure' with a little smile. Mr Felsach responded with a smile of his own and a bow and left the hall. Now that she'd been abandoned for a while Mrs Mooshaber could have a better look around.

It really could have been the Ritz itself. In fact not even the Ritz could have been more splendid. The ground was covered in many carpets of many colours, all of them huge, thick and with a softness that words cannot express. Several crystal chandeliers blazed from the ceiling and huge paintings in gilded frames hung on the walls. Rose-coloured gauze stood sentry to the deep red curtains of the windows and the room was amply served with armchairs, small tables and settees. The armchairs, table and settee that acted as courtiers around Mrs Mooshaber were even more splendid than the others. The armchairs and settee were decked in gold brocade while there was a gleaming glass cover for the table. At the end of the hall stood a staircase up to the first floor. Mrs Mooshaber had the feeling that it must be marble. At the foot of the staircase stood two statues of women wielding lamps in their hands, the lamps shining with a strange red light. There were several doors of dark polished wood by the staircase. Further away, on the other side of the hall, there were massive glass sliding doors, which were open at the time because Mr Felsach had just disappeared through them. Mrs Mooshaber managed a glimpse of what was behind those glass sliding doors from the depths of her armchair. There was a large room of some kind with a big sideboard, table and armchairs, most likely a dining-room. But the middle of the hall was what held Mrs Mooshaber's attention. This was where some kind of marble fish-pond could be made out. From it rose what looked like a metal or stone stalk which widened at the top, and out of this top came a splattering of water. That made it some kind of fountain, as Mrs Mooshaber could hardly fail to notice as soon as she'd come in. She couldn't take her eyes off this unusual and outlandish feature in the middle of the hall, but at this point Mr Felsach appeared through the glass door of the dining-room bearing a silver tray containing glasses and a couple of bottles. Mrs Mooshaber guessed that one bottle carried the water and the other was the bringer of her cure.

Mr Felsach approached the table, put down the tray and poured Mrs Mooshaber's liqueur into a glass.

'Please help yourself, Madam,' he said as he sat down.

Mrs Mooshaber thanked him with a faint smile and took a drink. It was a very good liqueur and for a while Mrs Mooshaber went silent. She looked at Mr Felsach with his tan and his lightish hair, his dark eyes and blue clothes, his white shirt and yellow tie, all of them facing her from the armchair, his face already looking less astonished than it had at the start. Mrs Mooshaber had the impression that it was even smiling now and that he was preparing himself to say something.

'Mrs Knorring said that I should pay you a visit today,' said Mrs Mooshaber, 'seeing that you'd be at home today. It's about your young lad.'

'Quite so,' said Mr Felsach with a nod. Now he really did offer a smile as he took in Mrs Mooshaber's necklace, her earrings and the feathers fluttering from her hat, 'yes, indeed. I turned to the Mother and Child Support Service about a month ago concerning my son Oberon. I needed someone who would be willing to come to us for three afternoons each week in order to keep an eye on Oberon, making sure that he was obedient and stayed at home. The thing is that the lad needs discipline, and according to our esteemed pedagogical experts this can only be acquired under supervision. I know Mr Witting, the Director-General of all the houses of correction in the area covered by our capital. He occasionally presents papers on the proper upbringing of children. He was the one who recommended and endorsed the course of action I have taken. Originally he proposed to find me an elderly and experienced guard from the state prison to look after Oberon. But Mrs Knorring from the Mother and Child Support Service expressed herself against such a move. She recommended you and I believe that she was not wrong to do so.'

Mrs Mooshaber listened, scarcely daring to breathe as she did so, but feeling a little better as she took in his words. Her heart almost missed a beat during Mr Felsach's last sentence.

'Mr Magnate,' she said, shaking the smallish bag in her white-gloved hand, 'it's true that I've been working for the Mother and Child Support Service for some twenty years now, and that means I do have some experience. But I have never worked inside a family. I would be willing to accept the position with you for three half-days each week, but I need to find out in advance what the lad is like and how I can be a positive influence on him. Of course Mrs Knorring from the Mother and Child Support Service has provided me with some information already.' Mrs Mooshaber glanced quickly around the hall and staircase.

'I will happily tell you what I can, Madam,' agreed Mr Felsach as he poured some water into his glass, 'in fact everything I know, although my information may not be exact. I only see Oberon now and then, because I'm away most of the time. I expect Mrs Knorring explained to you that I have business on the Moon and come back home perhaps once a month.' While Mrs Mooshaber nodded and took another sip of the fine liqueur, Mr Felsach continued:

'According to his school the boy is exceptionally talented. He's fourteen years old, but already so well-read that you wouldn't guess his age from the way he speaks. He expresses himself like an adult or even a writer. He's well ahead of anything they teach him at school, so he doesn't have to spend any time preparing for class. Instead he buries himself in other things, mainly the so-called occult sciences, although whether that is the right phrase to use I do not know. After all they already teach elements of these sciences in our universities and certain ministries. Anyway, he reads books about the occult and takes lots of notes. He likes to chat with the housekeeper about the subject, provided that she has the time to spare. She has to look after the whole house and do the cooking so she's not short of work, and when her work's finished she's entitled to a break or to go off walking on her own. But we've got two students living on the floor above. They're the sons of some friends of mine who live in the country. They're studying here at the university and lend Oberon their lecture notes, which he reads. He also likes talking about the occult to them. That's all to the good. Even the fact that he's got a sweet tooth and likes indulging it isn't such a bad thing, provided that it doesn't make him too disdainful of his greens, especially the seaweed and algae that our housekeeper so often purchases and prepares in so many different ways. Perhaps it's not even such a great defect that he has long black hair and dark eyes. That is just a fact of nature, though the length of his hair is a matter of human choice and the resourcefulness of any hairdresser. All the same, people say that his hair suits him and that many of our artists and scientists wear their hair long, and even one of our ministers, Scarola. What I think is worse is the very careful way in which he styles his nails. He leaves them to grow long, especially those on each little finger, where they almost curve back in on themselves. But the damning defect is discipline, the lack of which is where all the problems begin. It is apparently very difficult to get through to him where this matter is concerned. He appears to be disobedient, recalcitrant, insubordinate and non-compliant. When he's not buried in his books, he has a tendency to run out of the house in his black raincoat and spend the whole afternoon roaming around town. He ends up in the Pinetreestal district or the Elizabethan district – they're building some fine houses there right now – or he makes for the airport in the Stadium district or the Linde district. When he gets back home of an evening and the housekeeper reprimands him, he takes his revenge on her by pushing away the plate of seaweed she brings to the table and refusing to touch his food. That's if he doesn't do something worse, which happens from time to time, namely...' here Mr Felsach sighed and went silent for a moment while he took a drink of water... 'namely take hold of the plate of seaweed and bang on the table with it. The housekeeper breaks down when he does this and becomes extremely miserable. It seems that Oberon does other things to spite her that are much to be regretted. For example, he locks her in the cellar when she goes there for wine or plays other tricks on her to give her a fright. To give another example, over there in the piscina...' Mr Felsach pointed towards the marble fishpond with the split stem in the centre of the hall, 'there are three red fish that swim around in it, and he goes and throws in some ghastly artificial black fish to join them. When she sees it the housekeeper is frightened out of her wits. She's now afraid of him most of the time and so prefers not to find fault with him when he goes wandering away from home. I'm away for a whole month and during that time there's no one to keep an eye on Oberon and supervise what he does.'

'What about those students,' asked Mrs Mooshaber, 'I know a couple of students who live in a beautiful villa somewhere and they're very mature. Students can have a good influence on the lad.'

'I'm pleased to have them here,' agreed Mr Felsach, 'but I often get the feeling that the influence is more from him to them than the other way round. There's also the fact that they're not always at home. They set off for their lectures in the mornings and come back in the evening. Even if they are at home, they're upstairs studying in their own quarters. They have their own entrance and bathroom and they don't have to so much as show their faces if they don't want to. The housekeeper's glad to have them there, just as I am. She says that at least she doesn't feel so alone. All the same, it has to be accepted that they cannot supervise Oberon. They can talk to him and lend him their lecture notes, but they cannot make sure that he doesn't go roaming. It's simply not in their power to do so.'

'So, Mr Magnate,' said Mrs Mooshaber, finishing the last drop of her fine liqueur, 'you're worried about the lad.'

'I am worried about him,' confirmed Mr Felsach as a shadow fell across his tanned features, 'I'm afraid that if his defects grow too big he will turn into a troublesome individual. Perhaps you know what he'd have coming to him then....'

'Indeed I do,' said Mrs Mooshaber, taking another look at the fountain in the centre of the hall, 'only too well. First the school for troublemakers, then the house of correction, and he'll end up an unskilled pair of hands like as not hired for the day until he ends up behind bars.'

'Exactly so,' said Mr Felsach as the shadow fell once more across his tanned face, 'I mentioned as much to Mr Witting, the Director-General of the houses of correction. He assured me that there were many such cases.'

'Many,' agreed Mrs Mooshaber as she looked at the water gushing out of the split stem in the fish-pond, 'I know this from my own experience. My son Wezr has just come back from his third spell behind bars. Any minute now my daughter Nabule, who has recently married a certain Laibach and is about to buy a flat in the Elizabethan district, will find herself in the same place. My children have been getting into trouble since when they were tiny...' she went on, keeping her eyes on the fishpond, 'wandering off, beating up their schoolmates and stealing. They went to the school for troublemakers and the house of correction, despite the fact that I used to sing them a lullaby when they were little. Our caretaker Mrs Kralec knows that, as does Mrs Knorring. Wezr is twenty-five now,' Mrs Mooshaber was still keeping an eye on the fountain, 'Nabule is twenty, I had them quite late on in life...'

'You have had your share of troubles, then' said Mr Felsach, his suntanned features still under a small cloud of concern, 'you know all about this, Mrs Knorring said as much to me.'

'She may have said as much,' agreed Mrs Mooshaber as the feathers trembled on her hat, 'but she probably didn't tell you everything, Mr Magnate. When my daughter Nabule had her wedding not so long ago, she didn't give me a drop to drink, and they had wine and lemonade there...not to mention ham and salad and some kolaches which I baked myself for their wedding – I love baking, you see – she threw them out of the window for the horse in the courtyard to eat and then she threw me out of the reception. And I was in my best clothes for that wedding of hers.'

'What a terrible thing to hear,' said Mr Felsach in a bitter tone of voice, 'Madam, please help yourself...' and he proceeded to pour Mrs Mooshaber another glass of curacao.

'I understand that the lady of the house has died,' said Mrs Mooshaber as she looked at Mr Felsach, 'the lad has lost his mother.'

'She has died,' Mr Felsach confirmed, 'she died seven years ago, when Oberon was seven years old. But she'd been ill for a long time before that, so Oberon effectively grew up in the care of our housekeeper alone. His good qualities come from his mother, like his love of music. He has record players, radios and tape recorders on which to hear music. He even plays music when he's having his evening meal in the dining-room,' Mr Felsach continued while he gently indicated the broad sliding doors behind his back. 'The housekeeper doesn't prevent him – in fact quite the opposite. She says that when Oberon's listening to music he's calmer and more manageable. I have provided him with the very best equipment, of course,' said Mr Felsach with a smile, 'I would, wouldn't I? It is all concealed within the walls. This is my line of business.'

Mrs Mooshaber nodded, took hold of the glass in a white-gloved hand once again and looked around the hall.

'It is regrettable,' began Mr Felsach as he looked at the made-up cheeks, lips and eyebrows, 'it is regrettable that Oberon is not here right now. He went with the housekeeper to see some conjuror in the Kerke district. The performance began at four. It was something he'd been wanting to see. But there we are. You will get to know him when you start working here. However, there is one very important thing we have to talk about.' Mr Felsach smiled and reached into the pocket of his blue jacket and pulled out a shiny little notebook. 'You would be willing, Madam, to come three times a week, shall we say from three until seven?' When Mrs Mooshaber nodded, Mr Felsach continued:

'Your work will really boil down to this: be in the house and see to it that Oberon stays at home. He is allowed to be anywhere in the house – here in the hall, the dining-room, his own room or...if the students are at home and have time to spare, he can be with them. But he's not allowed into the garden, because then he can get away. Besides, it's already autumn, the days are shortening and there's an increasingly raw edge to the weather. The garden is already a rather desolate place, the leaves having fallen and the flowers faded.'

Mrs Mooshaber suddenly shook the bag in her white-gloved hand. 'What if he escapes from the house? Could he perhaps get away without my even realising that he's gone?'

'It's possible,' agreed Mr Felsach as he looked at the notebook in his hand, 'it's theoretically possible. You might be in some room or other and meanwhile he might run off. It could happen. I suppose it could happen once. I do not think it would happen a second time, because he wouldn't dare to do it twice. You would have won his respect by then, have gained influence over him and he would be afraid of you. I can't say that I know him that well. I could almost say that I don't know him at all, seeing that I see him only once a month. But I presume that you can talk to him about these occult interests of his, listen to him when he holds forth to you about them and then perhaps in return he won't run away. You can sit in the same room or in the next one, keeping the door open so that you can follow what he's doing. That way he won't escape. You can sit here in the hall and keep an eye on the exit. He won't be able to sneak past you here. And with all your experience you'll know all sorts of ways of striking fear into him. Mrs Knorring says that you'll certainly manage it.'

'I'll keep all that in mind,' said Mrs Mooshaber. The feathers trembled on her hat while she directed her attention to the wide glass doors leading to the dining-room. It was then that she noticed that they were essentially made of frosted glass rather like that of her own kitchen window. This meant that when the doors were shut she'd only get a murky view of what was behind them. She turned her attention back to the fountain in the centre of the hall, but Mr Felsach was already leafing through his notebook.

'I would like to revert to the main thing we had to talk about, namely the payment which I would like to offer you. I will give you...five guineas a month.'

Mrs Mooshaber gasped in her armchair and felt her head spinning. For a moment she couldn't believe her own ears. She shook her head, sending the feathers above it into a flutter. A white-gloved hand reached instinctively for the glass of water.

'Mr Magnate,' she began when she'd managed to moisten her lips, 'that is really a lot of money. I have always worked for the Mother and Child Support Service free of charge. I have a small pension on account of my husband having worked as a coachman for the brewery and in addition to this I've always had some money from my work in the cemetery. Five guineas a month is a lot of money and I will have to do everything within my power...to supervise the lad as best I can. So that he's brought into line...' Mrs Mooshaber shot another glance at the fountain, 'so that he doesn't escape from home and I can remove your worries. And so that I can prevent...' Mrs Mooshaber looked at the fountain and at its water-spurting stem...'prevent what might be coming to you if the lad were to continue growing up the way he is now. If I could know when to start...' she inquired as she looked once more at the stem in the middle of the fountain and now got a clearer understanding of it. The water spurted out of it twice. There was some kind of split in the stem making the water come out in two streams.

'Indeed,' said Mr Felsach as he took a look at the fish-pond himself, 'I was just thinking about that. I shall be staying here,' he went on as he consulted the notebook, 'for a week. I must definitely fly to the Moon before the national holiday which is two days before All Souls, on the last day of October. Madam,' Mr Felsach glanced up from his note-book, 'could you come on that day? On the national holiday? I think that I would need you then.'

'I will come on the national holiday,' Mrs Mooshaber agreed, 'I'll be here at three in the afternoon.'

'I would like to make an exception for the national holiday and make it five,' said Mr Felsach as he caught sight of the coloured beads on Mrs Mooshaber and was led from there to the earrings, the lips and the eyebrows, 'five in the afternoon on our national holiday, the thirty-first of October, and I will tell you why I ask for that... I would be particularly glad if my boy does not leave the house during the national holiday. There is a degree of unrest in our country,' Mr Felsach continued as he looked around the hall, 'there's an uneasy feeling among the people. When I spoke with Mrs Knorring a while ago, she told me about a sense of foreboding she had as well, and a national holiday is one of those days when anything can happen.'

'I know what you mean,' said Mrs Mooshaber. 'I heard the same myself from Mrs Knorring. I heard it for the first time when I was with her for the Eichen case, and then for a second time when it was the Linpeck case. She has some strange sense of foreboding. So you think that the lad should stay at home on that day.'

'On that day most decidedly so,' confirmed Mr Felsach as he contemplated his piscina, 'incidentally, it won't be that difficult. It won't be that difficult if he concentrates on the windows. We have quite a lot of them here and many will be decorated. Flowers, candles, cakes and glasses of wine, just as there always are on the national holiday in honour of our Thalian Princess. We even fill the house with incense. Oberon always likes that bit, so it will keep him occupied. The housekeeper will prepare dinner and the students may come too so you can join everyone here for the celebration of the national holiday and your first day with us. So to sum up, the housekeeper and Oberon will be waiting for you at five in the afternoon on the thirty-first of October on the occasion of the national holiday in honour of our dowager sovereign Augusta. The housekeeper will provide you with your monthly payment when you come.'

Mr Felsach helped Mrs Mooshaber into her stripey black-and-brown fur coat with its huge shaggy mane and helped her past his marble piscina, in which she could now clearly make out the fact that the stem from which the two streams of water flowed was enlarged and split at the top and probably made of metal. She also noticed that three red fish were swimming around in the piscina beneath the sploshing water. She took another look around the hall, glanced at the wide, frosted-glass doors into the dining-room, at the pictures in their gilded frames and at the dark, polished doors by the staircase, the three-piece suites and the crystal chandeliers and the two female statues at the bottom of the staircase, holding aloft the two lamps with their strange red lights...last of all she looked at the thick, soft carpet under her own flat shoes. Mrs Mooshaber shook her head and the smallish bag in her gloved hand as she bade farewell to Mr Felsach. He escorted her to the front door which he opened for her with a bow. His dark eyes had opened a little wider once again and his tanned face looked a little surprised. Mrs Mooshaber went out of the entrance between the two columns and then made her way along the wide path to the gate which led into the street. Mr Felsach watched her go for a moment, watched that striped fur, that great shaggy mane, those red and green feathers blowing in whatever there was of a breeze. When she reached the gate and found herself in the street, he in turn closed the door and went to his piscina in the middle of the hall. He watched the water streaming out of the split stem and the three red fish beneath the surface splashes and as he did so a great calm returned to his features. With a look of satisfaction he moved to the table and bore off the bottles and the glasses upon their tray of silver.

XV

Mrs Mooshaber reached her run-down old house feeling as if she was lost in a fog. But even if she got to the house in a fog, it was a fog that lay around her and swirled inside her head without affecting her senses. For instance, the light of the crystal chandeliers was still before her eyes, as was the red light coming from the lamps held by the statues beneath the staircase in the hall. As she went into the squalid entrance passage and made her way past the bricks, the 'barrow and the tub of lime, the dazzling red light still danced before her eyes. When she entered the kitchen and switched on the light, the clock above the stove was just striking half past six. Mrs Mooshaber removed the pins from her hat, took off her gloves, fur coat and necklace of bamboo beads, extracted the rings from her ears, changed out of her best dress and jacket and back into her old clothes...and throughout it all she could still see the dazzling red light from the villa right in front of her eyes. She filled the sink with water, washed the rouge, powder and eyebrow-liner from her face and then put her hat and best clothes into the wardrobe, while her jewellery and gloves went into the bedside table in her bedroom. The striped fur coat with a mane was the only thing to be laid out on the bed, so that she could return it to the caretaker when she dropped by later in the evening.

'She'll be amazed when she comes,' she said to herself in the bedroom. 'Five guineas! I must have misheard what what he said. When I tell her what it's like inside that place, about the light from the chandeliers and the red lamps...' Mrs Mooshaber returned to the kitchen and went to check the stove, to see whether the fire inside it was still alight, reaching into the scuttle to replenish it. But she'd scarcely been able to stoke the fire when she heard someone opening the door into the passage and before she knew what was happening there in the door to the kitchen stood Wezr, Nabule and the strange man looking like a black dog.

'At your service,' said Wezr, going straight to the table to sit down. With a snort of laughter Nabule also went to sit at the table and the strange black dog moved with her. As he went to sit at the table he smiled softly and threw a glance at Mrs Mooshaber.

Mrs Mooshaber was so taken aback by their sudden and unexpected arrival that she couldn't take a single step away from the stove. She remained rooted to the spot beside it, staring at them as if confronted by an apparition, one that had found its way into the vision before her eyes, past what was still left of those lights, dazzling white and red, the lights of the chandeliers and the lamps in the rich merchant's villa. She saw that Wezr seeemed to be if anything even more massive and powerful on this occasion, perhaps because of the red scarf round the nape of his neck, but mainly because he was wearing another new coat, not the new grey one he'd had the time before but a reddish-brown leather coat with a belt and buckles, like something that might be worn by élite military units or by firefighters. She saw that Nabule had a new coat too, not the light one with the blood-red buckle but a black one with a red collar and yellow buttons, while the black dog with his quiet smile was also in a coat that day, light-brown with a white lambswool collar.

'She's been knocked out,' spluttered Nabule from the table as she undid a yellow button, 'she's away with the fairies. We've turned up at her table like a bolt from the blue and like as not she thinks its messengers from Mars. She might have realised we'd be right back.'

'Be right back for our stuff under the sofa,' said Wezr, whose voice that day sounded dry and sharp as a razor.

'Not to mention that lunch which was supposed to be waiting for us,' said Nabule through foolish and exaggerated bursts of laughter as she eyed the stove, 'she must remember that she promised grub's up last time.'

Mrs Mooshaber stayed rooted to the spot next to the stove and didn't utter a single word. Nabule undid a second yellow button and went on:

'She doesn't move and doesn't speak. Have you got anything to cure her of this affliction?'

'I have,' said Wezr, nodding, while he took a cigarette out of the pocket of his leather coat and struck a match to it, 'I have, but I'm not saying anything about it today, not even dropping a hint. She'd pass out and we'd be even less likely to get anything out of her. She'd be out cold and wouldn't even put the food on the table.'

'Speaking of food,' shrieked Nabule, wiggling her hips and swaggering around, 'didn't we settle all that last time?'

At last Mrs Mooshaber began to come round by the stove and found her way over to the sideboard. She took in Nabule swinging her hips, swaggering and raising her eyes to the ceiling, she saw how Wezr fixed his cold pale eyes on her and she saw how the black dog with the shortish, unkempt mop of black hair above his low forehead was throwing her glances and silently smiling. She was on the point of finding speech when Wezr suddenly rose from his seat, grabbed hold of the belt of his leather coat and flicked the ash from his cigarette .

'We haven't time for this,' he said in that dry voice that was as sharp as a razor, while he flicked away the ash from his cigarette, 'there's people waiting to see us. So let's get on with the lunch and get the stuff. The stuff...' he pointed with the finger of his massive hand, 'the stuff under this sofa. I hope it hasn't got damp or been gnawed at by mice,' he went on as he approached the sofa. Then he put the cigarette into his mouth, bent over and began to pull out the packages.

'There they are,' yelled Nabule from her chair, 'just there, right where you put them. But we'd better take a look to make sure they've not been nibbled at.'

The cigarette still in his mouth, Wezr placed the packages onto the table and began to inspect them while standing there. Nabule also began to inspect them but rermained in her seat. And the strange black dog who was also sitting began to inspect them too. He was feeling the paper with his hand, especially at the corners. Then he looked towards the sideboard and began to speak.

'Madam,' he said in a soft voice that was as smooth as velvet, lifting those drooping corners of his mouth as he did so, 'you said that you would put mousetraps around these packages under the sofa so that the mice couldn't get at them. But it seems,' he went on smiling softly, 'that some mouse has been having a nibble after all. Look here,' he went on, pointing at one of the packages and still smiling softly, 'look here, Madam. Traces of little teeth.'

'A mouse has been at the packet,' shrieked Nabule, 'it's damaged goods. For all we know,' she went on shrieking, 'some mouse has been able to crawl inside. You'd better unwrap it and take a look,' she shrieked at Wezr.

'Stop yelling, we haven't time for that,' said Wezr in his sharp, dry voice, now seated in a chair once more, 'we can take a look at it when we get home. There are people waiting to see us right now. But if we were to find a live mouse in one of these packages...' a sudden flash lit his cold pale eyes and made Mrs Mooshaber's heart miss a beat by the sideboard...

'There isn't any mouse inside,' she blurted out, 'they're quite untouched.'

'Madam,' began the black dog in his soft velvety tones, 'how can you know that there isn't one inside? Surely you can't see through paper, can you? What if we were to unwrap it and one scurried out, what do you think would happen then? Someone could be frightened to death by a thing like that.'

'There isn't any mouse inside,' Mrs Mooshaber blurted out once again as she looked at the table, 'there's no mouse in them at all. The only way that could have happened would be if you'd put one inside yourselves.'

'Ourselves!' Nabule burst into peals of foolish laughter, 'Ourselves!'

'Madam,' resumed the black dog, glancing softly at Mrs Mooshaber by the sideboard, 'why would we put mice into packages ourselves, what would be the sense in doing that? After all being fences, as you called us last time, we want to sell these parcels and what would it do for our sales if we were to offer our customers mice in their purchases? Do you not think that it would be a catastrophe for us?'

'That's enough,' said Wezr, his voice still dry and sharp as a razor, 'enough. We haven't the time. We've still got a lot of things to sort out. It looks like she hid the packages well enough,' he went on, flicking the ash from his cigarette, 'perhaps there isn't any mouse inside them. And for that she'll get her reward. And so that she's got nothing to complain about, it'll be something even better than those copies of *Our Blooming Homeland.*'

Over by the sideboard Mrs Mooshaber all at once came fully to her senses. She felt as if she'd been doused with a cup of cold water. Suddenly she stepped towards the table and said:

'You swindled me. You swindled me with those copies. The ones you gave me were a week old.'

They fixed quizzical expressions of surprise on her, looking nonplussed. Wezr offered the cold pale eyes, the black dog gave her a sideways glance and Nabule produced an outburst of laughter.

'Yes, you swindled me,' Mrs Mooshaber exclaimed, 'if I hadn't run away, those people might have killed me. You palmed me off with old papers that were out of date.'

'Madam,' began the strange black dog, raising the downturned edges of his mouth as he spoke, 'what do you mean by saying we palmed you off? What do you mean by out-of-date? We were not palming you off with those papers, we put them right here on the table and Wezr gave you the official card to go with them. You should have gone with that to the editor of *Our Blooming Homeland* and you'd have had a few coppers in the palm of your hand. Did you even check the date on the top now that you're claiming they were a week old?'

'I didn't read it then but I know it for a fact now,' exclaimed Mrs Mooshaber, 'because people told me about it on the street corner. They even wanted to stone me, did you know that? In any case I have a few copies left and you can see the date for yourself.'

'Well well,' said Wezr, exhaling a cloud of smoke in front of him, 'well well, how unpleasant human nature can be. They will even swindle a newspaper seller, though not of course any old seller, only one that they can dupe. Any old saleswoman wouldn't do. Those people just wanted to have their paper for free and that's just what they got. She left those papers lying on the street corner and ran off, which is just what they were waiting for.'

'Just what they were waiting for,' echoed Nabule with her foolishly exaggerated laughter, 'she's so daft, she's everybody's fool. Those papers were too good for her. I wouldn't be surprised if she even left that good strong piece of cord along with the papers,' she went on giving one of her foolish cackles. 'And who knows how she went about selling those papers. You know perfectly well,' she went on as she threw Wezr a cackle, 'she's got no idea of how to sell things. And this stove of hers isn't even lit,' she continued, looking at the stove, 'there's no flame and not a morsel of food heating up on it. What's happened to our lunch?'

Wezr was silent for a while, Nabule swung her hips and swaggered as she reached for her red collar, and the black dog stranger glanced around the room smiling silently to himself. Mrs Mooshaber was standing near the table and shaking a little.

'I don't know,' began Wezr finally with a glance at his sister, 'I don't know whether, things being what they are, when a good deal has the skids put under it like this, we should say any more to her about the well.'

'I don't know about that either,' shrieked Nabule, 'In fact I think we shouldn't tell her. She'll only get it all wrong again. She'll give us away and ruin everything. We won't get a penny out of the well that way,' she yelled.

'I don't want to know about any well,' said Mrs Mooshaber, once again coming to her senses a little, 'it's all a matter of swindles and lies. Swindles and lies,' she shouted, 'I don't want to know about any well so don't get me mixed up in it. Besides,' she went on, 'there isn't any well.'

'See what she's like,' said Wezr to his sister with a sigh.

'There she goes again,' came the supporting shriek from Nabule.

'Madam.' The black dog was starting to speak softly once again, looking at Mrs Mooshaber as he did so, 'you are clearly a prophetess of some kind. I might even let bygones be bygones, namely your claims that these packages on the table here were stolen from the post office in the metro station and that Wezr has returned from prison. I don't want to remind you that you are always picking on Wezr, although you don't know anything about who he really is or what he does. But yes, you must indeed be a soothsayer,' he said with a quiet smile as he stared at Mrs Mooshaber, 'how can you know that there is no well, that it's all a lie? Before long you will start saying that there's no treasure in the well,' he went on with his quiet grin while fixing his eyes on Mrs Mooshaber, 'whereas in fact there's gold, silver and a sackful of money in that well. Madam,' he continued, still smiling quietly and seeking out Mrs Mooshaber with his eyes, 'how can you go on being so entirely mistaken?'

'I am not mistaken,' replied Mrs Mooshaber with what, curiously enough, amounted almost to a shout, 'I am not mistaken and I don't want to hear about any well.'

'Just listen to her.' Wezr threw his cigarette onto the floor and fixed his cold pale eyes on Mrs Mooshaber, 'listen to her. We haven't time to get into an argument. If there's a well, if there's treasure inside it and if you don't know anything about it, then that's your problem. We know what we know and we wanted to help you. If one day we empty that well of its contents, you can't reproach us for giving you nothing and keeping our lips zipped about it.'

'Zipping lips,' shrieked Nabule angrily as she tugged at a button, 'zipping lips and keeping mum. What's the point,' she yelled, 'when there's no convincing that mum over there? She'll stick to her story anyway.'

'Except - I know what would convince her.' As he spoke Wezr suddenly smiled and reached for the belt of his leather coat. 'I know what would convince her and then she wouldn't say another wrong word. Yes,' he went on, nodding, 'I'm afraid to say I know a thing or two about how to convince people.'

'Well go ahead and convince her, then' laughed Nabule, 'opportunity knocks for her. All she has to do is ask you-know-who,' she went on with a swagger and a swing of the hips, 'I dare say she knows where they live. But so far as we're concerned mum's the word.'

'We're saying nothing to her,' agreed Wezr, moving his massive hand from the belt of his leather coat to the table, 'I dare say she knows where they live, so let her go ahead and ask them. They'll confirm what we say and then she'll believe it. But that's something to think about, isn't it. She'll believe strangers but never us.'

'I don't know what you're talking about,' Mrs Mooshaber responded with a shake of the head, 'but I'm not going to speak to ayone about anything. I've already told you that it doesn't interest me.'

'Madam,' began the black dog, smiling and speaking in his soft and velvety tone, 'you say that you will ask no one anything and yet you don't even know whom we are talking about. Perhaps you can still recall those two students who were at Nabule's wedding…' he went on, the soft smile keeping up with the smooth talk, 'you must remember them. They were sitting next to you and you were talking to them right up to the moment when you suddenly rose and ran from the room. The question then is,' he went on smiling quietly, 'will you take their word or not?'

'I believe them,' said Mrs Mooshaber coolly, 'those students were decent people. But I never got up and ran out of that inn. Before I knew what was happening you were flinging me out as if that horse in the courtyard had joined the wedding party.'

'See what she's like,' said Wezr, 'see what she's like. We flung her out before she knew what was happening to her. And they were decent people, she says. If that's what you think, why don't you pay them a visit,' he added in sharp tones, 'ask whether they know about a well around here. A well containing treasure. Gold, silver and sackfuls of filthy lucre.'

'Do pay them a visit and ask them,' agreed the black dog, 'I advise you strongly to inquire of them yourself so that you can be persuaded. The only difficulty lies in the fact that we cannot wait for long. Nor do we need to do so. We can ask other people to help us, people who believe what we say at once and don't need to ask some students first. People who would be only too glad to help. It's just that Wezr wanted to make sure that you wouldn't then broadcast the fact that he shared the pie with others and didn't give a slice to you.'

Mrs Mooshaber took a step back towards the sideboard, fixing her attention on the corner of it before turning to the frosted glass window further away and staying silent. She was keeping a silence that could have seemed stubborn and wilful. Nabule put her palm over her bloated mouth and howled with laughter. The black dog fixed an offended stare on a corner of the ceiling. Mrs Mooshaber had the impression that she'd never seen him like this before. Meanwhile Wezr was looking impassively at the table. He too, she thought, had never looked that way before.

At that moment the clock above the stove struck eight. Wezr suddenly leaned against the back rest of the chair, put his hand onto the table to conclude the meeting in the way that public officials sometimes do, and with pale eyes fixed a cold stare upon his mother. 'It's time we took the parcels and were off,' he said in a dry and piercing manner while he rapped the table with his hand and pronounced 'so where's lunch?'

'It's the evening,' declared Mrs Mooshaber, 'the clock's just struck eight. There is no lunch. And for dinner I just made myself coffee.'

Nabule burst out laughing and did up the two unfastened yellow buttons. Wezr kept sitting and leaning on the back rest of the chair while his hand rapped the table. Then he said:

'Right then, never mind lunch, we won't ask you for any. But I'll be back soon and you'd do well to keep the matter we discussed in mind. Talk to the students. But don't take too long about it,' he went on, still rapping the table with his hand and looking at the parcels, 'if you don't make your mind up soon, I'll have had enough of waiting. Then you can go stuff yourself, living like a mule off the oats that give a certain gravedodging bitch eternal life.' He got up from the chair, reached for the buckle of his red-brown leather coat and took hold of a few parcels. The black dog also rose from his chair without a peep and quietly took a few parcels himself. Then Nabule got off her chair and wiggled her hips.

'And what would I have to do?' Mrs Mooshaber now asked but judging from the sound of her voice without much interest.

'What would you have to do?' Wezr shrugged his shoulders. 'Nothing. Sit in a basket on top of the well so that you can be lowered to the bottom. When you're down there you load the gold, silver and sacks of lucre into the basket and let yourself be pulled out again. End of story.'

'You want me to go down a well?' asked Mrs Mooshaber in astonishment and Wezr responded with a shrug of the shoulders. 'Why can't you go down a well? I'm sure you know how to lower yourself.'

'You might want to consider our offer,' said the smooth-smiling black dog, while with his free hand he caressed the lambswool collar of his light-coloured coat, 'such an opportunity only presents itself once. But then you seem to be set on wasting every opportunity that comes your way. We wanted to take you to the Ritz,' he went on, smiling as he looked at Mrs Mooshaber, 'but you went and hid yourself away in the caretaker's and then preferred to go to the park. Then we gave you newspapers to sell so that you'd have a bit of money in your pocket,' he continued with a smile as he stared at Mrs Mooshaber, 'you threw them on the ground by some street corner before running away. And now we are offering you access to a well full of treasure and you say that it's all a swindle. You believe that you're some kind of prophet and don't even want to make inquiries of the students. And that's without going through all your past errors once again.' Then he went on:

'You've given me no help so far with the mice, although I made you a decent financial offer. I only set one condition, namely that you bring your own traps. I've told you about this twice already, once even in writing, but it apparently means nothing to you. You know perfectly well that I'm a stonemason and that, as you said last time, you can easily find me among the masons at the cemetery gate, where you can perhaps find a certain Bekenmoscht. By the way, Madam,' he continued with a sudden glance at the sideboard, 'where have you put the *Moroccan*? The little white bag's nowhere to be seen today. You must have stashed it away in the larder, isn't that right?'

'She stashed her powder away in the larder and now there's more mice here than ever,' said Nabule as a foolish cackle burst out of her puffy features, 'I wonder if she's planning to move somewhere else.'

Mrs Mooshaber looked at her stupid swollen face exploding in laughter before nodding her head and saying in a sharp voice:

'You should mind your own business and sort out your own move to the Elizabethan district and give Laibach some money for that. You look as if you're rolling in money and I dare say he won't see a penny of it for the flat.'

'Why would I give him anything?' Nabule suddenly shrieked, though the shriek was immediately followed by an outburst of laughter. 'I reckon she's lost her marbles'.

'Zip it,' said Wezr sharply, 'zip it and stop shrieking.' Then he turned to Mrs Mooshaber and said:

'The papers say that a certain gravedodging bitch has decided to consider something. So you should do some considering yourself. We're off now.'

'Madam,' said the black dog stranger again with another quiet smile while the corners of his mouth curled up beatifically, 'we are leaving now, but I would like to say one more thing to you. Why on earth should Nabule give Laibach money towards the flat in the Elizabethan district? Why? Why should she when the day before yesterday she got divorced from him?'

And first Wezr, carrying parcels, then Nabule and finally the black dog stranger carrying parcels and wearing his quiet smile went out through the kitchen door into the corridor and then into the front passageway, passing the bricks, the barrow and the barrel of lime until before long the sound of their footsteps died away. Mrs Mooshaber remained standing by the sideboard, like an old withered tree rooted to the spot.

XVI

And on the third day in the afternoon Mrs Mooshaber went to the cemetery. It was past mid-October and autumn had set in by now. The leaves were shrivelling up even more, were even more yellow and more of them were falling than three days earlier. A cold dankness was hanging in the air. There was no need to water the graves any more or to trim the grass. It was enough to wipe the dust from the inscriptions and the headstones. Hence Mrs Mooshaber no longer had a watering-can or garden shears in her big black bag, just a brush and a bit of cloth. She wanted to use this day to prepare her graves for All Souls, so that the following week, when they issued her with grave decorations, there'd be less work for her to do. A few days before All Souls she normally went to the cemetery office to be issued with branches of spruce and one or two bouquets of artificial flowers, with which she could then decorate her graves. This was something people had paid for, it was part of the insurance they had taken out, and it would last until such time as the graves were forfeited and destroyed. Payment for some of the graves covered thirty years, for others fifty, for yet others a hundred and a few until the end of the world, the time of the Last Judgment and the Resurrection of the Dead. Mrs Mooshaber had only one grave which was covered till the Last Judgment and the Resurrection of the Dead. That was the family tomb of the Director of Education, the Baron de Schubauer. The happy mother Vincencia Cancer and her son the master builder were covered for a century, but the unhappy mother Therezia Bekenmoscht was only covered for thirty. In her ancient, long black skirt with the old waistless jacket and flat shoes, and in the winter coat she'd already been wearing for half a century and with the long black scarf in tow, Mrs Mooshaber made her way that autumn afternoon towards the cemetery, bearing her big black bag but half full. However, because she had it in mind to do something else that day, that is to say to go from the cemetery to Mrs Eichenkranz who lived on the boundary between the cemetery and the park, she did not on this occasion go to the cemetery from the Philipov area or even take the Blauental route, but instead went via Anna Maria the Blessed Square.

The statue of the princes' mother, who died a century old, was standing in the square next to the tall glass building of the station, beneath which somewhere in the depths lay Central Cemetery metro station with Mrs Linpeck's kiosk. Up in the square Mrs Mooshaber asked herself what Mrs Linpeck was likely to be doing. Perhaps she was sitting in her booth selling beer and lemonade, it being afternoon and after the lunch break, so she probably didn't have many customers. 'She must certainly be getting her alimony by now,' Mrs Mooshaber told herself up in the square, 'she certainly won't be wanting to throw herself under a train any more, though if the lad doesn't mend his ways, he'll be the end of her before she can go back to a career in the theatre. I wonder whether she's already bought him a winter coat and a hat, seeing that the cold weather's here already. Perhaps he's not in that green sweater of his any more and she'll get him skis for Christmas.' Then she had a sudden thought that since it was afternoon following the lunch break the lad would be in the refuge and wouldn't be taking his trolley up and down the platform till six. Mrs Mooshaber forced her gaze away from the huge edifice of the station and looked into the distance beyond it, at the kiosks with their glass and laminate. Perhaps there was no one standing there right now either. Then she looked at the row of apartment blocks in the distance and was reminded of the inn. '*The Golden Carriage* used to be there, yes it used to be there and now there's not a brick of it remaining,' she said to herself. She looked around the square once more, at the station building and at the statue which it overshadowed. Then she turned and made her way towards the gate of the cemetery. She laid eyes on a low building which she had never really noticed before, but now it drew her attention. That was the stonemasons' workshop. It was where they carved gravestones and engraved the inscriptions onto monuments and tombs. 'Perhaps the only son of that unhappy Mrs Bekenmoscht is still working there,' she said to herself, 'perhaps he is that stonemason who hangs around with Nabule and Wezr, the one who said "Come, Madam, rid me of my mice, you know where you can find me..."' At this point Mrs Mooshaber shook her big, black, half-empty bag and quickly turned away. She entered the cemetery and then came to a stop under one of the trees lining its main avenue.

She could now turn to the left and go to the grave of de Schubauer, the Director of Education, and from there to Vincencia Cancer and her son the master builder and then to Therezia Bekenmoscht. On the other hand she could go straight away to Vincencia Cancer and her son the master builder, thence to Therezia Bekenmoscht and finally to the Director of Education. Whichever she chose, she could first of all pass the tomb of the Loch family, where there was a water tap from which she sometimes had a drink during the summer next to a huge rubbish bin under a chestnut tree. Mrs Mooshaber decided that she would go to the Loch family tomb and from there move on to the Cancers, Therezia Bekenmoscht and last of all the Director of Education. And then, if she had any time left over, she'd go to little Faber's grave. She wanted to visit the lad's grave on All Souls in any case, but she might be able to fit an earlier visit in today. After all that was done she'd go to Mrs Eichenkranz while it was still light or at dusk, while her shop was still open. Mrs Mooshaber set off slowly walking straight down the avenue.

The trees were turning yellow and shedding their leaves even more by now. On the main paths through the cemetery, where the trees were biggest, there were already piles of leaves made damp by the moist air and the mist, which the cemetery workers, armed with long brooms, rakes and pitchforks, were loading onto wooden two-wheeled carts. The graves looked empty and forlorn, being always at their most abandoned in the period after mid-October, because the summer is long gone, the grass is no longer green and the flowers bloom no more. And All Souls, that last flourish with all its flowers and wreaths and candles, is still some way off. Even so, there were already people standing by many of the graves, cleaning them and in all sorts of ways putting them in order, preparing for All Souls and doing just what Mrs Mooshaber herself wanted to do that day.

Mrs Mooshaber reached a fork in the road where there was a pointed tomb looking like some kind of burial-mound. Then she remembered that it was round here that she'd once been searching for the lad with the blue-and-white stripey top with Mrs Eichenkranz. 'Mrs Eichen went to see whether he was on the other side of that burial-mound over there – and he wasn't.' Then Mrs Mooshaber spotted the small bench on which some bespectacled old lady with a lacework blouse had been sitting that day. Mrs Eichenkranz had asked her whether she'd seen the boy. 'But she hadn't seen him,' Mrs Mooshaber recalled, 'she was peering at some prayer-book.' The bench on which the old lady had been sitting was now as empty as all the other benches. It was autumn, it was past mid-October, a cold dankness was hanging in the air. At last Mrs Mooshaber reached the Loch family grave and the water supply – which amounted to a pipe with a tap above a huge barrel – next to a chestnut tree with a rubbish bin right underneath it. Mrs Mooshaber shook her big black bag and moved onto a smaller path which led to the grave of Vincencia and Vincencius Cancer.

When Mrs Mooshaber reached the grave, she stopped and examined it in one glance. Everything was more or less in order. A few dry yellow leaves had been brought by the breeze from the tree nearby and now lay on top of the oval-shaped gravestone. The only thing that appeared shabby was the gold inscription on the gravestone. Mrs Mooshaber opened her bag and took out a brush and a cloth. First she swept away the leaves on top of the grave and then she dusted the gravestone before proceeding to clean the inscription *Vincencia Cancer* and the inscription beneath *Vincencius Cancer, Master Builder.* When she had finished the inscription was so shiny that it could have been brand new. 'It will last a century and more,' Mrs Mooshaber said to herself as she returned the brush and cloth to her bag, 'what a happy mother. She lived to be eighty and succeeded in raising a good child.' Then she remembered something. 'I wonder about that son of the magnate, the one I'm going to see on the national holiday. I wonder how that one will turn out...' Mrs Mooshaber shook her head, bag in hand, looked around and then moved on. She slipped away onto the smaller path in order to get to Chapel Five where she'd find the grave of Therezia Bekenmoscht, but then she suddenly stopped in her tracks.

'What if first of all,' she thought to herself as she came to a sudden stop, 'instead of going to Therezia Bekenmoscht I was to go to the Director, what if I went to him first? True, it would mean making a detour, but what of it? I will still get to Mrs Eichen while the evening's drawing on, or just after dark anway, and the same goes for the Fabers.' So Mrs Mooshaber made an abrupt change of direction. She suddenly turned round and instead of going to Chapel Five and Therezia Bekenmoscht she went first of all to the grave of de

Schubauer, the Director of Education. In a short while she'd arrived at the section of the graveyard where there were big and beautiful marble tombs and that was where she found his. She contemplated the tomb for a while and shook her head. The grass in the plot was drooping, faded and yellow, damp and soggy from the mist. There was nothing that could be done about it now. 'When Spring comes I'll bring a spade,' Mrs Mooshaber said to herself, 'and then I will sow more grass. And in a week's time when the cemetery administration issues me with some branches of spruce, I'll cover it over and put some plastic flowers on top and a grave light.' Mrs Mooshaber opened her bag, took out the brush and cloth and began first of all to wipe the tombstone. She wiped the lamp for the eternal light, even the bit inside where you place the oil or a candle, and then took a look at the angel. A wing which had been damaged for a long time still remained attached, but Mrs Mooshaber had the feeling that as time went by its hold was becoming less and less secure and that it wouldn't be long before it fell down. 'What will I do then?' she wondered as she looked at the wing, 'I'll have to ask them at the cemetery office. They'll send a repairman or a mason here...' Mrs Mooshaber went on thinking with a nod and a sigh, 'the way the grave is, that angel will certainly never last until the end of the world which is what they paid for. It won't be able to hang on, not till the Last Judgment and the Resurrection. Assuming, of course,' it occurred to her while she carefully wiped the angel's wing, 'assuming that there is such a thing as a Last Judgment and a Resurrection. Perhaps the Last Judgment,' she went on, 'perhaps there must be one of those, but a Resurrection of the dead...?' Mrs Mooshaber finished cleaning the angel and then took out another cloth with which she began to clean the inscriptions on the tombstone. The lettering was gold and looked quite shabby, but Mrs Mooshaber knew that when she'd cleaned it it would shine like the letters on the tomb of the happy mother Cancer. She cleaned the inscription *The Family of the Director of Education Baron de Schubauer* and then another inscription *Director of Education, Baron Joachim de Schubauer, born 1854, died 1914* and then she cleaned a long row of names and numbers underneath, *Mathurin, Anna, Leopold, Rozalie.*

When she had finished, the inscription was clear and radiant, with a shine that made it almost as good as new. 'If he was still alive, this school director, I wonder what he would say to that defiant and disobedient son of the magnate who I begin working for on the national holiday,' she went on, remembering the matter all over again. 'I expect he'd be appalled, just as the boy's father the magnate is, or perhaps even more so.' Mrs Mooshaber shook her head and put her cloth and brush back into her bag. Then she took another look at the tomb and the angel's wing before moving on. Now she'd really be off to see Therezia Bekenmoscht.

Mrs Mooshaber left the part of the cemetery with the large and lovely marble tombs and went towards Chapel Five, retracing her steps for a while. Later on, at a fork in the path near to section 16 of the cemetery, she took a diversion towards some smaller graves. When the path, which was almost deserted and empty of the living, had all but taken her there, she suddenly caught the sound of bells. The bells were sounding from somewhere to mark a passing, and Mrs Mooshaber recognised that their tolling came from Chapel Five, which was not far from where she was. 'It will probably be a burial procession getting under way,' she said to herself from the empty, deserted path, 'they'll be setting off for the grave.' Mrs Mooshaber left the deserted path in order to approach the tombs and as she crossed the damp and yellowing grass she suddenly heard music too. She heard sounds and recognised that they were playing bugles and trumpets somewhere in the distance. 'It must be that burial,' she thought with a nod and a shake of her big black bag, 'the burial procession is underway somewhere, it's about four in the aftenoon.' And Mrs Mooshaber moved among the graves until she'd almost reached the small birch above the pointed tombstone of Therezia Bekenmoscht, and at that point she stopped. There wasn't a living soul anywhere around and there was something uncanny about the silence. The only sounds to be heard around her were the bells from Chapel Five and the bugles and trumpets in the distance. Otherwise an unusual deathly silence hung all about her. So uncanny was the deathly silence that Mrs Mooshaber, standing by the birch and the pointed tombstone, suddenly found herself unable to take another step.

All of a sudden Mrs Mooshaber thought she heard something moving nearby. She looked ahead of her beyond the grave and the small birch, to where thick bushes obscured the view of other graves nearby. The thick bushes were bare of leaves now, dried out to a point where you could see through them a little, and Mrs Mooshaber had the sudden feeling that someone was stalking her, lurking behind those bare dried-out bushes.

'I must be wrong,' she thought, 'who would be standing around and waiting there? Right next to this grave. I've been coming to this place for years. For the best part of a century.

And Mrs Mooshaber took a step forwards. She moved on and found herself under the small birch tree at the grave of the unfortunate Therezia Bekenmoscht. And she was just making up her mind to clean the grave and was on the point of opening her bag when all of a sudden a shot rang out.

Never in her life before had Mrs Mooshaber heard a gun being fired. She'd never done military service, never even been to one of the military parades which Prime Minister

Albinus Rappelschlund organised now and again in the city. She'd never been to a shooting range, a fancy fair or a cinema. Perhaps she'd heard cannonfire just once in her life, but she could scarcely remember that now. In reality this was the first sound of gunfire that had ever reached her ears. Mrs Mooshaber raised her head until she was looking at the sky through the branches of the birch hanging above the grave and listened out. All of a sudden she saw through the branches a flock of large black birds flying and listened to their cawing. There was no doubt about it, they were crows. And before she could pull herself together, another shot rang out and Mrs Mooshaber saw one of the crows, the one bringing up the rear, turn its wings upwards and plummet down to earth somewhere. At that moment Mrs Mooshaber's heart missed a beat. She'd remembered little Eichenkranz.

'It must be him,' she said to herself with a shake of her bag, 'they gave him back the rifle they'd confiscated and he's been firing it off somewhere nearby. He said they were vermin but that he'd never shoot them and even if he did he'd miss. And now he's shot and scored a bullseye.' And Mrs Mooshaber said to herself that as soon as she'd tidied the grave of this unhappy mother, she would go and see Mrs Eichenkranz on the boundary between the park and the cemetery and talk to her. 'Poor Mrs Eichen,' she thought, 'just what will she say? This lad will end up being the death of her after all. When I tell Mrs Knorring about it,' she went on to herself, 'they will take the lad away from Mrs Eichen, he's only there now on probation, and then who will help her out in the shop? The poor woman will be driven to distraction by this.' Suddenly it struck Mrs Mooshaber that little Eichenkranz might not have fired the shots. 'Perhaps it was someone working for the graveyard administration who was told to shoot the crows,' she told herself. 'That would be a great relief to Mrs Eichen and it's what I would wish for her.' And Mrs Mooshaber hurriedly opened her bag, took out her brush and cloth and set to work.

While she was wiping the pointed tombstone, on which some leaves from the small birch, not to mention the odd twig, had fallen here and there, she once again had the feeling that a person was snooping around somewhere near the grave. Yet everywhere around there was total silence, a strange and deathly silence which seemed to be even more marked and more peculiar after the recent shots. The sounds of music, of those bugles and trumpets, were still a constant refrain in the distance, but were noticeably fainter now. Evidently the funeral procession had moved on and was about to reach the graveside...even the bells of Chapel Five were growing weaker, evidently not in their case because they were moving further away but because whoever was tugging the rope to make them ring was pulling with less and less force...still Mrs Mooshaber could not rid herself of the impression that there was someone lurking somewhere near her. Cloth in hand she paused in her cleaning and looked once again at the bushes behind the grave, which in their dry and leafless condition permitted a peek through to the other side. But still she could not see anyone standing and lurking behind them.

Hurriedly she finished wiping the tombstone and took another cloth out of her bag with which to clean the inscription, the name of the unfortunate mother. Her hand reached out towards the inscription...and that was when the blow fell.

Mrs Mooshaber screamed, sensed the ground shudder beneath her and saw the sky spinning above her. The cloth fell from her hand... and then she felt herself falling.

At the last moment she must have pulled herself together and caught hold of something. Somehow she ended up on her feet again. She found herself staring right at the tombstone of Therezia Bekenmoscht, gazing and gazing while the ground was giving way beneath her and the sky was spinning above her. She had no idea what was happening to her.

For now Mrs Mooshaber was no longer looking at the tomb of Therezia Bekenmoscht, the unhappy mother, but at another tomb altogether.

It was not the tomb of Therezia Bekenmoscht standing before her now but that of Natalia Mooshaber. There it was, the inscription *Natalia Mooshaber*, engraved in letters of gold. *Keeper of Traps*, it continued, while right at the bottom, where you'd normally have a cross, a huge mouse had been carved into the stone.

Mrs Mooshaber was standing right in front of her own grave.

No one knows how long Mrs Mooshaber was standing there. It was not a tomb beside a path, so no one saw her. There was no one to see how her eyes bulged or how she was shaking or the way her head, her chin, her hands and her legs were all in a totter. No one saw the cloth lying at her feet, the big black bag or how pale she looked. No one even saw the sweat trickling down from beneath her old scarf. And as for her she heard nothing, not even the music of the funeral procession which had already reached a graveside somewhere and had fallen silent. She did not even hear the bells from Chapel Five, which had also perhaps had their

fill of ringing. She did not hear that there was some other living creature nearby, behind those thick, leafless bushes that concealed the other graves. She stared at the grave, at her own name, at the inscription and at the mouse, and she thought that she must be dead.

After an indefinite period she began to stir.

And then she suddenly rushed away from that terrible grave to find the path.

The path was deserted, empty of people as before, deserted, empty, just one solitary elderly fellow striding along in the distance... Mrs Mooshaber went running after him.

'What's going on,' the elderly man called out when he caught sight of her, 'what is it, what is it, what's happening...?' He was startled into a panic.

NATALIE
MOOSHABR

Alarm drove him to quicken his steps, almost to break into a run. Mrs Mooshaber ran, perhaps even a little ahead of him or perhaps at his side and then, pale as death, hot from their exertions and in a state of panic they came to a halt.

They had come to a halt at the graveside and with a scream Mrs Mooshaber pointed at the inscription.

Then came a third scream while her head was in a whirl and at the last moment the old man just managed to catch hold of her. The sight of the inscription on the stone made her delirious. It read:

THEREZIA BEKENMOSCHT

'What is it, Madam?' asked the elderly gent, 'what's wrong? Are you perhaps Therezia Bekenmoscht? But this is most strange,' he continued in a plaintive voice with a shake of the head, 'you said that you were someone else. In any case this doesn't make any sense.'

Mrs Mooshaber saw how the old fellow was shaking his head, on top of which a bowler hat was perched, and how the winter coat he was wearing remained unbuttoned and how in the waistcoat he was wearing there was a watch on a gold chain... and she saw how he shook his head, how he spoke, spoke in a voice that whined and lisped as he said:

'But it is something very special, something extraordinary that I, Klevenhütter, strange man that I am... did I not lose a gold coin from the pocket of my coat-tails?' And slowly he walked off.

Mrs Mooshaber picked her cloth up from the grass. Holding her big black bag she felt her head in a fever, her heart still thumping as it had not long before when she'd fled from the crossroads, and the sweat pouring down her forehead. 'Oh God,' it suddenly occurred to her, 'Oh God, I'd better go to the water pipe by the Loch grave and wash myself back into my senses...am I out of my mind?' At the very moment when she lifted her cloth and her bag from the grass, she heard a sound from behind those thick and dried-out bushes, and when she looked up she heard an explosion of laughter. Someone was laughing in a coarse and piercing manner, while a second laugh was more of a foolish and bloated screeching and the third source of laughter came quietly in tones as soft as velvet. And then she caught sight of three people through the thick dried-out hedge, one of whom was carrying some largeish tablet of stone under his arm.

XVII

No one knows what Mrs Mooshaber did at home in the evening, because no one visited her after she arrived from the cemetery that day. Not even Mrs Kralec the caretaker did. But as for what was going on in Mrs Mooshaber's mind, no one knows that either and no one will ever know. She may have stayed sitting still as a post on her sofa in the kitchen all night, looking straight ahead. Maybe this stillness on the outside reflected what was in her heart. She may not even have lit the stove, made tea or even heard the chiming of the clock. She may have spent that whole evening just sitting motionless on the sofa and looking straight ahead like an unseeing, shrivelled old tree. She may have finally gone to bed but whether she actually slept or stayed awake, no one knows that either, and no one even knows whether her sleep, if she had any, was broken by dreams.

Nor does anyone know what Mrs Mooshaber did on the following day. She didn't leave her flat from daybreak to dusk. Therefore she met neither the caretaker nor the masons, who were slowly bringing their work on the shabby old building to completion and removing the scaffolding. No one from the house came across her. She didn't leave her flat and in all likelihood no one knocked on her door either. It was the third day in the afternoon before Mrs Mooshaber, in her old clothes, her long black skirt, her black scarf, her old hat and her flat shoes, went outside carrying her smallish black bag.

She made her way down the three drab streets slowly, with her head strangely bowed, before emerging at the crossroads by the *Sunflower* department store. But she did not take the zebra crossing over the asphalt, nor did she glance towards the glass and laminate kiosks in the distance. Instead she took a different turn. Slowly and with head strangely bowed she made her way down a street which she would nomally only take in order to buy something from the co-operative. But she wasn't heading for the co-op. After a short while she turned into another street. And then she came to a stop in front of a pharmacy.

With its black marble tiling the pharmacy looked more like a funeral parlour than a purveyor of medicines. Small boxes filled the window display and a cross hung above the entrance. A black and yellow cross, because this was something to do with the name of the pharmacy... Notwithstanding this connection, there was something menacing, something macabre about this black and yellow cross over the entrance. So menacing and macabre that it could make the heart of many a passer-by skip a beat or freeze the blood in their veins. Mrs Mooshaber, in her long black skirt and her black scarf, her old winter coat and carrying her smallish black bag, headed straight inside.

A small and slightly built man stood behind the counter in a white coat. He had a little ginger beard and gold spectacles on his nose.

When Mrs Mooshaber entered, he looked at her through his spectacles while an expression of great sternness took over his face.

'What may I do for you?' he asked in a voice at once squeaky and stern.

'I am Nathalia Mooshaber from the Mother and Child Support Service, here is my licence.' Mrs Mooshaber extracted her card from the bag and handed it to the pharmacist.

The pharmacist gave it a glance before returning it to Mrs Mooshaber.

'Is it baby talc or soap that you want?' The severity had gone out of his squeak now. 'Or is it nappies you're after? You know, you can't get those in a pharmacy, you'll have to go to a textile store.'

'I don't want any nappies or soap,' said Mrs Mooshaber. 'I've come for some poison.'

'Poison?' The pharmacist blinked through his glasses and leaned his chest against the counter. 'Poison? Permit me to ask what for, Madam'

'For mice,' explained Mrs Mooshaber.

'Mouse poison.' The pharmacist pulled at his beard while he regarded Mrs Mooshaber, 'mouse poison. I can let you have that. I'll give you some *Moroccan*.' The pharmacist proceeded to spring away from the counter and was on the point of moving to one side of his store when Mrs Mooshaber shook her head.

'Not *Moroccan*,' she said brusquely, 'I've had my fill of that. I want something stronger.'

'Something stronger,' repeated the pharmacist as he once more took up position leaning his chest against the counter, 'something stronger? That will be for mice, will it?'

'Something stronger for the mice,' agreed Mrs Mooshaber. '*Moroccan* is too weak.'

'If you please, Madam, ' began the pharmacist, his eyes rising from behind his spectacles, 'what sort of mice do you have, if *Moroccan* is too weak? It must be rats that you have.'

'There you are, then,' agreed Mrs Mooshaber with a terse nod and a glance at the pharmacist, 'rats it is.'

The pharmacist tugged at his beard and took a good look at Mrs Mooshaber. It was a look that took in her old black scarf, her face and her winter coat, insofar as he could see it from behind his counter. He looked, he blinked some more and then he squeaked:

'I cannot give you anything but *Moroccan*. It's simply not allowed. Because I'm a pharmacist. Anything stronger could be life-threatening.'

'That's just what I need,' said Mrs Mooshaber drily, once more glancing around the pharmacy. 'I can't get rid of them with *Moroccan*. They eat it on the bacon and they're still there.'

'Put some *Metrazin* on your bacon, then,' squeaked the pharmacist, 'that stuff could poison a goat.'

'I used that twenty years ago,' snapped Mrs Mooshaber as she shook her head, 'that stuff's even weaker, it wouldn't even poison a mouse...I want something stronger, something that will guarantee their end. And so that no one has to suffer too much.'

'What you're asking for is a little tricky,' said the pharmacist, his tone severe again while he tugged anew at the little ginger beard, 'only *Rattenal* is that strong. It's a white powder like *Moroccan* and it's dangerous. Like *Moroccan*, it can be mistaken for sugar, but the *Rattenal* is three times as strong. You can see the difference if you put it on these scales here.' The pharmacist pointed at a counter with a pair of scales not far away. 'I cannot give you something like that. I'm a pharmacist. How can I be sure that you won't confuse it with sugar?'

'Why would I do something like that?' asked Mrs Mooshaber, now in very cold tones as she looked at the scales, 'I'm from the Mother and Child Support Service, you've seen my licence. I have an official stamp on it and the signature of Mrs Knorring herself.'

Once again the pharmacist examined Mrs Mooshaber through his glasses, her black scarf, her face, her old winter coat, insofar as he could see it from behind his counter, but he already had one hand opening a drawer and pulling out a folder of some kind. He placed the folder on the counter in front of him and said:

'Tell me, Madam, what is seven times seven?'

'About fifty,' replied Mrs Mooshaber in a cold manner. The pharmacist nodded.

'Good,' he said, 'and now can you tell me what the earth looks like?'

'What should it look like?' echoed Mrs Mooshaber with a shake of her bag.

'Is it a cube or a sphere or is it flat,' he went on, throwing in a few blinks, 'or is it perhaps a cylinder?'

'It's round,' said Mrs Mooshaber. 'That's why we speak of the globe.'

'Good again,' squeaked the pharmacist while he kept his eyes on Mrs Mooshaber. Then he blinked at the folder on the counter in front of him before squeaking:

'And what does this globe the earth rest on?'

'What should it rest on?' repeated Mrs Mooshaber.

'What does it rest on,' came the echoing squeak from the pharmacist, 'does it rest on some kind of ground or is it held up by some giant or is it carried on the back of a white elephant or a turtle...'

'It doesn't rest on anything and it isn't carried by anything,' said Mrs Mooshaber with a shake of the head, 'it floats.'

'In the sea?' inquired the pharmacist with a blink and a beard tug.

'In the air,' said Mrs Mooshaber.

The pharmacist blinked through his glasses and nodded his head. He rested his chest against the counter on which the folder lay and then went on:

'The earthly globe, Madam, does not actually float. It spins. It orbits around something, you see, around the sun. And the Moon, that place to which we send our rockets, that spins too. It orbits around the earth. And the sun, along with us on the earth, is part of our solar system in which there are billions of stars, and as for solar systems the universe contains many billions of billions of such systems, some of them far bigger than ours. Because the universe has no end just as time has no end, for it is everlasting. And here you are coming to me wanting mouse poison.'

The pharmacist propelled himself away from the counter and went to the side of his store. In a moment he came back bearing a small box with black and yellow stripes and a red label saying '*Rattenal*'. Beneath the word *Rattenal* was an impression of a skull and crossbones.

'There you are then, that's what you're looking for', said the pharmacist blinking through his glasses, 'you can see the skull here, meaning that this is highly poisonous. There's a quarter of a kilo in here, perhaps I needn't bother to weigh it on the scales. You could see off a regiment with this lot.'

'And how do you dose it?' asked Mrs Mooshaber in a cold voice.

'It says here on the other side,' squeaked the pharmacist as he turned over the box, 'the instructions are in three languages. Including Portuguese, if you happen to have some acquaintance with that,' he added with a blink. 'Just coat each morsel with some as you would with *Moroccan*.'

'And how long before it takes effect?' asked Mrs Mooshaber.

'How long,' echoed the pharmacist with a blink, 'that depends on the size of the mouse. With a little field mouse the effect would be almost immediate. But with a rat the size of a rabbit it would take a few minutes. The bigger the creature, the more flesh and blood there is to delay the impact. As someone who works at the Mother and Child Support Service,' he went on, still holding the *Rattenal* in his hand and blinking through his glasses at the folder on the counter, 'I take it that you know who Claparède was.'

'Cleopatra?' asked Mrs Mooshaber in surprise.

'Edouard Claparède,' the pharmacist continued. 'Or Pestalozzi. Or Rousseau. Or Comenius.'

MAROKAN
Rattenal

'I expect they were poets,' said Mrs Mooshaber. The pharmacist's head went up and down with his eyelids.

'Yes, poets,' he agreed. 'Poets. They were poets because they believed that a person could be improved by education. But that is not so, Madam, that was where they were wrong. Do you believe in God?'

'I do not,' said Mrs Mooshaber, shaking her head. 'I believe in Fate.'

'In Fate?' The pharmacist gave a quizzical blink and tug of his beard. 'That's rather strange. What does that mean, to believe in Fate but not in God?'

And when Mrs Mooshaber stayed silent, the pharmacist went on – still keeping a hold of the *Rattenal*:

'I am asking you what difference it makes, what this Fate of yours really is.'

'Fate,' began Mrs Mooshaber with a shake of the bag, 'means that what has happened was meant to happen and that what is meant to happen will happen. My own Fate, for example, was to have two unworthy children.'

'Well, and what of it,' squeaked the pharmacist, glancing at the scales nearby, 'to believe in something having happened or about to happen? That's not an article of belief. Everyone knows things that have happened as a matter of fact, you don't need any faith for that. And as for believing in things that will happen – that's just nonsense, seeing that you don't know what will happen and so you don't know what you're believing in. This is a strange faith of yours, Madam. You might as well believe in a house or in birds. Or,' he went on, eyeing the scales, 'in taking walks or in tomorrow being another day.' The pharmacist went quiet for a moment while he put the *Rattenal* back on the counter and looked at the folder.

'You say,' he continued again, straightening himself up while he kept an eye on the folder, 'that Mrs Knorring's signature is on this licence of yours.' When Mrs Mooshaber nodded, the pharmacist opened the folder on the counter to reveal sheets of music.

'Well, Madam,' squeaked the pharmacist, leaning his chest on the counter again, 'that lady is a great singer. She will sing the *Requiem* as part of a huge chorus of sopranos. I will also be singing there,' he squeaked, 'as a bass.' And with a glance at his score the pharmacist began to warble a few bars. Mrs Mooshaber stood in front of the counter, eyeing the sheets of music and the pharmacist but most of all eyeing the stripey box of *Rattenal*. Finally the pharmacist warbled to a halt and lifted his eyes from behind the spectacles.

'Do you know what a requiem is, Madam?'

At this moment the door opened and a customer entered the pharmacy. Some young man sporting a beard.

'A requiem,' began the pharmacist from behind his counter as he blinked at the young man, 'is a mass for the dead. The hardest to sing is the *Dies irae, dies illa*, that part, Madam, is sung *fortissimo*. 'Day of wrath and doom impending, David's word with Sibyl's blending! Heaven and earth in ashes ending!' So, Madam, that's what we sing. The bass voices are very important, always singing *fortissimo*. How may I help you?' the pharmacist went on, turning to the young man.

'I can wait,' said the young man with a sideways glance at Mrs Mooshaber.

'All right then,' said the pharmacist with a blink and a nod. He turned back to Mrs Mooshaber and went on:

'Have you ever sung in a choir, Madam? Do have the voice for it?'

'I used to sing a lullaby,' came the dry response from Mrs Mooshaber as she continued to eye the *Rattenal*.

'And do you know what the charioteer is?' the pharmacist asked.

'It's like the name of a pub,' replied Mrs Mooshaber. 'The name of the pub where I was married was called *The Golden Carriage*.'

'A pub,' squeaked the pharmacist, throwing a wink at the young man. 'A pub! It is the name given to a constellation of stars in the sky. It also refers to the driver of a means of transport on wheeels drawn by horses. It is a homonym, a word with many meanings to you. You do not believe in God, Madam, so you probably don't even believe in the Last Judgment or the Resurrection of the Dead. That is what a requiem concerns itself with.' The pharmacist looked at his musical score and began to recite:

Oh, what fear man's bosom rendeth,
When from heaven the Judge descendeth
On whose sentence all dependeth.
Wondrous sound the trumpet flingeth;
Through Earth's sepulchres it ringeth;
All before the throne it bringeth.
.....
Lo! The book, exactly worded,
Wherein all hath been recorded;
Thence shall Judgment be awarded.

And now, Madam, I will give you one more verse,' the pharmacist went on while blinking through his spectacles at the young man in the beard, who remained standing and waiting…'the last one:

When the Judge his seat attaineth,
And each hidden deed arraigneth
Nothing unavenged remaineth

So that's a requiem for you, Madam. A requiem,' the pharmacist went on as he blinked at the scales nearby, 'and here is your *Rattenal*. That will be two shillings and a penny.'

Mrs Mooshaber reached into her bag and pulled out some coins. The pharmacist took the money and wrapped the box in blue paper of some kind and passed it over to Mrs Mooshaber.

'This, Madam, will be the greatest requiem ever to have been performed in this land of ours,' he squeaked. 'One thousand singers and fifteen hundred musicians, conducted by Mr Scarone from Bosnia. After all, it has even made the headlines. There was an article about it in *Our Blooming Homeland* the other day. But as for when the première will take place,' here the pharmacist's eyes glazed over and he tugged once more at his beard, 'that remains unknown.'

Mrs Mooshaber stashed the parcel inside her bag, thanked him and left.

'Make sure you read the instructions,' the pharmacist called after her, 'they're in Ethiopian too, if you know that language, it's spoken in the Parrot Islands….' And then he looked at the young man while Mrs Mooshaber went out into the street.

XVIII

That evening Mrs Mooshaber went through her bedroom, the corridor and the larder picking up the traps she'd laid and taking them to the kitchen where she set them down on the ottoman. In several of the traps there were small dead mice with greasy whiskers and traces of white powder on their noses. For the time being, Mrs Mooshaber wanted to empty the traps into the ashes of the stove and then go back to the larder for the bacon, before once again filling the traps, and before finally taking another look at the little box with the black and yellow stripe, the warning notice in red and the skull and crossbones. Mrs Mooshaber wanted to do all these things that very evening, but at just that moment there was a knock on the front door. Mrs Mooshaber left the traps on the ottoman, while she hadn't yet had a chance to bring the plate of bacon from the larder. With the hint of a sigh she went to open the door.

'Mrs Natalia Mooshaber,' said a man in a leather coat as he took something out of his pocket.

Mrs Mooshaber opened her mouth in surprise.

'Yes,' the man in the leather coat went on as he put the licence back into his pocket, 'it is the police.' Mrs Mooshaber noticed that there was another policeman standing behind him.

'We haven't been to see you yet,' said the policemen, once they'd entered the kitchen and removed their hats. Mrs Mooshaber offered them chairs and said:

'The police have been here twice.'

'Twice,' echoed the policemen and setting down their hats on the table, 'but they were colleagues of ours. Perhaps you know why we are here, Mrs Mooshaber,' they went on, running their eyes over the kitchen and the traps on the ottoman. Mrs Mooshaber stood by the sideboard and nodded.

'Probably because of Wezr, Nabule and the stonemason,' she said in a dead voice, 'I mean my children and the stonemason who works by the cemetery gate.'

The police remained silent and continued to give the kitchen a visual going-over. The traps on the ottoman, the window of frosted glass, the stove and the clock. As they did so their faces remained completely inscrutable. Unlike the first and second deputations, this one wouldn't even raise a smile.

'I take it you're saying that Wezr has returned from prison,' said one of the policemen while he gave Mrs Mooshaber a searching look.

'He's not behind bars any more.' Mrs Mooshaber gave a nod of cold agreement. 'You always ask me about that. It's as if you don't believe me. Perhaps you think I'm lying.'

'No one is accusing you of that,' said the policeman and silence reigned awhile in the kitchen.

'Wezr is at large,' said the second policeman after a while, 'Wezr your son.' When Mrs Mooshaber nodded he asked:

'And he was here recently. What did he want from you?'

'He turned up with my daughter and the stonemason to collect some things they'd put under the sofa here.'

'That's of no importance,' said the second policeman with a wave of the hand, 'we need to know what he wanted from you, what he said to you. Kindly tell us.'

'He wanted me to climb into a well,' said Mrs Mooshaber.

'Mrs Mooshaber,' began the first policeman as he reached into his pocket and pulled out a notebook of some kind, 'if you don't mind we will be taking notes today. We have reason to think that it is necessary to do so.' He opened the notebook and took out a pencil before going on:

'So he wanted you to climb into a well?'

'He wanted me to climb into a well,' repeated Mrs Mooshaber in a cold voice. 'He would lower me down in a basket so that I could fetch the treasure inside. Then they'd lift me back up again.'

'And which well are we talking about?'

'Apparently there's one round here,' said Mrs Mooshaber from by the sideboard. 'I don't know of any myself. They told me that since I didn't believe what they were saying I should ask the students about it.'

'And which students are we talking about?' asked the policeman.

'Some students who were at my daughter Nabule's wedding, though when my daughter threw me out of the reception they got up and left too. But I felt so embarrassed that I hid from them in front of the building. They're decent fellows but I don't even know where they live, just that they rent rooms in a villa somewhere. I'm certain they don't know about any well. That's just one of Wezr's ruses, like everything else he does.'

'Mrs Mooshaber,' continued the policeman who was doing the writing in the notebook, 'allow me to ask you one question. Has Wezr ever been...in any way or at any time... a direct threat to your life?'

'Tell us,' added the other one, while a look of panic filled Mrs Mooshaber's eyes, 'whether you sometimes had the feeling that...to put it to you straight without any beating around the bush...he wanted to kill you?'

Silence took over the kitchen once again. The policemen gave Mrs Mooshaber a searching look while not a muscle moved in their faces. Mrs Mooshaber remained standing by the sideboard and strangely enough not a muscle moved in her face either. After a while Mrs Mooshaber broke the silence:

'The day before yesterday I went to to the cemetery to get the graves ready for All Souls Day.'

The policeman with the notebook made notes, while the other one went on asking questions and giving Mrs Mooshaber searching looks. Then the clock by the stove chimed half past eight and the policemen went quiet.

After a while the policeman who'd been taking notes resumed the inquiry. 'Mrs Mooshaber, we are not in fact here because of Wezr. We are not here because of a well that they wanted to throw you down. Nor are we here because of the grave of Therezia Bekenmoscht, where they changed the name in order to give you a fright. It doesn't even interest us that your daughter has got divorced. The main reason why we're here is something completely different.'

'And what might that be,' asked Mrs Mooshaber, who now took a seat of her own at the table, 'what...'

'What might that be...' repeated the policemen, 'what might that be. We came to see you in order to investigate.... how you live.'

Silence returned to the kitchen. Finally Mrs Mooshaber came to life in her chair.

'For God's sake,' she said coldly, 'you keep turning up to ask about that, don't you. In fact you've been here three times already. I've been living here for half a century and everyone here knows me. Kralec the caretaker, the Steinhägers, the Fabers, whose son fell to his death, their parents and even that doesn't stop you. Now you'll be wanting to ask me where I lived before this and about how I was a housekeeper for a few days and how I always wanted a kiosk and to sell things.'

'We already know all that.' For the first time the flicker of a smile appeared on the face of one policeman. 'These are things our colleagues have already ascertained. We are not going to ask you any more on that score. Not even when you were born, where you went to school, who your father and mother were, how you twice travelled from Fettgolding to Cat's Castle and how on the second occasion you witnessed a gamekeeper or a member of the domestic staff in one of the windows of the castle...' Mrs Mooshaber did nothing but hold her peace, eyes agog. She held her peace and stared at the policemen while sitting motionless in her chair. The policeman who had been taking notes then nodded and said:

'Yes, well, there you have it, the police have to keep abreast of every eventuality. That is what they are there for, Mrs Mooshaber. Perhaps you think that a bad thing, because it encroaches upon what is properly the domain of God. Or because it threatens people's privacy. However, a decent police force poses no such threat.'

'And in this particular case,' added the other policeman, the note-taker, 'it can only be in your interest for us to know a thing or two. The more we get to know, the better it is for you. That's why we're here. So then, you were born in Fettgolding in the foothills of the Black Forest and you visited Cat's Castle twice. You went to the Black Forest for kindling wood, but only as far as the edge, because you were afraid to go further. Your father worked on the ancestral estates of the Thalian princes. You left Fettgolding twice, once when you entered into employment as a housekeeper here in the Stadium district of the city, and the second time when you were married here to a coachman working at a brewery...'

'In the meantime you helped your father to look after rabbits and hens in Fettgolding,' said the second policeman, 'you planted trees in the forest and you cooked in the canteen for the children of the farm workers. You were perhaps twenty-five at that point. Mrs Mooshaber,' the policeman continued while he suddenly got up from his chair, 'just how old were you when you visited the Black Forest for the first time?'

'The Black Forest?' asked Mrs Mooshaber in surprise, 'how could I know? I would have been quite small then,' she went on while she shifted position a little in her chair, 'I would go there for kindling wood with my mother, the whole village used to go there, to get strawberries too. The Black Forest starts at Fettgolding, you see.'

'And the border of the forest extends for some twenty kilometers,' said the policeman speaking coldly and still set in a standing position, 'you were quite small, you say. You went with your mother for kindling wood or strawberries. How far did you go into the forest on those occasions?'

'How deeply in did I go?' said Mrs Mooshaber in amazement, 'How can I know that? All this was the best part of a century ago. And I've already told you that I stayed on the edge of it, nobody went any further into the forest. You could easily get lost in there.'

'Quite lost' agreed the policeman, 'the woods there are huge. And they are deep, dark and black and even...' here the policeman allowed a second smile to break through...'even full of ghosts. Mrs Mooshaber,' he said in a peremptory tone of voice, 'what did you come across in the forest on that occasion?'

'What did I come across?' Mrs Mooshaber blurted out, 'back then? When I first went there? When I was small?'

Mrs Mooshaber was sitting on the chair, her eyes fixed on the ground but looking at nothing in particular, as if she was deep in thought, deep in thought and shaking her head. 'What would I have come across?' she said with another shake, 'it's an age ago. How could I remember? Perhaps it was a dwarf or a ghost of some kind, how would I know?'

'What if it was...' began the second policeman, the one who was sitting and writing, '...a mouse?'

'A mouse?' asked Mrs Mooshaber in astonishment, 'a mouse? A mouse in the Black Forest? How would I ever know? I wonder whether there is such a thing as forest mice,' she went on, still shaking her head, 'but I wouldn't know the answer to that, would I?'

'Mrs Mooshaber,' began the other policeman, the one who was standing up, 'a mouse. And what if I were to tell you that it was a gigantic mouse?'

'You think it was some kind of rat?' asked Mrs Mooshaber.

'Even bigger than a rat,' the policeman said quickly, 'a mouse the size of a much bigger animal.'

'I just don't know any more,' said Mrs Mooshaber in a dead voice.

'I just don't know any more,' she repeated, 'maybe I did once read a fairy-tale in which something like that happened, but I'm not sure. Perhaps while I was at school in Fettgolding. But all I remember clearly from our reading there is a poem about a blind old lady. *Leaving church the blind old lady feels her way with stick unsteady. Forward with her stick she fumbles, Blind Old Lady often tumbles.*'

'Quite,' agreed the police, before the one who was standing up went on:

'All this concerns only your early childhood. But what about later? You were in the city for a few days working as a housekeeper before returning to your native village where you planted trees, helped at home and cooked in the canteen. During this time you never went to Cat's Castle any more. 'Do you know why it's called Cat's Castle?' he suddenly asked with features grown cold.

Mrs Mooshaber shook her head.

'It's a time-honoured legend. The legend was that there used to be plenty of mice there. Plenty of mice just like here where you live. Only there in the castle they didn't catch them with bacon but sent for the rodent exterminator. But this is a tall story of no importance, it means nothing... the poet Virgilius Cikl penned a poem about it. To cut a long story short, you never went to Cat's Castle a third time. Whether you went to the Black Forest at the time in question or not doesn't make any difference now. Just one question: did you ever see some huge beast at a later date, something in the shape of a mouse?'

'A huge beast in the shape of a mouse?' echoed Mrs Mooshaber in amazement as she shifted position a little in her chair, 'I really don't know any more. Where would I have seen something like that? I've never been to a menagerie, not even with the children or with my husband while he was still alive. He was a coachman in a brewery.'

'All right, we'll leave it there,' said the policeman who had been standing and now sat down again. 'We'll leave it there, that's enough for now. So you're getting your graves ready for All Souls Day.'

'I am,' said Mrs Mooshaber, 'I have to collect flowers and garlands. I also have to visit the Fabers' grave. And also go to the village of Drozdov by Etlichy. I may go there by bus this year. It'll be the first time in my life that I will have done that. I might be able to find the money for it this year.'

'Just so.' The policeman nodded as he took in the sofa and the mousetraps, 'Drozdov by Etlichy, that's where the grave of your husband is, the brewery coachman. He was killed in the short war that happened once upon a time.... And you are sure that he is buried there in that grave at Etlichy. You are sure that it is really your husband buried there?'

'For God's sake,' exclaimed Mrs Mooshaber as she rose from her chair, 'I must be hard of hearing because you just can't have said that. For God's sake,' she repeated as she got to her feet, but in a cooler and even a cold tone of voice, 'you're suggesting that my husband has not after all been buried in Drozdov by Etlichy and that I... for twenty years or however many it is, have been going to a grave where some marmot is buried.'

'Mrs Mooshaber,' said the note-taking policeman, 'you pointed out on the last occasion that when you got married you kept your maiden name. That it was your husband who took your name.'

'My husband took my name,' agreed Mrs Mooshaber drily as she resumed her seat, 'he became Medard Mooshaber.'

'And the name you had before you were married was...' inquired the other policeman.

'Mooshaber, for Christ's sake,' said Mrs Mooshaber, astounded. 'Natalia Mooshaber. Haven't I just explained to you that I kept my maiden name?'

'Indeed,' said the note-taking policeman. 'So it was your husband who had another name. What was he called before you were married?'

'Medard Kladrubsky, brewery coachman,' replied Mrs Mooshaber in frigid and dry tones which produced another round of silence in the kitchen.

Then the policemen resumed the conversation:

'Kladrubsky, that's a very strange name. A foreign name of some kind….'

Another bout of silence ensued.

'Very well then,' said the policemen, 'apart from housekeeping your desire was to sell things. From a kiosk.'

'From a kiosk,' repeated Mrs Mooshaber, 'to sell things from a kiosk. Ham, salad, lemonade. I've explained this already too. Everyone knows about it.'

'Exactly so,' agreed the policeman, 'but you were even saving up for that kiosk of yours.'

'I was saving up,' confirmed Mrs Mooshaber, 'I'd put by a guinea or two.'

'A guinea or two,' repeated the policeman, 'you'd saved this money when you were in Fettgolding for the second time and when you were planting trees, cooking for the children of the estate workers and perhaps you had a bit of money from the family in the Stadium district where you worked as a housekeeper. So why didn't you go on saving and then buy that kiosk?'

Silence flowed into the kitchen once again. Mrs Mooshaber rose from her chair once more and returned to the sideboard. She stood there with her eyes on the sofa and the traps keeping her silence.

'So why didn't you go on saving,' the policeman repeated after a while, 'why didn't you purchase that kiosk, since that was what you longed for? Did you change your mind, or was it perhaps more a case of...'

'I didn't change my mind,' Mrs Mooshaber finally answered with a shake of her head. 'It just wasn't meant to be. The guineas I'd put by for the kiosk, you see they... Wezr took them. He was seven years old at the time...'

The policemen sighed and there was another silent interval. Then the note-taker spoke:

'So you did go on saving even after you were married. And when Wezr took your money...did you stop saving then? Did you give up?'

'I didn't give up,' said Mrs Mooshaber, shaking her head, 'I went on saving. But only for a few years. When he was ten, the lad took my money once again. That was when I saw it was pointless. I'd never be able to save up for the kiosk. And even if I did, it wouldn't be any use. If I had a kiosk he'd destroy it or pilfer from it. I reckoned I'd be better off working for the Mother and Child Support Service.'

'So the kiosk idea led to nothing,' the policemen continued, shaking their heads and with serious expressions on their faces, 'it didn't come to fruition and nor did the plans to be a housekeeper. There's just this difference, namely that the kiosk plans went nowhere because Wezr took your money and the housekeeping plans went nowhere because working for this family in the Stadium district was too strenuous. You had to fetch grass for the livestock, feed goats and carry pails of water. So you took a job at the Mother and Child Support Service where no one got in your way and that worked out for you. And at the cemetery, where you have a job tending some of the graves...'

For a while the policemen looked down at the table in silence while Mrs Mooshaber matched their silence over by the sideboard. She said nothing while she went on looking at the traps on the sofa.

Finally one of the policemen, the note-taker, broke the silence.

'Mrs Mooshaber,' he began, 'you claim that you encountered nothing on that occasion when you were in the forest as a small girl. You claim that you are not aware of anything like that, that it was an age ago and you ask how you could possibly be expected to remember. You claim that you never saw any enormous mouse of monstrous proportions there. Imagine now,' he went on, 'that you were to meet a huge mouse that roared instead of squeaking.'

'For God's sake, I don't know what you mean,' said Mrs Mooshaber from the sideboard, speaking very curtly again and now showing signs of extreme impatience, 'I don't know. I've never seen such a beast. Not in the Black Forest and not even in a cage. I've told you a hundred times over that I've never even been to a zoo.'

'Just so,' agreed the policemen without hesitation, 'so just who was it that you came across in the Black Forest...just who was it that time...' said the policeman as he got up from the chair and narrowed his eyes, 'that time when you were little and went looking for kindling wood...whom did you meet there? I'm asking you, Mrs Mooshaber,' he repeated, raising his voice and adding renewed emphasis to his words as he stood by the chair, 'who it was that you met there all that time ago?'

From the sideboard came a sudden sigh as Mrs Mooshaber said in an expressionless voice:

'It could have been some young girl.'

The clock chimed beside the stove. It chimed nine o'clock to be precise, though no one noticed the fact. Not the policemen and not Mrs Mooshaber. The policemen were sitting down at the table now, one with his note-pad and the other one quietly surveying their hats on the table... Mrs Mooshaber was standing by the sideboard... silence was everywhere. After some time – it would be difficult to say how much – the note-taker spoke:

'You will soon have something to celebrate. Your birthday.'

'I will,' agreed Mrs Mooshaber, 'but I don't bother with such things. I never think about it. That's also something I explained last time.'

'When your husband was alive and the children were small, there might have been a time when you did bother about your birthday. They might have reminded you about it, perhaps they gave you something...'

'My husband might have done so,' said Mrs Mooshaber, shaking her head, 'perhaps a flower. He was a poor man. He worked as a coachman in a brewery. But the children – never. They weren't even at home. They were prowling around who knows where. We simply never did anything about my birthday or name-day.'

'And what will you do for the national holiday?' the policeman suddenly asked. 'That's coming up soon too.'

'I will go to where Mr Felsach the magnate lives,' explained Mrs Mooshaber, 'Mrs Knorring arranged a job for me there for three afternoons a week. I will be doing some supervision there.'

'Just a couple of questions more,' said one of the policemen. 'You say that you didn't celebrate your birthday. But did you at least observe national holidays? For example, did the family put things in the window to honour the birthday of our sovereign ruler the Dowager Princess? I mean flowers, candles, a goblet of wine, a cake...burning a little incense... the sort of thing that is done everywhere.'

'Everywhere,' agreed Mrs Mooshaber by the sideboard, her eyes still on the traps, 'even Mrs Eichen does it, and Mrs

Linpeck, Mrs Knorring – in fact everyone in this building does it too, the Fabers, the Steinhägers, the caretaker. But we didn't even do that. The things in the window would have been spilt, destroyed or thrown away by Wezr and Nabule, and any ritual involving burning would have been out of the question too.'

'So you won't even be putting anything in the window this year, not to mention burning incense' said the policeman.

'Not here,' said Mrs Mooshaber, shaking her head, 'I won't be here. As I told you I'm spending the national holiday where the magnate lives. They'll have things in the windows there, and they'll be burning incense too, the magnate's son and the housekeeper will see to it all. But not I...'

'There's an extraordinary level of interest in incense this year,' said one of the policemen, and Mrs Mooshaber had the impression that he was addressing his remark more to the other policeman than to her. 'It's in rather short supply and people are afraid that they won't be able to get their hands on any.'

'They're delivering bagfuls of it to all the pharmacies,' said the other policeman with a shake of the head, 'it looks like they'll have enough. But it's true that there's a rising tide of anxiety. A certain unease. So you will be spending the national holiday in honour of our sovereign the Dowager Princess at the Felsach residence,' he went on, turning to Mrs Mooshaber who stayed silent at the sideboard.

'I think we're just about done now,' said one of the policemen, 'We seem to have covered everything. So you don't remember any incident back in your youth involving the Black Forest and you encountered nothing strange later on.'

'I had no strange encounter,' said Mrs Mooshaber drily as she moved from the sideboard to the stove, 'I've told you everything I know.'

'Well,' said the policeman who was standing up, 'not everything and not exactly, Mrs Mooshaber. Not everything,' he repeated, 'and not exactly. But you don't need me to tell you that.'

'So now you're calling me a liar,' exclaimed Mrs Mooshaber.

'I'm not saying that you're lying,' said the policeman, 'no one is accusing you of that. I'm just saying that you are not saying everything and not saying it exactly. Tell me, Mrs Mooshaber,' the policeman continued as he eyed the stove, 'tell me one small thing. Our colleagues came to see you last time and that was the first occasion on which you remembered that you'd once been a housekeeper. You had never spoken about this on earlier occasions. You've been living in this house for half a century and never during those fifty years have you spoken about this, for example, to the caretaker, if we are to believe what you say. It first came back to you on that last occasion when our colleagues visited you. Of course this is just a small thing. However, I will now mention something more important. Mrs Mooshaber,' the policeman went on and for the second time – albeit after a long interval – a smile was creeping over his features, 'you did not meet any girl in the Black Forest when you were small. You met her when you were bigger. When you were already quite gown-up.'

'I've no idea,' said Mrs Mooshaber coldly from by the stove, 'if I remember rightly, I never said that I met her when I was small. What I know for sure is that I was after kindling wood.' The policemen nodded and remained silent.

'There is something else,' added the policeman who was always sitting and taking notes, 'one other thing. We mustn't forget that we have to write a few lines. A few lines to say that we dropped by. I have some paper and an envelope here in my pocket.'

'That's right,' agreed the other policeman as he sat down once again at the table, 'Mrs Mooshaber, we have to write a few lines and then pop them into a post box. It must be done in an official manner with a sealed envelope, indeed with a seal. You wouldn't happen to have some wax at hand or even a bit of candle, would you?'

'A bit of candle,' said Mrs Mooshaber from the stove, 'A bit of candle I do have. But not wax. You see I never write to anyone.'

'A bit of candle will be fine,' agreed the policeman as he set paper down on the table together with an envelope on which was affixed a stamp bearing the portrait of Albinus Rappelschlund. He then began to write something. Mrs Mooshaber opened the sideboard and placed a piece of nondescript yellow candle onto the table.

'That'll do,' said the other policeman, 'it's just a question of sealing the envelope properly. It's a requirement for a short official communication. You wouldn't happen to have a knife or some weight with which we can make a seal, would you?'

'I have a sealing-stick,' said Mrs Mooshaber, 'in the bedside table in my other room. I've never used it.'

'That'll do splendidly,' said the policemen, 'may we borrow it for a moment?'

Mrs Mooshaber went to the table in her bedroom and proceeded to remove a few rags, that terrible bonnet of hers with the bow, her spectacles and the sealing-stick. She took it to the policemen in the kitchen.

'Splendid,' they repeated. Then the one who was writing finished the letter, placed it in the envelope, closed it, flicked a lighter, heated up the candle and let the wax drip onto the envelope. Then he snuffed out the candle, took the sealing-stick and pressed it into the yellow wax firmly.

'That'll do the trick,' he said as he looked at the seal, 'you've been a great help to us, Mrs Mooshaber. You've saved us a lot of time, letting us do this here and not back in the office.'

'You've saved us a lot of time,' repeated the other policeman, 'please allow us to thank you and to return the candle and the sealing-stick.'

Both policemen were now really leaving their chairs, putting on their hats which had spent the whole time lying on the table, and saying:

'Please excuse us for the disturbance. You know that we've just been doing our duty. The junk by the front entrance should be gone by now, shouldn't it – especially that tub of lime.'

XIX

During the afternoon of 30th October the caretaker knocked at Mrs Mooshaber's door. Mrs Mooshaber, who was standing by the stove, heard the voice and knew whose it was. Outside the weather was cold and damp but the caretaker continued to sport a short cotton skirt and a bare neck – of course she was inside the house and had a roof over her head.

She entered Mrs Mooshaber's kitchen, sniffed the air and settled on the sofa. 'What a lovely smell,' she said as she sat and sniffed, 'and how pleasantly warm it is here.' Her eyes moved from the stove to the sideboard and the table before she went on without laughing:

'And all those things you have here, Mrs Mooshaber. Almonds, raisins, cream cheese. Vanilla, butter, eggs. Flour, milk, stirrer. It's just like being in a bakery when they're making coffee cake.'

'Making coffee cake,' repeated Mrs Mooshaber with a nod as she wiped her hands on her apron, 'I don't think I'll have enough left over for a coffee cake. I've got vanilla, almonds and raisins. Cream cheese and quite a bit of sugar too. The sugar is here' Mrs Mooshaber pointed at a small white bag on the table in a voice that was somehow distracted. 'It's a pity I won't be able to offer you any kolaches today. I won't be finished until late this evening.' Then she went to the stove and added:

'Once I...but you know it already...once I spent a whole day making kolaches like these.' There was silence until the caretaker broke it from her position on the sofa by saying:

'Mrs Mooshaber, you know, the Steinhägers may be coming. And Mrs Faber too. They are always asking me what you're doing and saying that they hardly ever see you around these days.'

'Hardly ever,' agreed Mrs Mooshaber from the stove as she began to mix the milk and cream cheese together in a bowl. 'They hardly ever see me. When I go outside I hardly ever meet them. I just never came across them, even that time when I went outside in those things of yours.'

'They wouldn't have recognised you in that outfit,' said the caretaker, laughing for the first time and reaching for her throat, 'they'd have thought it was some visitor leaving after coming to see you. An actress or the wife of a minister. You know, Mrs Mooshaber,' the caretaker continued, touching her throat again, 'I always find myself thinking about that villa and about how you will be supervising there. Crystal chandeliers, carpets, a fountain, just like I said it would be.'

'Just like you said,' confirmed Mrs Mooshaber, sounding a little distracted as she continued to mix the cream cheese and the milk together in her bowl. 'The pictures in their gold frames are just like in an art gallery, the marble staircase might have been in a church, the statues bearing lamps might have been in a ministry, except that the lamps in the villa have a red light. I sat down in this easy chair made of satin...' Mrs Mooshaber continued from by the stove, while she wiped her hands on her apron before leaning over to add firewood to the stove, 'an easy chair made of satin, but I could only make out part of the dining-room through doors made of frosted glass.'

'You'll see all of it tomorrow,' said the caretaker nodding, 'the dinner will take place there. After all, the housekeeper won't be serving dinner in the kitchen seeing that it will be your first day there, besides which it's a national holiday. But there's one thing I still can't get my head around. Can you guess what it is?' And when Mrs Mooshaber shook her head, the caretaker went on: 'It's that fountain. It stands in the middle of the entrance hall and water gushes out of it. How come the carpet doesn't end up getting soaked?'

'The carpet stays dry,' said Mrs Mooshaber, still mixing cream cheese and milk by the stove and now adding an egg to the concoction, 'the water runs back into a reservoir. It's like the one with a statue in the park, although instead of birds with beaks it's some kind of stem that's split at the end. It's just like the one in the park, only a smaller version.'

'As for that boy, that whatsisname...' laughed the caretaker, 'he throws black fish in there to frighten the housekeeper and locks her in the cellar when she goes there for something, that's really terrible.'

'Terrible,' agreed Mrs Mooshaber as she went to the table with her bowl of cream cheese, reached into the bag of sugar and threw a handful into the mixture, 'the water's boiling, I'll make you some tea. You say that dinner will be in the dining-room. I myself know how to set a table, as you know yourself I can lay a tablecloth, add the plates, I know how to do the whole works. I know how to set a table...and tomorrow I shall set the table there myself. That's what I will tell the lad and the housekeeper – I will do it myself. When I was a housekeeper for that family in the Stadium district I was feeding goats, fetching grass for livestock and carrying pails of water. I never set the table. Now I will be doing some supervising in the magnate's residence and I will set the table there.'

'Just you do it,' agreed the caretaker, 'it'll make up for the fact that you didn't set any tables when you were a housekeeper, and for the fact that when your Nabule got married you didn't lay the table either, seeing as it was part of the wedding package. You will do it tomorrow on the national holiday when you're at the magnate's. But Mrs Mooshaber,' the caretaker continued, 'when you go, you must wear that fur coat again. You must wear it because it will be your first day there and because it is a state occasion. And you must wear it because the housekeeper hasn't seen it on you and nor has that… that whatever he's called,' the caretaker continued with a laugh, 'that Oberon. Just think of what would happen if the widower said to the housekeeper what a beautiful fur coat you have and the housekeeper didn't see you wearing it. She'd wonder what on earth you'd done with it. You've got it somewhere in your other room…'

At that moment there was a knock on the front door and Mrs Mooshaber raised her head from her position by the stove. Curiously enough, she was perfectly calm.

'That'll just be the Steinhägers,' said the caretaker, 'please go on baking, I'll open the door myself.' And so the caretaker in her short cotton skirt and bare neck got up and went to open the front door. Soon after Mrs Faber entered the kitchen with the Steinhägers.

'I hope we're not disturbing you?' inquired Mr Steinhäger in a very agitated manner, an anxious look on his face as he surveyed the table, 'I can see that Mrs Mooshaber is busy baking.'

'You are not disturbing me at all,' said Mrs Mooshaber, 'please take a seat. It's a pity that the kolaches will not be ready until late in the evening, otherwise I would be able to offer you some. As it is, I can at least offer you tea.'

Ever uneasy, the Steinhägers set themselves anxiously down on the ottoman. The caretaker joined them there, while Mrs Faber sat on a chair at the table. She sat there stiff and reserved while she looked straight ahead and remained silent.

'Is something the matter?' the caretaker asked.

'Nothing's actually happening,' said Mr Steinhäger, sounding tense and uneasy, 'but there is a strange atmosphere outside. Perhaps there's something happening after all. Crowds have gathered in Anna Maria the Blessed Square by the cemetery and in Rappelschlund Square too. We've just come from there.'

'Maybe something's really happening out there,' said Mrs Steinhäger, full of apprehension. 'There's a crowd at the crossroads by the *Sunflower* department store too, though it's beginning to break up. Look at all the things you've got here, Mrs Mooshaber,' she continued, looking uneasily at the table and the sideboard, 'there's vanilla, butter, almonds, eggs and raisins...'

'And there's sugar here in this bag on the table,' said the caretaker, 'what are all these demonstrations about?'

'They're not demonstrations,' said Mr Steinhäger, shaking his head, 'it's just those crowds gathering and the police are doing nothing to disperse them.'

'There aren't even any police on the streets,' added Mrs Steinhäger, still full of concern, 'there's not a single uniform to be seen. Since you're baking cakes, Mrs Mooshaber, does this mean that you will put some things in the window this year? Will you burn some incense this time?'

'She'll be burning incense all right,' the caretaker put in, 'but not here. The thing is that Mrs Mooshaber is taking the kolaches with her tomorrow to the villa of a widower. She will put things in the window and burn incense while she's there.'

'Their housekeeper will do that with the young lad,' said Mrs Mooshaber pensively as she went to the sideboard to collect the mugs, 'at least it means the lad won't go missing before mealtime.'

'Mrs Mooshaber will be beginning her duties tomorrow in the widower's villa,' added the caretaker from the sofa, 'she will be starting as a supervisor. In a magnate's villa on three afternoons of each week. Tomorrow being the national holiday, there will be a festive dinner there in honour of our ruler the Dowager Princess at the same time...Has the widower already taken off?' she inquired.

'Certainly,' said Mrs Mooshaber as she poured tea into the mugs on the stove, 'he's already told me that he won't be there for the holiday.'

'When all's said and done,' the caretaker put in from the sofa, 'the widower is a Moon Magnate. He's up there more than he's down here. He's doing business in radios, casette recorders and lamps, not to mention heating systems and televisions. He's a wealthy man, I tell you. People on the Moon need heating, because otherwise they'd freeze to death. And they need their tapes, televisions and wirelesses, because it's impossible to survive up there without them.'

Mrs Mooshaber cleared a bit of space on the table by pushing the butter, vanilla, almonds and raisins to one side and brought over four mugs of tea. 'Here we are,' she said, 'the tea's already got some sugar in it, but if you want some more help yourself to the bag of sugar. In the meantime, I'll be getting on with the dough,' she added,' pointing at the sideboard.

The Steinhägers sipped some tea, as did the caretaker and in the end even Mrs Faber. She sat on the chair, forever stiff and aloof, not a muscle moving as she fixed her attention steadfastly in front of her somewhere in the direction of the door to the other room.

'And you say they live in a villa?' Mrs Steinhäger inquired in a manner at once distressed and discomposed. Mrs Mooshaber nodded.

'They live in a villa. At 6, Spring Street,' explained the caretaker from the sofa as she sweetened her tea with a little sugar from the bag, 'it's in the Blauental villa colony just a short distance from here. If you go out the back of this building it's right there. The villa has crystal chandeliers, carpets and pictures in gold frames just like in an art gallery. There's a marble staircase just like in a church, and beneath it there are statues holding lamps just like inside a ministry, except that the light from these is red. But never mind all that,' the caretaker went on as she waved her hand and fiddled with her throat, 'just think of the fact that right in the middle of the entrance hall there's a fountain with red fish swimming around in it.'

'There's a tank underneath,' explained Mrs Mooshaber by the sideboard while she worked on the flour and milk in a bowl....'it's a little pool, really. Water falls back into the pool from a sort of split stem, it's like a smaller version of the statue in the park.'

'And another thing' began the caretaker as she took a sip of tea, 'Mrs Mooshaber was sitting in the entrance hall in a satin chair and could see part of the dining-room through frosted glass doors. She will have dinner tomorrow in that dining-room and will see it all. I was right that it's just like being in the Ritz there. Aren't you going to set the table in that dining-room all by yourself, Mrs Mooshaber?'

'All by myself', confirmed Mrs Mooshaber from the sideboard as she poured some flour into a bowl. 'When I was sitting in the easy chair made from satin....'

'When she was sitting in that easy chair made of satin,' intervened the caretaker, taking up the tale from the sofa as she sipped more tea, 'the widower asked her what she wanted to drink and brought her some liqueur on a silver tray. You know it's a strange thing,' she suddenly went on while she turned to the Steinhägers, 'it's very strange that as you say there are so many people outside all over the place, while the police are nowhere. They're not actually demonstrating and so the police do not intervene.'

'I am afraid that something is about to happen,' said Mrs Steinhäger in her anxious and low-spirited way, 'apparently they're not demonstrating, just gathering around, and there's not a sign of the police on the streets or at the crossroads.'

'If you ask me,' said Mr Steinhäger, shaking his head, 'there's more in this than meets the eye.'

The Steinhägers sipped some tea again while they went on looking pictures of concern. Mrs Faber also drank tea in her stiff and aloof position, not a muscle of her face moving as she kept her eyes fixed on the door of the bedroom. Meanwhile Mrs Mooshaber went on working at the bowl, adding flour, pouring in milk and breaking eggs. Then the clock by the stove chimed half past three and Mrs Mooshaber said:

'The widowed magnate opened the door for me when I called.'

'The widower,' began the caretaker, jumping into the conversation while twiddling in the area of her throat, 'has lightish hair, now grey at the edges, and is quite tanned, probably from being on the Moon where he's always going, in fact he's there right now, and he's fifty years old. The arrival of Mrs Mooshaber and the banquet tomorrow will both take place without him. The housekeeper will be there together with that whatisname, that Oberon boy,' she laughed at this point, 'and there will also be the students who live there. Their families are friends of the magnate, but they only get home in the evening. But that Oberon,' she went on with another laugh, 'he's a proper little terror. Just imagine it, he's got black hair, dark eyes and long nails, the ones on his little fingers even curl, and he's very picky about his food. He doesn't do any homework because he already knows all there is to know, but what's worse than that is the mischief he gets up to. He runs away from home. He's not allowed out now, not even into the garden, in any case autumn's arrived and it's all gone to seed out there, I mean to say, Mrs Mooshaber, what could he do there? He takes off in this black coat of his and spends whole afternoons wandering wherever.'

'He takes off in this black coat of his and goes wandering,' repeated Mrs Mooshaber in a reflective tone of voice as she began preparing the doughy mixture on the sideboard, 'he goes wandering off. The Pinetreestal and Elizabethan districts...' Mrs Mooshaber poured some milk into the dough and added a few other things which were further back in the depths of the sideboard and so couldn't be seen very well, 'The area of the Stadium and of Kerke...'

'All the way to Kerke, just think about that,' said the caretaker from the sofa, 'but that's just the beginning. And there's worse to come. Tell us what he does to the housekeeper, Mrs Mooshaber,' she continued with a chuckle. You'd be amazed.'

'Well then, as for what he does to the housekeeper,' began Mrs Mooshaber with a nod from next to the sideboard while she kept preparing her dough, 'he plays nasty tricks on her, he terrifies her. He throws this spooky-looking black fish into the fountain where the other fish are, just to alarm the housekeeper, and he locks her in the cellar.'

'That's terrible,' said Mrs Steinhäger, sounding aghast, while Mr Steinhäger shook his head and said: 'Terrible. And he's the one you have to supervise, Mrs Mooshaber?'

'He's the one Mrs Mooshaber has to supervise,' the caretaker confirmed as she touched her bare throat, 'the widower himself gave Mrs Mooshaber some tips. She should go over his scientific interests with him and she can keep an eye on him from the next room if she keeps the door open.'

'I can keep an eye from the hall too,' said Mrs Mooshaber from the sideboard as she added a pinch of salt to the dough, 'he can't slip through my fingers while I'm in the hall either.'

'And you can put the fear of God into him,' chuckled the caretaker as she took a sip of tea, 'anyway Mrs Mooshaber will sort him out. Mrs Mooshaber could sort the devil out. But Mrs Mooshaber doesn't really know him.'

'I don't know him,' agreed Mrs Mooshaber, sounding as if she was absorbed in thought, while she added to her mixture yet more things taken from the depths of the sideboard where they could not be very clearly seen, 'I don't know him yet, I really don't.'

'Mrs Mooshaber has only heard about all this from the widower and from Mrs Knorring,' explained the caretaker from the sofa, 'the time when she went to see the widower the boy had gone to some circus performance. Mrs Mooshaber didn't even get to see their housekeeper. Truth be told, the housekeeper cannot cope with the lad and Mrs Mooshaber will be the one to mind him. Mrs Mooshaber will be his governess. But you've hardly touched a drop,' the caretaker said to Mrs Faber and the Steinhägers, 'drink your tea.'

'Do drink up,' said Mrs Mooshaber, still lost in her own thoughts as she wiped her hands on her apron and went to

the stove to add a bit of firewood, 'it's damp and cold out there today.'

'But all snug and warm in here,' laughed the caretaker, 'it's always very homely here in your kitchen, and so nice to sit down on the sofa here. And on top of that there's such a sweet aroma all round here today,' she went on as once again she surveyed the vanilla, the butter, the raisins, the almonds and the white bag of sugar on the table... and then she even cast her eyes in the direction of the sideboard where the dough was and, as she now noticed, a few other things which had come from the depths of the sideboard where they couldn't be very clearly seen. Furthermore she cast her eyes upon the stove where a bowl of cream cheese had been placed and she fingered her throat again. 'Mrs Mooshaber loves baking,' she went on as she reached for her throat, 'but it must have cost you money, these kolaches will be so good they could have come from the most exclusive bakery. Just look at what you've got behind the dough there on the sideboard...' The caretaker turned to the Steinhägers and Mrs Faber and the uneasy Steinhägers gave anxious nods. Mrs Faber, on the other hand, remained sitting in a stiff and aloof manner, not a muscle in her face so much as twitching as she looked ahead of her towards the door to Mrs Mooshaber's bedroom.

'That tub of lime has been here an eternity,' observed Mrs Mooshaber from the sideboard where she was now kneading the dough, 'goodness knows what would happen if someone were to fall into it.'

'The work out there is really coming to an end,' the caretaker responded, 'the scaffolding has almost been taken down. All that remains are those props in front of the window in your bedroom. But after the national holiday they will also disappear, together with the bricks, the wheelbarrow and the tub of lime outside your door. If someone fell in,' the caretaker went on, 'I really don't know what would happen to him. Maybe he'd just receive a whitewashing, or maybe he'd dissolve in it.'

'He wouldn't dissolve,' insisted Mr Steinhäger, 'even so he'd be soaked through and might possibly drown. I bumped into a couple of men in the entrance the other day,' Mr Steinhäger continued uneasily, 'they weren't by any chance policemen, were they?'

'They were coming to see me,' explained Mrs Mooshaber at the sideboard, while working the dough on a cutting board, 'it was their third time here.'

'May I ask you something?' the caretaker blurted out, touching her throat again, 'May I ask you what they wanted this time? Did they come here again to ask you where you were born and who your parents were and where you went to school and about Cat's Castle?'

'It was mainly about something else the third time,' explained Mrs Mooshaber, shaking her head, 'about when I went to the Black Forest. And whether something happened to me there when I was little. And whether I might have had some strange encounter there. With a giant mouse or a lion, or whatever...'

'A lion in the forest? Whatever next!' The caretaker rocked with laughter on the ottoman and even the Steinhägers had to join in the rocking since they were seated next to her. 'Fancy being asked that, as if there were any lions in the forest. Lions are to be found only in deserts, aren't they.'

'Lions are found in deserts and jungles,' said Mr Steinhäger, 'but not in our neck of the woods, except for caged ones in a zoo.'

'They also came to take a look at the way I live,' said Mrs Mooshaber while she went on kneading on her cutting board, 'this is the third time they've come to see how I live. 'They wanted to know how long I'd been living here. I told them it must be getting on for a century and that everyone here has known me for at least fifty years.' They also told me some legend about Cat's Castle and why it had that name. They said there had been hordes of mice there and that they used to have a ratcatcher on call to sort them out. They also asked me whether I visit my husband's grave in Etlichy. Now and again they dropped in a question about Wezr, as if they didn't really believe me when I said that he'd come back from prison, and this time round they even asked me why I'd never had a kiosk when it was something I'd dreamed of having. I had to tell them that Wezr always made off with my savings. Finally,' said Mrs Mooshaber, still working on the dough, 'finally they wrote their reports and wanted me to provide them with some wax. I gave them a candle.'

'Did they have to seal the reports?' asked Mr Steinhäger. Mrs Mooshaber nodded.

'In all likelihood they did,' laughed the caretaker. 'They're the police.'

'I gave them a sealing stick from the bedside table in my bedroom,' explained Mrs Mooshaber from the sideboard, after which she went to the table for vanilla and almonds.

'How decent the police are whenever they're visiting you,' the caretaker observed as she drank her tea, 'always so polite, Mrs Mooshaber, aren't they. They can't apologise too much for disturbing you.'

'They can't apologise too much,' agreed Mrs Mooshaber in a thoughtful tone while she covered the dough with a tea-towel in order to make it rise. Then she wiped her hands on her apron and sat down in a chair for a moment.

There was a short spell of silence in the kitchen. Then the clock by the stove struck four and at the same time the sound of knocking could be heard at the front entrance.

Mrs Mooshaber got to her feet, still keeping her calm.

'Whoever could that be?' she asked in a toneless voice.

'You stay here,' said the caretaker, 'I'll open the door myself.' And for the second time she got up from the sofa and went out into the corridor in order to open the door.

Suddenly there was the sound of voices in the corridor, voices which had never yet been heard in this corridor, and before you could say Jack Robinson three visitors had arrived in the kitchen. There was a slender and tallish woman with features at once delicate and prim, carrying some large black folder containing sheets of music. She was followed inside by two men.

'We must be disturbing you,' said the slender and tallish woman with the black folder as she surveyed the kitchen around her, 'I can see that you have guests.'

'They are tenants of the building here,' said Mrs Mooshaber, who could hardly believe her own eyes, 'this is the Steinhägers and this is Mrs Faber, perhaps you still remember them from the funeral... may I introduce Mrs Knorring from the Mother and Child Support Service and Messrs Smirsch and Landl. I'll just nip into the other room for a chair,' said Mrs Mooshaber, still trying to come to terms with what she could see before her.

The Steinhägers stood up from the sofa and bowed while Mrs Faber, who remained stiff and aloof sitting in her chair, tore her eyes away from the door and gave a nod. The Steinhägers, and perhaps even Mrs Faber, wanted to take their leave but Mrs Knorring shook her head.

'There's no need to disturb you,' she said, 'we're just dropping in for a moment. We were just coming back from choir practice. We had to take the crossing by the *Sunflower* department store and so we popped in here.'

In the meantime Mrs Mooshaber had brought some chairs from the other room and Mrs Knorring unbuttoned her coat before sitting down with the sheets of music clutched to her chest. In response Mr Smirsch and Mr Landl sat down too. Once again Mrs Knorring motioned the Steinhägers to sit down and the tense, uneasy couple resumed their seats on the sofa next to the caretaker.

'We popped in to see you,' began Mrs Knorring as she scanned the table, the sideboard and the stove, 'in order to tell you that the Mother and Child Support Service has already completed its move. We are now in a single-storey building in the Kerke district, the address of which I gave you the other day. Our former Mother and Child Support Centre is being used at this very moment as a prison. My former office and that of Messrs Rott and Kefr nearby, not to mention the waiting-rooms and corridors, and even the upper floor, are all part of this prison now and there are already people inside it. They didn't need to make any structural changes, they had the bars on the windows already, that was the reason they wanted the building in the first place. Perhaps,' Mrs Knorring went on as she looked around her, 'they will requisition some other places too. There's a refuge that belongs to the church consistory in a quiet side street. It's another place that has barred windows on the ground floor. But I do believe,' Mrs Knorring went on as she looked at the table and the sideboard, 'that Mrs Mooshaber is baking. Kolaches for the morrow. And how lovely their fragrance.'

'They're kolaches for tomorrow,' Mrs Mooshaber confirmed from the sideboard as she removed the cloth from the dough, 'It's such a pity that I cannot offer you any. It will be evening before I can finish baking. I've been doing it all day, adding vanilla, raisins, almonds and so on...'

'She's been baking kolaches all day,' echoed the caretaker from the sofa as she reached for her throat, 'she's already spent the whole day baking kolaches once before. But at least she will offer you some tea.'

While Mrs Mooshaber nodded and moved from the dough she'd uncovered to the sideboard and stove, the caretaker continued:

'The thing is that tomorrow in the evening Mrs Mooshaber will take her kolaches to the widower's residence. Just look at all the things she has here, there's butter as well. And I saw her put vanilla and almonds into them a moment ago over there on the sideboard. And besides, over there behind the dough she has even more things in bags and boxes. And there's sugar in this bag on the table,' she explained, indicating where it was.

'I am sure the kolaches will be very good,' said Mrs Knorring as she glanced at the sideboard and the table and shifted her score, which never left her hands, from one hand to the other, 'it's a pity that Mr Felsach won't be at home, seeing that he's already on the Moon. Only his boy and the housekeeper will be at home. Perhaps the students will be there too. I am curious,' she went on, while she glanced at Mrs Faber whose stiff and aloof stance was unyielding, and who was staring straight ahead again without moving a muscle, and also glanced at the Steinhägers, still nursing their disquiet and distress on the sofa next to the caretaker, 'I am curious to know how tomorrow's national holiday will turn out. There's so much discontent among the people...' she continued, now looking at Mr Smirsch, who kept mum as did Mr Landl, doing no more than look wordlessly around.

'There are crowds of people in Anna Maria the Blessed Square and in Rappelschlund Square,' said Mr Steinhäger uneasily.

'There's also some at the crossroads outside the *Sunflower* department store,' added Mrs Steinhäger with her own version of the unease that distressed them both, 'but as we went by they were already starting to disperse.'

'They're back again,' said Mrs Knorring thoughtfully as she looked straight ahead, 'they're at the State Opera House, in Darlinger Avenue and outside the *Tetrabiblos* theatre. They're in front of the Academy of Music and the Protestant chapel in Giuseppe Verdi Street and they're right outside Saint Quido of Fontgolland's Cathedral. They're also in front of the editorial offices of *Our Blooming Homeland*. What do you say to that?' Mrs Knorring went on, turning to Mr Smirsch, 'to what we've just seen outside the editorial offices of *Our Blooming Homeland*, Mr Smirsch...

'I don't know what I could tell you, Madam,' Mr Smirsch replied, shrugging his shoulders, 'there are always crowds of people in that place. They exchange stamps or talk about sport, organ transplants, the sky above...and just before the national holiday in honour of the princess there are always lots of people in the streets and squares, that's the way it's been for several decades now.'

'But everything is different this time,' said Mrs Knorring drily, as she shifted sheets of music between hands and kept her eyes on the clock by the stove, 'people are not exchanging stamps outside *Our Blooming Homeland* today. They're not discussing the different kinds of seaweed this time. There are more people everywhere today than in previous years and there's a very tense atmosphere in the city. Even the incense is in shorter supply this year than at other times.'

'There really is very little around,' echoed Mr Steinhäger uneasily, 'but they say that they'll stock up the pharmacies with sackfuls of it today.'

'My husband went to buy incense yesterday,' said the uneasy Mrs Steinhäger, 'and the pharmacist gave him only a quarter of a kilo. He said the man told him to come back today to see if there was any more. But there's enough wine for everyone.'

'Enough wine there is,' agreed Mrs Knorring, holding her score against her bosom, 'but it's true that the incense is in short supply. So you will be off to Mr Felsach tomorrow then, Mrs Mooshaber. You must be pleased...'

'I'm off tomorrow,' echoed Mrs Mooshaber in a pensive voice from the stove, while she poured the tea into three mugs.

'She's off tomorrow,' repeated the caretaker from the sofa, 'there will be an evening meal in the dining-room there. They will celebrate the arrival of Mrs Mooshaber and at the same time the national holiday in honour of the Princess. Mrs Mooshaber herself will be setting the table and the housekeeper and Oberon will burn incense together and place things in the windows, so at least he won't sneak off. The magnate widower,' continued the caretaker as she reached for her throat, 'said that the young man is not allowed out of the house on the national holiday. Isn't that what the magnate said, Mrs Mooshaber?' Mrs Mooshaber responded with a nod and put more mugs of tea onto the table.

'He's not allowed out, not even to the garden, especially before the meal,' said Mrs Mooshaber pensively while she transferred raisins from table to sideboard in order to make more room. Then she went on: 'Help yourself, Mrs Knorring and you too, gentlemen. If the tea's not sweet enough there's sugar in the bag.'

'And how are things with you, Mrs Faber?' Mrs Knorring inquired as she lifted her head.

Mrs Faber simply shrugged her shoulders and nodded, still a stiff and aloof fixture in the room, with not so much as a twitch of the muscles in her face. The only change was that she now took a mug and drank a little while the Steinhägers on the sofa offered light nods while they too sipped their tea.

'They are taking down the scaffolding,' said the caretaker, 'the work's already finished. After the holiday they will also take away the bricks, the wheelbarrow and the tub of lime outside Mrs Mooshaber's door. If soemone fell in that tub, they'd be soaked to the skin. Perhaps they'd even drown.'

'And go blind into the bargain', Mr Smirsch put in and drank his tea.

'There will be more work for you now, Mrs Mooshaber,' said Mrs Knorring while she brought a cup of tea to her lips with a hand that had been briefly freed from the task of holding the score, 'there'll be more work when you start going to the Felsach residence, but I'm sure you'll be able to cope.'

'Mrs Mooshaber will manage all right,' said the caretaker on the sofa, 'she needn't spend so much time in the cemetery now that winter's coming on, just do the All Souls, isn't that so, Mrs Mooshaber, you'll be collecting garlands and branches of spruce...'

'I've already collected them,' said Mrs Mooshaber as she tried to create some order on the sideboard from all the things surrounding her dish of dough, 'I've already done so and have prepared the graves. I've put the garlands and branches there already. There are only a few days left before All Souls. Only unfortunately I don't know...,' she went on as she continued to search for order around the dish on the sideboard, 'I don't know whether I will get to Drozdov by Etlichy at all this year. My husband's grave is there in the cemetery at Drozdov. He was a coachman working for the brewery.' And back at the sideboard Mrs Mooshaber proceeded to add a bit of flour to her chopping board before slicing off a segment of the dough and starting to make the kolaches.

'I can well believe that this will take you until the evening,' said Mr Smirsch as he looked at the sideboard, 'it's some task to make all those kolaches.'

'I can believe it too,' agreed Mr Landl, 'it's a lot of work, especially when you are only now chopping up the dough.'

'And adding so many different ingredients,' put in Mrs Knorring, 'you have a veritable sweet factory on the sideboard. But it's a bit dark over there and I can't make out all the things you're using, Mrs Mooshaber. Listen here, Mrs Mooshaber,' Mrs Knorring suddenly added while keeping her eyes on the Steinhägers, the caretaker and Mrs Faber, 'listen here, there's something I want to ask you. Do you by any chance know...' at this point Mrs Knorring rummaged through the sheets in her hands, 'do you happen to know a certain Mary Capricorn?'

The caretaker gave a start and a shriek on the sofa while Mrs Mooshaber interrupted her baking preparations at the sideboard.

'Mary Capri,' she repeated the name in astonishment, 'Mary Capri?'

'Mary Capricorn,' repeated Mrs Knorring and Mr Smirsch followed up with a 'Mary Capricorn' of his own and so Mr Landl had to repeat the name too.

'We must have asked Mrs Mooshaber this a hundred times over,' laughed the caretaker. 'I asked her the same thing once myself, it must have been some time back, that time when Nabule was getting married. And then there was that Mrs Eichenkranz asking you the same thing in the cemetery and also Mrs Linpeck, when we were in the metro at Cemetery station. Everyone asks about Mary Capricorn.'

'Our caretaker Mrs Kralec is quite right,' said Mrs Mooshaber as she continued to look in astonishment as did Mrs Knorring and Messrs Smirsch and Landl, 'there's no end to the way everyone is asking about Mary Capricorn. But I know nothing at all about her and I have absolutely no acquaintaince with her. All I know is that there is someone called Mary Capricorn and that she's a housekeeper somewhere – I think Mrs Linpeck told me that – besides that I don't know a thing. Do you know any more details about her, Mrs Knorring?'

'I know as little as you do,' said Mrs Knorring as she scanned her sheets, 'I know as little as do Messrs Smirsch and Landl. Now and then I hear someone mention her, but nothing more. No one knows her,' Mrs Knorring continued, shaking her head and looking fixedly into empty space, 'how very strange it all is. It would be understandable if someone knew a few more details, but the fact is that it doesn't matter whom you speak to, they never know any more than we do. When none of you knows anything either,' Mrs Knorring continued, her attention now fixed on the caretaker, 'and when not even Mrs Eichenkranz and Mrs Linpeck know anything, then it becomes odder still. You're certainly putting enough sugar into those kolaches,' she went on, looking at the sideboard where Mrs Mooshaber had resumed her baking.

'I am putting enough sugar in,' Mrs Mooshaber assured her with a nod, 'and also cream cheese. I really enjoy baking. But as you know I can only do it now and again. Most of the time I just eat potatoes and corn mash.'

'Now you will be eating ham and salad,' laughed the caretaker, 'and drinking wine and lemonade. Nothing will go badly for you now that you're going to supervise at the widower's.'

'Wine, lemonade, ham and salad,' echoed Mrs Mooshaber as once again she slightly shifted the stuff around the dish on the sideboard and added a little extra from something that had been positioned quite far away and hitherto out of sight, 'you could be right. But in any case I have never been able to work anything out where that Mary Capri is concerned. Who is she? A housekeeper, but what else? I really don't know her at all.'

'Don't bother yourself about it,' laughed the caretaker, 'you know what I said to you once. If you were to try to think about everybody it would fill your head to bursting, it just can't be done. But the widower's boy, that Oblong fellow,' she continued with a chuckle, 'he'll be a right terror and you haven't told us all that you know about him, Mrs Mooshaber.

He has long black hair, black eyes, long nails, wears a black coat, keeps running away from home and is so picky about his food…' the caretaker looked at the sideboard, where a small coloured box had suddenly manifested itself…'he's disobedient, he's as sulky as he's stubborn, he plays one trick after another on the housekeeper…when you think of what he does to her,' the caretaker went on, turning to Mrs Knorring and Messrs Smirsch and Landl, 'he puts this gruesome great black fish into the fountain and he locks her in the cellar. But Mrs Mooshaber…' the caretaker now turned to Mrs Mooshaber who was moulding some more kolaches on the sideboard, 'last time you said that there's something else he does. You said that when he's really annoyed he even pushes away the platter of food the housekeeper serves up for him and refuses to eat.'

'He shoves his plate to one side and won't eat,' confirmed Mrs Mooshaber as she moved to the stove in order to examine the cream cheese, 'he won't eat any of the seaweed specialities that the housekeeper gives him of an evening; he just sulks.'

'But then sometimes,' the caretaker said as she continued to chuckle and again threw a look at the little coloured box on the sideboard, which was now pretty much in evidence, 'sometimes he grabs hold of the whole plate and bangs it on the table. It drives the housekeeper out of her mind when he does that.'

'He drives her out of her mind,' repeated Mrs Mooshaber in a reflective voice, 'the thing was that she'd just scolded him about his running away. So after that she preferred not to scold him at all. He must be very disobedient and he must drive her to distraction. He's one who'll like as not end up in the school for troublemakers and then the house of correction. His father the magnate,' she said, still working on the kolaches at the sideboard, 'is afraid of what will happen to him. He could become a labourer, an unskilled pair of hands like as not hired for the day, before he ends up behind bars. But it's not as if I really know him, seeing that I haven't yet set eyes upon the young man.'

'I'm sure you will find your way around him,' affirmed Mrs Knorring as she consulted her notes, 'you will win his respect. Talk to him mainly about his scientific interests. Well then,' she went on as she revisited her sheets of music, 'the soprano part is really the most difficult of all. This piece...' Mrs Knorring continued as she glanced around...'is really demanding.'

'And pray what do you have to study?' inquired Mr Steinhäger, still uneasy and still as dispirited as his wife, 'a song of some kind?'

'A requiem,' explained Mrs Knorring, 'the biggest requiem ever to have been played here. A choir of two thousand will sing and three thousand musicians will play and the numbers keep growing. These gentlemen here,' she went on, indicating Mr Smirsch and Mr Landl, 'will be playing the horn.'

'Horns or to be precise French horns,' added Mr Smirsch as he took a sip of tea, 'it is indeed very demanding. The one advantage we have is that as an orchestra we don't need to know everything by heart. But the singers do. Madam, who is singing soprano, must know everything by heart as she cannot look at any notes during the performance and the same goes for the tenors and basses. The basses, Madam,' Mr Smirsch went on, 'turning to Mrs Knorring, surely have the best of it. Their part is the easiest.'

'You could be right,' said Mrs Knorring as she drank some tea, 'by the way, it is really strange what is happening. There is an air of tension in the city, as I said the people are showing their discontent, in the squares, at the offices of *Our Blooming Homeland*, at the crossroads nearby, in front of the opera house and the Terabiblos theatre and outside the Protestant chapel in Giuseppe Verdi Street. It's the same outside the Academy of Music and St Quido of Fontgolland's Cathedral. It all fills me with foreboding. A strange sense of foreboding.' Mrs Knorring lifted her head and looked at Mrs Faber, who remained stiff and aloof, sitting and looking straight ahead without so much as a twitch in her face, 'I've had such a sense of foreboding before, for instance the time when Mrs Mooshaber was with us concerning the Eichenkranz and Linpeck cases. I had such a sense of foreboding then,' Mrs Knorring continued as she surveyed the sideboard where Mrs Mooshaber was making kolaches, 'but today, on the eve of the national holiday in honour of the Princess our Sovereign, it is more pronounced. What we saw outside *Our Blooming Homeland*, Mr Smirsch, is not, as I said to you, something we are used to. What is going on in the squares and streets, in front of the opera house and the Academy of Music and St Quido of Fontgolland's Cathedral is not normal either. Mr Rott is right when he says that we must confront a problem head on and not always hide from it. Mr Rott has not come to work today. He excused himself saying that he was going to buy a rifle. Still, it seems that Mr Kefr has already been trained in our work by Mr Rott. He is well-versed in what we do and can take care of himself.'

'All I am trying to say, Madam,' Mr Smirsch put in as he glanced at Mrs Mooshaber, who was still preparing kolaches on the sideboard, 'all I am saying is that there are certain things I do not like to hear. He always goes too far in what he says and I don't like that in the home, let alone in the office. Once I said that it creates a lot of ill feeling.'

'And I've already given you my take on the matter,' added Mrs Knorring with a shake of the head as she glanced at the Steinhägers and the caretaker, 'what ill feeling can it create? People are in the city of their own free will today and they know how everything is getting worse and I have my hunches about that. Of course Mr Felsach is right to want his son to be at home tomorrow,' Mrs Knorring said to Mrs Mooshaber at her sideboard, 'he wants to be sure while he's on the Moon that here on Earth the lad's all right. He wants to be sure that the boy stays at home and doesn't get mixed up in anything. He's still too small to go out alone on the streets, so let him stay at home helping with the incense and putting things in the windows. Mrs Mooshaber will see to it all. Where you live, Mr Smirsch,' Mrs Knorring continued in dry tones, 'I am sure that your family puts flowers, candles, goblets of wine and kolaches in the windows to celebrate the national holiday in honour of our Princess, just as all the other families do, isn't that so? Or do you save all that for celebrating the national holiday in honour of Mr Rappelschlund?'

'Oh no,' replied Mr Smirsch, shaking his head, 'nothing like that.'

'There you are, then,' said Mrs Knorring and looked at the Steinhägers who were nodding, 'that's something, at any rate. The police,' Mrs Knorring went on as she looked at Mrs Mooshaber, 'the police are nowhere to be seen in the streets.'

'Yes, they're nowhere to be seen in the streets,' came the uneasy echo from Mrs Steinhäger, 'there's not a single uniform anywhere. We've just been speaking about it.'

'Just been speaking about it,' now Mr Steinhäger echoed his wife, 'there are no demonstrations as such yet and so the police don't break them up. But if you ask me,' Mr Steinhäger went on with a shake of the head, 'there's more to this than meets the eye.'

'Tomorrow the police will appear,' said Mr Smirsch, waving his hand, 'they are on general stand-by. It says in today's papers that Prime Minister Rappelschlund has received Scarcola, the Minister for Police, for a meeting.'

'Received for a meeting,' repeated Mrs Knorring with a smile in the direction of Mr Smirsch, 'as if that was a visit which could be refused. The truth is that the streets are empty of police and that between Mr Rappelschlund and Mr Scarcola there are certain areas in need of clarification.' Mrs Knorring gave another smile and the Steinhägers on the sofa nodded and even gave some slight smiles of their own.

'I think,' said Mr Steinhäger, 'that the police are being very restrained, that they don't want to let things get out of hand. I think that if something were to happen tomorrow, then our Prime Minister would ...'

'This is all rumour-mongering,' said Mr Smirsch in a rather abrasive manner, 'which is something I neither like nor wish to hear. It produces a disquiet which is no good to anyone. Yesterday Mr Rott said that people want to see the princess and speak with her and that the police will in all likelihood not prevent this from happening. But what is all this about?' Mr Smirsch went on in his prickly tone, 'Are the police not paid by the state? Are they not public servants?

Aren't they supposed to serve the state their paymaster in the way that soldiers are? I can only see the political manoeuvres and princess-seeking at work here as endangering the life of the state.'

'But Mr Smirsch,' intervened Mrs Knorring with a smile as she looked at the sideboard, where Mrs Mooshaber was still at work preparing kolaches, shifting her ingredients around, 'why should the state be in danger? Don't people have the right to find out at last what has happened to their princess? Is this something that must always be kept from them? Officially speaking she governs along with the Prime Minister, so let her show herself. Let us see whether she is in the palace or is in hiding or whether Rappelschlund is searching for her and wants her...' At this point Mrs Knorring went quiet for a while before raising her head and continuing...'wants her dead. Or maybe he took her life a long time ago, as some people say, and she is in a grave somewhere. After all these decades people want to know once and for all, rather than put up with being forever forbidden to speak about the princess. Or even worse, facing those threats that anyone who knows her whereabouts and doesn't turn her in will be shot together with their entire family. This has been going on since Rappelschlund took office. How can that be acceptable? Why is she a threat to national security when she is our sovereign? Why is she such a threat when she is on official portraits all over the place alongside Rappelschlund and when stories about her are in school primers and children study her family tree and when on her name-day people put flowers, candles, wine and kolaches in their windows and burn incense in their homes? Whereas on Rappelschlund's name-day, which is also an official holiday, there are only banners hung from the state offices and draping the statue in the square named after him. What is more throughout the capital and indeed the whole country there is not, if you will pardon the expression,' Mrs Knorring concluded with a smile and a glance around her, 'enough interest in him to make a dog bark.'

Silence reigned awhile in the kitchen. Mrs Mooshaber finished slicing up the dough on the sideboard for her kolaches, and moved to the stove for the cream cheese. Mrs Faber remained stiff and aloof in her seat, not a muscle moving, looking straight ahead of her, while on the sofa the caretaker and the Steinhägers produced nods. Mr Smirsch said nothing and Mr Landl followed suit. Mr Landl sipped his tea.

'Madam is quite right, 'Mr Landl said finally, 'it is just as she says. There is discontent among the people and the city is in a state of upheaval. There could well be an incident of some kind tomorrow.'

'To get back to that Oberon lad,' Mrs Knorring went on as she glanced at Mrs Mooshaber and her collection of objects at the sideboard, among which she now also discerned a little coloured box, 'as I was saying, you might like to keep him occupied by talking to him about his interests. About his studies in the occult.'

'I don't know the first thing about that,' said Mrs Mooshaber, back in reflective mode as she began to spread cream cheese over the kolaches, 'I'll just listen to what he has to say and maybe ask him a question now and again...'

'There are all those other scientific books he reads too,' the caretaker said, 'and he makes notes about them. He even reads the students' lecture notes and talks about them like an adult would. You'd think he was an a writer, seeing that he's just fourteen.'

'An adult, a writer,' agreed Mrs Mooshaber as she spread cream cheese on the kolaches, and now she was also adding some raisins and almonds. 'And he buries himself in the occult sciences, though whether that's the right way to describe...'

'He's too clever by half,' the caretaker suggested to Mrs Knorring from the couch, 'As soon as Mrs Mooshaber told me about him being some kind of prodigy, I knew it would be like that.'

This was the moment when the clock by the stove struck half past four and Mr Smirsch suddenly shook his head.

'I say!' All of a sudden Smirsch was speaking in a strange voice and surveying the kitchen, 'so very strange, everything...'

Mrs Knorring lifted her head and looked at him, as did the caretaker and the Steinhägers and only Mrs Faber kept herself stiff and aloof, looking straight ahead with not a muscle moving out of line. Mrs Mooshaber went on filling her kolaches, adding almonds and raisins to the cream cheese.

'What is strange, 'asked Mrs Knorring, 'the disquiet in the city?'

'Strange,' repeated Mr Smirsch with a shrug of the shoulders and a drink of tea, 'strange. Everything is somehow strange. So this Oberon Felsach has long black hair, dark eyes, nails so long they start to curl and likes best wearing a black coat and immersing himself in the occult.'

The voice of Mr Smirsch itself sounded very strange and everyone was looking at him, even Mr Landl. Only Mrs Mooshaber remained at the sideboard filling her kolaches with cream cheese, raisins and almonds, while Mrs Faber remained sitting stiff and aloof in her chair, staring straight ahead.

'Very well,' Mr Smirsch continued while he placed a finger on the table in front of him, 'and now let us bear in mind a certain Eichankrenz from the cemetery and a certain Linpeck from the Cemetery underground station. Now Eichenkranz, if I remember correctly what Mrs Mooshaber said about him, shot crows in the cemetery, talked to a squirrel, imitated a bird in flight and all of a sudden disappeared in the park as if he'd dropped through the surface of the earth. As for Linpeck, if I remember rightly, he talks to himself as if he's in conversation with someone else, has dreams in which he is flying and above all loves fire. And now this Felsach here,' at this point Mr Smirsch began to tap the table with the exposed finger, 'has long black hair, dark eyes, long nails, wears a black coat, is a prodigy and immerses himself in the occult. So it is somewhat strange,' he said. Then looking suddenly around the kitchen and speaking with a voice that was still itself strange, he stood up and went on:

'One talks to animals, flies around and manages to fall into the earth. The second talks to himself as if he's with someone else, flies in his dreams and loves fire above all other things. And the third has black hair, dark eyes, nails like claws, a black coat and a penchant for the occult. All three are twelve, thirteen, fourteen years of age. Well then,' said Mr Smirsch, remaining standing and looking somewhere in the direction of the stove, 'to me it has all been very strange. Strange now and strange for a very long time. Very strange for very long. It was strange when Mrs Mooshaber here was at the Mother and Child Support Service on account of Eichenkranz, and again when she was there on behalf of Linpeck, but I held my peace. Held my peace and didn't say a word. But now it seems to me that this is all too much. It seems to me,' Mr Smirsch went on as he looked round the kitchen, 'that these three cases were never mother-and-child cases when they came before us but something else. Matters concerning the State Tribunal.' At this point Mr Smirsch looked at the ground before continuing:

'These three should evidently be placed on the list of those who are in league with the Devil.'

Silence took over the kitchen. A deep and deafening silence such as had surely never been there before. Such as had never been there even when Wezr turned up. Such as had never been there even when the police arrived. The caretaker went pale and sat on the sofa dumbfounded. The Steinhägers stared at Mr Smirsch as if they were frozen with terror. Mr Landl was perturbed, confused and surprised as he looked at Mr Smirsch. Even Mrs Mooshaber, standing at the stove making kolaches, paused in her work and stood as rigid as a column of stone. And even Mrs Faber, who until this point had been on her chair all rigid and aloof, suddenly took her eyes off the door, looked at Mr Smirsch and a muscle twitched in her unrelenting face.

Mrs Knorring raised her head and looked at Mr Smirsch, her delicately prim face suddenly looking as if it had been turned to stone.

'Mr Smirsch,' she declared in a voice that sounded as if it was coming from someone else, while the sheets in her hands fluttered in agitation, 'first and foremost I would like you to take a seat.' And when Mr Smirsch had sat down again, Mrs Knorring spoke:

'What you are saying is so unexpected and so beyond my comprehension that my first thought is to doubt whether you mean it seriously. From time to time something happens in life which simply paralyses a person with shock. They do not know whether they are awake or dreaming, whether they are still among human beings or perhaps have been transferred to another astral plane. The next phase is usually a coma and if the person recovers their senses it is in a hospital bed. But you have made your utterance, you have made it here before us and not in a dream or in some hallucination, and so I must offer a response. And not only that. I must respond at once because of what I have just heard and because I do not want someone to be able to say one day that I remained silent in the face of such words. Now then, Mr Smirsch,' Mrs Knorring continued, her eyes fixed upon him while not a muscle moved in her face, 'what you have just said is utter nonsense. But at the same time it is the most serious charge that can be levelled against someone. Throughout my career at the Mother and Child Support Office, in all my twenty years there, on no other occasion have we had to do with something like this, and no one working for us has ever made such an accusation. Do you even know what you are saying, Mr Smirsch?'

'It is quite out of the question,' Mr Landl was now roused to say, 'many things are possible, but this is not one of them. Not this, Mr Smirsch. You really musn't say such a thing.'

'Good Lord, no,' echoed Mrs Steinhäger from the sofa in the distressed tones of someone worried out of their mind as she trembled all over, and Mr Steinhäger sitting beside her shook his head vehemently and said in a voice full of agitation: 'I don't know any of these boys but what you are saying, sir, cannot be right. Definitely not. You cannot mean this seriously.' And the caretaker, pale and struck dumb by what had been said, now began to find words again and with a touch to the throat blurted out: 'That cannot be. It cannot be. I don't know you at all, sir, but it seems to me that you're way off target there. I know Mrs Eichenkranz and Mrs Linpeck, and I know these lads from everything Mrs Mooshaber has told me about them and this is just out of the question.'

With another severe look in the direction of Mr Smirsch Mrs Knorring spoke again:

'Indeed it is out of the question. I would oppose a suggestion such as this with all my official authority. This is unacceptable. In twenty years of working at Mother and Child Support I have only had one case like that. That was fifteen years ago, a case involving an eight-year-old boy called Napoleon Stallruck who had neither mother nor father and you know how that case turned out. The whole country has been talking about it to this day. I firmly opposed the judgment. The whole of the Mother and Child Support Service opposed it.'

'And it still didn't make any difference,' said Mr Smirsch, staring at the ground.

'Quite right,' exclaimed Mrs Knorring her prim and severe face a ghostly shade of pale and the sheets shaking in her hands, 'quite right. Because he had been denounced to the Tribunal. Because some contemptible informer stuck his nose into the affair, someone who should have been brought to the Tribunal himself and publicly tried for what he did. That time,' Mrs Knorring went on, turning to the caretaker, the Steinhägers, Mrs Faber and Mrs Mooshaber by the sideboard, 'that time they arrested the boy after a tip-off from some dastardly criminal by the bridge in Linde, hauled him before the State Tribunal and he was put on the list. They questioned him, an eight-year-old boy mind you, for ten days and nights, they found him guilty of flying through the open air and throwing stones through mind control, although he originally came to us at the Mother and Child Support Service only because some miserable teacher handed him over claiming that he'd jumped over a high wall and broken a window with a stone... they proved to him that fire could indeed hurt him, at the Tribunal they put his hand in a barrel of boiling tar and found him guilty of having visions. How could he not have had them,' Mrs Knorring exclaimed, a severe and deathly pallor on her face and the sheets fluttering in her hands, 'how could he not have visions when they interrogated him for ten days and ten nights, an eight-year-old boy, and kept him in fetters all that time? When they left his legs in the stocks day and night and his hands in manacles. When they gave him water with vinegar to drink and just one bowl of oatmeal a day. When they doused his head with icy water and threatened to slice him in half and then in half again.

'But that's the way those things are done,' said Mr Smirsch, eyeing the ground, 'that's what they always do when someone is suspected of witchcraft. In the Middle Ages instead of the measures just described they used to burn such people, which was much worse. This lad even had legal representation.'

'Yes,' exclaimed Mrs Knorring, 'he did. And indeed his counsel protested his innocence and asked for clemency. But Rappelschlund turned him down. As in all the cases that come before the State Tribunal, this little lad was just another opportunity to say 'No', and Rappelschlund came within a hair's breadth of imprisoning the defence lawyer. He declared that being young and an orphan provided no excuse to anyone who sold themselves to the Devil. He directed that the poor lad should be quartered without being given drugs to relieve the pain and then flew off to spend a week on the Moon. Mr Smirsch,' declared Mrs Knorring, 'the things you have said…I could never have them on my conscience.'

'What you allege, sir, is out of the question,' said Mrs Mooshaber, at last intervening from the sideboard, 'in fact everything concerning these boys has already been explained. The Eichen lad was not swallowed up by the earth but hid himself inside a hollow tree – he showed me the spot himself. And he didn't talk to any squirrel. He made a noise at it just as you might cluck at a chicken. As for the Linpeck boy, he found empty spaces in fields to make fires during summer holidays, as kids do, and as for his flying that's just his dreams. He can't really fly, the only time he's gone up in the air is in a lift. As for the son of this magnate the widower,' Mrs Mooshaber continued as she shook her head and eyed her kolaches and the rest of her culinary collection on the sideboard, 'he is disobedient, gets up to mischief, is a constant vexation and perhaps the school for troublemakers and the house of correction await him, from which he will emerge an unskilled pair of hands, like as not hired for the day and he may well worry his father to death, but not this. Indeed these exotic studies are even taught in schools and long hair is even worn by a government minister these days.'

'Very well,' Mr Smirsch put in all of a sudden, 'I could be wrong. Perhaps I wasn't thinking. You are going there yourself tomorrow, Mrs Mooshaber,' he went on as he looked at the sideboard where the kolaches and sundry other things were on display…

Silence hung over the kitchen for a long time. Mrs Faber froze over once again in her stiff and aloof position, not a muscle moving in her face, looking straight ahead of her at the door of the room. The Steinhägers were also a little calmer, although the anxiety which both had brought remained with them. The caretaker was a little less pale, as was Mr Landl.

'It's quite intolerable,' Mrs Knorring resumed after a long interval, 'just frightful. I have some strange foreboding about what's going to happen. I'd rather not see what happens tomorrow. Somehow all this is just proving too much. That time when they quartered little Napoleon Stallruck in the square by the Tribunal, they had just sent three rockets to the Moon. I remember how their red and green lights slipped away into the sky above the city. In Saint Quido of Fontgolland's Cathedral the Cardinal Archbishop himself celebrated a requiem mass for the boy. Gogh, the minister of police at the time if you still remember, resigned in protest. What have you got in that little coloured box on the sideboard, Mrs Mooshaber?' Mrs Knorring was suddenly looking at Mrs Mooshaber standing by the sideboard, where she was once again spreading cream cheese, raisins and almonds on the kolaches-to-be and now adding a sprinkling of sugar besides. 'What have you got there?'

'What?' said Mrs Mooshaber, sudden and sharp in her response, 'what's what?'

'What's that little coloured box over there?' Mrs Knorring pointed at the sideboard. 'The one with the black and yellow stripe and something written on it in red. Isn't there a skull and crossbones underneath the label or whatever it is? I can't see that far very well.'

‘It’s nothing,’ said Mrs Mooshaber flatly, ‘the only reason it’s there is lack of space. When I’ve got vanilla, raisins, almonds, not to mention milk, butter, sugar, I just don’t know where to put it. It’s a powder for cleaning the windows… Right then,’ said Mrs Mooshaber, ‘time for me to stoke up the oven and start baking.’

‘And time for us to be going,’ said Mrs Knorring as she pressed her sheets to her bosom ‘we’ll be off.’ And so saying she rose from her chair.

Messrs Smirsch and Landl, the Steinhägers and bringing up the rear Mrs Faber all rose too.

‘The *Dies Irae* is perhaps the trickiest part of the whole Requiem,’ said Mrs Knorring as she stood with her head erect and quickly consulted her sheets of music once again, ‘would you say that our conductor Monsieur Scarone now appears to think that the French horns play with gusto? Do you think that by now Monsieur Scarone feels that there is a proper fortissimo?’ She turned to Mr Landl and Mr Landl gave a nod.

‘He appears to think so now,’ said Mr Smirsch, ‘in any case we’re doing our best. It’s being rehearsed so that it is correct, appealing and beautiful. Done in that way it sounds dignified, majestic and pure.’

‘Their playing is like peals of thunder,’ said Mr Landl. ‘Peals of thunder that bring a mysterious light to my eyes.’

‘This is the part that concerns the end of the world and the Last Judgment?’ asked Mrs Mooshaber in a pensive tone of voice as she wiped her hands on her apron, ‘the armageddon at the end?’

‘It is the terrible Last Judgment at the end,’ said Mrs Knorring, and closed her folder containing the score.

'And when will the première be?' asked Mr Steinhäger uneasily and anxiously, while Mrs Steinhäger whispered, 'the première, when will it be?'

'No one knows as yet,' said Mrs Knorring, 'your guess is as good as mine. But if you ask me, I'd say it will be earlier than we think. We will go past the crossroads,' she said to Mr Landl, 'I want to get a look at what's going on outside.'

When Mrs Knorring had left together with Messrs Smirsch and Landl, the Steinhägers and Mrs Faber, and only the caretaker was left in the kitchen with Mrs Mooshaber, the clock above the stove struck five. Eyeing the stove, the table and the sideboard, the caretaker said:

'I'll be off too, Mrs Mooshaber, seeing that you still have some baking to do. That was really horrible, you know. It beggars belief, and yet the man looked halfway normal.'

Then she went on: 'So tomorrow you must definitely take the fur. Take everything that goes with it. You're starting your mission there and at the same time it's a national holiday. Did you really say that you'll be doing all the preparations yourself?'

'All by myself,' confirmed Mrs Mooshaber as she looked at the sideboard, 'everything's in my hands. But there's something I want to remind you about.' And when Mrs Kralec the caretaker nodded, Mrs Mooshaber went on:

'Very well then, I want to remind you about the two black banners I have in the wardrobe in the corridor. They belong to you as does the pole. I've just had them for safekeeping. You do remember that the second is a spare if something happens to the first?'

'Please, Mrs Mooshaber,' said the caretaker as she laughed and caressed her throat, 'of course I know that. And I also know that they are both in perfect order.'

'That's right,' Mrs Mooshaber went on with the trace of a smile, 'but you don't yet know what I want to say. What I would like to do is borrow one of those black banners tomorrow...'

The caretaker left Mrs Mooshaber's flat just as the clock above the stove was striking, but that needn't have meant that a lot of time had elapsed, because that clock above Mrs Mooshaber's stove even struck the quarters. She left Mrs Mooshaber's flat in the way that she had come, in a short cotton dress and sporting a bare neck, but all the same a little different, because she was also wearing a large smile.

'I'm all consumed with curiosity,' she said as she smiled from the entrance to the building, touching her throat as she passed the tub of lime, 'when you come back tomorrow evening or maybe the following morning, you must tell me how everything went in the widower's villa. You must tell me, Mrs Mooshaber, how it went with the housekeeper and with whatsisname, that Oberon, and about how you set the table. And you needn't worry about that banner at all.'

XX

The evening passed, the night passed and then it was morning. The morning of the last day in October, two days before All Souls, the day of the national holiday in honour of the birth of the sovereign, the Dowager Princess Augusta.

No one knows what Mrs Mooshaber did in the morning of that day. She may have made something for her lunch, perhaps a little corn mash. It's also likely that she looked at the traps behind the sofa in the kitchen, behind the sideboard and the stove, and also at the traps in the corridor, the larder and in her bedroom, although she wouldn't normally do this every morning. It's likely too that she took mice out to the bin beneath the main stairs of the house located just behind the frosted glass window in her kitchen – that is, of course, if she had caught any mice during the night – and then added some new pieces of bacon to the traps, although even this was not a regular habit of hers every morning, done without exception. On the other hand, it is possible that she did none of this on the day in question. The only thing that's certain is that Mrs Natalia Mooshaber cleaned the flat thoroughly sometime after lunch, including the kitchen and her other room, not to mention the corridor, and that she started to get ready. To get ready for her first day of work with Oberon Felsach, the rich merchant's son, and to get ready for her dinner in the Felsach villa.

Because the Felsach villa was located in the Blauental villa colony not very far from the three drab streets, one of which contained the old and decrepit house in which she lived, Mrs Mooshaber didn't have to go to the crossroads by the *Sunflower* department store and make her way over the asphalt via the white stripes of the zebra crossing. Nor did she have to go to the grander avenues of the city which were always busy. And so she didn't go there or pass by. It was just like the first occasion when she went to see the merchant and she didn't go to any of the grand avenues or pass by them then either. And so she didn't even see what was happening in those busy and grander avenues of the city that very afternoon. On the way from the three shabby streets to the merchant's villa she passed only a few clusters of people in festive apparel, who were heading for the centre of town, some of them quiet and reticent, others merry and outgoing... and Mrs Mooshaber also knew only too well that all these people who were passing by, be they reticent and quiet or be they merry and outgoing, were staring at her, were turning around to face her and stare at her, she could feel the looks of all these people upon her whether they were ahead of her, behind her or passing beside her, and she knew why this was. Out of a shock of dark-brown mane, part of her brown-and-black striped fur, there peeped a hat with an old violet bow in it. It was a broad-brimmed hat with quivering red and green fuzzy feathers all of a flutter. The face framed by the mane was red and white with rouged lips and shadowed eyes. On top of this Mrs Mooshaber had her hands full this time. She was carrying some strange things in her white gloves. She had the big black bag with her, the one for her cloth, brush and watering-can (and even a spade in spring-time) which she used to take to the cemetery. She had all sorts of things inside it on this occasion too. And besides the bag she had some kind of big white parcel, tied up with some familiar cord... When she at last ended up in the villa colony and at the street entrance to 6, Spring Street where the merchant Felsach had his villa, she walked along a wide path through the garden overgrowths of autumn until she came to two columns marking the entrance to the building. It was five in the afternoon. She could hear the bells of some church tower ringing the hour.

An elderly woman arrived at the door to admit her.

The moment she stood in the doorway the old woman looked overcome with fright.

On the edge of the hall, which was already bathed in light, the old woman mumbled her name. Mrs Mooshaber was in the act of putting down her big black bulging bag and parcel on the carpet and unfastening her fur, so she didn't even catch what the old woman said. All she could work out was that this was probably the housekeeper, because she was wearing an apron of white lace and a bonnet of the same material. As for Mrs Mooshaber, she was still unfastening her fur, her neck was still entangled in a great shock of dark brown hair and her arms were outstretched while she finally managed to catch hold of her coatsleeves. That was the moment when right in front of her she suddenly spotted the boy.

He had the long black hair and dark eyes, but was not wearing the black coat. Being at home in the entrance hall of the villa, he was just wearing a dark suit. He looked at the great dark-brown mane of fur and at the green and red feathers on the hat which trembled and fluttered in the middle of the mane. He looked at the black and brown stripes on the coat, at the white and red on the face, at the lipstick on the lips. He looked at the big black bulging bag and the parcel on the carpet and then he had to have another look. This was when Mrs Mooshaber had removed the fur completely and passed it over to the housekeeper, which allowed the red earrings on their long shiny wires to announce themselves alongside the coloured bamboo beads hanging under the neck and over the waistless jacket. He looked at Mrs Mooshaber lost for words and Mrs Mooshaber was equally lost for words looking at him. The housekeeper found a coatstand for the fur and was the one who broke the silence.

'Madam,' she began in an unsteady voice, though whether it was unsteady with age or fear or worry Mrs Mooshaber did not know, 'I wonder, Madam, what I can do with this bag and parcel.' Mrs Mooshaber nodded, sending the feathers on her hat into another tremble, since as on the last occasion she had not removed it from her head, before saying:

'Just keep them here for the moment. Leave them next to the wall.' Then she finally managed the traces of a smile as she looked at the boy.

'So that's him,' she thought to herself, 'now I've seen him. He's not allowed to run off, not to the town and not even into the garden, I'll have to keep an eye on him. The main thing is that he's not allowed to run off before... (this thought was occurring to her for the first time) ...before dinner.' She then said out loud: 'So this is the son of Mr Felsach the magnate.'

Now the boy himself began to speak. 'The first thing I will show you, Madam,' he began in a voice that was calm and yet somehow firm, 'are some of the windows here on the ground floor. So that you'll see the decorations. We'll burn the incense right before dinner, once the gentlemen have arrived.'

'Master Oberon is referring to the students,' said the elderly housekeeper in an apprehensive voice and Mrs Mooshaber nodded. 'I'll take a look at those windows,' she said.

'I should be going to the kitchen,' the elderly housekeeper went on in timorous tones, 'I have food to prepare. I can offer Madam coffee and cakes to be going on with. I'll pop down to the cellar in order to see to it.'

The housekeeper bowed and headed towards the marble staircase. She turned off towards some dark polished doors and disappeared through one of them. That was when Mrs Mooshaber noticed how small, weak, fragile and elderly the housekeeper really was, and she thought to herself: 'It's no

wonder that she can't handle the lad. It's no wonder that he would run away on her watch. But he mustn't run off on mine, at least until dinner is over...' She nodded to Oberon and proceeded to follow him.

First of all he led her to a window in the hall beside a satin-covered three-piece suite. He drew back the long rose-coloured curtains in front of some blood-red drapes and showed her what was on the window ledge. As he did so Mrs Mooshaber noticed his nails. They were really long, particularly those of the little fingers which curled noticeably... Mrs Mooshaber turned her attention to what was on the window ledge. She saw a goblet of red wine, a plate with two cakes on it, a vase containing three splendid tulips and three large candles.

'I will light them when it gets dark,' said Oberon Felsach, 'now come and look at the window in the dining-room.' The boy covered the window with the curtain again and went through the hall towards the big glass sliding doors.

Still in her hat with the coloured feathers, earrings, beads and white gloves, Mrs Mooshaber followed him and kept a light hold on her black shiny skirt as she went. She looked at the fountain in the middle of the entrance hall, the water gushing out of the split stalk and falling back into the pool. She looked at the pictures in their gold frames on the wall and at the crystal chandeliers blazing with light as they hung from the ceiling. She looked at the statues by the staircase with their red lights. But Oberon Felsach was already opening the big frosted-glass sliding doors of the dining-room and stepping inside.

The dining-room contained a dark table and six red chairs. There was nothing covering the table and so a join on its surface was able to announce itself, showing that it could be opened out in order to seat more guests. Beside one of the walls stood a long, low sideboard on top of which a few vases of hyacinths had been placed. Beside another wall stood three smaller side tables. Two large dark paintings were hanging on the walls inside gold frames, each featuring a still life of some kind made up of pheasants, fruit and wine. Behind the chair which stood at the head of the table, right opposite the wide, frosted-glass doors, there was a window which evidently could be allowed to disappear behind some heavy dark-blue velvet drapes. It was to this window that Oberon Felsach headed, drawing aside the pink net curtains and opening it.

'See this here,' he said, pointing with hands which gave a glimpse of the long nails, 'another window. Take a look.'

Mrs Mooshaber saw three candles on the window ledge, three goblets with red wine in them, a plate of cakes and three vases. One of the vases contained tulips, a second hyacinths and a third had some kind of arrangement of white flowers... 'I'll light these here too,' explained Oberon Felsach as he pointed at the candles, 'when it's darker. Do you like our windows?'

‘I do,’ agreed Mrs Mooshaber as she glanced at the white flowers while the feathers on her hat trembled, ‘what are those beautiful white flowers? I know them. From where do they...’

‘From the co-op store,’ said the lad with a smile, ‘from Elizabeth Verdun. Take a look...’

The elderly housekeeper appeared in the wide doorway of the dining-room in her white lace apron and her lace bonnet. She was holding a tray in her hands. On the tray was a cup, a cafetière, a sugar-bowl and some small cakes.

‘Where would Madam like me to put this?’ she asked in a timid voice. ‘Should I serve Madam here or in the entrance-hall?’

‘In the hall,’ said Mrs Mooshaber and they all set off in that direction.

The housekeeper put the tray down on a small table and poured some coffee into the cup, while Mrs Mooshaber thanked her and sat down in an armchair. She recognised that it was by this very table and in this satin-covered chair that she had been sitting when she was with the merchant a week earlier. Oberon Felsach took a seat in another chair opposite her.

‘Here is the sugar-bowl, if you please,’ said the housekeeper as she pointed to a pair of gold sugar-tongs lying next to the bowl ‘I will let Madam help herself. And here...’ the housekeeper went on as she pulled something shiny out of her lace pocket...’here, if you please, is a bell. If there is anything that Madam wishes for, be so good as to ring and I will come.’ The housekeeper bowed and returned in the direction of the staircase and one of those dark polished doors. Mrs Mooshaber noticed that apart from the apron and bonnet of white lace she was wearing long, dark and very elegant clothes.

'The good lady who keeps house,' began Mrs Mooshaber as she spoke to Oberon Felsach sitting opposite her, 'has gone to the kitchen. Can the bell be heard even from there?'

'It can be heard anywhere,' said Oberon Felsach, smiling as he looked at the beads, earrings and hat of Mrs Mooshaber, 'it can even be heard from the cellar... anyone who can find their way around her can find out a lot of things from her. She's a psychic. But hardly anyone realises that. Perhaps she doesn't even recognise it herself. I don't do much work

of that sort with her myself. I have better sources of information,' he continued with a curious smile. Mrs Mooshaber looked at him and for the first time she became fully aware of how pale he was. His father the merchant was definitely far more tanned. Still it was possible that the lad's pallor was accentuated by his long black hair and dark eyes and even perhaps by his dark suit.

'She's a sidekick?' asked Mrs Mooshaber.

'A psychic,' the lad repeated. Then he pointed at the wall and asked her, still with a curious smile on his face, 'what exactly have you got in that big black bag and in that parcel?'

'I have some things there,' said Mrs Mooshaber as she calmly examined his pale face, 'some things for dinner. Even kolaches, good ones with vanilla, raisins and almonds... cream cheese too. I spent all of yesterday baking them, seeing that I like to bake. They'll be just the thing... for after dinner's over,' she added as she continued her calm examination of his face, 'you'll find them really tasty.'

'Help yourself,' said Oberon Felsach, pointing at the tray. Mrs Mooshaber thanked him, took the sugar-tongs in her white gloves and moved them to the bowl in order to add a sugar lump to her cup. She stirred the coffee with a small spoon and proceeded to drink in a thoughful manner.

'When you were coming here,' Oberon Felsach went on in what might or might not have been a somewhat inquisitive manner, 'did you come across anybody? Did you pass any groups, crowds even, people in a procession...'

'When I was on my way to see you,' replied Mrs Mooshaber, feeling slightly uneasy, though she made sure it didn't show, 'I only came across a small group of people. People would rather be home and not going out...I've heard it said,' she added quickly, changing the subject, 'that you don't need to do any homework. That you already know it all. But what exactly do you study at school?'

'What subjects do you want to know about?' asked Oberon Felsach as he leaned back in his chair and made himself comfortable. 'Geography, arithmetic, history...'

'Everything. The most important things you know,' said Mrs Mooshaber.

'Well right now when it's a national holiday like this, the most important thing to know about is the Prime Minister,' replied the lad. 'About him and about the Dowager Princess our sovereign Augusta.' Mrs Mooshaber nodded and twiddled the bamboo beads beneath her throat while she listened.

'Albinus Rappelschlund,' began Oberon Felsach as he made himself comfortable again leaning back in his armchair, 'Albinus Rappelschlund came to power fifty years ago, when he was promoted general and uncovered the traitors to the crown. From that moment he assumed absolute power, ruling jointly with the Dowager Princess, our sovereign Augusta. One important example of his many deeds is the short war during which he put a neighbouring state to the slaughter...he restored law and order, provided work for all the people and after the war founded a Museum of Peace, which contains one of the largest and most valuable collections of the instruments of war ever made. He built a huge launch pad for rockets in the Stadium district just outside the city, which is named after him and he is just finishing construction of a new state-of-the-art prison for five hundred inmates at the Einstein crater on the Moon. These are people who are not fit to continue living on Earth...and he has himself taken part in flights to the Moon five times. He has never suffered any thickening of the blood when landing.' Oberon Felsach fell silent for a moment and sported a strange smile. Mrs Mooshaber realised for the first time that he probably was very bright. 'This passage,' Oberon Felsach continued, still smiling strangely from the chair opposite her, 'this passage about Albinus Rappelschlund is something we have to be able to recite to order, doing so quickly, properly and without error – that's the regulation. If someone doesn't know it properly they might get interrogated. We learn it,' Oberon Felsach continued with a smile, 'because we have to. In the more junior classes they learn that he had been a tanner, a waiter, a soldier and a Protestant minister. Now I'll tell you what we learn about the princess in our class.'

Oberon Felsach again made himself comfortable leaning back in his armchair and Mrs Mooshaber now realised another thing, namely that he really spoke just like an adult, perhaps even like a writer, and that indeed he must be really clever. She nodded and went on thoughfully drinking her coffee.

'Princess Augusta,' said Oberon Felsach, 'was born the only heiress to the throne of her father Charles Napoleon, the Prince of Saas-Beer, and her mother Anna Maria the Thalian Princess known as the Blessed. Her childhood and youth were spent partly here in the capital and partly in various country chateaux which made up the ancestral Thalian estates. After the death of her mother Anna Maria, called the Blessed, who died at the age of one hundred, she ascended to the throne. She was fifteen years old at the time. From that moment on she has been our ruler. Since the time when the traitors were exposed – she was twenty at the time – she has governed jointly with Prime Minister Albinus Rappelschlund as our supreme sovereign the Dowager Princess Augusta. You may wonder why she was a dowager. Because at the age of twenty she got married, but her husband died very early, in fact just a few weeks after the wedding. He was a great nephew of Charles Napoleon and is buried in the royal palace.'

'Of course,' Oberon Flsach went on as he tapped on the armrest with his long nails, 'of course everything which I've told you comes from my schoolbook and is a fabrication. The princess does not govern. If Rappelschlund did exhibit the princess to the people from the balcony of the palace from time to time during these fifty years, it was a mannequin.'

'Mannequin?' Mrs Mooshaber shook her head and raised eyes surounded by make-up, 'You mean a monkey?'

'A mannequin, a dummy, an artificial copy,' Oberon Felsach explained, looking Mrs Mooshaber in the face, 'a mannequin is just a lie. A mannequin can stand on a balcony and can sit on a throne. It can be put on film and painted for official portraits. In the world of magic it is called using a proxy. For many years it has been said,' Oberon Felsach continued, now looking at the fountain in the middle of the hall, 'that Rappleschlund had the princess murdered or imprisoned in the palace. The truth is different – and that's what's being said now: the princess is alive and in hiding. I reckon,' Oberon Felsach continued as he looked at the coloured feathers on Mrs Mooshaber's head, 'I reckon that the police are now secure in the knowledge of where the princess is. In years gone by they hunted for her among various people who at one time knew her or had at least seen her once in their lives. They hunted for her among lots of people who had at some point in the past spoken a single word to her. They never stopped looking for her in all those years.'

'And now they have finally hunted her down...' inquired Mrs Mooshaber as she raised her eyes.

'They have hunted her down,' echoed Oberon Felsach with a smile, 'today they really know where the princess is. Let's say that right know she's at Cat's Castle.'

'At Cat's Castle in the foothills of the Black Forest?' asked Mrs Mooshaber in amazement, 'At Cat's Castle? However can she be there?'

'I'm sure of it,' said Oberon Felsach calmly, 'and for all I know she is there again right now. She's there right now frying mushrooms and doing a bit of lacework.'

'Is your housekeeper getting dinner ready?' asked Mrs Mooshaber, still sounding astonished.

'She is preparing dinner,' agreed Oberon Felsach, 'in the kitchen. She is preparing seaweed specialities for dinner, together with mushrooms and turtle soup. At the same time she is running to the cellar and is haunted by fear. She's frying fish...' Oberon Felsach went on as he looked at the fountain at the centre of the hall, 'she will extract every bone from them, for where fish are concerned it is not permitted for a single bone to remain. On a tray on the kitchen dresser she even has a few pieces of bacon,' he said, 'and then there's the kolaches you've brought...'

'Yes, kolaches' said Mrs Mooshaber with a nod and she looked at her big black bag and the parcel tied in string which lay by the wall, 'I spent the whole day baking them. I made them with vanilla, almonds, raisins... but there are some other things I brought too...' Mrs Mooshaber showed the hint of a smile at this point 'I not only like to bake but also to set the table. I would like to lay the table for you here in the dining-room today.'

'That will be all right,' agreed Oberon Felsach, 'the housekeeper will provide a tablecloth for you to lay.'

'I even brought a cloth myself,' explained Mrs Mooshaber with a shake of the head, 'and I brought some decorations. That's what the bag and the parcel are for. I hope it won't hurt the lady who is your housekeeper's feelings if I am the one to prepare everything.'

'If that's what you wish,' agreed Oberon Felsach as he looked at the green and red feathers on Mrs Mooshaber's hat, 'why should it upset her? There will be five of us at table including the students. Did you know, Madam,' he added hastily, 'that those long bits of fuzzy stuff on your hat, the green and red feathers, are the same colour as our rocketships? Our rocketships shine green and red too.'

'That could be so,' agreed Mrs Mooshaber while her feathers fluttered, 'I do see one of those rockets from time to time. And this necklace,' Mrs Mooshaber went on as she felt the beads under her throat, 'has the same colours as the trains in the metro, according to our caretaker. So the gentleman who is your father, the magnate, is now on the Moon. Have you ever been to the Moon yourself?'

'Not yet.' Oberon Felsach shook his head and ran both of his hands through his long black hair from the top. He really did have long nails, especially on the little fingers, and was very pale. 'But I know that I'll get to go there at some point. I know what it's like there. I hear reports, I've got illustrated books and we learn about it at school. It's rather sad up there.'

'But somewhere among those craters people are bathing in lava,' said Mrs Mooshaber.

'They only call it lava,' said Oberon Felsach with a smile, 'in reality it's dust and ash mixed with artificial water – in a word, mud. Dirt which liquefies in the sun before cooling a little – that's what the people up there bathe in. To treat their rheumatism, kidney complaints, hardening of the arteries and some mental illnesses. That's really ironic,'

Oberon Felsach continued with a smile, 'because they get these illnesses from being on the Moon. From the feeling of separation, loneliness and rejection...but there's no real lava on the Moon,' he pointed out, shaking his head, 'in volcanic terms the Moon is extinct. Building a spa or anything else up there is very costly, because everything has to be under glass in view of the changes in temperature. During the day it goes up to nearly a hundred degrees and in the morning just before sunrise it can go down to 157 degrees below zero.'

'That sounds like freezing,' agreed Mrs Mooshaber, 'that's why your father the magnate sells heaters there.'

'Not only heaters. He sells radios, cassette recorders, televisions and lamps,' Oberon Felsach explained, 'the people there listen in to the television and radio stations from Earth. I have here...' he pointed at the hall from his chair, but he was most likely referring to the whole villa, 'plenty of cassette recorders, televisions and radios. The radios are hidden in various places, mostly in walls. Even the housekeeper has a radio built into the kitchen walls so that she can listen while she's cooking.'

'The caretaker's told me about the Moon,' said Mrs Mooshaber, nodding her head, 'are there really seas and mountains there?'

'There are mountains there,' Oberon Felsach confirmed, 'whole clusters of them in mountain ranges made up of large pieces of broken rock. Some of it is of volcanic origin, but the volcanoes are extinct. There are no seas there, because there's no rain or water, it all has to be produced artificially. They're called seas, but it's just empty labels. There's a Sea of Showers, a Sea of Tranquillity and a Sea of Serenity. In fact they're not seas at all, just huge deserts too big to measure. Deserts of dust, ash and stone.'

'What about animals, plants and trees?' asked Mrs Mooshaber while she drank a little coffee.

'A few,' Oberon Felsach explained with a smile, 'but whatever there is is imported and raised artificially. Some countries build large irrigation channels on their parts of the Moon and then they can grow plants and trees, mainly pines and dwarf spruces. They've managed to keep some palm trees alive there, where the spas are located in the Einstein, Borman and Pestalozzi craters... there are even cacti and here and there some grass, but it's not possible, for instance, to grow hyacinths or tulips. And no one has succeeded in growing fruit trees so far, for example apple trees. So in the lunar Garden of Eden,' Oberon Felsach concluded with a smile, 'there isn't a single apple tree.'

'So the people there don't eat fruit,' said Mrs Mooshaber, 'and what about corn mash and porridge...'

'Everything is there,' Oberon Felsach said as he touched his long black hair, 'including fruit, for example oranges, lemons and figs. There are even tulips and hyacinths, not to mention corn, barley and hops, so they can even brew beer there. But everything grows under huge covers of unbreakable glass, where there is artificial irrigation and the temperature is controlled and the cosmic radiation is kept out. Otherwise nothing would work. Under an open sky everything would perish immediately during the day or freeze at night. If the trees are in a natural environment, like those pines, spruces and palms, they must be kept artificially cool during the day and be heated during the night. Every tree is fitted with its own electrical support system. Among the animals up there are camels, donkeys, beef cattle and it's possible to keep dogs and cats there, even lions... various birds too, for example peacocks and poultry, though all the different species can only go out in the open for a short while before sundown or shortly after sunrise, when the temperature is bearable. The peacocks, for example, go under the palms or as far as the edge of the wasteland of ash and dust, the donkeys stroll around on a patch of grass between the spruces...but only for a few moments. Then they must be back under cover, or else they'd die from the heat or the cold and be harmed by the radiation. There are horses there too.'

'That means a coachman can deliver the beer there,' said Mrs Mooshaber, raising her cup of coffee carefully with her white-gloved hand. She was about to add something else when the housekeeper came into the hall in her white apron and cap. Before she could get to the small table, Oberon Felsach had resumed his explanation with a smile:

'Everything there is moved around in cars, buses, helicopters and hovercrafts. The roads are made from heat-resistant metals and are not easy to build – the same goes for the homes. The dust, the cracked stones and the ash are all there is, they're everywhere and they never go away.'

The housekeeper had reached the small table and Mrs Mooshaber noticed how frightened she was. For a moment she couldn't even find words properly.

'Has something happened?' asked Mrs Mooshaber, raising her eyes.

'Prime Minister Rappelschlund is threatening martial law,' said the housekeeper, 'it's possible that he's already declared it.'

'So,' began Oberon Felsach as he moved quickly out of his chair, leaned towards the wall and pressed a button of some kind in it, 'so it's actually happened. I've been expecting as much since the morning,' he went on with a quiet smile on his pale face, 'I've been waiting since this morning, expecting that something would happen today... and now it has.' At that moment a voice could be heard from behind the wall, where there was evidently some kind of radio. The housekeeper took a small step backwards while Mrs Mooshaber raised her head a little.

'...in order that a dignified manner is maintained throughout the national holiday,' the voice from the wall explained before pausing briefly. Then the announcement went on: 'People will not be permitted to sow the seeds of discord, they must respect the need for quiet and orderly behaviour. The streets and squares must be empty by seven o'clock this evening. Otherwise the whole area will be secured by the army. It is not permitted to form mobs or to chant slogans hostile to the state. The national holiday must pass in an orderly manner, and so the army has orders to open fire if necessary. End of news bulletin.'

'What that means,' Oberon Felsach began with a quiet smile as he pressed the button, 'what that means is that the police are out of the picture. Rappelschlund has summoned the army. And what that means,' Oberon Felsach went on as he continued smiling and settled once more into a chair opposite Mrs Mooshaber, 'is that Rappelschlund does not trust the police. He's had various meetings with the Minister of Police, Scarcola, in recent days and as can be seen they turned out just as rumour had it. Badly. So it seems to me,' Oberon Felsach went on smiling, 'that everything is only just beginning, both in the city and in the country as a whole.' At that point Oberon Felsach looked towards the door of the hall in a very strange manner and as he did so Mrs Mooshaber was reminded of the fact that she was there in order to keep an eye on him and make sure that he didn't escape, at least before dinner, and she felt slightly uneasy.

'You'll soon be lighting the candles,' she said quickly, 'you'll be burning incense, the students will be arriving. There'll be five of us at dinner,' she went on, still talking rapidly, 'and I would also like to ask about the occult.' Oberon Felsach went on looking at the door to the hall for a moment before turning his attention back and saying:

'In a moment I'll switch the radio back on. I'll see what they will say.'

'If only the students were already here,' said the housekeeper in her timid voice always somewhere near at hand standing in her lace apron and cap, 'I hope that nothing has happened to them downtown.'

'They'll come to no harm at all, I'm sure of it,' said Oberon Felsach firmly and with barely a glance at the housekeeper, 'They'll be here. Surely you know that as well as anyone else.' The housekeeper shook her white-capped head, bowed and made a sharp exit. Oberon Felsach leaned comfortably against the back of his chair, looked at Mrs Mooshaber's hat and said:

'What do you want to know about the occult? There are so many aspects.'

'Just the main aspic,' said Mrs Mooshaber with a sigh of relief, 'you can surely tell me the most important bits.'

'Everything is important,' said Oberon Felsach as he ran his hands through his long black hair once more, 'there's nothing trivial in this area. Everything has a value and can be put to good use. The science of the occult comes in various forms. Some focus on the human brain and the mind, which make it possible to do things you wouldn't believe possible. Incidentally, these have been practised for the last thirty, forty or fifty years. Then there are types of occult practice which make it possible to exercise control from a distance in various ways, enabling you to eavesdrop and spy on people. The police and the army use these techniques, though there are ways of erecting defences against them. There are types which make it possible to connect with the next world, but these have been kept very secret so far and it's not possible to make regular use of them. And then there are the methods of telling the future. Using the flight patterns or the entrails of birds, especially crows which fly round cemeteries...' Oberon Felsach smiled, 'there are also crystal balls, though these are more of a prop to help you concentrate...and there's the reading of palms and hands, also called chiromancy. And of course there's reading the stars.'

'And can you find out Fate from the stars?' asked Mrs Mooshaber as the feathers fluttered on her hat.

'You can determine the contours of the future.' Oberon Felsach looked at Mrs Mooshaber and now his black eyes seemed to sparkle a little, 'but Fate is the wrong word to use in this instance.'

'A pharmacist told me,' Mrs Mooshaber explained as she raised the cup again with her gloved hand and drank a little, 'that it was foolish to believe in Fate. He said that you might as well believe in a house or in birds. Or in taking walks or believing that tomorrow is another day, he added. Still, I believe in Fate. I believe that what has happened was meant to happen and that what is meant to happen will happen...'

'That's just the point,' said Oberon Felsach, standing up from the chair and beginning to pace the carpet, 'Fate means everything that has happened and that therefore cannot be changed. By definition Fate cannot be changed. What can be changed are the consequences of Fate in the present and in the future. What still has to take place is not yet Fate, because it remains ahead of us, and is therefore a matter of choice. As soon as something happens, it becomes part of Fate, but not before. Right up to the last moment it is possible to change what will happen, at least within certain limits, because as I say the stars only provide a broad outline of the future. The past is not open to change, but the future is. That is in fact very fortunate for us.'

'And how can you get this broad outline from the stars?' asked Mrs Mooshaber.

'That is a very important question,' said Oberon Felsach.

At that moment one of the dark doors by the staircase opened again and the housekeeper appeared. She had a bowl of some kind in her hand. Oberon Felsach, who was constantly pacing around the table and chairs, went up to the wall and pressed the button. The housekeeper with the plate trembled by the staircase and then disappeared behind the door again. And from what was evidently a radio built into the wall a voice could be heard:

'Prime Minister Albinus Rappelschlund has just been in session at the royal palace. Army generals are attending. It is quite certain, Prime Minister Albinus Rappelschlund has announced, that the army will not have to apply martial law in the rural areas, the country people being educated, well-read and wise. There will be a further bulletin about proceedings in an hour's time.' There were a few seconds of silence before the announcer continued:

'In the capital there are reports of marches in the centre of the city and in the Kerke, Philipov and Stadium districts. There is less or no such activity in the Linde and Elizabethan districts. The commander of military forces calls upon citizens to disperse and to spend the rest of this national holiday in a dignified manner in their homes. And now some music by Giuseppe Verdi from his opera *Falstaff*.'

'It seems to me,' said Oberon Felsach as he turned down the music, 'that it's something serious. I also have the impression that there have been some hiccups concerning the declaration of martial law.' Once again Oberon Felsach threw strange looks at the door to the hall...and Mrs Mooshaber, who was well aware of these looks, once more felt uneasy... and quickly spoke up:

'It's already dark outside, will you get on with the incense now? Aren't you going to light the candles too?'

'Yes, I'll do it now.' Oberon Felsach removed his gaze from the door with a smile. 'Now is the time to light up.' He proceeded towards the window in the hall, which had been decorated, drew back the pink curtain and opened the window. Mrs Mooshaber watched him from her chair as he took a lighter out of his pocket, reached a hand across the goblet of wine, the tulips and the cakes and lit the candles.

'You can leave your drink for later,' he said to Mrs Mooshaber as he shut the window, 'come into the dining-room. I have to light up there as well.'

Mrs Mooshaber got out of her chair and followed the young man towards the wide frosted-glass doors. At the same time she threw another look at the pictures in their gold frames, at the statues below the staircase with their red lights and also at the fountain, in which the water quietly splashed out of the split stem and fell in a small arc into the pool beneath. Oberon Felsach opened the window of the dining-room, reached a hand over the goblets of wine, the dish of cakes and the vases containing the tulips, the hyacinths and the white flowers, and lit the candles.

'They're yellow, as you can see,' he said, 'they're left to burn right down till there's nothing left of them but a few pieces of wax...that will be all for the ground floor.' He shut the window and proceeded to draw down over it the dark-blue velvet drapes. Then he looked at the chairs and said: 'While we're here we can work out who sits where at dinner. I'll sit here,' he said, pointing at a chair on the right of the head of the table, 'the housekeeper will sit here,' he went on, pointing to a chair on the left, 'I'm afraid there's nothing to be done about that. The students will sit here,' he indicated, 'one next to me and one next to the housekeeper. You will sit at the head of the table, here with your back to the window. You will have the dark-blue velvet as your backdrop,' he went on, pointing at the curtain drapes, 'while in front of you,' he went on with a smile, 'you'll have the doors. The doors made of frosted-glass, which they also use now and again to make windows...you will sit at the head right opposite it because,' he added with a smile, 'you are the guest.'

'Shouldn't I already be setting the table?' asked Mrs Mooshaber.

'We've still got time,' said Oberon Felsach, shaking his head, 'wait till the students arrive. Then you can set the table while I burn the incense with them.'

Once again Mrs Mooshaber began to relax. She was almost sure that everything would work out as she'd hoped and wished. This Oberon Felsach clearly had no desire to take his black coat and abscond from the house into the streets. Like as not, he didn't even want to go out and explore the garden. The only thing was that after hearing the news on the radio he always looked at the door to the entrance hall in a funny way. Mrs Mooshaber was now almost certain that the young man would stay at least until dinner, and nodded her head. Nonetheless she quickly added: 'I would like to finish my drink. Can we not sit for a little longer in the hall?' Oberon Felsach nodded and went through the glass door into the hall.

'My Fate,' began Mrs Mooshaber when she was once again sitting in a satin-covered armchair, 'my Fate was to have two bad children.'

'Surely not,' said Oberon Felsach with a smile as he settled into an armchair himself, 'it's not possible. Tell me about it.'

'I will tell you about the not possible,' began Mrs Mooshaber as she looked at the sugar-bowl, 'my son has been in prison three times, on the last occasion for three months, and to this day I don't know for what offence, and my daughter will in all likelihood find herself there too. Not long ago she married a certain Laibach who was a mason, but since then she's divorced him. My children have been in trouble ever since they were tiny – getting into fights, wandering off and stealing. They went to the school for troublemakers and the house of correction, ending up as unskilled pairs of hands, like as not hired for the day and ending up behind bars, while they worried... worried their father to death. I've been at the Mother and Child Support Service for twenty years, from the time when Mrs Knorring had just begun there.'

'The Service has moved now,' said Oberon Felsach in a notably calm voice from his armchair as he looked at Mrs Mooshaber, 'their old centre has been turned into a prison.'

'That's right,' said Mrs Mooshaber while she looked at the bell, 'the Mother and Child Support Service is now in Kerke. They also want to turn a refuge in one of the little side streets into another prison, because it has barred windows too.'

'These children of yours,' said Oberon Felsach with a smile, 'do they live with you?'

'Not really,' said Mrs Mooshaber, shaking her head, 'they just show up from time to time and cause harm. Once they were sharing out stolen goods, I think they'd robbed someone by the Philipov cemetery, strange things happen there at night. On that occasion they tricked me with an invitation to a hotel. Another time they gave me stolen goods to keep safe for them, I think it was parcels from the post office at Cemetery metro station, this time they tricked me with some newspapers, the people in the street all but gave me a stoning. All I was left with was the cord used to tie the papers. On a third occasion they wanted to lower me into some well so that I could get hold of treasure for them. And a few days ago they set a trap for me in the cemetery at one of the graves which I look after, which suddenly had my own name on it. My daughter Nabule is divorced and I wouldn't be surprised if she wanted to marry again. The housekeeper is back,' said Mrs Mooshaber with a glance at the dark door by the staircase and Oberon Felsach got up, leaned against the wall and pressed a button.

'I'm so afraid,' wailed the housekeeper in her lace apron and cap, stopping some way short of the little table and the armchairs, so she was in fact wailing from some distance, 'I'm so concerned that the students haven't yet come. There are huge demonstrations, according to the radio.'

'...this is the final demand for citizens to disperse,' a voice on the radio had just announced, 'otherwise martial law will be applied and troops will begin to shoot. It is essential,' the announcer declared, 'that this national holiday, in honour of the birth of the Dowager Princess our Sovereign Augusta, passes in a dignified manner as it has in years gone by and as it is now doing in many towns and in the countryside, places which are peaceful and where the people are well-read, educated and wise. A meeting is in session at the royal palace, where the Minister of Police, Mr Scarcola, is expected to arrive...'

'You see,' said Oberon Felsach as he smiled at Mrs Mooshaber, 'he's not there yet. The Police Minister has not yet turned up to the meeting. Perhaps he is right now, shall we say, at Cat's Castle,' Oberon Felsach continued smiling, 'at Cat's Castle in the foothills. It will have taken him an hour to get there by plane. But one thing is obvious,' Oberon Felsach continued in a firm, clear voice and with another strange look towards the hall door…'the police are out of it. The police are keeping mum at the moment and between them and the military…' he went on looking at the door to the hall….'it could come to blows.'

The housekeeper again left the hall, disappearing through one of the dark doors, while Mrs Mooshaber added with a quick nod:

'You believe in the occult. Do you by any chance know what is foretold in the stars today? Our caretaker,' added Mrs Mooshaber, 'is very interested in the stars.'

'There are some strange things foretold in the stars.' Oberon Felsach switched off the radio and sat down again in an armchair, 'The stars foretell some great events. Rappelschlund is certainly aware of this, which is why he summoned the military. He brought in troops to meet the challenge. I've already said to you that what is still ahead of us can still be influenced and changed,' Oberon Felsach continued with a smile as he ran his hands through his long black hair, 'it is only when something has happened that it cannot be changed.'

'When my daughter got married,'said Mrs Mooshaber, carefully taking another sip of coffee, 'I baked some kolaches for the wedding. It took me the whole day and I made them with vanilla, raisins and almonds. Even cream cheese. And she grabbed them and flung them into the courtyard for the horse to eat. And then she flung me out too. The thing was that when they were small children I sang them a lullaby. And I wore my only best clothes to their celebration. This long and shiny black skirt, the one I'm in now, with the waistless jacket.'

'But you didn't wear this hat or the earrings and the necklace to that wedding,' Oberon Felsach suggested in a curious manner, though perhaps it was something else, while he looked at Mrs Mooshaber.

'No I wasn't wearing them at the wedding,' Mrs Mooshaber confirmed with a shake of the head, while she glanced around, taking in the hall, the red lights in the hands of the statues below the staircase, the split stem of the fountain and the wall where her big black bag and the tied parcel lay... I wasn't wearing them at the wedding. These students staying with you, have they been here a long time?'

'They have been here a long time,' confirmed Oberon Felsach 'they are friends from the countryside. They are at university here.'

'I knew some students too,' said Mrs Mooshaber, 'when my daughter was still a shop assistant, before she was dismissed. They once bought a tape recorder. They too lived in a beautiful villa belonging to some rich merchant and they were at my daughter's wedding. I was seated next to them.'

'Our students have never bought a tape recorder,' said Oberon Felsach, 'that's one thing I know. They'd never need to, because there are radios, televisions and all those gadgets in abundance here. They got a tape recorder from us.'

For a while Oberon Felsach fell silent and looked at Mrs Mooshaber. At her hat, at the coloured bamboo beads below her neck and at the red earrings on their long shiny wires. He looked at the red and white of her face, the lipstick and the eyebrow liner, and for her part Mrs Mooshaber glanced around the hall, looking at the split stem of the fountain, before reaching for the cup once more with her white-gloved hand and taking another sip. Since the time of her arrival she had been taking regular sips from the cup and yet she'd never refilled it. However, that wasn't something she was thinking about. From the moment when Oberon Felsach went quiet and looked at her, she'd had the impression that he was examining her and smiling in a strange way. The strange smile had been there from the beginning and Mrs Mooshaber had already noticed it several times. But she now had the feeling that the smile was becoming stranger still and she didn't know what to make of it. 'Perhaps he smiles like that,' she said to herself, 'because he knows that I was rather worried by the way he looked at the door. The way he always looked at it after the radio bulletins. He knows that I'm keeping an eye on him. He really speaks like a grown-up, he could be a writer, but on the other hand...' And now something entirely different occurred to Mrs Mooshaber. She suddenly had the feeling that what she'd heard about the lad from Mrs Knorring and from his father the rich merchant somehow didn't tally. Somehow it didn't fit with the way he appeared to her now. His supposed obstinacy, his disobedience, his need for discipline...Mrs Mooshaber made out that she didn't see his smile. But finally the lad himself spoke:

'I noticed that you arrived in a bizarre and beautiful fur. It had stripes like a tiger with a huge mane around the neck.'

'I hardly ever wear it,' said Mrs Mooshaber hastily.

'But you wore it today,' said Oberon Felsach, 'perhaps because of your visit to us and the national holiday. Listen a moment...' Oberon Felsach suddenly broke into a smile as he looked at the door to the hall...'Listen now. Listen.' As he looked towards the hall door his black eyes sparkled in his pale face. 'The students are here.' And the words were hardly out of his mouth before the door opened and two young men appeared at the entrance.

Oberon Felsach got out of his chair as the smile of elation broke out on his pale face.

'Good Lord, how did you know they were here?' asked an amazed Mrs Mooshaber.

Meanwhile the students walked into the hall. They had smart coats which they unbuttoned but didn't remove and delicate faces which wore a look of excitement. Even so, Mrs Mooshaber noticed, the students remained completely calm

of demeanour. Then suddenly her heart missed a beat. She could now see them well. In the light of the crystal chandeliers she recognised who was standing in front of her in the hall. It was Lothar Baar in his chequered jacket and silk shirt and his friend Rolsberg. The two students who'd been at Nabule's wretched wedding.

'Good evening, Madam,' said Lothan Baar, 'we were informed that you were coming. This is my classmate…we live here in Mr Felsach's house.' All at once Mrs Mooshaber had the impression that they were not waiting for her to introduce herself. She had the sudden impression that they hadn't even mentioned their names and indeed that they didn't recognise her and took her for someone else... 'of course,' she reminded herself, 'I don't look quite as I did at the wretched wedding. I look like an actress, a shopkeeper from those Parrot Islands, or the wife of a gentleman's gentleman. Even so when all's said and done they must know who I am, the magnate must have said that it is Mrs Mooshaber from the Mother and Child Support Service, and besides the boy Oberon Felsach knows who I am and so does their old housekeeper. Or could it be...' Mrs Mooshaber suddenly paused in her reflections, 'could it be that they are not really Mr Baar and Mr Rolsberg...'

'The city is in turmoil,' said the student in the dark chequered jacket...'the streets and squares are full of people.'

'It's like an uprising,' said his friend.

At this point the housekeeper appeared from a door by the staircase. Oberon Felsach stepped over to the wall and pressed a button.

'An uprising,' blurted out the housekeeper in her lace apron and cap, with a voice that trembled so much it could barely come out with words.

'Let us take our seats,' said Oberon Felsach and he motioned to the students and Mrs Mooshaber that they should sit down. Then he turned to the housekeeper and said:

'Why are you acting so surprised? You yourself know perfectly well that this has been expected. And you know other things besides.' The housekeeper nodded before moving closer and asking in a timid voice:

'May I bring you anything? Would Madam care for another coffee? Or the young gentlemen?'

'Thank you,' said the young man in the dark chequered jacket, 'but we will wait for dinner.'

'I still have some coffee,' said Mrs Mooshaber, her voice sounding strangely calm given all that had happened, 'and I've still got these nibbles.'

'If the lady or gentlemen require anything, would they be so good as to ring for it,' said the housekeeper. 'Dinner will be served in an hour. I still have some kolaches to finish.'

'You don't need to,' said Mrs Mooshaber, looking up, 'I've brought some myself. I spent the whole day baking them. I made them with vanilla, raisins and almonds...' Mrs Mooshaber looked at the students in their chairs, but not a muscle twitched in their delicate features. The housekeeper bowed and scurried back to the dark door which led to the kitchen.

'She doesn't yet realise,' began Oberon Felsach, 'that you like to bake and set the table. She doesn't yet realise that you will be laying the table yourself. There are many things she does know but not everything and she has hardly any faith in what she knows. It is here that her failings lie. So it's a rebellion?' he asked the students with a friendly smile on his face.

'Rebellion it is,' said the young man in the chequered jacket.

The sound of a radio was still coming through the wall, but it was just playing music. Oberon Felsach stood up and turned the sound down a bit before returning to his chair.

'It appears,' began the man in the chequered jacket with a side glance at Mrs Mooshaber, 'that everything started in front of the editorial offices of *Our Blooming Homeland*. About two hours ago there were five thousand people there. There was another gathering in Anna Maria the Blessed Square by the Central Cemetery. At five o'clock people gathering round the statue by the station started singing and Rappelschlund evidently saw this as a provocation. In front of the main cemetery gate Rappelschlund's mercenaries were chasing after some boy because he had an airgun but they didn't catch him. Apparently he disappeared into some tomb inside the cemetery. Crowds advanced towards the centre from the Stadium, Kerke and Elizabethan districts and gathered in front of the opera house, the academy of music and the *Tetrabiblos* theatre. Some former actress addressed the crowds from a balcony, declaring that this was the time to enact *In the Shadow of a Palm Tree* and topple Rappelschlund. Then his mercenaries were chasing another boy, a fair-haired one this time. God knows why they were doing so – perhaps because the woman on the balcony was his mother. He hid himself away inside some lift. Outside the *Severed Sky* patisserie in General Darlinger Avenue the crowds had overturned some military vehicles which contained the incense that had never arrived in the shops. We have just come from the cathedral where there are probably five thousand people.'

'Is the metro running?' asked Oberon Felsach.

The students nodded. 'The metro's running for the moment,' they confirmed. 'But there are masses of people on the platforms, even in the restaurants. There are soldiers there too.'

'Have they opened fire?' asked Oberon Felsach in a tone of voice that sounded curious but might have been something else.

'There was some shooting,' replied the young man in the chequered jacket, 'in front of the *Tetrabiblos* theatre while the actress was speaking from the balcony and they were chasing the boy. There was also shooting in Anna Maria the Blessed Square by the cemetery, when they were hunting the first boy I mentioned. People said in the metro that there had even been shooting in Rappelschlund Square, in front of the radio headquarters and in front of the State Tribunal.'

'It seems,' began the other student, 'that people are congregating in the streets and squares in order to move on to the Tribunal and the Royal Palace, where there's a meeting in session. They're chanting slogans against Rappelschlund as they go. The people want to see their princess.'

Mrs Mooshaber had the impression that the students held Oberon Felsach the merchant's son in respect, even though they were certainly quite a bit older than he. They spoke to him as if to someone their own age and readily answered his questions. Mrs Mooshaber looked at the students, at Lothar Baar in his dark chequered jacket and at Rolsberg, and she still didn't feel sure that they were who she thought they were. If they were, she didn't understand why they hadn't recognised her. How could they possibly not know that it was her, even though she didn't look quite the way she had at that wretched wedding? Indeed they must have known that she was coming, they must have known that she was Mrs Mooshaber from the Mother and Child Support Service, the person recommended by Mrs Knorring. She went on looking at the students and wondering at the fact that neither of them addressed her by name. Their delicate faces were friendly and glowing, but they eyed Mrs Mooshaber as if they were seeing her for the first time in their lives. Throughout this time not a muscle in their faces moved. Oberon Felsach renewed his strange smile every now and then. He looked at the students, he looked at her, Mrs Mooshaber, and he kept wearing that smile. Suddenly Mrs Mooshaber remembered once again that she was there on duty in order to supervise, and some of the sense of uneasiness returned. She wondered whether the young man might still change his mind, put on his black coat and make off. With a nod of the head she said:

'Gentlemen, will you burn the incense now while I go and set the table?'

It was Oberon Felsach's turn to nod. He took hold of the bell on the table, rang it once and then once again. In a jiffy the housekeeper had emerged from her dark doorway by the staircase in her lace apron and bonnet. The young man said to her:

'Mary, this lady will set the table for dinner. There's no need for you to bother with it. How are you getting on with the food?'

'The seaweed specialities are ready,' said the housekeeper in a voice that shook with fear, 'the mushrooms are ready too, as is the turtle soup. The fish are still frying. I am finishing baking the kolaches.'

'This lady has brought kolaches,' the boy retorted. 'She has already told you as much.'

'I've brought some other things to eat,' Mrs Mooshaber added, 'besides kolaches. We can eat them after the fish and the mushrooms. So that we don't lose our appetities before the meal...'

The housekeeper bowed and asked once again whether she could bring them anything. Oberon Felsach and the students shook their heads. Mrs Mooshaber did likewise and looked at the wall beside which lay her big black bag and the parcel tied with cord. The housekeeper bowed once more and scurried off to the kitchen.

'She's old and full of fear but she keeps running,' said Oberon Felsach, 'she's got a clock in the kitchen. She needs a new kitchen dresser. Now we will begin. We will light the candles upstairs where they are not yet lit,' he went on as he rose from his chair, 'we will begin to burn the incense. The lady will go to the dining-room and set the table.' The students and Mrs Mooshaber rose from their chairs. She reached with a gloved hand for the beads of her bamboo necklace, looked at the split stem of the fountain and went to the wall for her big black bag and parcel.

'We will begin with the incense upstairs,' said Oberon Felsach, 'and finish here in the hall. And finally end up in the dining-room at dinnertime. In the meantime this lady will set the table,' he repeated.

Mrs Mooshaber picked up the big black bag and the parcel tied in cord and nodded, setting the feathers aflutter on her hat. Then she went towards the big glass doors. She went through them into the dining-room and then closed the doors behind her.

Oberon Felsach went up the marble staircase with the students. They moved quietly and at a slow pace like the plenipotentiaries of an unknown king. Once upstairs in their own room the students first took off their unbuttoned coats. Then they went together with Oberon Felsach to the windows and reaching across the goblets of wine and the cakes and flowers they began to light the candles. They spoke little and in quiet voices while they did so, as you would on some solemn ceremonial occasion. They talked mainly about what was happening in the streets and squares of the capital and about whether the events would at last be shown on television, while they went on listening to the built-in radio behind the wall. There was no further news of the meeting at the Royal Palace, but on the other hand news did arrive of thirty thousand people assembling in front of the palace, cheering for the Dowager Princess Augusta and wanting her – if she was still alive – to appear on the balcony. There was also an announcement on the radio that the military commander of the capital had appeared on the balcony of the palace in order to pacify the crowd of thirty thousand in the name of Prime Minister Rappelschlund. He announced that the princess was alive but was not in the Royal Palace. 'She's not here,' he told them, 'she cannot come out onto the balcony and show herself, that is just a matter of common sense. You might as well ask to see an antelope in a place like this,' he announced. He said that the princess was spending the national holiday held in her honour in her ancestral home in the foothills at Cat's Castle. 'She is frying mushrooms,' the military commander of the city announced from the balcony, 'and doing some lacework.' Then the radio announcer went on to say that Scarcola, the Minister of Police, had not yet arrived for the official meeting. 'Maybe he's sprained his leg,' suggested the city's military commander.

When they had lit all the upstairs candles and had readied themselves to begin burning the incense, Oberon Felsach said:

'Nothing's been broadcast on television. That's curious, as well as being a pity. We should listen to the satellite stations. The satellite stations may have more to say.' He went to the wall and pressed some buttons. And from what came by satellite they were able to hear what was really happening in their city.

'The people do not believe the general when he says that the princess is alive, or at least they don't believe that she is at Cat's Castle,' came one announcement by satellite. 'The people insist that they must be shown the princess and be allowed to talk to her. Thirty thousand people have congregated in front of the Royal Palace.' Then Oberon Felsach went out into the corridor and through another smaller door next to the stairs. He came back to the students carrying a small white canvas bag. In the meantime the students had been preparing various bowls, a box containing charcoal and a phial containing a liquid of some kind.

Into each of the bowls they placed some pieces of charcoal, onto which they poured the liquid. Then they set the mixture on fire before sprinkling incense from the bag over it. Straight away white smoke rose from the bowls and a sweet aroma began to pervade the room. They moved into the corridor and lit fires in some other bowls. At that moment a radio behind the wall tuned in to a satellite channel announced that the thirty thousand people in front of the Royal Palace were cheering ceaselessly for their sovereign the Dowager Princess Augusta, wanting to see her and demanding ever more volubly that Prime Minister Albinus Rappelschlund himself appear on the balcony and explain what had happened to the princess. Meanwhile the corridor filled up with smoke and a sweet celestial aroma. The students and Oberon Felsach appeared in clouds of smoke as they went back into one of the rooms. When the smoke bearing its heavenly fragrance began to hang in the air even there, Oberon Felsach said that they should sit down for a moment. They sat on a settee and at that point it was announced on the radio behind the wall that troops were surrounding the thirty thousand people in front of the palace. Then pandemonium broke out. A hullabaloo of cries and screams could be heard coming from the radio.

And among the cries and screams could be heard the first dangerous words. 'This is the beginning,' said Oberon Felsach with his hands round the students' shoulders while their faces looked strange and unnatural. 'They are accusing Rappelschlund of her murder. They are saying that the princess is dead. They are accusing him of having had her killed and buried a long time ago. They are accusing him of keeping her alive and imprisoned in the palace. They are accusing him of having driven her into hiding some fifty years ago. I wonder what our radio is broadcasting...' said Oberon Felsach with a very serious but at the same time a calm expression on his face as he rose from the settee and turned the button.

...all such accusations are pathetic,' said the voice of the terrestrial radio station, 'the people in the city don't know what they're saying, the charges they make contradict one another, which is proof in itself that these are calumnies. There are wise, well-read and educated people in the provinces,' the terrestrial radio station announced, 'there is no one in our country who doesn't know how to read, write and count. In our country,' the voice on the radio continued, 'we produce delicious ice cream, we have kiosks made of glass and laminate and we can fly to the Moon. In our country we take care of young people and punish criminals. The Dowager Princess, our Sovereign Augusta, is in good health. She is fit as a fiddle,' the accouncer continued, 'today is her birthday. Together with Prime Minister Albinus Rappelschlund she has been our supreme and only ruler since the time of her accession to the throne fifty years ago. She is at Cat's Castle, eating mushrooms and doing lacework.'

'Unless, of course, she never acceded to the throne,' the student in the chequered jacket now put in.

'Unless she never began to rule,' put in the other.

'You know she did,' said Oberon Felsach with a smile, 'she wore the crown and got married at the age of twenty. Now we should slowly make our way downstairs.'

A moment later, bearing the bowls, the bag, the box of charcoal and the phial, they went down in a slow and restrained manner into the hall. At the bottom of the staircase, beside the statues with their red lights, they lit the first bowl and then moved in slow strides across the carpet and along the walls, passing the pictures in their gold frames and the windows with their pink net curtains and their blood-red drapes...they lit more bowls and continued to speak only a few quiet words...the hall slowly filled with smoke and a sweet celestial fragrance. They saw that the doors to the dining-room, the wide doors of frosted glass, were closed and behind them a light was on. They went around the hall and reached the fountain. Water splashed out from the split stem and fell back in a small arc to reach the pool below, in which three small red fish were swimming around. When they had set light to a further bowl, and looked almost like royal envoys standing beside a lake, a dark door beside the staircase opened and the housekeeper emerged in her white lace apron and her white cap. For a moment she stood rooted to the spot, stupefied by the pleasant smell, fixing her gaze on the water feature in the centre of the hall from which clouds of smoke were wafting their way upwards. Then she made her timid way towards the fountain and said:

'May I bring the food on a trolley now?'

'Do so,' agreed Oberon Felsach. 'The turtle soup, the seaweed specialities, the mushrooms and the fish. Use the best crockery and bring everything on a trolley using a plate warmer.'

'Mr Felsach,' said the housekeeper timidly as she moved ever closer to the fountain, 'there's also escalopes, jellyfish salad and octopus, not to mention fried molluscs. When should I bring those?'

'Put them all on the trolley,' said Oberon Felsach, 'those who want to can help themselves. But don't bring any kolaches.' Oberon Felsach took a deep breath to savour the aroma from the clouds of smoke wafting around them and looked at the pool. The housekeeper glanced in that direction. And at that very moment she gave a terrible shriek. The three fish swimming there had a large and ugly black companion carving its way through the water alongside them.

A moment later Oberon Felsach and the two students bearing the bag of incense, the bowls, the box of charcoal and the phial opened wide the big glass sliding doors of the dining-room, intending to go inside. As they did so they froze to the spot and a look of amazement suffused their features.

In her long black shiny skirt, held in place with the light touch of her gloved hands, and in her waistless jacket, her earrings and her hat with its long coloured feathers, Mrs Mooshaber stood at the head of the table beneath the window which lay concealed behind dark-blue velvet drapes. Plates containing some kind of food stood on the side tables while the table itself...

The table was covered in a big black cloth, one edge of which was formed by a wooden pole of some kind. It was indeed a large black cloth with a wooden pole at its edge, hanging down towards the floor. It was more reminiscent of a banner than a tablecloth. There was a vase on the black cloth containing ancient withered blooms of some kind. An old black and red ribbon lay around it bearing a black and gold inscription which had completely faded. Three bottles of wine and three magnificent bottles of lemonade had been placed around the display. Two plates of kolaches stood on the black cloth near to the head of the table. The kolaches on one plate had almonds in their centres, while each of those on the other plate had a raisin filling. A tall funeral candle was burning in the centre of the table.

XXI

When the housekeeper in her white apron and cap came through the wide door into the dining-room, she brought on the trolley plates and cutlery, soup, seaweed specialities, mushrooms, fried fish, escalopes and squid, shellfish, not to mention jellyfish and octopus salad on the trolley and the whole lot were shaking. The hands of the old housekeeper shook and all the rest of her shook with them. From her position at the head of the table in front of the dark-blue velvet drapery, Mrs Mooshaber watched her as she closed in with the trolley, watched her through clouds of smoke which were wafting up from three bowls on the sideboard, filling the room with a sweet celestial aroma. She watched her, this doddery little old woman, across the dried flowers in their vase and the candle, large, lofty and lighted, at the centre of the table. The housekeeper arrived at her right side with the trolley between her and the merchant's son, who motioned her to put everything onto the table. At first she put it all in front of Mrs Mooshaber at the head of the table. She put a plate containing the turtle soup, fried fish and seaweed specialities in front of her. Then she put the same in front of Oberon Felsach. Then in front of the student with the dark chequered jacket and the white shirt, who was seated on the other side of the merchant's son. Then in front of the other student, who was sitting opposite his classmate on the other side of the table. Finally she placed a plate in front of the empty chair on the left side of Mrs Mooshaber. This was her own place, the place for a frail and elderly housekeeper. Then she removed the plates containing the escalopes, squid, shellfish and the jellyfish and octopus salad, together with the plate warmer from the trolley. She put them on a low side table by the wall, next to some plates which were already there. She moved the trolley to the corner of the room before taking her seat to the left of Mrs Mooshaber. Then Oberon Felsach wished everyone *bon appetit* and they all started on the soup.

Her hands still in their white gloves, Mrs Mooshaber carefully tucked into her turtle soup at the head of the table.

Her red and white features looked completely calm now. Not a muscle twitched while she ate. All that could be seen was a little fluttering from the coloured feathers on her hat, a hint of a rattle from time to time among the bamboo beads of her necklace and a mild shaking of her earrings, while carefully and slowly and in silence she moved her white-gloved hand and ate. Then she pushed her plate and spoon to one side. Oberon Felsach, the old and feeble housekeeper and the two students followed suit. Quickly and timorously the house-keeper stood up and cleared the plates and spoons away onto the trolley. Then Oberon Felsach began to eat the fish and the seaweed salad, while the students and then Mrs Mooshaber followed suit. While they were eating Oberon Felsach got to his feet, went over to the wall and pressed a button. A voice could be heard, but it wasn't a news bulletin. The voice was announcing a piece of music.

'Mussorgsky's *Night on the Bare Mountain*,' the announcer explained, 'is played here by the orchestra of the National Opera...' Music flowed into the dining-room, the sound of *Night on the Bare Mountain*. Holding the fork in one of her white gloves, Mrs Mooshaber at the head of the table slowly ate fish, helping herself now and again to a mouthful of sea-weed, keeping her eyes on the spare banner which formed the black tablecloth, on the dried flowers and on the ribbon with the faded inscriptions, the two plates of kolaches near her hands and on the large flickering candle in the centre of the table. From time to time her attention turned to the bowls containing incense on the sideboard, whose slender stream of sweet-smelling smoke wafted through the surrounding air. Then Mrs Mooshaber spoke:

'*Night on the Bare Mountain*. I wonder how people on the Moon live, given that it's nothing but dust and ash. The caretaker says that it's miserable up there.'

'There isn't even air', added Oberon Felsach as he slowly ate his fish, 'just mountain ranges, sharp rocks and extinct volcanoes. We've already spoken about this. It's a place of long, dark shadows thrown by the rising or setting sun, a place where it isn't possible to light a fire, a place with very little gravity – a place where you can easily float around...' For a while Oberon Felsach went quiet and tucked into his fish. The silence engulfed Mrs Mooshaber and the others too. Only the music could be heard, playing through the wall *Night on the Bare Mountain* and a faint crackling from the incense burning in the bowls. Then Mrs Mooshaber went on:

'I heard that the people up there live in spice suits. A bit like those for swimming underwater.' She proceeded to take a mouthful from the seaweed selection.

'That's right,' said Oberon as he took a mouthful of the same, 'it's a bad place. There are constant meteor showers. Every day there's a cascade of a million shooting stars and meteors falling onto the Moon at a speed of fifty kilometres per second. It rains stones up there, enough to kill any living creature. That's why the people, plants and animals living there are all under these great glass covers. When they venture out under an open sky before sunset or shortly after sunrise they need to be wearing spacesuits. They need them in order to breathe and so that they're not overcome by the heat, the cold or the radiation. Then they can go out even during the day or night... the spacesuits also protect them when it's raining stones. So they really are like divers,' concluded Oberon Felsach with a look at Mrs Mooshaber.

He proceeded to savour the sweet aroma from the incense bowls before continuing:

'The lunar landscape is all black, white and grey, and despite the presence of certain trees, bushes and grassy areas that are sheltered from the open sky, the general terrain is one of dust, ash, stones and artificial mud in the crater spas. It's a landscape of death.'

Mrs Mooshaber pushed her plate of fish and her fork to one side and looked at the black tablecloth, the dried flowers and the large burning candle.

'It's a landscape of death,' she repeated.

The student in the dark chequered jacket also pushed aside his plate and fork before addressing the head of the table: 'Rappelschlund has put up a prison of pharaonic proportions there.'

'For prisoners who are not worthy to walk on the earth,' said the other student, addressing the head of the table, 'and for those who commune with the forces of darkness.'

'He considers that not one of those people should ever return to Earth,' said Oberon Felsach and there was something ominous in his voice.

The music on the radio faded away and the announcer's voice took its place.

'We are interrupting *Night on the Bare Mountain* for a few moments,' the announcer explained, 'to report that a crowd of insurgents has broken into the Albinus Rappelschlund Museum of Peace and attempted to destroy the rare collections of weapons which are housed there. However, military forces have cleared the museum and a large number of persons have been conducted to army barracks where they will not escape the severest of trials. In the countryside the national holiday is being celebrated in a dignified and sensible manner,' the announcer went on, 'it is a long time since we used to cut the rye with a scythe, sheave the wheat with our bare hands or use them to repair the wheels of our hay waggons. We have our modern technology to do that now. Even the sight of sheaves piled up in the fields is a thing of the past now. We have...'

Oberon Felsach rose from the table once again, went over to the wall and turned a knob. Another voice could be heard now, a voice from a satellite station.

'People made their way into the Albinus Rappelschlund Museum of Peace,' began the satellite announcer, 'they destroyed the weapons, got rid of all the rifles, machine-guns and tommy guns, the knives, sabres and daggers... they destroyed the cannons, howitzers and tanks in the exhibition halls. Then they set fire to the museum. The Albinus Rappelschlund Museum of Peace and its collections of weapons are in flames. An hour ago,' the announcer continued, 'crowds coming from the Pinetreestal and Philipov districts flocked in their thousands to join those already in Albinus Rappelschlund Square near the editorial offices of *Our Blooming Homeland*. We have just learned that these crowds have toppled the statue of the prime minister. Thousands of doves have been released into the evening sky. At the Albinus Rappelschlund launch site for space travel in the Stadium district people have pulled down commemorative plaques bearing his name and all flight conections with the Moon have been suspended. A meeting is underway in the Royal Palace where there is no sign as yet of Scarcola, the Police Minister. And our latest information,' the announcement went on, 'is that people are surrounding the State Tribunal. Thirty thousand people are in front of the palace calling for the princess and demanding that Rappleschlund appears on the balcony.'

The housekeeper cleared the plates of fish, the seaweed specials and the forks away onto the trolley in a corner of the room. Now the black table was free of plates, leaving only the decorations and, as an exception, the two plates of kolaches near the head of the table. Oberon Felsach turned a knob in the wall and the national radio station could be heard once more. It was playing *Night on the Bare Mountain* again...

'This year's national holiday in honour of the Princess,' Oberon Felsach began when he was sitting down at the table once more, 'is the most critical of all those that have taken place under Rappelschlund's rule. His museum is in flames, his statue and the signs bearing his name have been torn down. People are even surrounding that inhuman place, the State Tribunal. Rappelschlund has filled the city with his military, but the police are holding back. They said nothing about what has been happening at the meeting, but the police minister has not yet arrived. I think I might go to the crossroads and take a look...'

Mrs Mooshaber looked at Oberon Felsach from the head of the table... but didn't display any emotion. Oberon Felsach was sitting calmly. His face with the dark eyes bordered by his long black hair was pale. Nevertheless, he went on sitting calmly, inhaling the aroma of incense. Mrs Mooshaber looked at the students, the young man in the dark chequered jacket, who might have been Lothar Baar, and the other one who might have been Rolsberg, and then she once again fixed her eyes on Oberon Felsach.

'Go to the crossroads,' she repeated quietly. 'You spoke about certain occult sciences. It would very much interest me, not to mention our caretaker, to hear some more about them.'

Oberon Felsach gave a strange smile. 'As you please. I said to you that there were many occult sciences and that among them are those which work with the brain and with the soul. I said that everything could be made use of and in a good way. But I would like to add that everything can be abused too. Mrs Knorring,' Oberon Felsach went on, 'has told us about your life.' There was a moment of silence which allowed Mrs Mooshaber to look at the students once again. 'So,' she suddenly thought to herself, 'the penny must have dropped by now. They must realise that they know me from that wretched wedding of Nabule's in *The Land of the Elves*. They will see that it is I, Natalia Mooshaber, from the Mother and Child Support Service.' But the students kept looking at her at the head of the table with calm faces that looked wholly untroubled. 'Could it really be some others who are here and not Mr Baar and Mr Rolsberg,' she thought to herself, and then something suddenly occurred to her. Something very important. She looked at the students, smiled and said:

'I would like to ask something. To ask the students something. Gentlemen,' she began, leaning slightly on the black tablecloth, ' do you by any chance know about some well around here in Blauental which contains treasure? Gold, silver and a sackful of sovereigns? A well inside a courtyard of some sort?'

The students looked at each other across the table, across the vase of dried flowers and the burning candle, and shook their heads.

'We don't know about any well in Blauental containing treasure,' said the one who could have been Rolsberg, 'we only know about a street, this one, named after a spring. This is Spring Street.'

'We don't know of any well inside some courtyard,' said the student in the dark chequered jacket, who could have been Lothar Baar, 'besides, the city's water supply comes from the mains.' Mrs Mooshaber smiled at this and nodded and then turned to Oberon Felsach and said:

'I guessed as much. My children have tricked me again.' And she still couldn't make up her mind whether or not it was Lothar Baar and Rolsberg sitting there. Then she said to Oberon Felsach:

'Mrs Knorring told you all about me?'

'Not everything, of course,' said Oberon Felsach as he turned to face the bowls of incense on the sideboard, 'I have different information. You were born in Fettgolding near to Cat's Castle in the foothills of the Black Forest. Our Mary,' the lad went on, jerking his head forward and smiling his strange smile, 'our Mary will be interested in this. Make sure you tell us something about it,' he added, still smiling in the same way, 'it will make her happy.'

'I was born in Fettgolding near to Cat's Castle,' confirmed Mrs Mooshaber, speaking to the housekeeper as the feathers fluttered on her hat, 'my father worked on the estates. He cut the rye with his scythe and formed the sheaves into stacks. He also mended the wheels of the hay waggons. My mother looked after the house. We kept some hens and rabbits and had a small field, where we grew maize, potatoes, beetroot, cabbage too I think. From when I was little I used to go to the Black Forest to find brushwood. The police came to see me in my flat three times. They asked me how I lived. They also asked about Wezr (he's my son), who's just recently come back from behind bars... they asked me,' Mrs Mooshaber continued with a smile and a shake of the head, 'whether something had happened to me in the Black Forest and whether I had been to Cat's Castle...'

'Tell us what happened to you in the Black Forest and at Cat's Castle,' said Oberon Felsach, smoothing his long black hair with his hands for the first time in quite a while. Then he turned to the small and frail old housekeeper, who was all a-shiver and a-shake, and to the two students and then back to Mrs Mooshaber, 'tell us what happened to you in the Black Forest and at Cat's Castle,' he repeated in a voice that sounded strange to the point of unnatural, while his dark eyes were fixed somewhere around the dark lining of Mrs Mooshaber's eyebrows. She in turn looked at the candle burning on the tablecloth and at the two bowls of kolaches next to her hands before she went on:

'Nothing happened to me in the Black Forest. We only went to the edge of it. It's deep and full of ghosts. And I've only been to Cat's Castle twice, once when I was small and took part in a school trip. They took us there on a hay waggon and there was no one in residence so they let us enter some hallway lined with antlers, including those of deer, but we didn't speak to anyone. The second time I went there, that was when we'd returned to Fettgolding from the city and I went on foot to the castle. It took me one day to get there and another to get back. I slept in a haystack in some field overnight, or maybe it was a barn for storing grain. At any rate it was summertime and I took along a little maize to eat. But there was someone in residence at the castle and I couldn't get inside it. I walked around the park and saw some farm steward or servant appear in one of the windows. He was standing behind a curtain and looking at me, but I didn't speak to anyone there. When the police visited me they thought that something happened to me in the Black Forest and that I had in fact been in Cat's Castle on more than two occasions.'

'Perhaps they were right,' said Oberon Felsach, keeping his dark gaze fixed on Mrs Mooshaber, 'but perhaps you yourself don't even remember it.'

'How would I not remember?' asked Mrs Mooshaber with a smile. 'I still have a good memory. I never met any living thing when I was in the Black Forest collecting brushwood. Definitely not a lion, they don't live here but in deserts and jungles, or on the Moon for all I know. We've only got them in cages behind bars here... When I went back to Fettgolding I spent my time planting trees in the forest and cooking for the children of the farm workers. My mother was ill and soon passed away and then my father followed her. I had no siblings and none of my relatives is alive now, not my uncle, who would be over a hundred now, and not my cousin or nephew. Some of them were buried in the cemetery at Fettgolding. But the graves...' at this point Mrs Mooshaber looked at housekeeper on the left of her. The woman was even more afflicted by shakes and trembles than she had been earlier... 'the graves in Fettgolding have long since disappeared. They were dug up, leaving not a single brick behind. My graves in the Central Cemetery will last a long time yet. The grave of Therezia Bekenmoscht...' the face of Mrs Mooshaber looked quite calm at this moment... 'will be the first to go, after only thirty years. The grave of Vincencia Cancer and her son the master builder will last a hundred. And the tomb of the Director of Education and his family will last an eternity, until the end of the world and the Last Judgment. Until the Resurrection of the Dead,' added Mrs Mooshaber as she looked at the black tablecloth, at the dried flowers, at the ribbons by the vase and at the burning candle. 'I do not believe in the Resurrection of the Dead or in the Lord God... I might believe in the Last Judgment though,' she continued as she looked at the plate of kolaches, 'perhaps that will come one day. Perhaps it even needs to come...'

'This lady,' Oberon Felsach explained to the students, 'believes not in God but in Fate.'

At that very moment something went quiet in the dining-room. It was the music that had been coming from the radio in the wall. *The Night on the Bare Mountain*. Instead a voice could be heard.

'News of the meeting in the royal palace,' began the announcement.

'About time,' said Oberon Felsach as he rose from his chair. Both the students got up with him. Meanwhile the housekeeper next to Mrs Mooshaber lifted her head in apprehension.

'Scarcola, the Police Minister, has finally arrived for the meeting,' the announcer continued. 'The crowds under incitement in front of the Royal Palace have been shouting his name and that of the Dowager Princess, our sovereign Augusta. They have been holding our Prime Minister, Albinus Rappelschlund, to account for the murder or imprisonment of our dowager sovereign. They have been calling Albinus Rappelschlund a child murderer. They have been accusing him of the murder of Napoleon Stallruck. Who could allow such calumnies to continue? Such accusations are pathetic and preposterous. Albinus Rappelschlund has brought us order. It is he who once waged a victorious war against a neighboruing state. It is he who has given everyone work. He founded a Museum of Peace. He built our spaceport in the Stadium district and has flown to the Moon five times, without suffering from any thickening of the blood. He knows foreign languages, even Portuguese, and in the Elizabethan district he is at this very moment building beautiful new homes for fifty families... and now Albinus Rappelschlund has ordered the Police Minister to make the police force join the military and open fire, for who could tolerate such offences with impunity? Not even a blind mole. The Minister for Police went out onto the balcony,' the voice continued, 'and briefly addressed the crowds. He announced that the police could affirm unreservedly that the Dowager Princess, our sovereign Augusta, had neither been killed nor imprisoned in the Royal Palace. She is very much alive. The Police Minister personally refuted the pathetic accusations and criminal slanders against our Prime Minister which the crowd had been incited to make. How is it then possible that this very same minister then proceeded to announce from the balcony that he was not obeying Prime Minister Rappelschlund's command and would order the police to refrain from protecting so-called murderers? That amounts to a dereliction of duty which should be dealt with by the court. But his action is of no significance,' the announcer continued, 'and will not help the insurgents. In the rural areas the national holiday is being celebrated in a dignified and sensible manner. It is a long time since we cut the rye with a scythe or sheaved the wheat with our bare...' Oberon Felsach turned the knob and silence reigned for a moment in the dining-room. Smoke from the bowls on the sideboard still hung in the air, though it had evidently begun to disperse. The students remained standing, calm but tense, and the old, frail housekeeper in the white lace cap was all a-tremble beside Mrs Mooshaber. She really was an aged, weak and feeble creature. Then Oberon Felsach turned the knob again and the voice of the announcer could be heard once more.

He explained that the music would return until there was a further news bulletin.

'We have wonderful theatres,' he announced, 'like *Tetrabiblos*, where they are playing *The Trapeze*. And the national opera, where Hector Berlioz' *Symphonie Fantastique* is being performed.'

'Now the uprising begins in earnest,' said Oberon Felsach, 'the city is igniting.' He glanced at the students and at the wide open door leading into the hall.

Mrs Mooshaber registered his glance but once again displayed no emotion. She gave a quick nod and began to speak:

'Yes, I believe in Fate, a pharmacist told me all about it. You also...' she went on, nodding quickly at Oberon Felsach, and when he and the students resumed their seats at the table she sighed inwardly with relief. But then she quickly started talking again:

'When I was small,' she began, nodding quickly at Oberon Felsach, 'there was a farm worker or perhaps it was a steward, I can't remember any more, who said to me that I shouldn't believe in God. There wasn't one anyway, and I should believe in Fate and grow turnips, because they were at least something to live on. When I was small I had a friend called Maria... her father was a farm steward in Fettgolding who wore a gold watch and used to ride to Cat's Castle. She was from a rich family, lived close to the school and was loved by the children. She got married and took the name of her husband, but he died a few weeks after the wedding. She then became a housekeeper for some rich family here in the city, where she stayed for two whole generations. I haven't seen her for all of fifty years. I've always wanted to be a housekeeper like her and as a matter of fact I once was one. But when I stayed with the family I had to feed goats, fetch grass for the livestock and carry heavy pails... I wanted to set the table, but in the end I took ill and left. I also wanted to be a stallholder and sell things. Like ham and Italian salad...' now Mrs Mooshaber glanced at the sidetables, on which there lay a few plates containing the food which she had brought in her big black bag, and at the bottles of wine and lemonade on the table '...but it all came to nothing. I saved some money, but Wezr always got his hands on it... in a moment we'll put these plates onto the table,' she went on, indicating the sidetables, 'and we'll open the wine and lemonade. And in another moment we'll start on the kolaches,' she continued, pointing at the two plates.

'Madam,' began Oberon Felsach as he focused his dark gaze on Mrs Mooshaber at the head of the table, 'you went to school in Fettgolding and you had a friend called Maria there who came from a rich family. She married, took the name of her husband and became the housekeeper of a wealthy merchant family for two generations. You have not laid eyes upon her for half a century. That housekeeper is sitting right here at the table on your left hand side.'

Mrs Mooshaber jerked her head to the left and looked at the housekeeper. At the old, weak and frail housekeeper in a white lace cap and a white lace apron, who was trembling through and through. And strangely enough, although Mrs Mooshaber was in a very calm frame of mind that day, she stared for a moment and her heart missed a beat.

'Maria?' she gasped, still staring at her.

'Yes, it's me,' said the old housekeeper in a whisper as she trembled all over and barely managed to find words, 'it's me, Maria from Fettgolding. My father was a farm steward who wore a gold watch and rode to Cat's Castle. We lived next to the school and the children loved me. I got married but my husband died soon after. I took his name and I have been the housekeeper for Mr Felsach the merchant from one generation to the next. That's who I am, Maria from Fettgolding. But I...' now the housekeeper suddenly appeared to be in a state of great agitation as she looked Mrs Mooshaber over and could scarcely manage to speak, 'but I... I... the thing is, Madam.... I don't know you at all. I have never seen you before in my life. You didn't go to school with me at Fettgolding. You weren't my friend there. Madam, you have never...' the housekeeper couldn't even speak now, she was trembling so much, 'you weren't in Fettgolding...'

A deep silence took hold of the dining-room. A deep and oppressive silence. Only the music went on playing the *Symphonie Fantastique* from within the wall, while the incense in the bowls of charcoal went on crackling softly and the big high candle went on burning in the centre of the black table. Oberon Felsach was calmness itself. Even the student in the dark chequered jacket stayed quiet, as did his fellow-student. Only the housekeeper was all a-quiver, trembling from head to toe and looking Mrs Mooshaber over while Mrs Mooshaber remained stiff.

At last Oberon Felsach began to speak.

'Yes,' he began, 'that is indeed Maria from Fettgolding. Mary, tell us your real name. You already introduced yourself in the hall when Madam arrived, but perhaps she didn't catch the name. Tell us your real name and then we will know the truth.'

'I am,' began the housekeeper as she sat up in her chair while Mrs Mooshaber, who was entirely stiff and motionless, now noticed the beads of perspiration starting to flow from beneath her white lace cap, '...I am Mary Terra from Fettgolding, bound in marriage to a man who went by the name Capricorn. I am Mary Capricorn.'

'Mary Capri,' gasped the motionless Mrs Mooshaber, 'Mary Capri...' and everyone recognised that the shudder and the look of complete astonishment which she gave were no pretence.

'Yes,' Oberon Felsach finally confirmed, 'Mary Capricorn. The Mary Capricorn. Capricorn,' he repeated with a nod as he stroked his long black hair and a deep period of silence returned to the dining-room.

When the silence had lasted for a long time, broken only by the *Symphonie Fantastique* coming from within the wall, the weakening crackle of the incense in the bowls and the candle burning on the table, Oberon Felsach looked at the students whose deathly pallor was matched by his own.

And then the sound of music from inside the wall died down and was replaced by another bulletin.

'Long live Prime Minister Albinus Rappelschlund,' roared a voice, 'long live the Prime Minister!' And then the announcer read out a poem:

Fly away, blue-grey bird, fly into the blue beyond, Albinus Rappelschlund is there, protecting you from every wrong

Then some other voice could be heard:

'Listen carefully. This is an important announcement,' the voice began and then an uproarious shout could be heard through the wall of the dining-room:

'Prime MinisterAlbinus Rappelschlund has just been placed under arrest in the Royal Palace. He will be tried and executed.'

At last everyone at the table came alive.

The students' delicate faces and eyes contrived to shine splendidly despite their lingering deathly pallor. The old, frail and feeble housekeeper Mary Capricorn, deathly pale and trembling from tip to toe, still managed to move and remained among the living. Oberon Felsach was pale, but he was pale at the best of times, and now he was completely calm and smiling. Even Mrs Mooshaber was completely calm now at the head of the table.

The voice from the radio filled the dining-room with the news not once, twice or three times but over and over again, while it evidently spread through the whole country, the wider world and must even have reached the Moon and been heard by the people there. Prime Minister Albinus Rappelschlund was under arrest. On this very day, the thirty-first of October, a national holiday in honour of the birth of our Thalian Dowager Princess, at twenty-five to nine in the evening on the steps of the Royal Palace, and after a failed attempt at rallying support, Albinus Rappelschlund, who for fifty years appeared to govern the country along with the Dowager Princess Augusta, although in reality he was the only one to govern, having pulled off what was beyond belief and robbing the princess of her throne when she was still a young girl, has been placed under arrest. He wanted to rob her of life itself, and for half a century she remained in hiding from him. He has been trying to hunt her down for fifty years, weaving a web of pretence and lies, filling his country with prisons and in the end even building one at the Einstein crater on the Moon... and he didn't even shrink from executing children. It was at his bidding that the State Tribunal to Investigate Dealings with Demonic Powers was established, it was at his bidding that a Diabolical Dossier was produced each year, always with several names on it, and it was at his bidding that several years ago poor little Napoleon Stallruck was quartered. It was at his bidding that people were not allowed to search for the Princess, at his bidding that familes suspected of knowing where she was staying were shot and at his bidding that the worst enemy of mankind – fear – was allowed to stalk the land. Now at last, on the seventy-fifth birthday of that unhappy Dowager Princess our sovereign Augusta, Albinus Rappelschlund has been placed under arrest following the order he gave for the army to open fire on the people. This brings matters to a close. He has been arrested, he will be tried and he will be executed. Throughout the country our people are cheering for the Thalian Dowager Princess Augusta.

Then there was another announcement through the wall of the dining-room.

'Police Minister Scarcola,' began the announcement through the dining-room wall, 'has provisionally assumed supreme power in our country on an interim basis.' This was followed by a proclamation:

'In order to avoid any unfortunate events occurring or crimes being committed during these happy and at the same time fateful times, and in order to maintain peace and order, I am assuming as of this moment supreme control of all the military, police and administrative authorities in this country until such time as, by the will of the people, our rightful sovereign the Thalian Dowager Princess Augusta is once again seated on the throne. I am ending with immediate effect the martial law which was declared by the fallen dictator, and I proclaim an immediate amnesty for all political prisoners both here and on our lifeless satellite in the sky.'

General Leo Scarcola, Commander-in-Chief of the Armed Forces and Minister of the Interior.

'So we'll move these plates onto the table here,' said Mrs Mooshaber with a shake of the head that made the coloured feathers on her hat tremble at the top of the table, while her earrings quivered on their long wires and the bamboo beads round her throat went clickety-clack... and before the old housekeeper Mary Capricorn could find her feet Mrs Mooshaber herself had stood up and had moved to the sidetable, her gloved hands fetching the plates and distributing them on the main table. She put plates in front of Mary Capricorn, in front of the students and in front of herself. And on the plates was ham and Italian salad.

'And now we will also drink some wine,' said Mrs Mooshaber from the head of the table as she fingered her coloured beads, 'some wine and then the best thing of all, lemonade by the name of Limo... and to finish off there'll be the kolaches,' said Mrs Mooshaber as she smiled at everyone from the head of the table, 'I spent the whole day baking these, I made them with vanilla, with raisins, with almonds...'

Mrs Mooshaber ate the ham and salad slowly at the head of the table while she took dainty sips from a full glass of wine. Oberon Felsach took a piece of ham and a spoonful of salad. The students followed suit, as did the housekeeper, Mary Capricorn...

'I always wanted to have a kiosk and sell this sort of thing,' said Mrs Mooshaber as her white-gloved hands made their way through the ham and Italian salad, 'I've never eaten it in my life before, or once only if you count my wedding, that was all of fifty years ago. We were married in the town hall on Anna Maria the Blessed Square. There was no great glass railway station there at that time, just a small chapel of some kind. We travelled there on the underground from around here in the Blauental district, we went both there and back by underground. We sat down and had to hold on because of the way you get thrown about in those tunnels. I've never been on the underground since then. Once I thought I was going to get a ride in a taxi... anyway, we had our reception in *The Golden Carriage* behind the town hall. That's another place that's no longer there – modern apartment blocks have replaced it. Not a brick of that old inn, *The Golden Carriage*, has been left standing.'

'Life passes quickly,' observed Oberon Felsach as he rose to his feet and approached the bowls on the sideboard, 'what are a few decades when set against eternity? In one life,' Oberon Felsach continued as he took some more charcoal out of a tin, put it in the bowls, added a few drops of liquid and lit it, 'a few decades is an awfully long time in the life of an individual, but is just a drop in the ocean of eternity.' Now he sprinkled incense onto the charcoal. 'The joys and pains of a single life melt away in eternity and disappear in a puff of smoke like the little clouds that are beginning to form here.' He finished speaking and went back to sit at the table, while Mrs Mooshaber slowly made her way through her ham and salad and her wine while she thought to herself, 'it's true, he really does talk like an adult, like a writer.' Then Oberon Felsach breathed in the sweet and heavenly fragrance, smiled strangely and spoke:

'But there's another thing, Mrs Mooshaber. There were never any Mooshabers at Fettgolding. You, Mrs Mooshaber, have never been at Fettgolding. In point of fact...' here Oberon Felsach smiled his strange smile and once again inhaled the heavenly aroma from the bowls which was now permeating the whole dining-room, '...there were Mooshabers in Fettgolding. He cut corn with a scythe in the fields, he sheaved the wheat and he repaired wheels, while she looked after their cottage... but the couple never had any children. That much has been found out by now from the old parish records. No one ever took you to Cat's Castle in a hay waggon while you were at school in Fettgolding, for the simple reason that you never were at school in Fettgolding. The truth is that you went to Cat's Castle once, when you were twenty-five, and that was a long time after everything had happened... you went there once and I suppose you wouldn't have gone inside even if they had let you. You went only to the park and saw a steward or one of the servants behind a curtain in one of the windows. At that moment you beat a rapid retreat. The truth is that a long time before that you used to go to the Black Forest, though not from Fettgolding but from somewhere far from there, somewhere almost on the other side of the forest. And it wasn't for brushwood that you used to go there. And once, when you were about twenty and it was just after your wedding, you went once again to the Black Forest. Suddenly some monstrously big animal with a mane around its neck emerged right opposite you, coming to the edge of the forest from outside it, a monstrous mouse with a mane. You were terrified and fled from the creature. Because it was running at you from the edge of the forest, you had to escape it by running further into the forest, further and further into the depths. It ran after you until there came a moment when with a terrible voice it cried out to you. Its voice was so shattering that the heavens above echoed its booming roar, the trees trembled and the earth beneath you shook. It cried out that you should not believe in God, that there was none, that you'd do better to grow turnips because one can at least live on turnips... that was no farm steward or farm worker addressing you, that was a monstrous great mouse. And then it vanished from your sight as if it had been swallowed up by the earth itself.'

Mrs Mooshaber finished eating her ham and salad and finished drinking her wine. She looked at the black tablecloth and at the burning candle, she looked at the dried flowers in the vase and at the ribbons below with their faded gold and silver inscriptions and she looked at the two plates of kolaches next to her hands. She looked at them all and was silent. The beads around her neck gently nudged each other, the rings in her ears vibrated on their long wires and the green and red feathers in the hat on her head quivered. But not a muscle twitched in the features of that red and white face. Mary Capricorn was all of a tremble on her left and the students, still deathly pale and silent, were looking towards the head of the table.

'A monstrous mouse vanished from your sight at one point.' Oberon Felsach once more breathed in the fragrance around him and placed his hands with their long nails on the table, 'it was in the depths of the forest, with not a living soul for miles around. It vanished all of a sudden and at the very same instant you met a young girl there. Or rather you saw a young girl. I wonder what she looked like, Madam...' Hands on the table, Oberon Felsach looked at Mrs Mooshaber with his dark eyes.

'Young Master,' began Mrs Mooshaber with a smile as she eyed her kolaches on their plates, 'I really cannot tell you. It is too long ago. I was just twenty at the time – you said it yourself.'

'Yes, twenty,' agreed Oberon Felsach as he took another gulp of the sweet aroma coming out of the bowls and floating through the dining-room, 'you were twenty and had just got married. I am not asking what the girl looked like, but how she was attired.'

All went quiet for a moment in the dining-room. The only sound was the music coming weakly through the wall and the soft hiss of the incense in the bowls. Mrs Mooshaber looked at the burning candle while a halo of incense hovered above her head. Then she said:

'I don't even know whether any of this really happened. To me it seems like a fairy-tale which I read once. She was a village girl and she was looking for brushwood in a forest.'

Oberon Felsach smiled at the students in their deathly pallor and at Mary Capricorn as the beads of sweat escaped from under her bonnet.

'A village girl was looking for brushwood in a forest. That is significant. If you'd said that she wasn't a village girl but was wearing a crinoline dress, things would have been clear. But what you have actually said,' Oberon Felsach continued with a smile, 'makes them even clearer.'

At this point the music was interrupted by another an-noucement.

'Minister Scarcola has ended martial law and has an-nounced an amnesty for all political prisoners. Minister Scarcola has abolished the State Tribunal, the abolition to have immediate effect. A moment ago certain mercenaries in the service of the arrested despot Rappelschlund, demons who have the taking of innocent lives on their consciences, were themselves placed under arrest. Their names are Conrad Melz, Vincent Sutin, Lena Vites, Martin Tatrman and Wezr Mooshaber, the former warden of the State Prison. His sister Nabule, a prostitute, was also placed under arrest, as was a stonemason, a foreigner apparently going by the name of Aureus Bekenmoscht and commonly known as the Black Dog. He, however, ran himself through with a dagger a moment after his arrest. Wezr Mooshaber was infamous for his manner of torturing prisoners, namely by admonishing blows between the eyes with his fist. His sister and the dead mason were his accomplices. The three of them shared the inmates' stolen belongings among themselves. They committed various offences involving fraud with impunity. While the police were aware of the miscreants' activities, no arrests were possible on account of their position as demons in the service of the former ruler now under arrest. Now, like he, they will get the rope. They will be,' the voice concluded, 'hanged by the neck until dead.'

A deep silence fell over the dining-room. The students and Mary Capricorn looked towards the head of the table with staring eyes. Oberon Felsach was breathing calmly and looking at the black tablecloth, while his hands with their long nails perched there. Meanwhile Mrs Mooshaber at the head of the table was looking at the kolaches on their plates and not a muscle of that red and white face so much as stirred.

'What a terrible thing it is,' she said in a quiet, dry voice after a while as she eyed her kolaches on their plates, 'what a terrible thing it is when parents have children that go bad. Children who go to schools for the troublemakers and young offenders... and what do they end up as but unskilled pairs of hands, like as not hired for the day until they end up... how terrible it is for the parents and for the children too. The children drive their parents to distraction and an early grave, while what awaits the children is death by hanging. We will now proceed to the kolaches.'

Mrs Mooshaber pulled the two plates closer with hands covered in long white gloves and gave a nod. Oberon Felsach on her right, and Mary Capricorn on her left, could clearly see now that the kolaches were of two different kinds. On one plate lay kolaches with raisins, and on the other kolaches with almonds.

'Be my first guest,' Mrs Mooshaber said to Oberon Felsach, not a muscle of her face moving as she spoke, 'I spent the whole day baking these, I made them with vanilla, with raisins, with almonds and with lots of sugar, yes, lots of sugar... choose from the ones with almonds.' Frozen-faced, she passed the plate of kolaches with almonds to Oberon Felsach... and Oberon Felsach, his eyes fixed on the black tablecloth, took one and began to eat. Mrs Mooshaber watched him for a while, watched him eat and watched him swallow, and a profound silence fell upon the dining-room at that moment. There was just a murmur of music playing through the wall and a crackle of incense in the bowls and the little clouds hovering above the table, the candle burning beneath them. And then Natalia Mooshaber took a kolache too. She took a kolache topped with a raisin... The students and Mary Capricorn, who were looking at her, had the impression that she was smiling. She swallowed a mouthful and then reached into a pocket lying somewhere in her long, black skirt. She pulled out a bottle opener and helped herself to a lemonade.

Oberon Felsach ate a kolache topped with an almond while the students suddenly had the impression that he'd undergone some kind of metamorphosis. 'I would like to conclude,' he began, 'by saying that life may be long, but measured against eternity it is but the blinking of an eye. You met, or rather saw, this young girl in the forest, this young girl who was not in a crinoline dress. She was a village girl hunting for brushwood. If it had been the other way round,' Oberon Felsach went on with a smile while he looked at the tablecloth, 'then as I said everything would have been clear. But this way round,' he went on with a simle, 'it is even clearer. Because that young girl in the forest was you and that young girl in the crinoline dress – was you. The thing is,'he went on after a moment's silence, during which the music played softly through the wall, the incense hissed to itself and the candle went on burning...and Oberon went on eating his kolache, 'the thing is that whichever you were it doesn't change anything. It doesn't matter whether you say you were the village girl collecting brushwood or the girl in the crinoline dress. And that's because at the moment when that monstrous mouse in a mane vanished before your eyes in the depths of the forest, you were suddenly both girls. There weren't two girls, you and some other, they were both of them you. You were never at Fettgolding, but Mary Terra was someone you knew and liked in your childhood, perhaps she was even your one and only friend, even though you didn't ever speak to each other, not once in your lives... and your husband wasn't Medard Mooshaber, some coachman for the brewery. Your husband was never buried in Drozdov by Etlichy. The coachman Medard Mooshaber was not your husband but a stranger who later took lodgings with you and also took the name which you had chosen to adopt. You never married him in the town hall. You were a widow at the time and didn't want to marry again. You considered that it would be sinful to do so. Hence you didn't have the pension you would be entitled to as the widow of a coachman in the brewery. You lived for the whole of your very long life on nothing more than the few guineas given you for tending graves. Mooshaber died in the war and is buried in Drozdov. Fond of you he was, but he wasn't your husband. And Wezr and Nabule Mooshaber were not your children either, you never had any children. They were total strangers whom you adopted, and their adoption came at a terrible price.'

Mrs Mooshaber went on sitting at the head of the table, her face red and white, her eyebrows lined and her lips red, her earrings on their wires and her coloured bamboo beads around her neck, her hat still with its long fluttering feathers and her gloves long and white. She sat and she ate her kolache with the raisin on top while her face remained motionless and calm. For a few moments she watched Oberon Felsach while he ate his kolache topped with an almond. Then she turned her attention to the students who sat looking pale and didn't budge an inch, before looking at Mary Capricorn, the housekeeper and her friend from childhood days, the one who didn't know her and had never spoken to her in her life... and then she looked at the candle burning on the tablecloth, above which a small cloud of sweet smoke sat hovering in the air, and at the dried flowers in the vase with the ribbons around it. Now the sound of voices cheering for the Dowager Princess, the sovereign Augusta, could be heard from the radio through the wall, while interspersed among the hundreds of thousands of voices could be heard the sound of military marches. And then a new ingredient was added to the military marches and the voices of hundreds of thousands of people – the sound of bells. But none of this was heard by Mrs Mooshaber. She was looking at Oberon Felsach eating his kolache topped with an almond while she finished her own kolache with the raisin on top and she was looking at the burning candle above which the cloud of incense hung in the air. Then she spoke:

'I learnt a little poem when I was young.'

Slowly she began to recite against a backdrop of military marches and peals of bells:

Leaving church the blind old lady
Feels her way with stick unsteady
Forward with her stick she fumbles
Blind Old Lady often tumbles

Then she went on:

'When Wezr and Nabule were little, I sang them a lullaby.' And for the first time she took a drink from the bottle marked Limo and sang slowly against the backdrop of pealing bells and military marches:

Now it's good evening and now it's good night
Now by the power of angelic might ...
.....
Tomorrow in the morning-time
You will once more rise and shine

And then the doorbell rang.

Mary Capricorn wrenched herself out of her chair and ran from the dining-room into the hall. Old, small and frail, she was trembling like a leaf. As she ran, even Oberon Felsach got to his feet as he slowly came towards the end of his kolache... he was very pale but also calm. Even the students got to their feet.

Mrs Mooshaber smiled and spoke to them from the head of the table:

'And just how could I have been friends with this Maria when I never even spoke to her? How could I have been friends with her when I never set foot in Fettgolding. How...'

'It is possible to have friends,' began Oberon Felsach by the chair, still slowly working through his kolache and turning ever paler, 'it is possible to have friends and at the same time never to have spoken to them once in your life... it is possible to have friends and to see them seldom and only then from a distance, through a window. You were never in Fettgolding, but from when she was small Maria Terra used to ride sometimes with her father to Cat's Castle...'

'And who then was my husband?' asked a smiling Mrs Mooshaber from the head of the table. 'Who was he, if not Medard Mooshaber of Drozdov by Etlichy, and where then is he buried...'

The ever more pallid Oberon Felsach, still finishing his kolache with the almond, repled:

'Your husband died a week after your marriage. He was the great nephew of Charles Napoleon and is buried in the Royal Palace.'

At that moment Mrs Mooshaber saw the wide doors of the dining-room leading into the hall fly open. Ushered into the hall by Mary Capricorn in her white lace bonnet and apron was a posse of people, people in top hats, dark clothes and uniforms, headed by a general with longish grey hair and a messenger.

Mrs Natalia Mooshaber looked at Oberon Felsach, whose kolache was now completely gone and whose deathly pallor now looked terrible against the backdrop of his dark hair and clothes, and then spoke calmly:

'Once a street mob wanted to stone me.'

Then she went on:

'According to legend once upon a time there were many mice in Cat's Castle. The things have dogged me throughout my whole life. I wonder if there are mice on the Moon as well.'

The almost colourless Oberon Felsach, standing beside his chair, smiled and shook his head.

'The Moon may be in dust and ashes,' Mrs Mooshaber responded with a nod from the head of the table, while the military marches and pealing bells remained in the background, while the coloured feathers on her hat went on quivering and the rings in her ears kept vibrating and the bamboo beads round her neck went on nudging each other, 'there may be nothing but desert, rocks bare and sad, it may be a landscape of death... but if there are no mice there, then it is still the land of the blessed.' At this moment she swallowed the last mouthful of her kolache.

And now all those people in the hall were standing in front of the wide sliding doors into the dining-room facing Mrs Mooshaber who was at the head of the table, and the messenger gave a bow before saying:

'The Honourable Police Minister, Count Scarcola'

At this point the general with the longish grey hair removed his hat, bowed deeply and said:

'Your Highness, the golden carriage awaits you outside.'

From the radio came the sound of people shouting for joy and cheering for their Thalian Dowager Princess, the Sovereign Augusta, while the military bands went on playing and the bells went on pealing...the students, the one in the dark chequered jacket who might have been Lothar Baar, and the other who was also nicely dressed and might have been Rolsberg, knelt on the ground beside their chairs next to the dining-room table, and the gentlemen in the dark clothes, top hats and uniforms also knelt in the hallway in front of the sliding doors of the dining-room and the deathly pale young man Oberon Felsach with the long black hair and dark eyes and over-extended nails, knelt with the students beside the dining-room table. And somewhere in the corner of the dining-room old, frail Mary Capricorn, all shakes and sobs, knelt too, still in her white lace bonnet and apron. And Mrs Natalia Mooshaber rose from her chair at the head of the table, placed a white-gloved hand upon the black tablecloth, glanced at the dried flowers in their vase, at the ribbons with their faded gold-and-silver markings and at the burning candle, above which a heavier cloud of incense had now formed. Then she smiled, reached for the little bottle of lemonade marked Limo and took another drink, before pointing at the plate of kolaches topped with raisins and saying:

'Those should be destroyed. The ones with raisins. They're poisoned.'

Then she looked at the people on their knees in the dining-room, at Oberon Felsach with his deathly pallor, at the students with their echoing pallor and at Mary Capricorn, wretched and weeping, and then she smiled and said:

'There's just one thing I still don't know. Are they the same students or not?'

And then against a background of exhaustive military marches and pealing bells she moved slowly towards the former Police Minister at the entrance to the dining-room. She moved slowly in those flat shoes of hers, the feathers fluttering in her hat, the rings in her ears vibrating, the bamboo beads round her neck nudging each other with a click... while with one of her white-gloved hands she was holding up her long black skirt. She moved slowly, oh so slowly, and she already knew precisely how far she would get. She was a few steps in front of the minister and the kneeling throng. And here she stopped, smiled and spoke:

'By the power that is mine I order and decree a pardon for Albinus Rappelschlund. I also order and decree a pardon for Wezr and Nabule Mooshaber.' And she reached into the pocket of her long black skirt and handed an ancient seal of some kind to the minister.

Then she collapsed onto the carpet like an old withered tree that had finally been felled, and those kneeling closest to her were able to catch her final softly-spoken words.

'All of this was my Fate. May God have mercy upon my poor soul.'

Late in the evening on the same day, the thirty-first of October, two days before All Souls, the announcement came that the country's sovereign the Thalian Dowager Augusta, Princess of Saas-Beer, had passed away. She died having succumbed to the effects of poison, on her seventy-fifth birthday, at the very moment when after half a century she

had returned to the throne. The golden carriage in front of Oberon Felsach's villa bore only the painted corpse of an old woman in a long, black shiny skirt, waistless jacket and shoes that had spurned heels... with a bamboo necklace, earrings, a hat with red and green feathers that fluttered of their own accord and fluttered even more from the bumpy ride above the wheels, covered by the brown and black stripes of a fur wrap with a huge shaggy mane. On the following day they played the greatest *Requiem* ever to be performed in the country, with five thousand singers and musicians. It was sung in the cathedral of Saint Quido of Fontgolland and the Thalian Cardinal Archbishop presided over the requiem mass. Monsieur Scarone directed the music. Among the sopranos was Mrs Magdalene Knorring from the Mother and Child Support Service and reverberating among the French horns was Mr Joachim Landl and somewhere or other perhaps even Mr Zepheus Smirsch. During the *Dies irae* the cathedral was flooded with light.

From a dilapidated old house in the Blauental district a black flag hung on a hook over the front entrance, as it did from every building throughout the city and the whole country. The scaffolding around the shared balconies in the courtyard had already been taken down and the trio of 'barrow, bricks and barrel of lime had already departed. When the caretaker came to after a week in the Blauental infirmary, the first words she came out with were:

'What a bundle of nerves that poor woman was. Always under such pressure to play a part.'

And that was one thing the caretaker was right about.

AFTERWORD

By the time of the first publication of *Myši Natálie Mooshabrové* (Of Mice and Mooshaber), in 1970, Ladislav Fuks was well established as one of Czech literature's leading contemporary writers. His first book, *Mr Theodor Mundstock* (Pan Theodor Mundstock), a psychological novel about an elderly Prague Jew awaiting deportation to Auschwitz, had appeared in 1963. That year – also noteworthy for the publication of the first books of major fiction by Bohumil Hrabal, Ivan Klíma and Milan Kundera, the return to publication of Josef Škvorecký and the first performance of Václav Havel's *The Garden Party* – signalled the beginning of a period of cultural liberalization, during which an unprecedented number of Czech creative artists secured international recognition. Between 1964 and 1967, Fuks cemented his reputation as the outstanding interpreter of the German occupation in Czech literature. Born in 1923, he drew on his own late adolescent memories in *Variations for a Dark String* (Variace pro temnou strunu), while in *The Cremator* (Spalovač mrtvol) he imagined an apparently respectable Czech's descent into collaboration.

By 1970, the situation in Czechoslovakia had changed. The Warsaw Pact military intervention of August 1968 heralded the end of liberalization, and in April 1969 the 'reform-Communist' leadership was replaced. The change affected Fuks directly when Juraj Herz's internationally acclaimed film version of *The Cremator*, which was co-scripted with Fuks, but replaced the delicate black comedy of the novel with more overt moralizing and horror, was withdrawn from cinemas shortly after its release in March 1969, and not shown again publicly in Czechoslovakia until after the fall of Communism in November 1989.

Judging from remarks by Fuks in interviews, the writing of *Of Mice and Mooshaber* pre-dates the events of 1968 and 1969, but it finally reached readers as the policy of 'normalization' intensified, with extensive purges of those associated with calls for reform. In its mood of uncertainty, unease and threat, the novel unquestionably resonated with the atmosphere of the time. The reader may well have expected another work about the German occupation, perhaps encouraged by the possibly Jewish-sounding surname of the title character and the Jewish names of her children, Wezr and Nabule. Fuks certainly employs the same disorientating, hallucinatory techniques that he had used previously to communicate the anxiety and psychological pressure of the Occupation. Quickly, however, the stable reference-points of time, space and even genre are removed. The German-sounding names conjure up Vienna more than Berlin and the fictional dictatorship described, with its ubiquitous police and the overweening Care, seems more implicitly Eastern Bloc. Though the novel, published a year after the Apollo moon landing, appears set in the future, when interplanetary flights are commonplace, Fuks sets these motifs of science fiction against the mundane, stereotypically Czech realia of cakes, parks and housing blocks, in an otherwise technologically unremarkable society. The contrast seems wryly to reflect how little the state's scientific and military-industrial achievements affect the lives of ordinary people.

Fuks may have conceived the novel as an allegory of Socialist Czechoslovakia before 1968, but its implicit message of solidarity and succour resonated even more in the post-1969 context. That message is founded in two key allusions to classics of Czech literature. First, Mrs Mooshaber's name calls to mind the poem 'Záhoř's bed', from the 1853 cycle *Kytice z pověstí národních* (A Posy of National Folk Tales) by Karel Jaromír Erben (1811–70). In German, Mooshaber literally means 'one who has moss'. In Erben's poem, a pilgrim wandering in deep despair passes through a thicket of hornbeams (*habr* in Czech) to discover a terrifying forest man lying on a bed of moss inside an oak. The wanderer tells the forest man that he is on his way to purgatory (the legendary

Purgatory of St Patrick), and the forest man allows him to pass on condition that he returns and tells him what he sees there. The wanderer eventually returns and reports that the ultimate punishment is called 'Záhoř's bed'. Suddenly stricken with fear, the forest man, whose name is Záhoř, confesses to the wanderer that he has murdered many men. The wanderer tells the forest man that, to atone, he must kneel on the bed of moss inside the tree and pray to God for forgiveness until he returns. Many years later, the wanderer returns, as an old man, and finds Záhoř apparently inside a giant tree-stump completely overgrown with moss and brambles. He grants Záhoř peace and the stump crumbles into dust, rather as Mrs Mooshaber falls 'like an old withered tree that had finally been felled'. The souls of both men fly to heaven as two white doves. We may assume that Mrs Mooshaber, having 'gathered moss' over a lifetime of penance, will do the same.

Secondly, the closing description of the deceased Mrs Mooshaber as 'that poor woman' ('ta ubohá žena') would remind any Czech reader of the pastoral national classic, *Babička* (Granny, 1855), by Erben's friend, Božena Němcová (1820–62). In Němcová's novel, the eponymous grandmother uses these words to describe the tragic Viktorka, who years before had been seduced by a stranger and then abandoned. Viktorka drowned her new-born child, and – either driven insane or as an act of penance – lived out her days in the forest, until one night she was struck by lightning, which the villagers interpret as a merciful gesture from God. By contrast, at the end of Němcová's novel, the local duchess describes the deceased grandmother as a 'happy' or 'blessed' woman ('Šťastná to žena!'). Despite the inverted epithets, Mrs Mooshaber resembles the wise, pious, patriotic, self-sacrificing grandmother far more than Viktorka. In Němcová's novel, it is not the duchess, but the old peasant woman, the guardian of tradition and solver of problems, loved, respected and sought out by everyone, who is the real ruler in the novel.

Following the events of 1968 and 1969, the choice of references seems prescient. Both *Kytice* and *Babička* were written and published in the wake of the imposition of martial law in Bohemia in 1848, during the clampdown in Austria that followed the 'year of revolutions'. For Erben, Němcová and other Czech patriotic intellectuals, this period seemed to signal a return to the perceived Austrian suppression of Czech nationhood and national identity of the seventeenth and eighteenth centuries, and both sought through these works to comfort and give courage to the nation in a difficult time. Erben alludes in the opening and closing poems to a nation in despair, orphaned and seeking a mother, or headless like a damaged statue on the Stone Bridge in Prague, while in letters, Němcová describes how she retreated into the embrace of childhood memories of her grandmother for consolation at a time of personal and national misfortune. *Of Mice and Mooshaber* seems to address its reader in a similar way at a similar time. Ironically, however, as in other novels, notably *Nebožtíci na* bále (Dead Men at a Ball, 1972) and *Vévodkyně a kuchařka* (The Duchess and the Cook, 1983), the most un-Steinbeck-like Fuks implicitly finds comfort in nostalgia for the monarchy and Austria.

The hope at the end of *Of Mice and Mooshabr* is ambiguous. Mrs Mooshaber attains release only moments before she dies, bequeathing a message of forgiveness to her land, the future of which remains uncertain. The message is therefore close to Erben's poem, which is commonly read as an expression of faith in God's infinite mercy and the promise of redemption for sinners who repent, written in response to the 1836 poem *Máj* (Spring) by the leading poet Karel Hynek Mácha (1810–36), in which the after-life is portrayed as an abyss of nothingness. By alluding to 'Záhoř's bed', Fuks implicitly evokes a Roman Catholic vision of terrestrial existence as suffering, self-sacrifice and self-denial, a time of waiting which ends in the rebirth to new life implied by Mrs Mooshaber's first name. He thus reasserts the Czech Baroque tradition, which merged with Enlightenment thinking in Czech literature of the first third of the nineteenth century and was revived at the end of that century, but had been marginalized in supposedly 'realist', 'rationalist' Czech fiction since the war. Its influence is evident in *Of Mice and Mooshaber*, and throughout Fuks's writing, in the essentially comic, 'small' perception of the human being, the use of mysteriously interlinked, recurring images and motifs, the presentation of life as a conflict between good and evil, and the portrayal – particularly in the figure of Mrs Mooshaber – of goodness, a discredited 'bourgeois', 'religious' stereotype in the Marxist-Leninist-Stalinist ideology of the time.

The Judeo-Christian motif of waiting that pervades *Of Mice and Mooshaber* and recurs in Fuks's work separated him from the dominant rhetoric of action that paradoxically united supporters and opponents of 'reform-Communism' and pro- and anti-government intellectuals during the Normalization. Fuks was not prominently involved in the cultural politics of the late 1960s, though his portrayal of life under German occupation easily invited interpretation as an allegory of an even more recent period of repression. Throughout the 1960s, his work could be read simultaneously as undermining and conforming to prevailing ideological expectations. During the Normalization, therefore, while other writers, like Havel, Klíma and Kundera, found themselves unable to publish, it was possible for Fuks to remain a 'sanctioned' writer and lend credibility to the decimated ranks of contemporary Czech literature. His willingness to do so was seen as a betrayal by opponents of the Normalization government, who considered his work after 1970 both artistically and morally compromised.

Of Mice and Mooshaber pre-dates the works of the mid-1970s that most exercised these critics, and indeed for conformist Normalization reviewers the novel retained too much of the 1960s' perceived preoccupation with style over ideological clarity. In 1977, in order for the book to be republished without substantial alteration, Fuks had to append an essay in which he effectively insisted that the fictional dictatorship should be read as a reference not to Czechoslovakia, but, for example, to far-right dictatorships in Latin America. While most see this essay as a low point in Fuks's subordination to the demands of Party ideologues, it has also been read as a parody of Normalization rhetoric. Aleš Kovalčík highlights Fuks's use throughout his writing of 'masks', which he hopes an ideal implied reader will see through. Fuks's central characters, including Mrs Mooshaber, are easily understood as authorial self-characterizations. They are generally solitary, eccentric, inscrutable figures, hiding from oppression, preparing for the worst, too weak to resist actively, but – with the important exception of his cremator – refusing to collaborate. Kovalčík notes that Fuks's central characters frequently wear disguises, and cannot risk revealing their true identity. For Kovalčík, this feature may be linked as much to Fuks's experience as a homosexual as his experience as a writer in highly politicized times.

Fuks died in 1994, perhaps too soon to enjoy the re-evaluation of his whole body of work. Over recent years, as authors' biographies are replaced by their texts, and Czechs move away from the binary oppositions of collaborator and resister or conformist and dissident towards a more complex understanding of responses to dictatorship, so Fuks has perhaps unexpectedly emerged as potentially the most lasting, rich and interpretable voice of the lionized generation of the 1960s. His novels, nearly all of which have now been re-published, consistently analyse the individual human being's psychological experience of oppression, in all its ambiguity. The oppression is real and external, but intensified and perpetuated by those oppressed, and release comes only moments before death. Faced with this 'life-sentence', some characters, like Mrs Mooshaber, find the resources privately and solitarily to resist oppression, while others – notably Fuks's cremator – falter and turn oppressor. Fuks's work may be understood in terms of Czechs and Jews during the German Occupation, of writers or ordinary people under Communism, of Christians in an increasingly secular Europe, of actual or spiritual aristocrats in an increasingly plebeian Europe or of homosexuals in twentieth-century Czechoslovakia, but ultimately the context is less important than the experience, the response and the underlying expression of solidarity. Through his writing, Fuks seeks to communicate secretly with the oppressed, providing comfort and a sense of community among those who understand what lies behind the façade. For a moment, the meek seem to inherit the earth.

TRANSLATOR'S NOTE AND ACKNOWLEDGEMENT

Like any politician or football manager, a translator has to make choices. Whatever he decides, he will be applauded by some and derided by others.

It will probably please no one that I chose a form of semi-anglicisation, changing some names, half-changing others and leaving a few unaltered. It was a question of trying to maintain the atmosphere of the book while conveying meanings when I felt that the author wanted them conveyed.

There were also some issues that were unique to Fuks. The deliberate repetition, for instance, especially where Mrs Mooshaber is concerned, which means the translator must rein in any desire to show that he has a broad vocabulary and stick to the task of giving voice to an elderly woman who may indeed be prone to the repetition that age brings, but is also deliberately hiding her identity. Moreover the repetition does not stop there. We are constantly reminded of certain mannerisms, like the caretaker touching her throat or Oberon Felsach smoothing his hair. We are constantly reminded who is speaking, even when there can be little or no doubt about it. Here again, a translator can't simply cut the text down like an over-zealous editor. He has to respect the wishes of the author to create an atmosphere through repetition.

On top of that, the translator has to have some idea of the sort of book he is translating – but what sort of book is this? Is it an allegory of modern men and women lost in an alienated and totalitarian society? Is it a surrealist myth, combining modern technology with primitive ideas of evil and magic? The names problem is relevant here too. What are we to do with Rappelschlund and the Thalian Princess and villages with names like Fettgolding? Where are we? Are we in Liechtenstein or in Ruritania? Where are we with Count Scarcola? In Italy? In Transylvania, perhaps. Or are we lost inside a Lévi-Straussian *bricolage*? Or perhaps (I write this in Brussels) we're trapped inside some multi-cultural burlesque anticipating the European Union.

Others with much more knowledge about literary theory than I can better answer these questions. For a translator one of the most important things – in fact I think the most important - is to like a book, to be translating something you'd want to read anyway. I can certainly admit to that – Mrs Mooshaber never ceased to be compelling. And there was an element of mission in what I was doing too. After reading this book, can anyone possibly doubt that Fuks could be funny or that he had no time for the pretensions of communism?

Without the help of my wife Lenka Zdráhalová it would have been impossible to produce a translation. She was indispensable, indubitably when correcting my Czech, occasionally when correcting my English. Without the time she spent sorting out my mistakes the translation itself would have been in Ruritanian. I would also like to thank Lucie Johnová for her wit (I owe the elks and elves to her) and wisdom. Finally I would like to thank Martin Janeček for his patience in awaiting delivery of the manuscript, which took nearly as long as those workmen on the scaffolding outside the Mooshaber apartment.

CONTENTS

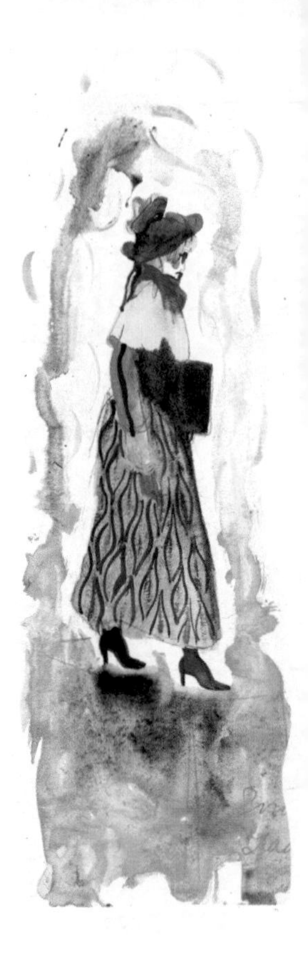

OF MICE AND MOOSHABER
LADISLAV FUKS

English translation by Mark Corner
Afterword by Rajendra A. Chitnis
Illustrations by Jiří Grus
Layout by Zdeněk Ziegler

Published by Charles University
in Prague, Karolinum Press
Ovocný trh 3–5, 116 36 Praha 1
http://cupress.cuni.cz
Prague 2014
Vice-rector-editor
Prof. PhDr. Ing. Jan Royt, Ph. D.
Edited by Martin Janeček
Typeset by DTP Karolinum Press
Printed by PBtisk, Příbram
First English edition

ISBN 978-80-246-2216-3